Joseph Wilcocks

Roman conversations

A short description of the antiquities of Rome

Joseph Wilcocks

Roman conversations
A short description of the antiquities of Rome

ISBN/EAN: 9783742832801

Manufactured in Europe, USA, Canada, Australia, Japa

Cover: Foto ©Andreas Hilbeck / pixelio.de

Manufactured and distributed by brebook publishing software
(www.brebook.com)

Joseph Wilcocks

Roman conversations

ROMAN CONVERSATIONS;

OR

A SHORT DESCRIPTION

OF THE

ANTIQUITIES OF ROME,

&c.

ROMAN CONVERSATIONS;

OR

A SHORT DESCRIPTION

OF THE

ANTIQUITIES OF ROME:

INTERSPERSED WITH

CHARACTERS OF EMINENT ROMANS;

AND

REFLECTIONS, RELIGIOUS AND MORAL,

ON

ROMAN HISTORY.

BY THE LATE

JOSEPH WILCOCKS, F.S.A.

THE SECOND EDITION, CORRECTED:
With a PREFACE, containing
SOME ACCOUNT OF THE AUTHOR:
ALSO
A TRANSLATION OF THE QUOTATIONS,
A GENERAL INDEX, AND
A PLAN OF ROME.

IN TWO VOLUMES.
VOL. II.

Exemplum cernitis insigne Mutationis rerum humanarum: Vobis hoc præcipuè dico, Juvenes!——LIVII. Hist. L. XLV. 8.

London:
PRINTED BY P. NORMAN, DUNSTAN's HILL, TOWER STREET,
FOR R. BICKERSTAFF,
(SUCCESSOR TO W. BROWN,)
CORNER OF ESSEX STREET, STRAND.

MDCCXCVII.

CONTENTS.

OF THE

Second Volume.

BOOK III.

CHAP. IV.

A 3   Massacres;

CHAP. V.

Saxon

CONTENTS.

CHAP. VI.

CHAP. VII.

SEVENTEENTH DAY'S CONVERSATION 112

Hospitals,

CONTENTS.

CHAP. VIII.

It's

CHAP. IV.

Canopus

CHAP. V.

Meffalina.—

CHAP. VI.

CHAP VII.

Reflec-

ROMAN

ROMAN CONVERSATIONS.

Book III.

C H A P. IV.

FOURTEENTH DAY'S CONVERSATION,

ON the bank of the *Tiber*, in the place anciently known by the name of *Pulchri Littoris*, ftands a fmall and round *antique* temple, generally fuppofed to be that of *Vefta*. It's beautiful circular portico is fupported by twenty fluted columns of the *corinthian* order, all of white *parian* marble. The temple itfelf is entirely compofed of the fame rich material; the feveral parts of it being fo curioufly joined, that the whole fabric muft have originally appeared as one fingle mafs of marble: a circumftance, as the young nobleman obferved, not to be paralleled in any other building at *Rome.*

If the architecture of this building gave *him* fuch pleafure, *Crito's* pupil was not lefs agreeably entertained with the pleafantnefs of it's fituation, and with the feveral poetic ideas which here rofe in his memory. Looking to the river, he immediately recollected *Horace's* exact defcription of this fpot*.

> *Vidimus flavum Tiberim, retortis*
> *Littore etrufco violenter undis,*
> *Ire dejectum monumenta regis,*
> *Templaque Veftæ.*

But with far more pleafure did he turn his eyes to the other fide of the temple of *Vefta*, towards the pleafant *Palatine* hill, the folemn ruins of which were much enlivened by the frefh beauty of the many intermingled fhrubs now all in leaf or flower; then towards the ancient fquare white fabric of *Janus Quadrifrons*, and the circular brick temple of *Romulus*. It was not without fome claffical enthufiafm, that he faluted all thefe places with the following lines of *Virgil:*

---

* CARM. lib. i. od. 2. 13. The oppofite bending fhore is part of *Etruria*, of which the *Tiber* was the ancient boundary, and the adjoining oblong temple was built by *Servius Tullius*, the fixth king of *Rome*. See book i. p. 35. See alfo the learned *Abbate Venuti's* Antiquities of *Rome*, vol. ii. p. 29, 30.

Di patrii Indigetes, *&* Romule, Veſtaque *mater,*
Quæ tuſcum Tiberim, *&* romana palatia *fervas**.

CRITO was as highly ſatisfied with the view
of this antique building as any of the younger
part of his company; though for a very different
reaſon.

THIS elegant fabric, ſaid he, is thought, by
ſome antiquarians, to have been the temple of
Cybele; by others, that of *Apollo,* or *Hercules.*
It is marked as the temple of *Portumnus* in the
map before *Kennet's* Antiquities; which book indeed we have generally found to be very accurate. But, amidſt all this incertitude, the opinion
which ſeems to prevail moſt at preſent, and which
fixes on this fabric as one of the temples of *Veſta,*
is perhaps the moſt true. Suppoſing this to have
been really the caſe, how venerable ought this
edifice to appear to us! The temples of *Veſta* were
indeed far more aweful than any other of the ancient religious edifices in *Rome:* for though the
worſhip of *Veſta* was heatheniſh, yet her temples
never contained any ſtatue, or image, which
might *ſtriƐtly* be called an idolatrous repreſentation of the Supreme Being.

GEORG. i. 498.

AFTER

AFTER fome refpeftful paufe, on uttering the laft expreffions, *Crito* propofed to his young friends, to take a fhort ftudious walk along the valley, which leads from this temple of *Vefta* to the forum.

DURING that walk, his pupil repeated the following lines of *Ovid.*

Effe diu ftultus Veftæ fimulacra putavi:
  Mox didici curvo nulla fubeffe tholo.
Ignis inextinctus templo celatur in illo;
  Effigiem nullam Vefta nec ignis habent*.

ANOTHER of the young gentlemen fpoke of the *natural* fire, at *Pietra Mala*, in *Tufcany*. It is faid, added he, that there was anciently a temple of *Vefta* on *that* fpot; though I cannot fay, that I remember feeing there any remains of fuch a building, or even any marks of it's fituation. If a temple of *Vefta* really ftood there, it was probably in fome refpefts fimilar to the fire temple, which *Hanway* defcribes at *Baku*, on the coafts of the *Cafpian* fea.

THE converfation now wandered to *Perfia.* *Crito* mentioned, not without fome marks of doubt

----
* FASTOR. lib. vi. 295.

and difapprobation, the very favourable manner in which Dr. *Hyde* fpeaks of the ancient *p ·fian* religion: he began alfo to confider the celebrated charaĉter of *Zoroafter;* when, recolleĉting how far that digreffion might lead him from his prefent bufinefs, he brought again the difcourfe to it's former claffical fubjeĉt.

EVERY *curia* or *ward* of ancient *Rome,* faid he, had it's particular temple * dedicated to *Vefta.* The edifice, which we have been juft now viewing on the banks of the *Tiber,* was probably *one* of thefe temples.

ANOTHER of them ftood on this fide the *Capitoline* hill, near the church of *Santa Maria della Gratia,* and the hofpital of *Santa Maria della Confolatione.* It was probably *that* temple of *Vefta,* which *Nero,* even in the height of his wickednefs and power, trembled to enter †.

BUT the *chief* temple of *Vefta* ftood in the forum, on your right, where you fee the church of *Santa Maria Liberatrice.* We cannot be miftaken in it's fituation, as *Statius,* in his defcrip-

---

* See *Dionyfius Halicarnaffeus.*
† See *Tacitus, Ann.* lib. xv.
Adiit Capitolium veneraturus deos. Cum Veftæ quoque templum iniviffet, repente cunĉtos per artus tremens, feu numine exterrente, feu facinorum recordatione nunquam timore vacuus.

tion

tion of the *roman* forum*, defcribes it ftanding
oppofite to the temple of *Concord*.

AT *that* church, if you pleafe, we will finifh
our walk : we may fit down on fome of the blocks
of marble, which lie near it's porch ; and, as the
place is at prefent very folitary, you will perhaps
permit me to trouble you there with one of my
papers.

QUINTUS MUTIUS SCÆVOLA,
PONTIFEX MAX.

IF this hand, *this moft unworthy hand,* fhould be
ever employed in delineating the charaƈters of any
great and truly chriftian ecclefiaftics, my *principal* endeavour certainly would be, to defcribe
their conduƈt in their profeffion ; their *paftoral*
care of the people committed to their charge; and
their diligence in *religious* ftudies.

BUT, in the charaƈter of this *heathen* high-
prieft, the cafe is totally different.   We muft pafs
over in filence his conduƈt in his pontificate, and
fpeak not of his learned labours, which were relative to his falfe religion †.

MOST

---

* *De Equo Domitiani,* ver. 31. to ver. 36.
† Some fragments of *Scævola's* works in this kind are
preferved by *Tully* and *St. Auftin.*   See on this occafion *Le-
land's*

Most heartily indeed might it be wished, that *Scævola*, as well as the elder *Metellus*, the *Valerii*, and other ancient worthies of this city *, had been enlightened with the true faith. His temperance, and other moral virtues, would not have been unfuitable to the highest rank in the church.

But, laying aside his pontifical character, let us confider his conduct in *other* flations.

The duties of the christian priesthood are so numerous and so important, as to afford the most industrious ecclesiastic sufficient employment during his whole life. Λατρευειν ΘΕΩ εν οσιοτητι και δικαιοσυνη πασας τας ημερας της ζωης †.

But it was otherwise among the heathen: their flamens and pontifices, without being supposed to run any hazard of neglecting the proper work of their profession, were generally engaged in *other* business: sometimes even in *military* employments; frequently in the conduct of *civil* affairs relative to the *state*, and in the labours of the *law*.

land's Advantage and Necessity of the Christian Revelation, shown from the state of religion in the ancient heathen world, vol. i. p. 132, 157, 197, 255.

* See the Conversation *on this same spot*, book i, vol. i, p. 131. See also book ii, vol. i, p. 219—20.
† Luke i. 74, 75.

IT was the cuftom here at *Rome*, as you very well know, dear fir, continued *Crito*, addreffing himfelf to the eldeft of the young gentlemen,—a cuftom as ancient as this city itfelf, that the youth of the principal families fhould be all educated in fome knowledge of the laws of their country, and in fome practice of fpeaking before the public affemblies of the people. By thefe means, thofe among them, who were endowed with a proper degree of genius and induftry, had it in their power, when grown up, not only to be of fome real fervice to the public, in the great work of legiflation,—for how can any one pretend to make new laws, who is not acquainted with the old?—but alfo, in private life, to be very ferviceable to many perfons and families of inferiour rank, under their patronage.

AT the public tribunals, the young noblemen pleaded the caufes of thefe their clients *gratis.* The beneficence of this employment is placed by *Tully* in a very ftrong light. *Quid tam regium, tam liberale, tam munificum, quàm opem ferre fupplicibus, excitare afflictos, liberare periculis, retinere homines in civitate?*

THE *elder* part of the nobility, befide prefiding in the feveral courts of juftice in their offices of prætors, &c., employed themfelves alfo in
giving

giving gratis to their clients their learned opinions and friendly advice in matters of law. *In civitate amplissimus quisque & clarissimus vir senectutem suam ornabat tali juris interpretatione. Domus eorum velut oraculum civitatis erat, maximâ frequentiâ civium celebrata. Stipabant illorum fores, ut ait Ennius,*

> *Suarum rerum incerti, quos ego ope meâ ex*
> *Incertis certos, competosque consili*
> *Dimitto, ut ne res temere tractent turbidas.*

DR. *Burnet,* in his life of lord chief justice *Hale,* takes notice, that his lordship greatly admired this custom among the *romans.* Let me read to you some of his own words. *The jurisconsults were the men of the highest quality, who were bred to be capable of the chief employments in the state, and became the great masters of their law; and whose resolutions were of that authority, that they made one classis of those materials, out of which Trebonian compiled the digests under Justinian. Lord chief justice* Hale *thought it might become the greatness of a prince to encourage such a sort of men and of studies: in which none, in the age he lived in, was equal to the great Selden; who was truly, in our english law, what the old roman jurisconsults were in their's.*

BUT

BUT let us return to *Scævola*. He excelled in each manner; I mean, if I may ufe the expreffions, both as pleader, and as chamber-council. He mixed and tempered together the qualifications both of jurifprudence and eloquence, fo as to become, in *Tully's* opinion, *inter juris peritos eloquentiffimus, inter oratores juris peritiffimus.*

PARDON me, dear fir, faid *Crito's* pupil, for this interruption; but, when we reflect, that *Tully* was the *fcholar and difciple of Scævola*, we ought not furely to forbear expreffing our pleafure in hearing this his encomium on his beloved *old* mafter. Many other fimilar paffages in *Cicero's* works crowd into my mind; particularly one, in the beginning of his *Amicitia. Pontificem Scævolam unum noftræ civitatis, & ingenio & juftitiâ præftantiffimum, audeo dicere.* But pray proceed.

SCÆVOLA'S love of juftice and of beneficence, my dear pupil, continued *Crito*, extended much farther than to the limits of his own city and country. He accepted the office of governor of *Afia Minor*, on purpofe to increafe his power of doing good.

I LISTENED with much pleafure yefterday morning, in the *Negroni* garden, to the reflections

of

of fome of this company on the fubject of provincial government; and fhould be very glad, if that converfation were now refumed. It fhould feem indeed probable, from feveral circumftances, particularly from fome expreffions of *Tully*, which I met with yefterday afternoon in turning over his *Oration de lege Maniliâ*, that *Afia Minor* may juftly be confidered as the *Mexico* or *Peru* of the *roman* empire.

CRITO faid this with a kind of intention to revive that fubject, on which the eldeft of the young gentlemen had yefterday fpoken with much laudable ardour; but the worthy youth modeftly declined the compliment, and defired rather to attend to *Crito's* lectures, than to interrupt them. Some fhort mention indeed was made, on this occafion, of the famous bifhop of *Chiapa;* of *Peter de Toledo,* the great *peruvian* viceroy and legiflator; and of feveral other *europeans,* who are faid to have acted well in other parts of *America:*—but the converfation foon returned to *Scævola.*

IN your late *roman* ftudies, continued *Crito,* you have often had occafion to obferve, that the provinces of the empire, in this age of degeneracy, were groaning under the heavieft and moft fhameful oppreffion. Their governors were far

from

from looking on the high office, by which fo large
a part of mankind was moft folemnly committed
to their care, in it's true and noble light. Inftead
of this, their only views were plunder and rapine.
They confidered their patents of government
merely as licences for repairing their fortunes,
broken and ruined by luxury; and for fully fa-
tisfying their tyrannical pride and avarice. In
vain did the oppreffed provincials cry for protection at the tribunals of *Rome.* The judges
there were generally perfons connected with their
oppreffors, and deeply ftained, themfelves, with
the fame crimes. For the governors willingly
fuffered thefe *roman* judges to join, by their
agents, in plundering the provinces, on condition that they themfelves might be mutually protected by them, from all accufations on that head,
with the greateft impunity. But with what different views did *Scævola* enter on his government!
With what indignation did he look down on fuch
leagues of iniquity as thefe! His maxim of government was, not to be himfelf burdenfome in
the leaft to his provincials, or to fuffer any other
perfons to be injurious to them. He ferved this
important office *gratis :* never accepting any thing
whatfoever from the *afiatics ;* but refiding among
them far from his own country ; diligently labouring for their benefit ; and in the mean time living
on his own fortune, eating *his own bread* among
them

them with frugality, contentment, and the greateſt joy. The conſciouſneſs of his own integrity enabled him alſo moſt intrepidly to defend the *aſiatics* from other oppreſſors, and to bring his countrymen themſelves to juſtice. For theſe proud and cruel men were equally brought before the tribunal of *Scævola;* condemned there with the moſt juſt and impartial ſeverity, and dragged thence to priſon, or to death, by the hands of the very perſons over whom they had tyranniſed. A ſpeƈtacle, moſt unexpeƈted, but moſt welcome to the poor *aſiatics:* A ſpirit of government, which regained to *Rome* the love of all it's provinces and allies; and crowned *Scævola* himſelf with the greateſt though unſought and uncoveted glory *.

CRITO now pauſed, and for ſome time fixed his eyes in ſilence on the ground;—his uſual attitude, when beginning to think on any ſubjeƈt that was particularly ſolemn. His countenance for ſome inſtants bore the marks of concern and pain: but a ſweet tranquillity and humble reſignation ſoon enſued in his mind, and ſoftened all his features.

---

* The *aſiatics*, in honour of his memory, eſtabliſhed a perpetual yearly feſtival, called the *Mutian Feaſt.* (Vide *Cic. Verres* xi. 51.) *Et in ipſâ etiam Româ, gloriâ maximè illuſtris erat Scævola, utpote qui provinciam tam ſanƈtè & tam fortiter adminiſtraſſet. Senatus etiam, magiſtratibus deinceps in eam provinciam ituris, exemplum atque formam officii Scævolam decreto ſuo propoſuit.*

THE more good, faid he, that *Scævola* thus did to others, the better was he enabled to bear adverfity himfelf.

THE time was now come, when the mifery which *Rome* had inflicted on other nations, was to be retaliated on herfelf. *The cup of the anger of the Lord* had been carried round many regions*, and this city was now to drink the dregs of it herfelf.

O MY dear fellow ftudents, in turning over the hiftory of the world, both ancient and modern, what do we find to be in great meafure it's contents? alas! wickednefs, and the punifhments thereof: *fcelera, & pænas.*

BUT in perufing the difmal hiftories of the punifhment of wicked and hardened nations, we muft not wonder, if we fhould fometimes find feveral *good* men partaking of the national calamities, and fuffering with their refpective country. In the prefent condition of things, and clofe connexion of mankind one with another, fuch accidents feem inevitable.

LET me correct my words. It is wrong to call thefe events *accidental;* fince Providence

---

* Vide *Jeremiam,* c. 25:

feems

feems often by the fame means, and at the fame time, to punifh fome men, to correct others, and to try the good, and by fuch trials to exalt their characters. *Didici etiam ex hoc infcrutabile Tuum judicium expavefcere; qui affligis juftum cum impio, fed non fine æquitate & juftitiâ*.*

LET us endeavour to confider the hiftory of the *romans* in this light; fo far at leaft as the circumftance of their being pagans may perhaps permit us.

CRITO now rofe from the block of marble, on which he had been fitting, and fixed his eyes on the adjoining forum.

IF I be not miftaken, faid *Crito's* pupil, many were the bad men, who in thefe times greatly contributed to increafe the plagues of their country. Such were *Carbo, Cinna,* and young *Marius.* But the chief inftruments of the divine juftice feem to have been *Sylla,* and the elder *Marius;* themfelves the moft wicked of men, and confequently the moft proper to torment others.

Whofe hearts, nor yells of mothers, maids, or babes;
Nor fight of priefts in holy veftments bleeding,
Could pierce a jot.

* *Imitatio.* lib. iii. c. 50.

YOUR

YOUR quotation, replied *Crito*, is very applicable to thefe times.   In the horrid maffacres, which, as the various factions prevailed, were then frequently repeated in this city, all regard to juftice or humanity was overthrown by thofe wicked men, and their affociates.   For how, then, did *this* forum appear?   It's rich pavement was all ftained with blood; while many mangled bodies were dragged through it, and the neighbouring ftreets.   How horrid a fcene! *There* was the *Capitol;* half of it lay then in ruins and afhes: in the remaining part of it,—in *that* afcent to the temples of *Concord* and of *Jupiter Optimus Maximus*, were expofed to view the *tabularia* of the empire, covered with long profcriptions. *Here* ftood the *Roftra*, like a flaughter-houfe, crowded with the heads of many principal perfons; of feveral in particular, who had done great good to their fellow-citizens in this very place:

————*Simul ora virûm præfixa videbant,*
Nota nimis miferis, atroque fluentia tabo*.

A.C.
82 IN one of thefe maffacres *Scævola* retreated to the temple of *Vefta;* to that temple, which ftood in the very place where you are now feated. *Scævola* expected, perhaps, that the place, his office, and above all the great notoriety of his

* ÆNEID. ix. 471.

excel-

excellent character, might be some protection to him: or perhaps, he was willing to die, as *Merula* did some few months before, in a place generally esteemed holy.

SCÆVOLA had always behaved with the greatest regard to his country,—with the greatest firmness and disinterestedness. In the height of his prosperity and power, when conful, he had opposed the improper exaltation of his friends; for ill-judged principles of friendship, and the proftitution of the honours and offices of truft in the public ftate to such principles, were indeed great causes of the national ruin. In the height of danger he had refused to enter into the civil wars, or to take up arms againft his enemies, who were also his fellow-citizens. *Scævola*, like the prieft, whom *Josephus* juftly celebrates, seems to have thought it much better to remember always, that he was the high-prieft of his country; whose office it was to pray for all, to endeavour to unite and reconcile all, to bless and benefit all. He died in the veftments of his priefthood! He died *on this spot. Quia servare cives per compo-sitionem volebat, ipse ab iis interemptus eft* *:

Dum paci medium se offert,—justissimus unus!

* Cic. *pro Rosc. Amerino,* c. 12. vid. etiam, Virg. *Æneid.* vii. 536.

TEARS feemed now to be ftanding in *Crito's* eyes: he wiped them, and proceeded with the following words.

AFFECTING as the fate of *Scævola* is, thus murdered at the feet of the altar of *Vefta;* yet, O my dear friends, if *Scævola* had been a chriftian;—if on this fpot had ftood at the time of his death, not a pagan temple, but, as now, a chriftian church; how much more exalted might have been your meditations in this place!

MIGHT we not then, perhaps, have prefumed to compare him, in fome inferiour degree, to *St. James,* the bifhop of *Jerufalem,* who was flain in or near the temple; or to *Zacharias,* the fon of *Barachias,* who was flain between the temple and the altar?

BUT, let me check thefe prefumptuous thoughts: thofe names indeed are too holy for fuch a comparifon.

CRITO now paufing, the young gentlemen refumed the converfation. *Crito's* pupil, and his elder friend, made feveral obfervations on the murder of *Scævola.*

IT is fome comfort, faid the young nobleman, to reflect, that *Scævola's* great moral virtues feem

to

to have been rewarded by the long profperity of his family. The houfe of the *Marchefi Mutii* is ftill, to this day, remaining here, in an honourable rank and plentiful circumftances*. Is it not very remarkable, that no war during the time of the *roman* republic; no tyranny of the emperors; no fword of the *gothic* or *lombard* invaders; no other accident, in the courfe of fo many ages, has been fuffered to extirpate the families of *Publicola*, *Fabius*, and *Scævola?*

* * *

BY *Crito's* defire the company now ftept into their coach,—which ftood waiting for them at fome diftance,—and took a fhort airing for an hour or two in the country, on the eaftern fide of *Rome.* During this excurfion they frequently looked towards the diftant hills of *Palæftrina*, A.C. 82 and recollected the bloody end of young *Marius* in that unhappy city.

As they were re-entering *Rome* by the *Porta Salaria*,—which ftands either on the fpot, or near the place of the ancient *Porta Collina*,—*Crito*

---

* It is certain, that the *Marchefi Mutii* are of a very ancient family, and have fubfifted thefe laft eight hundred years, with this title, and this tradition of their pedigree. Their prefent eftate is about 1500*l. per annum.* They have two good palaces, and feveral fiefs in land.

reminded

A.C. reminded them of the great battle fought on that
82 fpot between the armies of *Telefinus* and *Sylla;*
in which fifty thoufand men perifhed on each
fide!

FROM the *Salarian* gate they drove again down
towards the *Capitol;* and turning fhort on their
right at the *venetian* palace, procceded along the
Corfo towards the *Piazza di Spagna.*

IN paffing by the *venetian* palacc, *Crito* obferved, that on that fpot ftood the *Villa Publica**,
where *Sylla,* immediately after his victory over
Telefinus, perpetrated an act of horrour, far more
atrocious than the flaughters of any field of
battle†.

BUT why, faid he, fhould I thus lead you,
ftep by ftep, along the bloody track of this cruel

* See *Abbate Venuti's* Defcription of *Rome,* vol. ii. p. 40.
Tempio di Bellona era fotto il Campidoglio, &c.
† *Octo hominum millia Sullæ fe dediderant. Eos in villam
publicam ingredi juffos, quafi inter fuos milites defcripturus,
eodem tempore quo fenatum in ædem Bellonæ convocari jufferat,
crudeliffimè trucidavit: multique fimul pagani, qui forte eodem
venerant, etiam fullanarum partium homines, perierunt. Corpora in Tiberim projecta funt. Dum tanta multitudo cæditur,
ipfe verba in fenatu faciebat: patribufque ad horribilem tumul-
tum ac clamorem, tot quem millia indignè moritura edebant,
exterritis; eodem quo dicere cæperat vultu vocifque tenore;
Hoc agite, inquit, patres confcripti, pauci feditiofi juffu meo
puniuntur. Quâ tantæ acerbitatis voce, vix quidquam ab ullo
homine dictum puto truculentius.*
                                    Freinfh. Supp. lib. lxxxviii. c. 17, 18.

man

man? Every part of *Rome*, every part of *Italy*, witneſſed ſome of his dreadful deeds. Your minds, I am ſure, loath the ſubject. Let us haſten to our lodgings: let us finiſh there this morning what remains of *Sylla's* hiſtory; and then —never mention his name more.

ARRIVED at his pupil's lodgings, the company went into *Crito's* apartment; and ſeating them-ſelves round his table, gave their attention to ſome papers, which he read to them. Theſe chiefly conſiſted of extracts from *Freinſhemius*, relative to *Sylla's* dictatorſhip.

IT is true, ſaid *Crito*, that ſome of the laws, which were made by *Sylla*, when poſſeſſed of that ſupreme magiſtracy, were wiſe and ſalutary to the ſtate. Several cruel uſupers and tyrants,—even our own *Richard* the Third, may make the ſame boaſt. But *Sylla's* conduct in other reſpects was very oppreſſive, and very mean. How mean was his private life at that time! It was paſſed in the ſociety of the loweſt, and the worſt of men. How tyrannical was his public behaviour! *Ne neſciatis, quirites.—Monitos volo victos, ne tertiùm inſani-entes opus incendio habeant.* A ſpeech ſuitable only to the tutor of a *Cataline*.

C 3   *SYLLA,*

SYLLA, in the third year of his dictatorship, resigned that office. *An ipsum jam pigebat raptæ potestatis? & quum recordatio delictorum seræ pœnitentiæ morsibus consciam mentem cruentaret, quantas miserias, quàm vile ob præmium, perferret, experientiâ monstrante perfenserat? Nam priusquam cupitis potiretur, in his omnem inesse & solidam animi felicitatem crediderat. Adeptus deinde, quum se pejus etiam excruciari deprehenderet, odisse atque fastidire cœpit, quod anteà, per tot bella civilia, flagrantissimè appetiverat. Hæc exempla docere mortalitatem poterunt, ut priusquam sese præcipitent unde regredi non liceat, consilio regant affectus, iisque rebus quærendis adhibeant, quas, ubi consecuti fuerint, nullo deinceps pudore pœnitentiâve torqueantur*.*

THESE observations of *Freinshemius* are certainly in a great measure very true, and very important. But so far as relates to *Sylla*, I am in some doubt whether or not he ever intended to continue his dictatorship longer, than till he had established the aristocratic party in the state, and had fully glutted his own vengeance. His ruling passion seems indeed to have been, not ambition ; but that infernal temper, revenge.

* *Freinsh.* Supp. lib. lxxxix. c. 37, 38.

HE

HE died foon afterwards. — In faying thefe words, *Crito* laid afide his papers; and entered into a converfation as ferious, as if the company had been then fitting round the bed of *Sylla*, juft after he had expired.

* * *

AFTER fome confiderable time paffed in meditation* on this folemn fubject, the company rofe, and retired to their feveral apartments, in order to drefs before dinner. As to the manner in which they paffed the remainder of the day, it may be fufficient to take notice only, that foon after dinner they parted.

CRITO fhut himfelf up among his books and papers, in order to prepare for to-morrow's lecture.

THE intended fubject of this lecture was the character of that great *roman*, QUINTUS SERTORIUS; who with very extraordinary ability fupported himfelf, and his profcribed friends in *Spain*, againft all the power of *Sylla's* party,

---

* *Forbear to judge; for we are finners all.*
Clofe up his eyes, and draw the curtain clofe:
And let us all to meditation.

Shakfpeare, Henry VI.

during

during the dictatorſhip, and for above five' years
after the death of that tyrannic uſurper.

Q. SERTORIUS was a hero, whom adverſity never funk, and proſperity never corrupted.
He was illuſtrious, not only for his conduct,
activity, and courage; but for his generoſity
alſo. Though an enemy of the bloody *Sylla,*
yet had he oppoſed the return of *Marius* to
Rome. He was remarkable for a ſtrong love
of his country, and for his earneſt deſire of
peace.

FROM his life, written by *Plutarch, Crito* had
collected ſeveral extracts, which he thought
would be peculiarly agreeable to his good pupil.
The firſt of theſe extracts deſcribed the filial
tenderneſs, which *Sertorius* bore to his aged
mother. Λεγεται ɤκ ηκιϛα της πατριδ℧ επιθυμειν δια
την μητερα, τραφεις ορφαν℧ υπ' αυτη, και το ϲυμπαν
αναϰειμεν℧ εϰεινη, &c. The ſecond contained an
account of his intended retreat from the horrid
ſcene of civil war to the *Fortunate* iſles: a project, from which *Horace* poſſibly might have
taken the hint of his ſixteenth epode :—a project
very feaſible for ſo ſmall a number of perſons, as
would probably accompany *Sertorius* in ſuch an
expedition; though very romantic, when applied

to

to fo large a multitude as mentioned by the lyric poet.

Great, perhaps, might have been the event of that expedition: perhaps *Sertorius* might have pufhed on the expedition fo far, *as to make that great difcovery*, which prince *Madoc* is fuppofed to have done; and *Columbus* certainly did, feveral centuries afterwards.

In compiling a paper from thefe materials, *Crito* was very agreeably engaged; when he was at once fuddenly damped, by the recollection of the *ofcan* children*, and the impofture of the ftag. Reflecting on thefe moft unworthy parts of *Sertorius's* hiftory, *Crito* threw afide the paper of his character, and determined to pafs over his name in filence; a name, which, if not fullied by thofe unhappy circumftances, would have been certainly one of the very brighteft in the catalogue of *roman* worthies.

While *Crito* was thus employed, the eldeft of the young gentlemen alfo was giving feveral hours of the afternoon to ftudy. His induftry was not, as ufual, exercifed in the cultivation of fome branch of parliamentary fcience, it was totally confined to the *roman* hiftory.

* Mr. *Hooke*, in the third volume of his *Roman* Hiftory, p. 192, exprefles much doubt of the truth of that ftory.

During

DURING the firſt hour, the objeƈt of his ſtudy was the civil war of *Lepidus;—Fax illius motûs,* ſays *Florus,* a Syllæ rogo *exarſit:*—a war, which, during it's ſhort continuance, threatened *deſtruction* to this city.   Yeſterday evening, while at *Ponte Molle,* he had recolleƈted the *happy* viƈtory, which *Pompey* had *there* gained over the army of *Lepidus.*

HE then proceeded to the hiſtory of *Spartacus,* whoſe inſurreƈtion produced a kind of *civil* war*, almoſt as deſtruƈtive to the inhabitants of *Italy,* as either the *Social* or the *Marian.*

IF, thought he to himſelf, ſome able political writer were to take a general view of the hiſtory of *Italy,* during the twenty years which intervened between the beginning of the *Social* war,

---

* This great inſurreƈtion was begun by about ſeventy gladiators: it was augmented by numbers of perſons in the ſame condition of life, and by multitudes of *gallic* and *german* ſlaves.   But the *bulk* of the *vaſt* armies, which followed the ſtandards of *Spartacus,*—that able general, *Cui nihil ad eximii imperatoris tuendum nomen deerat, præter humilitatem ſortis,*—ſeems moſt probably to have conſiſted of the inhabitants of *Italy.*   Such alſo appears to have been the army of ſeventy thouſand men, which he commanded in *Campania;* and that of one hundred and twenty thouſand, with which he once dared to march towards *Rome.*   On this account, the war of *Spartacus* may perhaps not improperly be conſidered as a kind of *civil* war. Ηδει ο Μιθριδατης Ιταλιαν Σπαρτακω μονομαχω συςασαν επι ςωμαιης.

Appian's Mithridatic war, edit. *Hen. Steph.* p. 240.

and

and the conclusion of that of *Spartacus ;* might he not with justice consider those annals, as the most dreadful examples of the misery and havoc which mankind has ever suffered from civil distractions? The thirty years civil war in *Germany**, —if the hostilities of that country may be called by that name—seems not to have been half so bloody.

The two following hours he employed in turning over *Appian's Mithridatic* history : a book, which he had formerly read with due care. The first fifty or sixty pages of that history he now surveyed in a very cursory manner; but, as he drew near the conclusion, his attention became gradually more engaged. With pleasure he regularly perused most part of *Lucullus's* and the whole of *Pompey's* campaigns in the *East,* whether against that mighty king, or against other states.

A.C. 65

It now drawing near evening, he rose from his studies, and took a walk towards that place in the *Campo Marzo,* where *Pompey* erected, in gratitude for these victories, his temple to *Minerva.* The church, which now stands on that spot, is called *Santa Maria sopra Minerva.*

* See the history of the wars and negotiations which preceded the treaty of *Westphalia,* compiled by *Pere Bougeant,* from the memoirs of the compte *d'Avaux.*

FROM

Thence he continued his walk to the *Campo del Fiore*, where fome remains of *Pompey's* theatre are ftill exifting, though covered by the modern palace of the prince *Pio*.

In returning to his lodgings from this walk, he fell into deep thought on the *civic* characters of *Pompey, Lucullus, Craſſus,* and *Julius Cæſar* *. The fenatorial profeſſion of this *engliſh* gentleman unhappily made it almoft neceſſary for him, in his hiftorical ftudies, to give much time to the confideration of *fuch* characters. In order to prepare himfelf for what he was to fee in parliament, he was forced to give diligent attention, though not approbation, to the conduct of thofe men; whofe abilities were great, and actions fometimes good; but their intentions in general not upright†.

Such was not the cafe of *Crito's* pupil. His moft happy difpofition of mind had inclined him to a ftate of life, far removed from thofe *great* objects, which excite the turbulent paſſions; and from that variety of negotiations, and hurry of diftractions, under which the moft virtuous often find it difficult not to lofe fight of their God. His ftudies alfo flowed in a far more pleafant

* At the time of *Pompey's* triumph, *Julius Cæſar* was about thirty-eight years of age.
† See Introduction to the firft book, vol. i. p. xxvii.

channel,

channel, in a much fmoother and purer ftream. He always rofe from them with a better idea of mankind, and of human nature; for his literary amufement was not hiftory in general, but an exquifitely felect biography. The daily perufal and reperufal of the lives of fome few of the very beft men, who ever exifted, were his principal *amufement:* pious reading, meditation, and prayer, were his *bufinefs* and *delight.* Happy, happy youth! Of whom, in fome degree, it might truly be faid, *Ejus cor & cogitatio non cum popularibus & communibus hominum viis erant; fed cum angelis in cœlo, aut cum perfectis viris in terrâ.*

If at any time other objects offered themfelves to his confideration, he gave them, comparatively, but a flight attention. Accordingly this afternoon he paffed indeed half an hour in turning over fome leaves of *Freinfhemius,* but diligently employed all the reft of the time in ftudies more fuitable to his own happy genius. In the evening he walked to the *Capitol:* he turned afide there, to view for fome moments the fragments of the coloffus of *Apollo,* which *M. Lucullus* brought from *Apollonia* to *Rome:* But he foon left them, and croffed over the court to the Mufæum. On afcending the ftairs, he turned into the room on the right, where the brazen vafe of *Mithri-*

dates

dates is preferved; and thence went on to the PHILOSOPHIC chamber.

THE young nobleman, who had come to table at dinner time very richly dreffed, paffed the afternoon and evening in making vifits to fome of the moft diftinguifhed perfons in *Rome.* Indeed, throughout this whole tour it was remarkable, that though he never flighted his countrymen, whom he accidentally met with abroad, yet in general he chiefly kept company with the *italians* when in *Italy*, as with the *french* while in *France.* Among thefe alfo he was very careful with whom he made acquaintance. He lived, wherever he came, with the great and eminent; with men honoured and reverenced in their feveral countries, not fo much for their birth and wealth, as for their virtue and knowledge.

CHAP.

C H A P. V.

FIFTEENTH DAY'S CONVERSATION.

SEVERAL noble villas are fituated within the walls of *Rome*. Among thefe the villa *Ludovifi* bears a *principal* rank, in regard both of it's greatnefs and beauty.

IT's buildings are enriched with fome capital paintings and fculptures, the labours of *Guercino* and *Bernini*. It's gardens are about a mile in circuit; and contain many pleafant walks, fome of which are filled with a great number of *antique* ftatues.

IN one of thefe walks the *englifh* company met this morning. After half an hour paffed in admiring the beauties of the place. *Crito's* pupil obferved, that feveral of thefe antique ftatues were found in digging on the fpot. How glad, added he, would the proprietors of fome *englifh* country-feats be, if in digging their ground for new plantations, or moving the foil for other purpofes, they had any chance of finding fuch plenty of antique

tique fculptures; fuch elegant ornaments for the embellifhment of their woods and lawns!

IT is no wonder, faid the young nobleman, that fuch treafures of *virtù* fhould be found on this fpot; as fome part of thefe gardens anciently made a part of the famous *Horti Salluſtiani.* You remember in what manner our learned antiquarian defcribed the great extent of thofe *Salluſtian* gardens, and the magnificent ſtruĉtures with which they were adorned.

THE converfation now wandered to the charaĉter of *Salluſt.* The eldeſt of the young gentlemen made feveral obfervations on this fubjeĉt. He afterwards proceeded to that *far more worthy topic,* the confideration of *Salluſt's writings;* particularly his hiſtory of the *Catalinarian* confpiracy.

How noble an idea, faid he, *here* prefents itfelf to our imagination! I mean, the idea of that grand debate in the *roman* fenate, the defcription of which was perhaps compofed by *Salluſt in this walk.* On that important day, three perfons of the higheſt names in the *roman* hiſtory eminently diſtinguiſhed themfelves in the houfe. How auguſt muſt have been the appearance of that parliament, in which *Cicero* prefided, while the debate

A.C.
63

bate was fupported on one fide by *Julius Cæfar*, and on the other by *Cato!*

IF I be not miftaken, *Cato* was then a *very young* member *. How pleafing, how encouraging is *this laft* circumftance, to perfons who may be entering the *britifh* fenate at the fame early period of life!

IN which of thofe celebrated characters, replied *Crito*, with a benevolent fmile, would you, dear fir, if you had lived at that time, have chofen to have appeared? In refpect of eloquence, notwithftanding the high abilities both of *Cato* and *Cæfar*, you certainly would on the whole have given the preference to *Tully*. As to patriotifm, I need not afk you on whom you would have fixed your choice: your ardent looks and language fufficiently declare in favour of young *Cato*.

IN converfing thus the company arrived at the further end of a winding moffy walk, where they found a perfectly undifturbed recefs, thickly fhaded with ilex and pine.

* *Hic tribunus plebis defignatus,* adhuc admodum adolefcens, *pæne inter ultimos interrogatus fententiam tantâ vi animi atque ingenii invectus eft in conjurationem; fic impendentia publici ftatûs pericula expofuit; ita confulis virtutem amplificavit, ut univerfus fenatus in ejus fententiam tranfiret, majorque pars ordinis ejus Catonem profequerentur domum.*
VELLEIUS PATERCULUS.

IN this retired fpot ftands an antique fenatorial ftatue. Leaning on it's bafis, the eldeft of the young gentlemen took out a pocket *Salluft*, and read to his friends, not without entering into the warmth and fpirit of the orator himfelf,—the fpeech of *Cato* in that great debate.

How could I wifh, added he in the conclufion, that I had brought with me hither to-day a pocket volume of *Tully's* works, particularly *Orationes illas Catilinarias, tam luculentas, tamque utiles reipublicæ!* We fhould have had the greateft pleafure in comparing thofe orations with this of *Cato;* particularly as our kind tutor would have affifted us with his remarks on them.

FAR be it from me, replied *Crito,* to pretend to judge of the eloquence or other *political* talents of thofe illuftrious *roman* fenators. It is much more fuitable to my profeffion, as well as to the defign of our prefent courfe of ftudies, to endeavour to learn what was good in their *moral* characters.

I WISH you would give me leave to afk your opinion, this morning, in relation to the moral character of *Cato.* If you pleafe to take your feats in this pleafant and fhady fpot, I will defire the liberty to trouble you, for a quarter of an hour,

hour, with fome extracts of his life. Thefe extracts are chiefly made from *Plutarch*, but fome are taken from *Salluft*. The latter will be particularly agreeable to you *here;* as, perhaps, according to your obfervation, this garden may be really the place, in which *Salluft* compofed fome part of his hiftory.

C A T O.

P A R T I.

THERE is not, in the whole *roman* hiftory, any virtuous character, which has been fo highly celebrated either by orators and poets, or by philofophers and hiftorians, as that of *Cato.* *Finxit illum ipfa natura ad honeftatem, gravitatem, temperantiam, magnitudinem animi, juftitiam; ad omnes denique virtutes magnum hominem & excelfum.* This excellent natural difpofition he greatly ftrengthened and improved, by fettling his aim always on *one* moft noble object: which was to attain to the moft exalted degree of virtue.

HE condefcended not to ftruggle for the low prizes, for which *Lucullus* or *Craffus*, *Cæfar* or *Pompey* were then contending. In that age of general luxury, avarice, and ambition, *non luxuriâ certabat cum luxuriofo, non divitiis cum di-*

vite,

vite, non factionibus cum factiofo: His elevated defign was to excel in that which is moft *excellent;* to copy, and if poffible to furpafs, the *beft* examples. *Amore fapientiæ, & moralis præcipue philofophiæ certabat cum fapientibus; virtute certabat cum ftrenuis, pudore cum modeftis, abftinentiâ cum innocentibus.* Or is *Cato* faid, in this noble emulation, to have thirfted for the praife of men. *Quanquam enim facta ejus erant bona, divina, egregia, totiufque vitæ ejus maximus fuit fplendor & gravitas; tamen effe quàm videri bonus malebat. Itaque, quo minus gloriam appetebat, eò magis illam affequebatur.*

Such is the character of *Cato,* according to *Salluft,* and feveral other ancient writers. On an impartial furvey of his hiftory, you will find many of thefe particulars to be very true: but, on the whole, you will have reafon to abate fomewhat of the panegyric.

Perhaps there never was a man,—continued *Crito,* addreffing himfelf to the eldeft of the young gentlemen,—to whom his *country* was more obliged for kind and noble *intentions,* and willing *labours in her fervice.* We fhall be ftrongly inclined to this opinion, if we examine his conduct in the many public characters, which at different times he fuftained.

Sorry

SORRY ought I to be, that I am obliged to obferve, that in one unhappy part of his life he carried his regard for his country much too far. Commanded by that country,—if the affemblies of the people, under the influence of a *Clodius* deferve *that* name,—to take the management of an unjuft war againft the king of *Cyprus*, *Cato obeyed*. He obeyed, though unwillingly, *it is faid by fome writers* *, in order to prevent feditions and farther confufions at home.

IN the execution of this office he reftored peace and tranquillity at *Byzantium*. He endeavoured to foften the fate of that unhappy prince againft whom he afted. With the greateft fidelity he delivered into the public treafury all the fpoils of the war, and all the treafures and furniture of the royal palace of *Cyprus*. Of thefe he accepted nothing for himfelf, except a ftatue of *Zeno*, which he brought to *Rome*.

HE refufed all honours from his country, and all rewards. As his only recompence, he defired that he might be permitted to give liberty to fome of the unhappy captives.

---

* Ανεκραγοντ᾽ δε τ᷉ Κάτωνος ως ενεδρα το πραγμα, και προπηλα-
κισμ᷉, ου χαρις εςιν, υπερηφανως ο Κλωδι᷉ και ολιγωρως: Ουκ᷉ν,
ειπεν, ει μη χαριν εχεις, ανιωμεν᷉ πλευση. Και προελθων ευθυς εις
τον δημον, ΕΚΥΡΩΣΕ ΝΟΜΩ την εκπεμψιν τ᷉ Κατων᷉.

Plutarchus, Catonis Vita.

D 3

THESE actions, certainly, are marks of a good mind; and yet, they are not sufficient to justify him for having engaged in this unjust war. *Ptolemy* might deserve to be punished for his vices; yet surely *Cato* must have been greatly deceived, in thinking that *Rome* had any authority to dethrone that king.

BUT let us turn our eyes from this *probably indefensible* part of his history. In most of it's other parts we shall find his love of his country to deserve very high commendations.

THIS paper, which I now take in my hand, contains some imperfect *extracts from Plutarch,* relative to *Cato's* conduct in four or five different public stations. Permit me to read it to you; and to add my strong wishes, that you could find time to-night, before you sleep, to peruse *Cato's* life, *as written by that good man.*

1. PART of *Cato's* life was military. He had at several times the command of considerable bodies of forces. In that station he is said to have behaved very nobly. Highly esteemed indeed he was by all men, but he was particularly beloved and almost adored by his soldiers; for he kept up his authority, but added to it persuasion and instruction. He was continually bestowing

on

on them either rewards or punifhments, according to their deferts. Whatever he commanded to be done by others, he himfelf took part in performing *. In diet and labour he made himfelf equal to the common foldier; in love of difcipline, in courage and conduct, he was equal, if not fuperiour, to moft of the generals of *Rome.*

But, what was much more important, he reformed the avarice and cruelty of the *roman* army, which was very infamous at that time for it's oppreffions, both public and private, on the country. *Cato* looked on it as a fmall matter, fingly to fhow *himfelf* virtuous. He endeavoured to make all *his* foldiers like himfelf. In a word, he rendered *his* forces fo well difciplined, that it was hard to fay whether they were more valiant or juft. Under his guidance, they were formidable to their enemies, but peaceable and courteous to all others: they were fearful to do wrong, brave and forward to act nobly.

In relation to this conduct of *Cato* towards the foldiers, as well as that of *Scævola* towards the

---

* The like excellent character is given of the *fpartan Lycurgus;* of whom *Juftin* fays, *Nihil, lege ullâ,* in alios *fanxit, cujus non* ipfe *primus,* in fe, *documenta daret.* "He ordained nothing by law concerning others, of which he did not firft fet them a pattern, in his own behaviour." HISTOR. lib. iii. c. ii.

publicans,

publicans, I find on my papers a reference to the
third chapter of *St. Luke*, verſes 12, 13, 14. But
let u. proceed.

2. *AS tribune, and as prætor, Cato* aĉted with
great ſpirit;—the ſpirit, not of turbulent faĉtion,
but of true patriotiſm ; of eager contention in the
cauſe of liberty. Conſcious of his own innocence
and virtue, he was continually ſtemming and reſiſting the general luxury and corruption of the
times. With the greateſt conſtancy and fortitude,
he was intrepid in reſiſting all faĉtions: unmoved
by the tumults and violence of the people, and
by the threats and hatred of the great, whether
ſeparated in their intereſts, or combined together
againſt him. He was invincible by all temptations which could be propoſed; and far ſuperiour
to all the affronts and ridicule, which could be caſt
on him by thoſe, who at the ſame time really moſt
envied his glory.—In public, indeed, as well as
in private life, you will always, dear ſir, find the
knaves endeavouring to repreſent the honeſt men
in a ridiculous light.

3. ON the *tribunal of juſtice, Cato,* as you well
know, was above all influence of corruption or
fear. He was reſpeĉted by all: he was dreaded
by the guilty: yet his ſeverity to them was *in*
reality

reality the mere confequence of his compaffion for the public.

H E fupported *the majefty of the laws*, above the power of *Pompey*, or the intereft of any other great men. In all thefe things he fhowed the moft firm attachment to juftice and truth.

How could fuch a man, faid the eldeft of the young gentlemen, mifs obtaining the higheft honours in the ftate? How much was it to be wifhed, for the fake of his country, that he had fucceeded in his election for the confulfhip! In that high office he might perhaps have prevented the civil war, which broke out, if I miftake not, in the following year.

His lofs of that election, replied *Crito, feems* indeed to have been a very great misfortune to the public. But it was no perfonal affliction to himfelf; for he bore the lofs with fo much magnanimity, as to turn that event to his ftill greater glory. The fplendour of virtue is, as his example fhowed, independent of the fuffrages of the people. It is far fuperiour to all honours; and, on the other hand, no popular ignorance or injuftice can tarnifh it's luftre. *Horace* perhaps alluded to this part of *Cato's* hiftory.

Virtus,

Virtus, repulfæ nefcia fordidæ,
  Intaminatis fulget honoribus :
    Nec fumit aut ponit fecures
      Arbitrio popularis auræ *.

But let us proceed to the confideration of *Cato's*
merits, in fome other public ftations, in which he
was really placed.

4. In the office of *quæftor, or manager of the*
public treafury, Cato exercifed the greateft diligence, abilities, and fidelity.   He reduced the
national accounts, from a ftate of confufion, into
good order : he took care, that the public during
his adminiftration of the exchequer, fhould neither
do nor fuffer wrong : he punctually exacted what.
ever was due to the treafury,—forcing, particularly, feveral of *Sylla's* blood-hounds, to refund
the fpoils of their rapine and cruelty ; and on the
other hand, he with great readinefs paid all perfons, who had juft demands on government. On
the whole, he left the treafury in a flourifhing
condition ; and made it evidently appear, how
the ftate may be made rich, without oppreffing
the people.

5. I wish, dear fir, that I were able to defcribe, in a proper ftyle, the conduct of *Cato*

* CARM. lib. iii. od. 2.

in

in his greateſt public ſtation, *in his ſenatorial office.*

IN the *roman* ſenate, *Cato* was much admired for his *eloquence.* He was ſtill more reſpeɛted for *thoſe other talents,* without which all ſtrength of genius, all ſweetneſs and charms of language, are very inſufficient qualifications for a ſenatorial life: I mean *induſtry* and *integrity.*

FROM the firſt day on which he took his ſeat in the houſe, he applied himſelf to *buſineſs* with the moſt indefatigable diligence. He was continually employed, either in informing himſelf on ſome matter of moment, or in doing his duty by communicating his lights to others:

Vigilando, agendo, bene conſulendo.

BUT his ſenatorial *integrity* chiefly merits your attention. It gained him general veneration while alive; and during all ſucceeding centuries, it has made his name the ſymbol of patriotic virtue.

ON a ſubjeɛt ſo well known, I need to ſpeak but little. Suffer me only to obſerve, that *Cato* was in the ſenate, uniformly, the ſame honeſt man as when ſeated on the bench of the judges, or

when

when employed in any branch of bufinefs, whether of public or private life.

*   *   *

CRITO here paufed,—fome converfation *accidentally* rifing, relative to the glorious charaĉter
of integrity, which the judges of *England* have
acquired, in a degree far fuperiour to the judges
of *France,* or to thofe of feveral other countries.

IT was not long however, before the young
nobleman defired *Crito* to continue his leĉture.

I FIND in my memorandum-papers, faid *Crito,*
two inftances of *Cato's fenatorial* conduĉt particularly marked down: one to be confidered as an
example of his love to his country; the other, as
an inftance of his juftice to the reft of mankind.

1. HE very greatly affifted *Cicero,* in faving
Rome from that deftruĉtion, with which the *Cati-
linarian* confpiracy threatened it. But it is needlefs for me to trouble you with any refleĉtions on
this head, as it has been the fubjeĉt of your converfation this morning.

2. THE fecond particular is related by *Plutarch*
as follows.

JULIUS

JULIUS CÆSAR attacked the *germans*, who at that time were at peace with the *romans*; and put three hundred thoufand of them to the fword. His party made a motion in the fenate, that a public thankfgiving fhould be proclaimed on the occafion: But *Cato*, on the contrary, earneftly argued, that *Cæfar* fhould be given up by the *roman* government to the vengeance of thofe nations, whom, probably without any command from his country, he had invaded. " By fuch a " facrifice, faid he, let us endeavour to expiate " the injuftice of this war. It is highly proper, " however, that the motion for a thankfgiving " fhould be approved, fince we have great reafon " to thank the gods. They have as yet fpared the " commonwealth; and not taken vengeance on " our armies, for the cruelty and wickednefs of " our general."

NOBLE was this fentiment;—but it would have been far more noble, if *Cato* himfelf had been fo happy, as never to have feen the fhores of *Cyprus*.

IF I be not miftaken, faid the eldeft of the young gentlemen, a fimilar fentiment is exprefled by *Livy*, in one of the fpeeches of *Paulus Æmilius* *. But pray proceed.

* *Livy*, book xxxviii. c. 45, 46.

WE

*   *   *

WE have been fuperficially confidering, replied *Crito*, the conduct of this celebrated patriot,
during the period in which the *roman* republic
ftood.   For fome time the commonwealth fupported itfelf, though fhaken to it's loweft roots
by the continual ftorms of faction and anarchy;

———— *illa ufque minatur,*
Et tremefacta comam concuffo vertice nutat *,

BUT, foon after the conclufion of *Cæfar's* gal-
lic and *german* campaigns, that fatal civil war
broke out, which *Cato* had long foretold, and laboured to prevent.

THE conduct of *Cato* in the civil war feems,
in feveral refpects, very fimilar to that amiable
behaviour of lord *Falkland*, which you, dear fir,
have often admired, in the fourth and feventh
books of *Clarendon's* hiftory.

CATO, like lord *Falkland*, was always figh-
ing and labouring for peace. Αει μεν ειχετο μιᾶς
γνωμης, ελπιζων διαλυσεις.

———————————————
* VIRG. *Æn.* ii. 628.

WHEREVER

WHEREVER *Cato* had the command, he was very merciful to the inhabitants of the country which was the feat of war.

BY *his* perfuafion it was agreed, at a council held in *Pompey's* camp, that, during the courfe of the campaign, no city fhould be facked, and no *roman* fhould be killed, but in the heat of battle.

IN the progrefs of the war, *Cato* bore patiently much fatigue and diftrefs. In the few engagements at which he was prefent, he fhowed much perfonal courage; and animated his friends with a confiderable degree of the fame fpirit: Yet never did he rejoice for any victory.

IMMEDIATELY after the obtaining of any fuccefs, *Cato* vifited with forrow the field of battle; he there bewailed that curfed ambition, which was the deftruction of fo many of his countrymen: he fhed tears on the corpfes even of *Cæfar's* fol-diers.

INDEED, from the day on which this civil war broke out, to the day of his death, *Cato's* countenance was filled with a fixt melancholy, a perpetual fadnefs; unchanged by any fuccefs, which at any time attended his own party.

ON the other hand, in all the heavy misfortunes, and repeated defeats, which at laſt totally ſunk it, he was himſelf unmoved; but condeſcending to thoſe of his friends, who were willing to make their peace with the conqueror. He was anxious and indefatigable, to his laſt breath, in doing every thing in his power, that could be beneficial to them.

Can any thing be thought of for their ſervice?
Whilſt I yet live, let me not live in vain *.

* * *

SCARCE had *Crito* repeated theſe lines, when his pupil's ſervant came, to acquaint him, that at the garden-gate there was a perſon, who was deſirous of ſpeaking to him, if he were at leiſure. On this notice *Crito* immediately roſe, and went with the ſervant to the gate. The young gentlemen alſo quitted their moſſy ſeats, and employed a quarter of an hour in walking about the garden.

DURING this walk, *Crito's* pupil obſerved, that the firſt four acts of the tragedy of *Cato* were compoſed by Mr. *Addiſon during his reſidence at*

---

* ADDISON's *Cato.*

Rome.

Rome. Is it not probable, faid he, that *Addifon* then frequently vifited *thefe Salluftian gardens,* and compofed here fome of the moft fhining paffages?

But oh! my friends, your fafety fills my heart
With anxious thoughts: a thoufand fecret terrours
Rife in my foul: how fhall I fave my friends?
'Tis now, O Cæfar, I begin to fear thee.

HAD *Cato,* replied the eldeft of the young gentlemen, any juft reafon to fear *Cæfar* on this account? *Cæfar* was indeed a man of *blood,* and had in his former wars deftroyed fome millions of his fellow-creatures; but yet, in general, his behaviour to his enemies, in this conteft with *Pompey,* had been full of clemency.

THIS learned young gentleman began now to expatiate on *Cæfar's* mercy, contrafting it with the cruelty of *Sylla* in the foregoing civil war. He proceeded next to confider *Cæfar's* courage, activity, and aftonifhing abilities of mind. He fpoke much of feveral of his great exploits: he concluded however his reflections on the life of this moft famous man, by repeating fome of *Addifon's* verfes.

——— *'Tis an impious greatnefs;*
And mixt with too much horrour to be envied*.

DURING this part of the converfation the company arrived at the garden-gate. They found
Crito there with the *irifh* painter, who had been
lately relieved by the young nobleman's generofity. This was the firft day of his venturing
abroad, after his late illnefs: he was ftill very
weak, and far from well; yet he had been at his
noble patron's lodgings already this morning; and
hearing that he was gone to the *Ludovifi* gardens,
had followed him thither, being very defirous of
taking the earlieft opportunity to exprefs his gratitude.

IT is needlefs to add, that on this occafion the
young nobleman behaved with all poffible politenefs and humanity. After fome time they feparated: the painter returned to his lodgings, and
our *englifh* company proceeded to the adjoining
circus of *Salluft.*

---

* A noble modern writer, the author of the Dialogues of
the Dead, fums up *Cæfar's* charaƈter in the following manner:

" *Cæfar's* courage and talents were equal to the objeƈt to
" which his ambition afpired,—the dominion of the world:
" and he exercifed a fovereignty unjuftly acquired with a
" magnanimous clemency. But it would have been better
" for his country, and for mankind, if he had never ex-
" ifted."

So extenfive were the gardens of *Salluft*, as to contain, 'befide many other buildings, a large circus. Of this there are to this day fome confiderable remains *. On it's fouthern fide is to be feen an antique octangular temple, rendered at prefent a kind of grotto, by the ruins of other ftructures, which have fallen on it, and almoft buried it. *Salluft*, probably in compliment to his patron *Julius Cæfar*, confecrated this temple to *Venus*.

THIS fabric, faid the young nobleman while entering it, feems to have been a kind of monument, erected by *Salluft* in honour of *Cæfar's* exploits. The ftatue of *Venus*, which was placed in this temple, was adorned, if I be not miftaken, with a corflet of *britifh* pearls. Thefe pearls came, I fuppofe, from *Sandwich*. About two or three years ago I was on a vifit at a gentleman's houfe in that neighbourhood. We rode one morning, I remember, to the old *roman* walls at *Rutupiæ*: another morning we rode towards *Deal* and *Dover*; frequently recollecting in the way the defcription of that coaft in *Cæfar's* Commentaries.

I HAVE alfo had the pleafure, faid the eldeft of the young gentlemen, of taking the fame ride.

* See *Abbate Venuti's* Roman Antiquities, vol. i. p. 86, 87.

The

The fummer before laft I made the tour of the coafts of *Kent* and *Suffex.* My *principal defire* was to fee the ground, on which *Julius Cæfar* had trodden.—I was not then fatiated with *roman* antiquities. I had alfo fome curiofity to vifit the fhore in *Kent,* where the *faxon Hengift;* and in *Suffex,* where the *norman* conqueror landed. Ought not our pride to be humbled, when we refleƈt how often in ancient times our ifland has been invaded and fubdued?

Each of thefe conquefts, replied *Crito,* though they might juftly appear very heavy calamities at the times when they happened, yet in their long confequences have produced very confiderable benefit to our ifland.

To the *roman* conqueft *Britain* owes, perhaps, it's firft civilization; certainly it's firft converfion to chriftianity.

To the *faxon* conqueft we are indebted for that fyftem of *government,* which is to this day the bafis of *englifh* liberty. Many good effeƈts of *faxon piety* alfo are ftill great bleffings to us.

To the *norman* conqueft we owe not perhaps fo much refpeƈt. Yet we may be certain, that

Providence

Providence intended some real good by that great event.

You were mentioning your journey to *Suffex*: Give me leave to recollect, that many years ago, when I was a very young man, I was also in that county. From *Brighthelmstone* I made with some friends a short voyage to *Dieppe*. During that voyage, we often thought of the hostile fleets, *roman*, *faxon*, and *norman*, which in various ages have crossed, or rather filled the *british* channel. The *Portus Iccius*, indeed, was then at a considerable distance from us, but the port of *St. Valery en Somme*, whence *William* the Conqueror set sail with eight hundred vessels*, lay but some few leagues to the northward of our track. We landed at *Dieppe;* and during the few days that we passed there, had great pleasure in reading the latter part of sir *William Temple's* introduction to the history of *England:* we had fortunately brought that book with us from *Bright-helmstone.*

Did you go up any higher into *Normandy?* said *Crito's* pupil. I have heard it is a very fine country, and very like to *England.*

---

* The fleet of *Julius Cæsar*, and the fleet of *William* the Conqueror, each consisted of above eight hundred sail.

WE

WE went up no farther than *Rouen*, replied
Crito. The country feemed to us to refemble the
open parts of *Northamptonſhire:* it has however
greatly the advantage of that country, by being
fituate at leaſt four degrees more to the fouth.
It abounds with apple-trees, planted, not in orchards, as in our cyder-counties; but in ſtraight
rows along the roads, or fcattered up and down
in the corn fields. You would have great pleafure in making a ſhort tour through that province
of *France*, efpecially as in various parts of it you
would probably fee many marks, ſtill remaining,
of it's conneſtion with *England* in former ages.

SIMILAR obfervations occurred to me, faid
the eldeſt of the young gentlemen, in the firſt part
of our prefent long tour; I mean, while we were
in thofe parts of *Germany*, from which our *faxon*
anceftors came.—But furely, dear fir, you have
at prefent an opportunity of favouring us with
fome very noble refleſtions. Thefe gloomy and
folitary *roman* ruins cannot fail of fuggeſting to
you a train of important fentiments; efpecially,
if you be of our noble young friend's opinion,
that this edifice was built partly at leaſt on occafion of the firſt connexion of *Britain* with the
roman empire,

I AM

I AM by no means capable, replied *Crito,* of fupporting the dignity of that topic. Befides, it is now late in the morning: if you pleafe we will return to our lodgings. You may there meditate at leifure on all the various changes which have happened to our country. But why do I fay *happened?* I remember a noble reflection of *Bof-fuet,* towards the conclufion of his univerfal hif-tory. *Ne parlons plus ni de hazard ni de fortune; ou parlons en feulement comme d'un nom, dont nous couvrons notre ignorance. C'eſt DIEU, qui pre-pare les effets dans les caufes les plus eloignées; & qui frappe ces grands coups, dont le contrecoup porte fi loin.*

* * *

THE company now walked to their lodgings. During that walk, and at dinner-time alfo, the converfation chiefly dwelt on the ftate of *Britain* in *Cæfar's* time. It afterwards returned to *Cato's* character; the young nobleman politely reviving that topic, in compliment to *Crito.*

I COULD wifh, faid he, that the ftatue of *Zeno,* which, as you informed us this morning, *Cato* brought hither from *Cyprus,* were ftill preferved in fome of the *roman* mufæums. In that cafe, I

E 4

fhould

fhould have been very glad of the pleafure of attending you on a vifit to it this afternoon.

THERE is in the *Capitoline* mufæum, replied *Crito's* pupil, a noble ftatue of that philofopher. You *muft* remember it; it is the moft remarkable piece of fculpture in the *ftanza dei filofofi.* It was found in the ruins of the villa of *Antoninus Pius.*

Poffibly, faid the young nobleman, it may be the identical ftatue; at leaft we may fancy it fo, and vifit it with that idea. If you pleafe we may walk thither in the evening, as foon as we have had our tea. I fhould be very glad to take a walk to that part of the town, as I want to call at the print fhop, at the upper end of the *Corfo.*

*   *   *

THE bell of the *Capitol* clock ftruck three and twenty *, when this *englifh* company arrived there. They went up ftairs into the mufæum; and paffing through feveral of it's apartments, proceeded to the *ftanza dei filofofi,* where they fat down, being much heated by their long walk.

CRITO'S pupil was the firft, who recovered his fpirits after this fatigue.

* FIVE, in the afternoon.

THERE

THERE is not, faid he, with peculiar earneftnefs, any part of the *Capitoline* mufæum more
pleafing, or more inftru&ive, than this apartment ;
this *philofophic chamber*, as it is *juftly* called, from
it's being filled with two fuch noble ranges of near
an hundred antique bufts of moft of the learned
men of *Greece*, particularly the philofophers of
Athens.

I CAME hither alone yefterday afternoon, and
perufed in this chamber part of *Milton's* Paradife
Regained.   I then confidered myfelf as prefent,
not only

On the Tarpeian rock, the citadel
Of great and glorious Rome, queen of the earth,
So far renown'd, and with the fpoils enricht
Of nations.

But what is a far more pleafing idea.

Ω Χαιρ' Αθηνων, Χαιρε Φιλτατη πολις.

Athens, the eye of Greece, mother of arts,
Of eloquence, and fage philofophy,
From heav'n defcended to the low-rooft houfe
Of Socrates !——

* Par. Reg. b. iv. 240 and 273.

Saying

Saying this, he approached the buſt of *Socrates,* which is placed near that of *Homer,* fronting the entrance.——How deſervedly—continued he, addreſſing himſelf to his noble young friend—may the buſts of theſe two great men claim their ſtation in all ſuch muſæums as this; one at the head of all the philoſophers, the other at the head of all the tragic and lyric poets of *Greece!* Theſe two indeed, *gave breath to all the reſt.* How fortunate is the education of thoſe young men, who in poetry chiefly ſtudy the one, in philoſophy the other of theſe moſt exalted geniuſes!

THINKING of this, I was highly pleaſed juſt now, when, in paſſing through the firſt apartment of this muſæum, you ſtopped to admire the elegant deſign of that marble ſepulchre, found in the villa of *Alexander Severus:* at one end of which is *Homer,* receiving his book from the genius of poetry; at the other, *Socrates,* attending to the inſtructions of a veiled figure, which leans on a column, and repreſents moral philoſophy: the whole front of the monument being filled with the ſtatues of the nine *muſes,* all of the fineſt ſculpture.

WHILE you were ſo happy here yeſterday, in the company of *Milton,* ſaid *Crito,* I was not leſs ſo at home, in that of *Xenophon.* You left your

Xenophon

Xenophon on your table, open at the conclusion
of one of his *Socratic* discourses. I could not
help taking it up, and reading with great pleasure
the last sentence, which breathes such grateful
affection to the memory of his beloved master,
exceeded only by a still greater love and thirst of
virtue. Εγω μεν δη κατανοων τ8 ανδρ℗ τηντε σοφιαν,
και την γενναιοτητα, ουτε μη μεμνησθαι δυναμαι αυτ8,
8τε μεμνημεν℗ μη 8κ επαινειν. Ει δε τις των αρετης
εφιεμενων ωφελιμωτερω τινι Σωκρατ8ς συνεγενετο, εκεινον
εγω τον ανδρα ΑΞΙΟΜΑΚΑΡΙΣΤΟΤΑΤΟΝ νομιζω. Or
could I help reflecting then with due gratitude,
how *we* are all blessed with *that high happiness*,
the idea of which *Xenophon* regarded with such
admiration; and with a desire, which seems to
have something of divine inspiration. We have
all of us an instructor and leader in the path of
virtue, *far superiour* to *Socrates*. Let us then
make the best use of all these lights so graciously
bestowed on us. In the study of ethical institu-
tion from the moralists of *Greece*, let us principally confine ourselves to the study of the doctrines of the *benevolent* and *humble Socrates:* in a
far superiour study, let us apply ourselves principally to learn and imbibe the character and
temper of it's most *beneficent*, and most *humble*,
though DIVINE founder. Happy, truly happy,
are those, whose education is founded *on these two
bases!*

BUT,

BUT, at prefent, let us have the pleafure of following you round this room; and of making with you a fhort vifit to thefe feveral philofophers, who were almoft all of them men of great genius, though none of them equal to *Socrates*.

SAYING this, and paffing by *Epicurus*, he ftopt a confiderable time in filence before the bufts of *Plato* and *Ariftotle*. He then proceeded to the ftatue of *Zeno*.

AFTER hearing the obfervations of his young friends relative to the fculpture of this ftatue, he drew a chair near to it's pedeftal; and fitting down, defired leave to finifh in that place thofe papers relative to *Cato's* charaĉter, which he had begun to read to them this morning in the *Ludovifi* gardens.

C A T O.

PART II.

THE charaĉter of *Cato* is fo famous, that in forming a catalogue of *roman* worthies, his name could not with any propriety be omitted. At the fame time the truth of hiftory will oblige us to own, that in feveral particulars this great man was much mifled.

HE

HE was certainly fo, as we obferved this morning, in the affair of *Cyprus*. Probably, a miftaken principle of obedience to the commands of his country engaged him in that unjuft expedition.

THE other principal objections to his character are the feveral marks, which appear in it, of harfhnefs and feverity, of pride and want of condefcenfion in accomodating himfelf to thofe cuftoms and manners of the age, which in themfelves were indifferent. Add to thefe, fome great errours in family-life; and above all, the moft unhappy cataftrophe of his laft hour.

A.C.
46

BUT, on the other hand, how many circumftances are there to be found in his hiftory, which evidently fhow, as *Tully* obferves, *quòd hæc omnia non à naturâ Catonis erant!*

CATO'S temper, though full of fpirit and refolution, was far from being deficient in tendernefs, or mercy. This is plain, not only from his amiable conduct during the civil war, which was mentioned this morning, but alfo from many other of his actions. He was conftantly difinclined to all unneceffary punifhments. He always fhowed the greateft gentlenefs, courtefy, and good-nature to *all* in private life. *Eâ conditione Cato nobis in*
hoc

hâc civitate natus eſt, ut ejus opes & ingenium, præſidio multis etiam alieniſſimis: vix cuiquam inimico exitio eſſe deberet. Bona M. Catonis, quæ ille adeptus eſt, ut multis prodeſſe poſſet*. His perſon and lands were devoted to the ſervice of his friends. The ſweetneſs of his temper is, above all, moſt viſible in that regard, which he bore to his brother; and which was continually increaſing, even from his moſt early years : never perhaps was there a more amiable and beautiful ſcene of fraternal love, than that which is contained in *Cato's* hiſtory.

IN point of pride, he certainly was *in general* averſe to flattery. He often refuſed honours, and ſeems to have done ſo from a motive of real humility : for when every one thought him worthy of the higheſt honour, he alone was of the contrary opinion.

AS to want of condeſcenſion in accommodating himſelf to the times, he certainly often ſhowed great wiſdom in yielding, as far as he thought he might, in order to prevent greater evil.

I WISH I could be totally ſilent in regard to the diſmal, and never ſufficiently lamented end of

* See *Tully's* oration for *Muræna.*

Cato's

Cato's life. Moſt unworthy was it of his former fortitude and virtue; and far inferiour to the example, which the pontifex *Scævola* had ſhown here at *Rome*, or to that which *Regulus* had ſhown in *the ſame african* country;—for *Carthage* was almoſt within ſight of *Utica**. On this ſubjeɛt I ought to ſpeak moſt unwillingly: yet let me obſerve, that ſome kind of deſpondency, or fear, is always the original motive of ſuicide; fear either of ſhame, pain, want, or ſomewhat ſimilar; —a paſſion, which ſurely never had a place in *Cato's* natural conſtitution.

To what cauſe then are moſt of the ſtains, in the charaɛter of *Cato,* to be attributed? Probably to his inſtruɛtors, the ſtoics; for in their writings, moſt of theſe capital defeɛts are deſcribed as moral excellencies.

Let us attend to what *Cicero* ſays in various places on this ſubjeɛt. *In Marco Catone hæc bona quæ videmus divina & egregia, ipſius ſcitote eſſe propria. Quæ nonnunquam requirimus, ea ſunt omnia, non a naturâ ſuâ, ſed a magiſtro. His enim tot tantiſque ejus virtutibus acceſſit adjumentum doɛtrinæ, non moderatæ, neque mitis, ſed aſ-*

* See the comparifon of the charaɛter of *Regulus* with that of *Cato* in this refpeɛt, in *St. Auſtin's* book *de Civitate Dei,* lib. i. c. 24.

perioris

perioris ac durioris. Stoicorum scilicet discipli-
nam auctoribus eruditissimis inductus arripuit, &
talium præceptorum (Zenonis præsertim, summo
ingenio viri, magistri sui) studiis flagravit. How
much is it indeed to be wished, *ut ad alios magi-*
stros aliqua te fortuna, Cato, cum illâ naturâ de-
tulisset!

YET, seated as we are at present by *Zeno's*
statue, let us not omit to do proper justice even
to the stoics themselves. Many of their doctrines
are very noble, very exalted; many of their examples deserve our study, and claim our imitation. But, at the same time that we acknowledge
this, let us again and again bless Providence, for
having assisted *us* with other examples, far more
perfect than those of any *roman* worthy: with
other instructions, far more correct and complete
than this *grecian* philosophy, which thus abounded with many errours, mixed with much wisdom,
and taught great vices, mixed with great virtues.

CRITO now began to consider the christian
religion, in contrast with the stoic philosophy.
There is no need to insert here the particulars of
his discourse: they seem indeed to be in some
measure foreign from the subject of these *Roman*
Conversations. It may be sufficient to observe
in general, that his discourse was, in it's beginning,

ning, cool; it was throughout learned and judicious; but in it's progrefs, his heart became gradually warm; and at the conclufion broke out
into a pure *flame* of piety.

THE chriftian charaĉter, faid he towards the
clofe, is not only more grand, than any imagined
perfeĉtion in this fo much celebrated philofophy;
but it has alfo a grace, amiablenefs, and beauty,
which never adorned any ftoic vifion. Much
fuller is it, than ftoicifm, of the fpirit of true juftice, but infinitely fuller of benevolence and
mercy: fuller of the fpirit of juft inflexibility
in what is right; but ftill more full of condefcenfion and fweetnefs: fuller of fortitude; but infinitely more abounding in patience, refignation,
and hope: greater as to exaltation of mind; but
infinitely greater in humility, and in the moft
grateful acknowledgement, that all it's virtues are
the gifts of heaven.

All that we have and are, we have received, O
    Lord, from Thy grace:
All that we defire and hope, we humbly expeĉt in
    Thy glory.

INDULGE me, my dear fellow ftudents, in thefe
refleĉtions. The grace of heaven is the great
diftin-

diftinguifhing bleffing of the chriftian difpenfa-
tion: we cannot employ our meditations on a
fubject more fublime.

I REMEMBER, that about laft *Whitfuntide* I was
taking a folitary walk in this part of *Rome,* and
paffed by a church fituated in one of the narrow
lanes at the foot of *this Capitoline* hill. The
hymn of *Veni, Sancte Spiritus,* was then performing there, fet to moft affecting folemn mufic. In attending to fome of the notes and words
of that heavenly harmony, I could not avoid
recollecting a paffage in a very venerable writer;
who, though fomewhat barbarous in his language,
—as he lived probably about the time of our
king *Richard* the Second,—yet in his fentiments
is generally very exalted; far more fo, on the
whole, than *any of thefe* philofophers.

*O verè cæleftis Gratia, fine quâ nihil doctrina,
nihil eloquentia, nihil ingenium valet, in confpectu Dei!*

*O beatiffima Gratia, quæ pauperem fpiritu,
virtutibus divitem facis: & divitem multis bonis,
humilem corde reddis!*

*Veni! defcende ad nos! Tu fortitudo noftra.
Tu auxilium confers, & confilium. Tu lumen
cordis.*

cordis.   Tu fugatrix triſtitiæ, & ablatrix timoris. Tu devotionis nutrix.

Tu nos ſemper prævenias, & bonis operibus jugiter præſtes eſſe intentos*.

* *Imitatio Chriſti.* lib. iii. c. 55.

CHAP.

CHAP. VI.

SIXTEENTH DAY'S CONVERSATION.

THE character of *Cicero* being the intended subject of this day's conversation, the company agreed to meet early in the *Farnese* gardens, which cover most part of the summit of mount *Palatine;* and, after passing an hour there, to set out from them in their coach, and dine at *Frescati,* a town about twelve miles distant from *Rome.*

THE *northern part* of the *Farnese* gardens was the appointed place of their meeting. *Crito* walked thither about nine o'clock,—according to his *english* watch *,—and found his beloved company all arrived there before him.

THE young nobleman had seated himself on a projecting part of the hill, and was taking a sketch of the narrow valley of the *Forum Romanum,* which lay beneath him, and of the opposite *Clivus Capitolinus.*

* Or *fifteen* o'clock, in modern *Italy.*

His

His pupil was leaning againſt a cyprefs, and ſilently ſtudying an octavo, which contained ſome of *Tully's* rhetorical and philoſophical works.

THE third young gentleman was walking with a volume of the Orations in his hand; ſometimes reflecting wtih high pleaſure, that *Tully's* houſe ſtood in *this part* of the *Farneſe* gardens *; ſometimes repeating aloud ſeveral of that great orator's ſhining periods.

CRITO liſtened to him for a conſiderable time with great attention, and then, being always ready to partake of the ſatisfaction felt by any part of this good company, he turned round to the young nobleman, and admired all the merit of his drawing.

HE afterwards ſat down under the cyprefs by his pupil's ſide.

THE company now deſired him to favour them, as uſual, with the contents of one of his papers.

BEFORE I begin, ſaid he, to ſpeak of the character of *Tully*, which has been repreſented by ſeveral eminent writers in *very different* lights, I

---

* See Abbate *Venuti's* Roman Antiquities, vol. i. p. 15.

ought

ought to premife, that I by no means think myfelf a competent judge of the queftion: my judgment is far too weak, my knowledge far too fu-
perficial. When I compofed this paper, I lay
under another difadvantage alfo, being in great
want of proper books to confult on the occafion.
Neither can a traveller carry a library with him,
nor muft he expeﬓ to have this want fupplied at
the bookfeller's fhops, in the towns through which
he paffes. The only book of the kind, which I
could then procure, was a *Middleton's Cicero,*
which I bought at *Modena;* and which had belonged to a *fcottifh* gentleman, who died there on
his travels.

THE paper in my hand, as you will therefore
expeﬓ, confifts of little more than mere extraﬓs
from Dr. *Middleton.* In fome future year of
your lives, you may perhaps allot fome leifure
time for thorough and impartial examination of
Cicero's charaﬓer. You will be greatly affifted
in that examination, by fome books which have
been lately publifhed in *France* and *England,* and
by others which are faid to be now preparing for
the prefs. Long before that time, you will have
totally forgotten, that I ever troubled you with a
paper on the fubjeﬓ; otherwife it would be proper, that I fhould make an apology for it. Indeed, when I recolleﬓ the criticifms made by

                                            fome

fome learned perfons on *Cicero's* conduct, I am afraid, that in this paper his defects are too much concealed or palliated: and on the contrary, when I take up Dr. *Middleton,* I have the greateft reafon to think, that in this my very imperfect compilation I have not done juftice to the hundredth part of his merit.

C I C E R O.

P A R T I.

IT feems a confiderable mark, not only of a goodnefs of heart, but alfo of real ftrength of underftanding,—and a very proper method for improving both thefe qualities,—if, in the confideration of any great and exalted character, the ftudent obferves indeed it's defects, yet neither dwells too much on them, nor views them in the moft unfavourable light; but candidly confiders the whole character together, and then applies his attention more peculiarly to the ftudy of thofe parts, which are the moft noble or beutiful.

THE character of *Cicero* has, for many ages, excited the attention, and, *generally fpeaking,* the admiration of mankind.

IN

IN difcourfing on fuch a chara&er, let us be as filent as poffible in relation to it's imperfe&ions; and, according to the generous fcope and intention of thefe our *Roman* Converfations, endeavour to improve ourfelves as much as we can, by diligently ftudying it's real excellencies.

LET us confider, that though *Cicero* lived in one of the moft corrupt ages that ever was known, yet he was totally free from any ftain, either of avarice, or luxurious debauchery.

As to pride, the third great vice of thofe times, *Cicero* had nothing of that cruel *roman* haughtinefs, which was the occafion of much mifery to *Rome*, and to thofe nations, who had any connection with her. *Cicero* was not proud of any actions, which were vicious in themfelves, or hurtful to other perfons. He was not proud of riches or power. It muft be indeed acknowledged, that he was vain, very vain, of the great abilities of mind, which he really poffeffed, and of the important fervices, which he had really performed for his country. This vanity is one of the univerfally acknowledged weakneffes in *Tully's* character. Had he been more *humble and lowly in his own fight*, he certainly would have been not only a much happier, but a much better man:

for

for humility in itfelf is a great virtue, and is alfo the foundation of many others.

BUT humility was an excellence little known in the heathen world.

LET us then turn our thoughts to thofe virtues, which may, with more probability, be expeƈted in a heathen charaƈter.

IN private life, *Cicero* was a kind and gene-rous mafter; he was an excellent father; he was grateful to his benefaƈtors, and fincerely zealous for his friends, whether they were in profperity or in adverfity. His works abound with thefe noble fentiments, and his life is full of examples of them. On this head, permit me, my dear pupil, to refer you to the beginning of the twelfth feƈtion in Dr. *Middleton's* hiftory.

CICERO loved his country: Φιλοπατρις ην, as even *Oƈtavius* owned: he laboured to fupport it's ancient conftitution and liberty. He fome-times fhowed great intrepidity in refifting the at-tempts of it's enemies: at other times, it muft be acknowledged, he feems to have been filent, as if over-awed. Perhaps this might be real weak-nefs of mind. On the other hand, it may poffi-bly, and with juftice be urged, that *Tully* might
think

think he beſt ſervcd his country, by occaſionally
ſuſpending an uſelefs oppoſition to the irreſiſtible
power of thoſe, who had uſurped the national
authority.   He might deem it more patriotic, as
well as more prudent, to ſoften them by patience
and ſubmiſſion; and by propér management to
conduct them into ſuch a train of thought and
action, as might produce ſomething conſiderably
beneficial to the public.

Bu t however this may be, the faireſt method,
certainly, of paſſing judgment on the political
charaᵍter of *Tully*, is to examine how he behaved,
when he himſelf was in power.

I t was then, indeed, that the ſplendour of his
character ſhone forth in it's true luſtre.   At thoſe
times his appearance in the hiſtory of his country
diſcloſes itſelf with as much dignity, as attended
the *founder of this roman empire;* when, according to the deſcription which you, my dear pupil,
have often admired in *Virgil,*—he diſcovered
himſelf, in the fulleſt majeſty, before the tribunals
and ſenate of *Carthage.*

Scindit ſe nubes, & in æthera purgat apertum:
Reſtitit Æneas, claráque in luce refulſit.*

* Æ N E I D. lib. i, 591.

LET us confider his conduct while governor of *Cilicia:* we fhall find in it much patriotifm, much philanthropy. He had in his youth behaved very well, while quæftor at *Syracufe;* but this *afiatic* government produced a very confiderable addition of honour to his character.

CICERO feems to have followed, in a great meafure, the glorious plan of government, which his mafter *Scævola* had obferved in *Afia Minor*.

CICERO principally directed his attention to avert the grievances of his province, by lightening that heavy load of debts, with which the avarice of his predeceffors had incumbered it: and by remedying all the other evil confequences of their bad government. The *afiatics*, who had joined with the former governors to opprefs and plunder their country, were by *Cicero* obliged to refund whatever they had thus extorted. He protected the province alfo from all *roman* oppreffors; from fome, in particular, who were of the higheft rank in *Rome*, and otherwife greatly connected with himfelf. Nor was he lefs affiduous to avert evils arifing from other caufes; he alleviated the fcarcity of provifion, which at that time afflicted *Cilicia* and *Cyprus* like a famine. He prepared with great fpirit to defend the fron-

tiers

tiers again{t the threatened, and *then moſt formidable* invaſion of the *parthians.*

H E permitted the natives of his whole province,
to uſe their own laws.   He was kind and affable
at all times to all: indeed, the ſpirit of every
part of his government, like that of every part of
his life, was moſt mild and merciful, though at
the ſame time very prudent, and very active.
Nor was he leſs remarkable for his noble diſinter-
eſtedneſs.   For, as he ſupported the dignity of
his office of proconſul liberally, not ſumptuouſly,
he had no temptation to exerciſe fraud and rapine.
He was able to refuſe the immenſe perquiſites,
preſents, contributions, *&c.*, with which his predeceſſors had diſgraced their adminiſtration.   He
accepted only the moſt juſt and moderate emolu-
ments of his office; and even from theſe his law-
ful appointments, he beſtowed ſeveral thouſand
pounds for the relief of diſtreſſed individuals or
communities in his government.   At his departure he declined the acceptance of ſeveral of the
then cuſtomary public honours: he declined alſo
the great free-gift, which was ſpontaneouſly
offered to him by the province; and which is
ſaid, on the whole, to have amounted to upwards
of two hundred and fifty thouſand pounds ſterling.   You ſeem ſurprized, dear ſir; but the
                                                    generoſity

generofity of *Cicero* in his government of *Cilicia*
was much *greater* in other articles,—according to
two extracts which I have made from Dr. *Middle-*
ton's narration.   The fum mentioned in the fecond
extract is indeed fo exceffive, that I fhould apprehend there muft be fome miftake in the calcu-
lation.

ALL the wealthier cities of the province ufed
to pay to their proconfuls large contributions,
for being exempt from furnifhing winter quarters
to the army: *Cyprus* alone paid yearly, on this
fingle account, two hundred talents, or about
forty thoufand pounds: But *Cicero* remitted
this *whole* tax to them, which alone made a *vaft*
revenue*.

IN his province of *Cilicia*, he faved to the
public a full *million* fterling, which all other
governors had applied to their own private ufe†.

WHILE *Crito* was reading thefe noble particulars relative to *Tully's cilician* government, the
whole company grew warm in his praife; they
totally forgot the blemifhes in his character, and
were almoft as much engaged in his favour as Dr.

* See *Middleton,* vol. ii. p. 53, 4to edit.
† MIDD, vol. ii. p. 513.

Middle-

Middleton himfelf. *Crito* alfo partook of the ardent pleafure expreffed by his young friends; and proceeded through the remaining part of his lecture in a much more elevated ftyle.

As to the great offices of ftate, with which *Cicero* was intrufted *here* at *Rome,* one inftance will be abundantly fufficient, to demonftrate the excellency of his adminiftration; I mean, that ever memorable work of his confulfhip. Οτι μεγιϛ۞ ην των πωποτε νεωτερισμων, ϐτ۞ ελαχιϛοις κακοις ανευ ϛασεως και ταραχης κατεσβεσε*.

How feel you this noble idea, my valued friends? If we have, really, any fparks of patriotifm in our hearts, how ought they now to burn!

DIRECTLY on *this* very angle of the hill, *on which we ftand,* was the houfe of *Tully.* On the evening of the defeat of the confpiracy, he was moft honourably condu&ed hither from *that Capitoline* hill, acrofs that valley of the *Forum Romanum,* by a general proceffion of the fenate and people of *Rome:* with the acclamation of many thoufand voices, proclaiming him the general deliverer.

* *Plutarchus, in vitâ Tullii.*

O MY

O MY dear friends! how often have you, while at *Weſtminſter*, wandered about the great hall of the tribunals of *England*, and about the avenues of both houſes of the *britiſh* parliament, thinking on the hiſtory of thoſe great men, who in each of thoſe venerable edifices have in ſeveral ſucceſſive ages, by their wiſdom and eloquence, by their juſtice and integrity, done much ſervice and honour to our country?——A ſcene of the ſame nature, and of at leaſt equal dignity, is now before your eyes.

LOOK at *thoſe* three lofty columns of the temple of *Jupiter Stator!* It was there, that *Cicero* confounded all the fiercenefs of the conſpirators, by the thunder of his firſt *Catalinarian* oration. Look, again, on that ſtill remaining portico of the temple of *Concord!* There all the glory of *Tully* was completed and crowned; when, in full ſenate there aſſembled, *Catulus* and *Cato* both in ſo ſolemn a manner ſaluted him with the higheſt ſtyle and title of *Father of his country. Salve, Cicero;* primus omnium *Pater patriæ appellatus* !*

---

* The firſt *Catalinarian* oration, as it appears from the concluding paragraph, was ſpoken in the temple of *Jupiter Stator.* The ſecond and third from the *Roſtra* in the *Forum.* The fourth probably in the temple of *Concord;* which was the moſt uſual place of aſſembly for the ſenate during theſe *Catalinarian* troubles.

How

How aweful a ceremony was this! How auguſt the ſpeſtacle! — How happy, my poetic pupil, might you be, to repoſe for ſome hours beneath the ſhade of theſe cypreſſes; would the *genius of the place* but condeſcend to bleſs your ſlumbers with a dream, reviving in your imagination the ancient grandeur of this part of *Rome*, and re-preſenting to you in full viſion ſome of theſe ſcenes!

But let us, continued *Crito*, taking up his paper of notes, proceed to other parts of *Tully's* hiſtory.

_{A.C. 44} Soon after the death of *Julius Cæſar*, *Cicero* vigorouſly exerted himſelf in the direſtion of the affairs of the republic. His conduſt at that period is in general thus repreſented by Dr. *Middleton*.

" With the univerſal conſent and joy of the
" people, *Cicero* accepted the care of the govern-
" ment, then in extreme danger. He laboured
" in forming and executing ſuch a plan of policy,
" as ſeemed moſt likely to ſave the ſinking ſtate.
" At leaſt, it was to his counſels, and to his
" authority, that *Rome* owed that laſt effort
" which was then made for her liberty. *Cicero*
" with great reſolution reſiſted *Antony*, a tyrant
" much

" much worfe than *Julius Cæfar.* *(I could wifh*
" *however that there was not fo much rancour ex-*
" *preffed in the Philippics.)* *Cicero* with great
" wifdom converted *Hirtius,* *Panfa,* and other
" powerful men to the caufe of their country,
" (he hoped to do the fame with *Octavius)* and
" directed and united all their power to his de-
" figns for the public good. He endeavoured to
" reftore general concord and quiet among all
" parties, by * wifely propofing a general act of
" oblivion for what was paffed. Far was he
" from being difcouraged by the great dangers,
" which he faw impending over his head; he
" knew not now the fenfe of fear, of which
" weaknefs he was fometimes juftly accufed; he
" defpifed all perils. The government was in
" his hands, and he fupported it with the fame
" wifdom, with the fame heroic intrepidity, which
" he had fhown in the times of *Cataline.* *Nullum*
" *locum prætermifit monendi, agendi, providendi;*
" *hoc denique animo erat, ut fi in hâc curâ atque*
" *adminiftratione vita illi ponenda effet, præclaré*
" *actum fecum putaret."*

Such indeed was his fate; and moft happy
and honourable may we juftly efteem it. For

---

* *Illud decreti Athenienfium celeberrimi* (relatum a Cice-
rone) *oblivionis præteritarum rerum decreto patrum compro-*
batum eft. *Vell. Paterculus,*

let us look round on the other great men of thofe turbulent times, who almoft all died a violent death, and compare their laft hours with that of *Cicero*. *Pompey's* death is furely a ftriking leffon of the inftability of the greateft human grandeur and power: but yet confers no honour on himfelf; it being uncertain, whether he were brought to that cataftrophe by a fpirit of love for his country, or by that of mere and mean private ambition. *Cæfar* and *Craffus* died in a bad A.C. caufe; *Cato* and *Brutus* in a bad manner. *Cicero* 43 died undeniably in the caufe of his country: He fhowed however his regard to natural duty, by declining death as far as he might; but, when the laft ftroke came, he met it with joy and fortitude, equal to any of the above-mentioned, or any other of the moft celebrated heroes of *Rome.*

*   *   *

CRITO now clofed his notes. I compiled this very fhort and imperfect paper, faid he, partly at *Modena,* partly at *Bologna.* For while I was at *Modena,* my imagination was ftrongly affected with the *latter* part of *Cicero's* hiftory; and in my road from *Modena* to *Bologna,* I faw with horrour the infamous fpot of the *Ifola Triumvirado.*

As

As foon as *Crito* had folded up his notes, he fat down, and meditated for fome moments in filence on the dreadful fcenes, which appeared *in this part of Rome* at the time of that bloody profcription, which was the confequence of the negotiation near *Modena ;*—a profcription more bloody, if poffible, than any of the maffacres of *Marius* or *Sylla.*

THE reft of the company, whofe youthful imaginations were more lively, thought they faw all the carnage really before them; dogs tearing the carcafes, and flocks of vultures fcreaming from the roofs of the adjoining temples*.

AFTER fome time, *Crito* took up the volume of *Tully's* works, which his pupil had been perufing, and turned to the beginning of the third book *de Oratore.* With a melancholy accent he began to read the following lines from fection 3.

In his ipfis roftris, in quibus ille rempublicam conftantiffimé conful defenderat, pofitum caput illud fuit, à quo erant multorum civium capita fervata.

---

* Διων⊙. Βιβ. μζ.

Γυπες επι τα νεω τα γενικια τα δημα, και επι της Ομονοιας παμπλη-
θεις ιδρυθησαν. και αυτων ενταυθα ετι, ως ειπειν, οντων, αι τε σφαγαι
εκειναι εποιηθεσαν, και η πολις απασα νεκρων επληρωθη.

As

As foon as *Crito* had read thefe lines, he ftretched out his right hand, pointing to a barn, which ftands in the middle of the narrow valley, between the northern point of the *Farnefe* gardens, and the *Capitoline* hill*.

O my dear pupil, cannot you imagine, that you now fee, *there,* the pale face and lifelefs hands of *Tully?* The head which meditated, the hands which wrote all the noble *philofophic* treatifes in this volume!—Of the *Philippics,* let us not think at this trying moment.

Such an idea muft peculiarly affect *your* good mind. A recollection of the mangled head of *Craffus* or of *Pompey,* lying on the fands of *Parthia* or of *Egypt,* cannot affect you in the like manner. The vanity of the greateft riches and power will give *you* but little concern, in comparifon of the thought—that genius and learning perifh alfo. But take comfort: There is one accomplifhment of the mind *which will never fail, though tongues may ceafe, and knowledge vanifh away.*

---

* On this fpot ftood the ancient *roman Roftra,* till the time of *Auguftus Cæfar,* who removed them about a ftone's caft nearer to the *Palatine* hill. Adjoining to the northern point of the *Farnefe* gardens are to this day ftill remaining feveral high brick walls, faid to be the remains of the fabric of the *Roftra* built by *Augnftus.*

One

* * *

ONE of the young nobleman's fervants now coming, to acquaint his mafter, that the coach, according to his order, was waiting in the *Campo Vaccino*, the company concluded their morning ftudy, and fet out for *Frefcati*. On the road their converfation was frequently diverted to various topics, and as frequently it returned to the *roman* hiftory; the great events in *Tully's* times having deeply engaged their attention.

As they drew near to *Frefcati*, the young nobleman looked out of the coach-window on the right, towards *Albano*, and began to talk of the antiquities in *that* neighbourhood.

You remember, faid he, the ruined monument, which ftands in the middle of the high road near *Albano;* I mean the monument with five fmall pyramids on it's top, which is commonly called the tomb of the *Horatii* and *Curiatii;* but which is fuppofed by more learned antiquarians to be the fepulchre erected by *Cornelia* to the memory of *Pompey*. I could wifh that we were to pafs by it to-day. In the prefent difpofition of our minds, the fight of *Pompey's* fepul-

chre

chre would be a very pleafing, though melancholy objeɛt.

SOME of the admirers of the Night-Thoughts, faid *Crito's* pupil, I believe would not have been forry, if that poem had been written in *Italy.* How would *that* author have moralized, while leaning on the monument, that contained the afhes of *Pompey* the Great!

Regnatorem Afiœ! jacet ingens littore truncus,
Avulfumque humeris caput, & fine nomine corpus*.

I KNOW not, replied *Crito,* how to reconcile the different opinions of the ancients, relative to the afhes of *Pompey. Plutarch* exprefsly fays, that they were buried by *Cornelia,* at *Alba.* On the other hand, if we ftriɛtly follow the opinion of *Martial* and *Lucan,* that fepulchre muft be a *cenotaph* only :—for *Pompey's* remains, as *Lucan* very diffufively defcribes, were in his time ftill in *Egypt. Martial* alfo fays,

———*ipfum*
Terra tegit Libyes, fi tamen ulla tegit.

Perhaps *Pompey's* head, which was prefented to *Julius Cœfar* at *Alexandria,* might, agreeably

———————
* VIRG. Æn. ii. 557.

his

to his ufual humanity, be fent by him to *Cor-*
nelia, and by her be interred at *Albano**. The
remainder of his duft is probably loft, amidft
the common fand and mud of the *egyptian*
fhore.

THE converfation now again diverted itfelf
to other fubjeċts. About noon the coach arrived
at the gates of *Frefcati:* the young nobleman
fent a fervant into the town, to order dinner at
the inn to be ready, according to the *italian*
cuſtom of dining early, in an hour and a half;
and then told his coachman to drive, in the mean
time, to the neighbouring monaſtery of *Grotta*
Ferrata.

THE road from *Frefcati* to *Grotta Ferrata*
is very pleafant: the former part of it is a fhady
wood; the latter is an open corn field, adorned
with feveral oriental plane trees, which, from
their vaft fize, feem to be fome hundreds of years
old.

PERHAPS, faid *Crito's* pupil, thefe may be the
defcendants of that plane tree of *Craffus,* which
Tully defcribes with fuch pleafure; *Ad opacandum*
hunc locum *patulis diffufa ramis*†. But let us

---

* See *Efchinardi's* defcription of the *Agro Romano,* p. 302.
† See *de Oratore,* lib. i. c. 7.

not

not think of *Craſſus:* we are now near the country-houſe of *Tully* himſelf.

GROTTA Ferrata, ſaid *Crito,* is, you know, commonly ſuppoſed to be the place of *Tully's Tuſculan* villa. *Addiſon* and *Middleton* ſtrongly embraced that tradition: but ſome *italian* antiquarians are of a contrary opinion; and produce ſeveral weighty arguments, proving it's ſituation to have been rather at the *Ruffinella,* which is about two miles nearer *Tuſculum **. There are indeed ſcarce any remains of antiquity in the neighbourhood of *Tuſculum,* that are not imagined, either by the vulgar, or by ſome antiquarians, to have belonged to *Cicero.* Perhaps of all theſe their different opinions, ſome one may be true. In the midſt of this uncertainty, let us however have the pleaſure of walking to the *Ruffinella* in the afternoon; and, at preſent, of viſiting *Grotta Ferrata.*

WITHIN about half an hour the coach arrived at the convent. The monks who inhabit it are of a *greek* order;—the *baſilian.* They received our *engliſh* company with great civility; ſhowed them certain ancient marbles in the cloiſter, as ſome kind of proof, that *Tully's* villa might have

---

* See *Eſchinardi's Deſcrittione dell' Agro Romano,* p. 274, 275, 276.

been

been fituate there; and then conducted them to
the other curiofities of the place; particularly
Domenichino. paintings in the chapel. The
young nobleman ftudied thefe pictures for a confiderable time, not without expreffing the greateft
admiration.

HE afterwards got into his coach, thanked
the monks for their civility, and returned with
his *englifh* friends to *Frefcati* to dinner.

* * *

AFTER dinner the eldeft of the young gentlemen, who had fat up moft part of the night to
read *Plutarch's* life of *Cato*, laid himfelf down
on the couch to fleep. The young nobleman diverted himfelf with finifhing the drawing, which
he had begun this morning; and *Crito* retired
with his pupil into the next room, to their *cicero-
nian* ftudies.

ABOUT two and twenty o'clock the company
walked out. Juft at the edge of the town their
roman fervant fhowed them a rough mafs of ftone,
faid to be the remains of *Lucullus's* maufoleum.
Thence they walked up to the *Ruffinella*.

THE *Ruffinella* is fituate half-way between the
pleafant town of *Frefcati*, and the rocks and ruins
of

of the ancient and lofty city of *Tufculum.*
No waik can be more agreeable than the afcent
from *Frefcati* thither, through the groves, and by
the numerous cafcades of *Villa Pamphili.* On
one fide of it, towards the plain, appear the beautiful fhades and ftreams of *Villa Conti,* formerly
the habitation of *Lucullus;* and on the other fide,
the road planted with laurel, which leads towards
the fteep hill of *Monte Portio,* the family feat of
Cato *.

BUT far elevated above all is that venerable
open grove of lofty pines near the *Ruffinella,*
which crowns the ridge of the *Tufculan* mountains, and fhades the fpot where *Cicero's* villa and
rural *Lycæum* once perhaps ftood.

. IN the field on the fide of this grove, are yet
to be feen many marks of terraffes, and a large
and broad mofaic pavement, ftill entire. This
pavement perhaps, as the young nobleman pleafed
himfelf with imagining, might belong to *Cicero's*
library; the centre of it being ornamented with
a large defign of the head of *Minerva* †.

---

* *Anni fono, della parte di Frefcati che riguarda Monte Por-*
zio fu trovato il fepolchro antiquiffimo della famiglia Porzia
reportata' del Bellori & dal Volpi.   *Abbate Venuti.*

† *Condamine,* in his tour to *Italy,* p. 42, fpeaks of this
pavement, as the moft beautiful work of the kind remaining; and of this head of *Minerva,* as executed in the nobleft manner.

How grand and how delightful is the fituation of this apartment, faid the young nobleman ; and *how properly adapted to the charaƐer of it's great inhabitant!* Cicero, though the moſt ſtudious and moſt learned man of his times, yet perhaps never, amidſt all his pleaſures and labours, forgot his favourite objeƐ in them all ; — beneficence to *Rome*.*

Let me continue to indulge myſelf for ſome moments, in ſuppoſing this apartment to have been his *library.* To the ſouth, how ſolemn a profpeƐ opens itſelf, over the foreſts of *Algidum,* the mountains and lakes of *Alba,* and the ſea-coaſt ; quite to the woody iſland of *Aſtura,* where *Cicero* had another reſidence, deſigned for ſtill more retired ſtudy ! To the north, he might here have always before his view the magnificence and ſplendour of *Rome,* which is even now widely ſpread over the *Campania* before us ; together with all thoſe great works of public utility, thoſe many grand and everlaſting paved roads, and thoſe many long and lofty aqueduƐs, which — like his own deſigns — ſtretch from all ſides a-croſs this vaſt plain, to their great and common centre.

---

* Λογι☉ ανηρ, ω παι, λογοις και φιλοπατρις.
See the concluſion of *Cicero's* life by *Plutarch.*

WHILE

WHILE the young nobleman was thus fpeaking, *Crito* turned to him with a look of refpect and love; and—How happy fhould we have been, faid he, if, fo foon as you had finifhed this afternoon your drawing of the temple of *Concord*, you had favoured us with your company in the next room. Your loving and worthy friend, whom I know not whether I ought to call my pupil, or my tutor, was then affifting me to prepare and finifh this fecond fhort paper on *Cicero*'s character. He reminded me of feveral paffages, tending to fhow, that *Tufculum* was always *Cicero*'s *favourite* country-feat; from which he wrote *with the greateft pleafure* feveral of his epiftles; in which he compofed *with the greateft fpirit* feveral of his orations; and which he made the fcene of feveral of his rhetorical and philofophic dialogues: particularly of thofe two, the *principal* perhaps of each kind; the books *de Oratore*, and the *Tufculan* queftions.

So fond indeed was *Tully* of this his rural retirement, as frequently to expatiate with pleafure on the defcription of perfons and places in the neighbourhood. *Monte Portio* was the farm of *Cato* the elder, the principal fpeaker in the dialogue *de Senectute*. At *Villa Conti* was the famous library of *Lucullus*, which is the fcene of the dialogues in the third and fourth book *de Finibus;* and

and in which thefe two illuftrious country neigh-
bours, *Cicero* and *Cato* the younger, both then,
and probably often, *really* met. *Ibi Catonem fe-
dentem inveni, multis circumfufum libris: erat
enim in illo inexhaufta aviditas legendi, neque fa-
tiari poterat: & malo, mihi dixit, hunc pue-
rum Luculli* [the pupil of *Cato* and *Cicero*], *his
libris, potius quàm omni reliquo villæ ornatu de-
lectari* *.

MODERN *Frefcati*, replied the young nobleman, notwithftanding all it's beauty and fplendour, is I apprehend much inferiour to *Tufculum*,
as it appeared in the times of *Tully;* when the
fides of thefe hills, and all the environs, were
covered with the country palaces of the *roman*
fenators. At *Cafal Morena*, was, I have heard,
Muræna's villa : at *Villa Magna*, one of *Pompey's*
houfes. But the feats of *Cicero* and *Lucullus* feem
to have been the principal buildings of this place:
they were far fuperiour, I fuppofe, to *Villa Conti*,
Villa Pamphili, or *Monte Dragone* itfelf.

SCARCE ever was any country place, faid *Crito's*
pupil, adorned with two fuch famous libraries.
That of *Lucullus* was, I fhould imagine, the moft
expenfive; that of *Tully*, the beft-chofen collection.

* De FINIB. l. iii. c. 2.

THE

THE young nobleman now began to fpeak of the *ornaments* of *Tully's* library, particularly the *Hermathenæ**; when, obferving a paper in *Crito's* hand, he fat down, and defired him to favour the company with it's contents.

C I C E R O.

PART II.

Quid dedicatum pofcit Apollinem
Vates? Quid orat de paterâ novum
Fundens liquorem?

HOR. carm. lib. i. od. 31.

WHAT ought to be the *principal* wifh of a young man, who has already had the happinefs to be entered on a courfe of good education?—For what bleffing may we fuppofe *Tully* to have principally petitioned in his youth, at the fhrine of *Apollo;* of this, his favourite patronefs *Minerva;* or of any other of thofe deities, who were imagined to prefide over the improvement of the human mind?

---

* *Quod ad me de Hermathenâ fcribis, per mihi gratum eft; & ornamentum academiæ proprium meæ; quod & Hermes commune omnium; & Minerva fingulare eft infigne ejus gymnafii. Quare velim, ut fcribis, cæteris quoque rebus quàm plurimis eum locum ornes. Signa illa omnia in Tufculanum deportabo.*

Ep. ad Atticum, lib. i. ep. 4.

FOR

For the spirit of perpetual industry.

STUDIOUS diligence, by which I must be understood to mean that of the best kind, is one of the great principles of growth to the human understanding, which thus it continually forms, replenishes, and extends; correcting and healing whatever in it is amiss; guarding it from many unnecessary worldly cares; supplying it's defects; and improving it's excellencies.

SUCH is it to the mind. Nor is it, really, any way hostile to the health of the body; especially when attended by temperance, and moderate exercise; each of which greatly strengthens the mental, as well as the corporeal frame.

IF we look into the life of *Cicero,* we shall find it *filled* with labour and industry. His indefatigable application far surpasses what we generally conceive of study,—and seems almost incredible. It is said, that the time, which other young men of his age gave up to pleasure and diversion, was by him regularly added to his studious hours; that he never devoted one leisure hour to absolute idleness; and that all the intervals of his great labours were generally applied to some good purpose:

THIS

THIS *ſtudious diligence* was the means indiſ-penſably neceſſary to qualify, even ſuch a genius as *Tully,* for his great literary attainments. Let us not be diſheartened by this conſideration; but rather with pleaſure reflect that *Cicero,* by this moſt careful management of his time, made every day produce ſome valuable addition to the vaſt fund of his knowledge.

IN relation to the *fruits* of theſe his learned labours, I am by no means able to ſay any thing worthy your attention. Permit me to read to you ſome ſhort extracts from Dr. *Middleton,* relative to this ſubject.

" No man," ſays he, " whoſe life had been " wholly ſpent in ſtudy, ever left more numerous " or more valuable fruits of his learning, in every " branch of ſcience and the politer arts."

BUT let us confine our thoughts at preſent to his *philoſophic* works.

ROME, though in the time of *Cicero* ſuperiour to all the nations of the earth in power and dominion, yet was comparatively very deficient in knowledge; particularly in the knowledge of that which is the ſummit of all literary glory,—moral philoſophy. *Cicero's* great deſign was, to ſup-

ply

ply this moſt important *deſideratum*. He laboured
to increaſe the knowledge of his countrymen, by
adding to it whatever was wiſe or noble, in the
ſeveral *grecian* philoſophies. He laboured, above
all, to place before their eyes, in the ſtrongeſt
light, thoſe five great principles of natural religion and morality, on which the happineſs of
mankind ſo much depends :—The exiſtence of
GOD; the reality of a Providence; the immortality
of the ſoul; the future ſtate of rewards and puniſhments; and the eternal difference of good and
evil. *Reipublicæ causâ, philoſophiam hanc ro-
manis hominibus explicandam putavit ; magni ex-
iſtimans intereſſe ad decus & ad laudem civitatis,
res, tam graves, tamque præclaras, latinis etiam
literis contineri.* It is needleſs to obſerve, how
nobly he executed this great deſign. Happy is
it, that the compoſitions, which he originally thus
deſigned for the benefit of his country, have extended their good effects much farther, to many
other ages and nations.

BUT, it may be peculiarly uſeful for us to obſerve, that *Cicero himſelf* ſeems to have received
great benefit from theſe his ſtudies, at *ſeveral different periods* of his life.

FROM his early youth he had applied himſelf
diligently to the ſtudy of moral philoſophy. Soon

indeed did he difdain, and with indignation re-
ject, the mean doctrines of the *epicurean* fect;
but he induſtriouſly took all opportunities, both
at home and on his travels, to imbibe the principles of ſome other much more exalted ſyſtems.
At *Rome,*—let me repeat his own words—*totum ſe
Philoni tradidit, admirabili quodam ad philoſophiam ſtudio concitatus.* During his travels, which
on the whole took up about *two years,* he reſided
no leſs than ſix months in Athens, at the houſe of
Antiochus, the principal philoſopher of the old
academy * : at *Rhodes* alſo he ſtudied philoſophy
with *Poſidonius,* the moſt eſteemed and learned
ſtoic of that age.

It is a pleaſing reflection, my dear fellow-travellers, and may it prove alſo a good omen to
ſome of this company, to recollect, that *Cicero,
in the year following his return from theſe his
travels,* acted very nobly *in his firſt public office,*
—the *ſicilian* quæſtorſhip.

Let us conſider his life at *another* period.
About his forty-ſecond or forty-third year, we
find him paſſing great part of his time with much

* *Cum veniſſem Athenas, ſex menſes cum Antiocho, veteris
academiæ nobiliſſimo ac prudentiſſimo philoſopho, fui; ſtudiumque
philoſophiæ nunquam intermiſſum, à primáque adoleſcentiâ cultum, & ſemper auctum, hoc rurſus ſummo auctore & doctore re-
novavi.* De Claris Oratoribus, c. 91.

ſatisfac-

satisfaction *here at Tusculum. Ex omnibus molestiis & laboribus hoc uno in loco conquiescimus. Tusculano ita delectamur, ut nobismet ipsis tum denique, cum huc venimus, placeamus**. Cicero was at that time very eager in making a collection of *greek* books, and forming a library. Such an employment is sometimes the work of mere ignorant vanity; but with a *Tully* it must have been far otherwise. He was fully sensible, that on the learned furniture of *this* room, properly arranged and digested, would depend, in a great measure, the usefulness of his present time of life, as well as the comfort of his old age. It seems highly probable, that *Tully* took *this opportunity* to refresh his memory in relation to some of his former studies; and that by this refreshment he was enabled to achieve the patriotic actions of his famous consulship, in the next year, which was the forty-fourth of his life.

About ten years afterwards we find *Cicero* resuming his studies with particular application. In his fifty-third year he frequently retired from the tumults of *Rome* to his country villas; passing his time partly at *Cumæ*, partly at *Tusculum*. He was then employed in his great work, *de Republicâ*, of which the *Somnium Scipionis* is the conclusion. When he had finished the first two

---

* *Ep. ad Attic.* lib. I. ep. 4, 5.

books

books of that work, he read them to some of his friends here in his *Tusculan* villa. *Sallust* was one of the company*.

PARDON, dear sir, this interruption, said the eldest of the young gentlemen: but how fortunate would it be, if ever in ploughing up these fields a chest should be discovered, containing the manuscript of those books *de Republicâ*. A chest of *Numa's* manuscripts, I think, was discovered on the *Janiculan* hill in the same manner. But pray proceed.

IN his fifty-fourth or fifty-fifth year, continued *Crito*, *Tully* wrote his treatise *de Legibus*, after the example of *Plato*, whom, of all writers, he most loved to imitate. This work was designed as a supplement, or second volume, to his other, *de Republicâ*.

IN his fifty-sixth year he was governor of *Cilicia*, the beneficent protector of a happy people committed to his care. O my dear friends, does it not seem highly probable, that *Cicero's* studies, during the three preceding years, had excited in his mind many noble sentiments, which he put in practice during that glorious government?

* *Ep. ad Q. Fratrem*, lib. iii. 5.

LET

LET us confider him again at a *fourth* period. *Cicero* in his fixty-firft, fixty-fecond, and fixty-third years, was, more deeply perhaps than ever, engaged in literary labours. He was then bufy in works of greater dignity in themfelves, and of greater utility to the world, than thofe which in modern times have been the happy fruits of the retirements of a *Clarendon*, or—I had almoft faid, a *Bacon*. During thefe three years *Cicero* was employed in writing his hiftory of the life of *Cato*; his treatifes *de Confolatione*, *de Amicitiâ*, *de Senectute*, *de Gloriâ*; his *Hortenfius*, *vel Cohortationes ad Philofophiam*; his books *de Academicis*, *de Finibus*, *de Naturâ Deorum*, *de Fato*; his tranflation of *Plato's Timæus*, on the nature and origin of the univerfe;—and, to crown all, his *Tufculans* and his *Offices*.

WHAT a long and fplendid catalogue of literary labours! But what muft have been *the fpirit of that induftry*, by which fuch numerous and excellent works were planned and perfected? *Credibile non eft quantum fcribam die, quin etiam noctibus*, fays *Tully*, in one of his letters at that time.

IT alfo moft highly deferves our notice and admiration, that at the fame time, and in thefe retirements, *Tully* ftrongly and intimately con-

H 3 · nected

neēted himſelf with the learned *Varro.* The deſign, with which theſe two great men joined and
united their literary labours, was the ſupport of
the cauſe of virtue.

Your minds, I know, my dear friends, are
filled with the two ruling principles of love of
ſtudy, and love of doing good. Let us then here
pauſe a little; and, ſeated as we now are, perhaps in the very library of *Cicero,* let us endeavour to excite in ourſelves ſome meditations
worthy of the place and ſubjeēt.

Venerable as is the memory of *Cato,* yet
how much more wiſe, noble, and good,—at leaſt
in one reſpeēt—was the conduēt of *that* great
mind, *quæ hìc cogitabat?* Amidſt the moſt heavy
public calamities, *Cicero* did not deſpair, or
abandon that exiſtence, in which providence had
ſtationed him. Driven from the tribunals and
the ſenate, yet he ceaſed not his labour of doing
good to the utmoſt, by thoſe other means which
ſtill remained in his power:—I mean his *philoſophical* ſtudies. For the cultivation of theſe he
moſt indefatigably exerted himſelf in *this* retirement: and their growth ſo proſpered, as to produce to the world infinitely more benefit, than
whatever had ariſen from his former *oratorical*
and *political* abilities.—Such are the fruits of *re-
ſignation,*

fignation, and of perfeverance in doing good!—
Such, as a young poet might fay, in thefe poetic
regions, was the reward of the pious *Æneas* himfelf; who, upon the fall of the kingdom of *Troy*,
did not give himfelf up to defpair, or flay himfelf on the ruins of *Priam's* palace; but, after
having bravely done his duty to his country,
patiently refigned himfelf to the will of provi-
dence*. He retired, with fome few companions,
to thefe very plains; and here became the founder
of all the grandeur and glory of the immenfe empire of *Rome.*

BUT not only *to the public* was *Cicero* fo happy
as to be thus ufeful. By thefe, the laft and moft
noble of his ftudious labours, he muft have
greatly comforted, ennobled, and exalted his *own
mind.*

SUCH ftudies muft have been, from their general tendency, very ferviceable in correcting thofe
defects of character, by which, it muft be owned,
Tully fometimes funk much lower than could be
well imagined of fo great a man. I mean, his
propenfity on the one hand to pride, on the other

---

* *Teftor, in occafu veftro, nec tela, nec ullas*
Vitaviffe vices:——
————*Nec fpes opis ulla dabatur:*
Ceffi.——

ÆNEID. ii. 432, 803,

H 4   to

to timidity: and, confequently, his too great dejection in adverfity; and too much confidence
when in a profperous ftate.

THESE defects feem to have grown upon *Tully,*
while he continued deeply engaged in public and
private bufinefs. Much converfe with the world
is indeed generally found to be very prejudicial
to the heart, by weakening it's virtues, and in-
flaming it's bad paffions. The world is full of
contagion, and *aria cattiva.*

ON the contrary, *Tully's* moral ftudies in retirement feem to have been the conftant medicine
of his foul. This grove feems to have been, at
leaft *in fome degree,* his Ψυχης Ιατρειον.

HAPPY would it have been, if the moral ftudies
of this great man had been ennobled with a proper
fpirit of *piety* and *humility.*

IN relation to *piety,* it is difficult to conceive
the infinite improvement, which that heavenly
grace might have produced in fuch a character as
that of *Tully.* Let me remind you only of two
expreffions, which were read to you about this
time yefterday evening:—*Fugatrix triftitiæ; ablatrix timoris.*

IN

IN relation to *humility*, let me read to you half a dozen lines, which I find written in my memorandum-book, and dated at *Venice* in the beginning of laſt *ſeptember*. During our ſtay there, by accident I went one day into the church of *St. George in Algâ*, and heard part of a ſermon. The preacher was ſpeaking of *Laurence Juſtinian*, the famous patriarch of *Venice**; and obſerved, that the moſt ſincere and profound humility was the firſt thing, in which that prelate laboured to ground his religious diſciples.

LAURENCE JUSTINIAN taught his ſcholars, that humility inſpires the ſoul with true courage and reſolution, by directing her to place her intire confidence in God alone, the only foundation of her ſtrength. He compared humility to a river; which is low and ſtill in ſummer, but loud and high in winter. So, ſaid this pious prelate, humility is ſilent in proſperity, never elated or ſwelled by it; but it is high, magnanimous, and full of joy and invincible courage under adverſity.

---

* *Laurentius Juſtinianus, patriâ venetus, dignitate patricius, canonicus regularis S. Georgii in Algâ. Triginta annis in regulari vitâ exactis, venetiarum epiſcopus conſtitutus eſt; poſtquam nullas non artes, ut onus impoſitum excuteret, adhibuiſſet. Vir infucatâ ergà Deum pietate, prodigâ in pauperes charitate, & ingenti religionis zelo meritò celebrandus.*
Cave's Hiſtoria Literaria, Sæculum xv. p. 133.

THERE feems, indeed, fomething of falfe tafte in the fimile; but the doctrine itfelf is of high importance: it affected me peculiarly at that time, as in our late journey from *Bologna* to *Venice,* I had been often thinking on *Tully's* character.

HAD *Tully* directed his moral ftudies to the acquifition of fuch a virtue, his life, no doubt, would have been far more laudable and exemplary.

BUT, however imperfect his moral ftudies might be, they certainly were of *great* fervice to him. Though not αριςοι, they were καλοι πρ⊙ αρετην, και σωφροσυνην συμμαχοι.

By their affiftance he repaired *in fome meafure* the breaches in his mind, and fortified himfelf with new and noble refolutions. Thus animated, he refumed in old age his political labours, for the fervice and affiftance of the republic, then in her defperate and laft agonies. In *that* difmal fervice *Cicero* fhowed no marks of timid dejection:—you will pleafe to remember that I am fpeaking from Dr. *Middleton:* — and he concluded all his labours, by death in the caufe of his country; a death full of refignation, and unobfcured by fymptoms either of oftentation or of fear.

APPIAN

APPIAN vifited that fpot: χωριον καθ' ιϛοριαν τϐδε τϐ παθϐς ειδεν. In our journey next month to *Naples*, we fhall neceffarily pafs near it. *Cicero's* fepulchre is, as I have been informed, in the vineyard or olive-garden, on the right-hand of the entrance of *Mola*,—the ancient *Formiæ.*

BUT to conclude. The moral ftudies of *Cicero*, imperfect as they were, feem ever to have amended and exalted his character, in proportion to the diligence with which he applied to them. They were to him, in fome degree, like a frequent renewal of the *Eleufinian* myfteries, which to the initiated are faid to have been * *reverà initia vitæ*. From them—to ufe his own words—he was inftructed, not only how to live with more real happinefs, but alfo how to die with a better hope :— *Sed etiam, cum meliore fpe, moriendi.*

* * *

CRITO now rofe from the bench, and pro-pofed to his young friends to return to *Frefcati*, before the evening dews came on; but in walking down the hill, he could not refrain from expreffing the following fentiments.

* See *de Legibus*, lib. 2.

IN

IN concluding our reflexions on *Cicero's* moral fludies, and confequent actions, we muſt with forrow repeatedly own, that they were both very imperfect. His conduct, *even at it's beſt periods,* I am afraid, was not free from faults: his opinions, relative to fome very important points of moral and natural philofophy, were often wavering.

THESE conſiderations have very greatly abated the veneration, which I ſhould otherwiſe have felt, in treading on that pavement, which, as our noble young friend with probability imagines, was often traverfed by *Tully* in his ſtudious meditations.

I MUST acknowledge, that I have been much more affected, in feveral parts of our travels through *France* and *Italy,* on entering the libraries of fome perfons famous in modern hiftory; who, though they were of abilities far inferiour to thofe of *Tully,* yet infinitely exceeded him in the general uprightnefs of their conduct, as well as in the happinefs of their chriftian faith. Never indeed do I enter the library of a wife and good man, without feeling fome kind of fecret awe. Wife and good ſtudy is juftly efteemed, next after prayer, the higheſt exaltation of the human mind: and confequently, the library of the vir-

tuous

tuous man is, next after the church in which he prays, the moſt venerable and ſacred place.

Nor is it only by wiſe ſtudy, that it is thus, as it were, conſecrated. In it are all his works of public and private beneficence generally planned: in it the virtues, which he owes to himſelf, are continually examined and enlarged; and from it, his moſt private, and perhaps moſt fervent devotions are daily aſcending to heaven. I remember part of a copy of verſes, tranſlated from the *italian* by my dear pupil, on a ſimilar ſubject.

Balm of the mind! hail ſtudious ſolitude!
O bring with thee calm peace, wiſe piety!
Bring ſelf-correcting, ſtill improving virtue!
Bring charity, for ever meditating
To all, in juſt degrees, the higheſt good.
  Hail! ſolitude! that from eternity
Waſt preſent at the glorious throne of God;
And, in his bounteous mind revolv'd, could'ſt trace
Creation's plan: how vaſt! how wiſe! how good!
Inhabitant of heaven, and friend of man,
With all thy kindred virtues, hither come!
And, if aught human may become thy train,
Let faireſt ſcience on thy footſteps wait.

I FOR-

I forget the words of the next ftanza; but they were expreffive of the poet's wifh, that fcience might come accompanied always by humility. Humility is indeed the beginning, the middle, and the end of all true knowledge, both in this world and in the next.

* * *

Scarce had *Crito* pronounced the laft words, when making a fwift tranfition to other fubjects, he began to talk of the pleafantnefs of the weather, and the beauty of the country. The young nobleman admired with him the various tints of the trees, and the picturefque effect of feveral objects in the profpect. The eldeft of the young gentlemen furveyed with pleafure the beautiful and pure azure of the *italian* fky over their heads. *Crito's* pupil wifhed for fome *englifh* clouds, to variegate it; and for an *englifh* twilight, to lengthen out the evening.

Discoursing on thefe, and other fimilar topics, they arrived at *Frefcati* about dufk, and finding their coach, with the horfes ready harneffed, ftanding before the inn door, got into it as foon as they had paid the dinner bill, and drove to *Rome.*

THIS

THIS fhort night-journey was very pleafant. There was indeed no moon, but the whole fky was filled with ftars; multitudes of lights alfo were fcattered over many parts of the *roman Campania*, the fields being at that hour full of countrymen, getting in their harveft as ufual, during the coolnefs of the night. Thefe lights on the ground feemed to be, as it were, the reflection of thofe bright luminaries in the heavens.

ABOUT an hour before midnight the company arrived fafe at their lodgings on *Monte di Trinita.*

CHAP.

C H A P. VII.

SEVENTEENTH DAY'S CONVERSATION.

ENCHANTED, as this company was, in daily treading the *circle of the antiquities* of *Rome*, yet they forgot not, to pay a due attention to other great and worthy objects.

FROM the first outfet on their travels, *Crito* had been conftantly induftrious in examining the *real* religion, the natural hiftory, and ftate of literature in every country ; but he was peculiarly attentive to thefe three fubjects, during his refidence in the *roman* territories.

THE young nobleman, as has been frequently obferved, had been bufy in the contemplation of the fine arts, efpecially painting: he had ftudied it with continually-increafing ardour in the *flemifh, lombard, venetian,* and *roman* fchools.

HIS elder companion, with exceffive diligence, had laboured in the political mine ; fearching deeply into the laws, police, manufactures, commerce,

merce, funds, and forces of every ftate, in which he for any confiderable time had refided. Nor was he blind to the great *" capabilities"* of the ecclefiaftical ftate in thefe feveral particulars *.

CRITO'S pupil had propofed to himfelf another field of inquiry; viz. the various kinds and degrees of public beneficence, and the different workings of humanity and chriftian charity in different parts of *Europe.* Scarce a day paffed, in which he had not·made fome progrefs in this work; either by digefting into proper order his former obfervations, or by acquiring frefh materials. He was indefatigably active in making due inquiries after every wife law of mercy; after every judicioufly-charitable inftitution : efteeming all thefe labours as fuperabundantly repaid, if by thefe means he could, at a future time, be able to introduce in his own country any one new method of doing good.

---

* The ecclefiaftic ftate, as all travellers obferve, is in a very poor condition. It's governors, *even when well intentioned,* feem ignorant, or inattentive to the various means of improvement. Indeed, as *Addifon* remarked in his travels, " to fpeak truly, they are here fo taken up with the " care of men's fouls, that they neglect the care of their " bodies:" and it has often happened, that the fovereign of this country has paft moft of his days in a convent,— or in fome other religious or ftudious retirement from the world.

SUCH had been his darling object throughout the whole courſe of his travels,—and eſpecially during his reſidence at *Milan,* and at *Rome.*

AMONG other articles of public beneficence, he was particularly deſirous to acquire ſome ſenſible and true memoirs, relative to the management of the beſt-regulated *hoſpitals.* He even diſdained not to make ſome inquiries as to the care of the *priſons.*

THIS morning, while he was happily employed in tranſcribing and abridging ſome papers, *on the laſt ſubject,* he was viſited by his tutor, and his two young friends. They ſurveyed the bundles of papers, with which his table was covered: and then fixed their eyes on him, with the complacency, with which angels look on one of their celeſtial brethren, while ardently engaged in ſome eminent work of benevolence.

THEY were beginning to expreſs their ſentiments on the occaſion, but were prevented by him. Turning to the elder of the young gentlemen, After all, ſaid he, the greateſt *temporal* charity, is the charity of a wiſe government;—which, by a judicious encouragement of induſtry, in agriculture, in manufactures, and in commerce,

both

both by fea and land, is able to clothe comfortably and feed *millions* of it's fubjects. In this great charity there is not perhaps a country on the face of the univerfe fuperiour, or even equal to *Great Britain.* But in the fecondary, though very important and laudable charities, fuch as *hofpitals for the fick and aged,* and other inftitutions of a fimilar nature; although our country is richly adorned with many noble foundations of this kind, yet I know not whether other nations of *Chriftendom* may not juftly claim an equal fhare of honour.

I HAVE often, both at home and abroad, heard our countrymen obferve, perhaps with a patriotic partiality, That no country was equal to *England* in fuch works of charity: But let us fee what *Keyfler,* though a *german,* fays of the *italians.*

CRITO'S pupil now took up a volume of *Keyfler's* travels, which lay on the table open, at the article " *Milan,*" and read feveral paffages in it, to the point in queftion.

HOWEVER this may be, continued he, yet certainly all travellers, notwithftanding their feveral political and religious differences, muft acknowledge both the magnitude and variety of

charitable

charitable inftitutions, which are to be feen in all parts of *Italy*, efpecially at *Milan*, and here at *Rome*.

I could wifh, faid *Crito*, that there was a good account publifhed of all the *italian*, and indeed of all the *european public charities.* A faithful and judicious defcription of the various inftitutions of mercy throughout *Chriftendom* would undoubtedly be a very pleafing book, as well as a very ftrong teftimony to the excellence of the chriftian religion, by difplaying thus it's beneficent genius, and happy operation in the world *. For it feems well worthy of obfervation, that all thefe noble inftitutions of mercy were utterly unknown in *Europe*, during the times of the ancient grecian or *roman* dominion: and have all rifen on *chriftianity*, as their true foundation. Even. *mohammedanifm* has copied it's fpirit in this particular.

Such a book, faid *Crito's* pupil, might perhaps be ferviceable to another good purpofe.

Is it not ardently to be wifhed, that the different nations of *Europe* would mutually ftudy

---

* The laft fixteen verfes of the twenty-fifth chapter of *St. Matthew* might perhaps be not improperly placed as a frontifpiece to fuch a book.

and

and imitate each other's moral excellencies? It was a wife principle of heathen *Rome*, never to think herfelf perfect in the military art; but conftantly to obferve, and to adopt, whatever was truly laudable and ufeful in the neighbouring ftates. By this principle, and by this practice, fhe attained all her grandeur. And by the fame means *England*, no doubt, might very confiderably improve herfelf in the higheft kind of true glory,—chriftian beneficence. Her public charities might thus be rendered the moft abundant and complete, the moft beautifully variegated, and the moft wifely felected of any in the univerfe.

IF I be not miftaken, faid the young nobleman, fome great new charities,—the *Foundling, Lying-in,* and *Magdalen* hofpitals,—were in this manner *lately imported* into *England.*

THERE is another charitable inftitution, faid *Crito,* which, if properly regulated, might juftly be efteemed far more honourable and ufeful than any of thefe three. I mean that charity, which you know flourifhes fo much in *Italy,* particularly here at *Rome, the charity of giving portions to poor young maidens in marriage*.* It has at different

---

* The legacies to this charity have been at *Rome* fo very ample, that there is fcarce a poor young woman in the

I 3

whole

different times made feveral attempts to eftablifh
itfelf in *England.* Archbifhop *Laud* fet an example of it in his native town of *Reading:* where,
according to his fmall fortune, he bequeathed a
legacy, out of which young women who have
ferved a certain time in the fame family, with a
good charaĉter, are now apportioned.

AMONG all the *roman* charities, faid the eldeft
of the young gentlemen, there is one, which I
have often thought might be as deferving of imitation as any. I mean the *Convalefcent* hofpital;
which receives poor patients, cured in other hofpitals, and fupports them for fome weeks with
comfortable provifion, till they have recovered
their ftrength, and are able to return to their
work. If I miftake not, you have an account
of that hofpital among your papers.

IN turning over the papers of *Crito's* pupil, to
find that account, the young gentleman fixed his
eyes by accident on a memoir relative to the mo-

whole city, of a creditable charaĉter, but what may be a par-
taker of them. The portioning of maidens makes indeed a
part of many ecclefiaftical funĉtions there. Once in the
year no lefs than three hundred maidens appear in proceffion at the church of *Santa Maria foprà Minerva.* They
come there to receive their marriage portions; all dreffed
in long and flowing white robes, fuch as are feen on feveral
antique ftatues of *roman* matrons; and their faces in particular are covered exaĉtly in the fame manner as fome of the
moft famous bufts.

dern

dern *roman prifons.* I could heartily wifh you, faid he, to extract from this memoir fome hints that may be ufeful at home. There is perhaps no part of the *britifh* police, in which there are more *defiderata.* I heard lately from *London,* that a propofal for rebuilding *Newgate* is foon to be laid before the houfe of commons.

THE converfation now dwelt for fome time on this topic, when *Crito's* pupil requefted the company to take an hour's walk with him. He wifhed they would permit him to be their conductor this morning; as he had a great defire to vifit the remains of the two moft noted prifons of *ancient Rome.* The company readily confented to his propofal.

*　　*　　*

SOME fmall remains of the ancient *Carcere Tulliano* are ftill to be feen, at the foot of the fouth-eaft fide of the *Capitoline* hill. Going down a flight of fteps under the church of *S. Giufeppe Falegnami,* the company entered into the dark fubterranean apartments of that fearful fcene, and defcended from dungeon to dungeon*.

___
* See Abbate *Venuti's Roman* Antiquities, vol. i, p. 58.

THE loweſt of theſe is a round, low, ſmall vault*. In this diſmal place it is ſaid *Plemminius* died†; *Jugurtha* was ſtarved to death‡; and *Cethegus* and the other murderers and incendiaries of *Cataline's* band were all ſtrangled§. This vault ſeems indeed, from it's ſituation, ſhape, and dimenſions, to anſwer *Salluſt's* deſcription of the *Tullianum;* and the floor, walls, and roof being all compoſed of very large ſtones, it is at preſent, perhaps, exactly in the ſame ſtate, as formerly.

WRETCHED as that ſet of villains were, and moſt deſerving of their fate, yet how often, ſaid *Crito's* pupil, has this gloomy cavern confined perſons of a *quite* contrary character! In the republican times, how many foreign generals and patriots, the brave defenders of their country againſt the *roman* invaſions, have, after undergoing all the bitterneſs of the triumph, taken their ſeats on *this* ſtone bench, in expectation and de-

---

* It nearly reſembles the deſcription, given by *Diodorus Siculus,* of the dungeon at *Alba Marſorum,* in which *Perſes* was impriſoned. Vid. *Photii Bibliothec.* edit. *Rotomag.* p. 1156.

† See *Livy,* book 34, c. 44. *In inferiorem demiſſus eſt carcerem, necatuſque.*

‡ See *Freinſhemius,* book lxvii. c. 19. *Ibi demum loci; ſextum in diem, cum fame & vitâ luctans, ſpiritus expulſus eſt.*

§ In this ſame priſon *Sejanus* died; the ſenate being aſſembled for his condemnation in the adjoining temple of *Concord.* *Simon Gioras* alſo. See *Joſephus,* b. vii. c. 5.

fire of fpeedy death! In the lower ages, under *imperial* tyranny, how many virtuous *romans* have fighed againft the walls of this vault; and mixed their tears with that cup of their affliction,—the fpring which rifes in the middle of this floor!

O mon fils, mes amis, qui l'eut penfè jamais
Que nous habiterions ce fejour des forfaits ?
Ah! fans doute, avant nous, ces chaines fletriffantes
Ont courbé fous leur poids les Vertus gemiffantes*.

PLACES and conditions, at which human weaknefs would moft tremble, and human pride would moft difdain, have often been the fcenes of the moft amiable and exalted virtues. Not to fpecify other countries, the two moft venerable characters in the *athenian* hiftory, *Socrates* and *Phocion*, lived in poverty, and died as malefactors in prifon. *Carcer illorum*,—a *Seneca* might fay,—*omni curiâ fanctior.*

LOOK at the infcription on that wall: It fays, that this vault was the dungeon even of the *apoftle of the gentiles*,—and that to this very pillar were fixed his chains.

* * * * *

* *Siege de Calais,* act 4.

THE

THE infcription adds, that *St. Peter* alfo was confined here. I know not what degree of credit fhould be given to this tradition: however, we are certain, that thofe holy apoftles did, in fome place or other, *really* undergo fuch treatment*.

BUT let me not trefpafs on my tutor's province, who can fpeak on this fubject fo much better. Perhaps under his guidance we may make a fecond vifit to this place, when advanced in his courfe of lectures to the time of *Nero's* reign.

LET me add this reflection, my dear friends: Surely, we fhould never difdain to confider, and to commiferate the fufferings, *even of malefactors in prifon;* fince both by facred and profane hiftory we are affured, that perfons of the HOLIEST CHARACTER have been contented even to live and die with them there†.

* * *

THESE fentiments of charity, expreffed by *Crito's* pupil, rofe fincerely from his heart.

---

* See, in particular, the twelfth and fixteenth chapters of the Acts of the Apoftles.

† Our Saviour himfelf died among malefactors; one of whom reviled him in his laft moments. The other, by penitence, obtained a bleffing, far fuperiour to all the riches and honours of this world.

Often

Often while in *London* had he, unknown to any perfon, vifited *Newgate;* alleviating the miferies of fome of the felons, and releafing fome of the debtors confined there *.

THIS fincerity of heart added fuch powerful energy to his expreffions, as affected all his audience with a heavenly fympathy. Every heart was melted: every eye fwelled with a tear.

FULL of thefe fentiments, they re-afcended the dark and narrow ftair-cafe, and came foon within hearing of the organ in the church, which is built over thefe dungeons. The young nobleman turned round to *Crito*, and afked him if he knew what feftival it was to-day? It is, I believe, replied he, the eleventh of *june;*—the feftival of the *charitable St. Barnabas†.*

---

* The perfons whom he releafed were chiefly thofe, who were committed thither for fmall debts, by the Court of Confcience. He had often been happy in difcharging feveral of thefe, who were parents of large families; and who, for debts of *fome few fhillings only,* were committed prifoners to that difmal place for three long months! As the Court of Confcience is a *new inftitution,* perhaps it may not be improper to fuggeft to well-difpofed perfons, that here is *a new method of doing good.* Very fmall fums thus difpofed may fometimes fave whole families from deftruction.

† Many have been the happy perfons who have literally obeyed our Saviour's words; " Sell whatever thou haft, and give to the poor." *St. Barnabas* is the firft *recorded by name,* who for this purpofe fold his landed property. See *Acts* iv, from ver. 32, to the end.

DAYLIGHT now broke in full upon them. How glorious a fpectacle, faid the eldeft of the young gentlemen, muft *that* fun be, to perfons long confined in the gloom of fuch difmal dungeons! What occafion is there ever to deprive prifoners of the benefit of light and air? How inhuman muft that government be, which would grudge fome little expence in affording them this confolation!

CRITO'S pupil now repeated fome lines in the beginning of *Samfon Agoniftes;* and then propofed to his friends to continue their morning walk; if not too fatiguing, as far as to the other noted prifon of ancient *Rome,*—the gaol of the *Decemvirs.*

*　　*　　*

THE gaol of the *Decemvirs* ftood near the *Forum Olitorium* *. In that prifon was performed the famous action, known by the name of the *roman* charity. In memory of fuch an inftance of filial piety, the fenate ordered *that* part of the prifon, which was thus diftinguifhed, to be pulled down, and a temple to be erected on it, named on this account *Templum Pietatis.* The church

* See Abbate *Venuti's Roman* Antiquities, vol. ii. p. 33. See alfo *Pliny's* hiftory, book vii. c. 36.

of

of *St. Nicolo in Carcere* now ſtands on the ſame ſpot.

THE company arrived there about noon, and finding the church at that hour quite ſolitary, walked about it at their leiſure.

Is it not probable, ſaid the young nobleman, that ſome of theſe marble pillars once adorned the temple of *Filial Piety?* I could wiſh that a plan of that temple were now extant. But give me leave to expreſs another, more rational wiſh ; I mean that our tutor, I hope he will permit me to uſe that name, would favour us with ſome of his ſentiments on the excellent action here performed.

I AM much obliged to you for your politeneſs, replied *Crito;* but I am not worthy of that title.

I HAVE attended you to this place with very great pleaſure; but am certain, that there is no occaſion to trouble you with any of my reflections on the ſubject of the *roman* charity; the hiſtory of that action being ſo well known, and it's excellence ſo happily diſplayed by every one of this company.

GIVE me leave, however, in this place, to congratulate my pupil on the purchafe, which, by your kind affiftance, he has lately made :—I mean, the fine picture of *Guido* on that fubject. He purpofes to fend it foon to *England.* With the greateft pleafure will his father certainly receive it, and place it at the head of his gallery of family pictures; as a moft pleafing mark of his fon's goodnefs, and as a ftanding leffon and emblem of that filial love, which ought to fubfift in all families from generation to generation.

* * *

IN this manner ended the morning's converfation; and they parted for the remainder of the day. At night the company, meeting at fupper at the young nobleman's lodgings, were informed by *Crito's* pupil, in what manner he had paffed the afternoon and firft part of the evening.

IT is needlefs to add, that *Crito* gave his attention with the greateft pleafure to the following account; and, by the firft poft to *England,* made the parents of his pupil happy, by a full relation of it.

I CAME

I CAME home, faid the young gentleman, this
morning, from the place of the ancient temple of
Filial Piety, full of the idea of the work of charity
there performed. I fat down in my room, oppofite the picture of *Guido.*—Would to GOD,
that the thoughts, which then arofe in my mind,
may always be kept alive there, and continually
increafe in ardour! In the afternoon I again fat
down before the fame picture; and in that fituation, often cafting my eye on a fpectacle fo pa-
thetic, I made the following extracts; partly
from the epiftles of *Seneca*, and his book *de Beneficiis;* partly from a volume of the difcourfes
of *Socrates.*

" IT is not eafy to conceive how any man can
" receive from any of his fellow-creatures greater
" benefits, than thofe which all children derive
" from their parents; by whofe means they begin
" their exiftence, are admitted as fpectators of
" all the magnificence of the univerfe, and made
" partakers of all the temporal and eternal boun-
" ties of GOD. Let us endeavour to proportion
" our gratitude to fuch benefits received! Let us
" earneftly labour, let us at leaft fincerely defire,
" to be, if poffible, of as much benefit to our
" parents, as they have been to us! *Hoc agite,*
" *optimi juvenes! Pofita fit inter parentes libe-*
" *rofque honefta contentio, dederint majora, an ac-*
                                        " *ceperint.*

" *ceperint. Quod certamen tam optabile! Felices,*
" *qui vicerint! Felices, qui vincentur! Quid eo*
" *fortunatius sene, qui omnibus ubique prædicabit,*
" *a filio suo se beneficiis victum? Quid eo adole-*
" *scente præclarius? Nullâ enim vi verborum,*
" *nullâ ingenii facultate exprimi potest, quàm lau-*
" *dabile, quamque nunquam à memoriâ hominum*
" *exiturum, posse hoc dicere; parentibus meis*
" *parui: cessi: imperio eorum obsequentem, sub-*
" *missumque me præbui: ad hoc unum contumax*
" *fui,—ne beneficiis vincerer.*

" *Nec desunt tam pulchro certamini duces qui*
" *per vestigia sua ire nos cohortentur & jubeant.*
" Many fons have defended the old age of their
" parents from want and injury; many have fuc-
" cefsfully laboured to crown them with honour,
" and to blefs their latter days with great joy, and
" greater hope; many have moft ardently fronted
" the greateft dangers to fave their parents from
" harm; many have even had the happinefs of
" returning life for life. Happy fons! But how
" much more happy muft be their parents! *Non*
" *enim tantùm vivere, quantûm a filiis suis vitam*
" *accipere lætabuntur; & longè majorem ex animo*
" *prolis, quàm ex re ipsâ percipient voluptatem.*"

AFTER I had made thefe extracts, I took a
folitary evening walk to that fame temple of *Filial*
Piety,

Piety, which we had vifited this morning. Meeting the fexton in the church, I had an opportunity of feeing the fubterranean chapel under the communion-table: which chapel was one of the dungeons of the ancient prifon.

TWICE, if I be not miftaken, that pious and charitable a&ion was there performed. Two different *roman* matrons, at two different times, there nobly incurred the hazard of their own lives, in order to fave thofe of their parents :—A&ions of charity, which, though performed by perfons in private life, and in circumftances of indigence and obfcurity, were yet *moft highly* honoured and rewarded; the prifoners in each cafe being pardoned, and releafed, for the fake of the eminent goodnefs of their children.

HAVING fully indulged and fatisfied myfelf in meditation on the fubje& of that ftory, I left the church of *St. Nicolo in Carcere,* and walked to the *Capitol.* I fat down on the terrace, behind the *Palazzo del Senatore.*

THE view of the *Roman* Forum, and *Via Sacra,* from that terrace, made me recolle& fome of my tutor's refle&ions relative to the chara&er of *Metellus Pius.* I recolle&ed at the fame time feveral other *roman* heroes, whofe names are immortalized by their goodnefs to their parents.

Nor could I help reflecting with pleafure, that this noble virtue of filial piety fubfifted even in A.C. thofe difmal times, to which in the courfe of my 43 tutor's lecture we yefterday arrived; I mean the times of the fecond, accurfed triumvirate.

In the midft of all the horrours of cruelty and black perfidioufnefs, with which this city was then overwhelmed, filial love frequently fhone forth with peculiar luftre,—*velut erumpente inter nubila vehementiore fole.*

I remember what *Velleius Paterculus* fays on the occafion; and indeed, the inftances of fidelity fhown in that time of terror, by wives to their hufbands, and by fervants to their mafters, were very remarkable*; yet furely thofe performed by
children

* It feems not unfuitable to the defign of this work, to infert here, in a concife abridged manner, fome few of thofe examples, as copied by *Freinſhemius* from the writers of antiquity.

Tanuſia virum fuum T. Vinium conditum in arcâ, in ædes liberti Philopœmenis tranſtulit, ibique occultavit. Tum per Octaviam fororem Cæfaris, quæ multis eo tempore faluti fuit, Cæfari rem indicavit. Ille impunitatem conceſſit omnibus; Philopœmenem quinetiam equeſtri dignitate poſteà decoravit.— Lucretium, Ligariumque & Antiſtium celaverunt conjuges.— Acilium

children to their parents were not lefs worthy of commendation.

Having in my pocket a fmall *french* tranfla-tion of *Appian's* civil wars, I turned to the fourth book; and—the place where I fat being then quite folitary, employed the half hour before fun-fet in perufing the happy fate of *Ignatius;* the goodnefs of *Geta*, of *Adrian*, and of *Metellus;*—fo worthy to be called by his anceftor's glorious title.

Acilium uxor redemit à militibus, omni fuo mundo dato.—L. Cæfar à forore fuâ fervatur.—Servorum fumma ergà heros fides erat; Hirtii præfertim & Ventidii: fed Panopionis & Menenii fervi fe percufforibus etiam obtulerunt pro dominis.— Ligariorum & aliorum fratrum fumma erat inter tot terrores caritas.

Perhaps alfo it may not be improper to infert in this note fome abridged extracts from *Appian,* relative to the exam-ples of *filial* piety; efpecially confidering *Velleius Pater-culus's* ftrange affertion on that fubject.

Ἣν σπɣδη και αρετη γυναικων τε και ΠΑΙΔΙΩΝ και αδελφων και θεραποντων περισωζοντων τε και συμμηχανωμενων πολλα και ΣΥΝΑ-ΠΟΘΝΗΣΚΟΝΤΩΝ.

Ιγνατιοι, πατηρ και υἱ⊙̇, συμφυεντες αλληλοις, δια μιας πληγης απεθανον, και αυτων αι κεφαλαι μεν απετετμηντο, τα δε λοιπα σωματα ετι συνεπεπληκτο.

Γεταν ο υἱ⊙̇ εν ευρυχωρω της οικιας εδοξε κανειν, και λαθων εν αγρω νεωνητω κατελιπεν.

Αρριανου εν τη στηη κεχολαπτο εκ διαθηκων. "Τον ενθαδε κειμενον "υἱ⊙̇ ɣ προγραφεις προγραφιντα εκρυψε τε και συνεφυγε και περιεσωσε."

Μετελλω ηστην υἱ⊙̇ τε και πατηρ. διακρινοντι τω Καισαρι τɣς αιχμα-λωτɣς, ο πρεσβυτης ηγετο κομης τρ εμπλεως και δυης και ρυπου. Ο υἱ⊙̇ δε μολις επιγνους τον πατερα ανεθορεν εκ τɣ συνεδριɣ (Καισαρι γαρ συνεστρατευετο και συνηδρευεν) και ησπαζετο συν οιμωγη. Ουτος μεν σοι πολεμι⊙̇-γεγονεν ω Καισαρ, εγω δε συμμαχ⊙̇. αιτω δη σε τον πατερα σωζειν δι'εμε, η δι'εκεινον εμε συγκαταχανειν. Οικτɣ δε εξ απαντων γενομενɣ, μεθηκε σωζεδαι τον Μετελλον ο Καισαρ, και τοι πολεμιωτατον.

I WAS

I was peculiarly affected with the behaviour of another young man, a near relation to *Cicero*. He was imagined indeed,—if I be not miftaken, —not to have behaved quite well formerly to his parents; but at the time of the profcription, he nobly atoned for all his former faults. Moft carefully did he hide his father from the purfuit and fearch of the affaffins; and moft patiently did he himfelf endure the moft cruel torments, even to death, rather than difcover him. The father,— in hafte to deliver his *now beloved* fon from fuch torture,

> ———*nec fe celare tenebris*
> *Amplius, aut tantum potuit perferre dolorem.*
> *Me! Me! Adfum qui feci. In me convertite ferrum!*
> ———*Nihil ifte, nec aufus,*
> *Nec potuit.*———
> *Tum fuper exanimem fefe projecit amicum*
> *Confoffus, placidâque ibi demum morte quievit.*
> *Fortunati ambo * !*—

At the fame time *Oppius*, a very rich fenator, —a friend, I believe, both of *Tully* and *Varro*, received the fatal news, that his name too, though he was of the *Cæfarian* party, was inferted in the bloody profcription. Worn down as he was with age and ficknefs, he intended quietly to fubmit

* VIRG. *Æneid.* ix. 425, 444.

to

to his fate, and patiently to expect his murderers; but he could not refist the tender zeal and tears of his fon.

THE affecting fcene of *Anchifes* and *Æneas* was then revived. After much earneft follicitation of the fon, and bleffings and tears of the father, young *Oppius* appeared with the precious burden of his parent on his fhoulders, ftaggering along the ftreets of *Rome*, and acrofs the forum.

—— *Nec me labor ifle gravabit:*
Quo res cunque cadent, unum & commune periclum,
Una falus ambobus erit *.

O MY dear young friends!—you, who fo lately admired even with tears an action of the fame kind, nobly reprefented in one of *Raphael's* great works in the *Vatican*:—and *you* my dear tutor, who from my infancy have been a tender and truly *fpiritual* father to me; and have diligently inculcated the duty upon me, in all our ftudies, and on all occafions, which I owe to my real, and much-loved parents:—tell me, if you can, what *muft* have been my fentiments; feated as I then was, by the walls and ancient pillars of the *Roman Tabularia*, where thofe bloody profcriptions were

* ÆNEID. ii. 708.

K 3

fixed; and imagining, that I faw the moft excellent young *Oppius* thus traverfing the *Forum* before me!

CRITO'S pupil here paufed for fome moments;
and then proceeded, as follows.

No wonder, that the *romans*, who defervedly
prided themfelves in the belief of their defcent
from the ancient pious hero of *Troy*, fhould be
moved with *fo ftriking* a refemblance;

Atque animum patriæ ftrinxit pietatis imago * !

No wonder, that they fhould ardently have protefted, and loudly, as well as tenderly, applauded
this aftion. The bloody *triumvirs* durft not
venture to attempt any thing further againft the
life of fuch a father, and fuch a fon. Young *Oppius*, even at mid-day, fafely traverfed the midft
of the city; and then—after having paffed the
gates,—fometimes helping the old man to walk a
little, fometimes with tears of joy taking him again
on his fhoulders, quietly at length reached *Oftia*,
and there embarked with him for *Sicily* †.

No

---

* ÆNEID. ix. 294.
† During the reign of *Auguftus*, *Oppius* being returned to
Rome, and living there in private and very narrow circumftances, on the day appointed for the eleftion of *ædiles*,
the

No wonder, that the *ficilians* fhould kindly receive him in their ifland. They were moved to it, by their refpeft for *Sextus Pompeius*, the common patron of all the profcribed: they like-wife probably recollefted, how much their own country alfo was celebrated, for an aftion of the *fame* moft moving and moft laudable kind. You remember, my dear young friends, that noble ftory, as it is told in *Seneca* and in *Pliny*. You reminded me of it one day, while we were view-ing the paintings of the *Farnefe* gallery :—*Duo ficuli juvenes, cum Ætna, majore vi peragitata, in urbes, in agros, in magnam infulæ partem ef-fudiffet incendium, vexerunt parentes fuos ;—pa-trem fcilicet alter, alter matrem. Difceffiffe cre-ditum eft ignes ; et utrimque flammâ recedente, limitem adapertum, per quem tranfcurrerent ju-venes digniffimi.*—

the people, by a fudden refolution, would have him for their *ædile*, notwithftanding all the objeftions he could urge againft it. As he was by no means able at that time to bear the expence of this office, all the companies of the dif-erent trades in this vaft city, probably by *Auguftus's* volun-tary and glad confent, engaged to provide and furnifh *gratis* all the fhows of the theatre, *&c.*, for him. On the laft day of the fhows, and at the conclufion of the laft play, the whole ftage was on a fudden covered with heaps of money, which the numerous fpeftators in that vaft theatre, with the loudeft moft heart-felt acclamations, fhowered down on it on all fides, for the benefit of this their beloved *Op-pius.*——Εως τον ανδρα ϰατεπληϲτιϲαν.

Vid. *Appian*, lib. 4.

K 4   Tht

THE fame kind of heavenly protection, which was faid by *Virgil* to have been vouchfafed to Æneas, when entering on the fame glorious work.

Defcendo: ac ducente Deo flammam inter & hoftes
Expedior: dant tela locum, flammæque recedunt*.

* *Æneid.* ii. 632.

CHAP.

C H A P. VIII.

EIGHTEENTH DAY'S CONVERSATION.

—

THIS morning, being *faturday* the 13th of *june*, the young nobleman propofed to make a vifit to the fmall antique arch near the *Forum Boarium*. The company *readily* confented: fuch eafinefs of temper is indeed an indifpenfible requifite, for the mutual happinefs of a fet of travellers.

AT this arch the young nobleman paffed half an hour, taking, as well as he could, a drawing of fome of it's battered bas-reliefs. He then obferved to his young friends, that one of the figures of thefe bas-reliefs feems to have been imitated by *Raphael*, in his cartoon of the facrifice at *Lyftra*.

WHEN he had finifhed his defign, he walked acrofs the way, to the oppofite fquare fabric, commonly called the arch of *Janus* *.

I KNOW

* *Un' antica fabrica qui fi vede chiamata volgarmente l'arco di Giano; con* 12 *nicchie per ciafcuno dello quattro facciate. Quefto monumento e di tale ftruttura di fabrica compofta de fmifurati*

I know not, faid he, whether this grand building were originally defigned as an exchange for the
roman merchants,—according to the opinion of
moſt antiquarians; or according to the popular
tradition, as a temple of *Janus. Donato* is of
the latter opinion *.—Perhaps it may have ſerved
for both purpoſes. In relation to it's plan, I
cannot help thinking, that as, in the other neighbouring temple of *Janus* in the *Argiletum, Janus's* image was ſo formed, as to expreſs by it's
fingers the number of the days in the year; ſo
perhaps *this* fabric was built with a *ſimilar emble-
matic deſign.* It's four fronts might be alluſive
to the four ſeaſons; and the twelve niches in each
front may perhaps have contained the figures of
the twelve months.

Your conjecture, replied *Crito,* ſeems to
carry ſome probability: But I ſhould doubt
whether the repreſentation of the months was repeated on all the four fronts. Perhaps on one of
theſe ſides might be placed the ſtatues of the twelve
Dii conſentes urbani:—which *Varro* † deſcribes
as

---

*furati pezzi di marmo Greco congiunti inſieme, che e ſor pren-
dente Ogni ſuo angolo e di palmi* 102: *onde in tutto e di palmi*
408.   *Venuti,* vol. i. p. 5.

* *Exſtructa ſunt templa quadrilatera Jano quadrifronti.
Unum hodieque cernimus, apud S. Georgii in Foro Boario.*
         Donato, p. 208.

† *Eorum imagines ad forum auratæ ſtant: ſex mares, & fœ-
minæ totidem.*   *De re ruſticâ,* lib. i.

See

as ftanding in his time near the *Forum*,—and on another fide, the twelve *rural* gods, whom *Varro* invokes in the beginning of his treatife *De re ruftica.*—*Duodecim deos,* I think thefe are his words,—*qui maximé agricolarum duces funt.*

EXCUSE my impertinence, dear fir, faid *Crito's* pupil; but you were mentioning to us laft night after fupper, that the next name in your catalogue of illuftrious *romans* was that of *Varro.* Why may we not be *here* favoured with your lecture on his character? *Janus's* temple is furely no improper place for fuch a converfation; whether we confider *Janus* in his mythological character, as patron of all the *rural* labours of the year; or whether we endeavour to view him in an hiftorical light, as the firft founder of this city, many ages before the birth of *Romulus.* *Varro,* in ftudying the primæval antiquities of *Italy,* muft often have had occafion to examine the obfcure hiftory of *Janus.*

IF, replied *Crito,* my paper on the character of *Varro* had been ready for your perufal, my intention was to have prefented it to you, fome day, when you fhould be paffing by the church

---

See in reference to this fubject, the defcription of the temple of *Nifmes,* given by *Montfaucon* in his journey to *Italy.*

of *St. Salvator in Tellure*, at the foot of the *Ef-quiline* hill. The temple of the *Earth* is fuppofed by *Montfaucon* to have been fituate in that place. *Varro* makes it the fcene of one of his dialogues *de re Ruftica.*

But perhaps *this* place might have been more proper. However that may be, I muft beg leave to defer, for fome time, the offering you my notes on the fubject of *Varro's* life; they are as yet by no means fitly digefted for your perufal.

Yesterday afternoon I met, walking on the terrace of *Monte di Trinità*, your acquaintance the *french* marquis, with fome gentlemen, his countrymen, who were lately returned from *Naples*, by way of the convent of *Monte Caffino*. When they did me the honour to join company with me, they were talking of the vifit they had made to that famous abbey; they fpoke much of it's library, chapel, and other fplendid ftructures. From that fubject their converfation changed to the *antiquities* in the neighbouring town of *Caffino*. Near thofe ruins, faid one of the company, *dans un baffin formé par la retraite de la montagne, fut le lieu, qu' occupoient la maifon de campagne & les jardins du Varron.*

I COULD

I COULD have wifhed, that their converfation had dwelt on a farther defcription of the place: but it went off to other topics.

I TOOK leave of the company in about half an hour. On my return to your lodgings, I immediately confulted *Montfaucon* on the fubject* ; and then indulged myfelf in imagining the pleafure, which you, with your two worthy friends, will certainly feel, when in your return from *Naples* you will be paffing two or three days at *Caffino*.

YOU remember, my dear pupil, what *Tully* fays of that place, in his fecond Philippic †. *Studiorum fuorum M. Varro fundum Caffinatem voluit effe diverforium. Quæ in illâ villâ dicebantur? Quæ cogitabantur? Quæ literis mandabantur?—Jura populi romani, monumenta majorum, omnis fapientiæ ratio, omnifque doctrina.*

YOU will recollect this paffage with double pleafure, when you fhall be walking on the banks of the clear and deep river at *Caffino*. I wifh you may be able to trace out the fituation of *Varro's* mufæum there ‡.

* See *Montfaucon's* Journey to *Italy*, c. 22.
† Sect. 18.
‡ *Habeo fub oppido Cafino flumen, quod per villam fluit liquidum & altum—ubi eft mufæum. Circum hujus ripas ambulatio fub dio lata pedes denos.* De re Ruftica, lib. 3.

BUT,

BUT, on the other hand, you will be affected with much concern, when you turn your eyes to the prefent ftate of agriculture in that part of the kingdom of *Naples.* In *Varro's* time, *Italy* was in general the beft cultivated region of the known world. *Nulla quæ tam tota fit culta*. Arboribus confita Italia eft, ut tota pomarium videatur.* But how fadly different is it's prefent ftate! From what thefe *french* gentlemen were faying, it appears, that the delicious country between *Cafino* and *Frufinone,*—that rich and fertile territory, which once flourifhed under *Varro's* eye,—lies now almoft defolate. Even the fields of *Varro's* farms are now, in part at leaft, abandoned.

BUT let us defer talking further on this fubject, till we fee the place. When we are on that fpot, we may, *with the utmoft propriety, converfe on the topic of Varro's character.* In the mean time I may perhaps be able to collect fome memorandums relative to it. At prefent I am by no means prepared to fpeak on the fubject.

ACCORDING to the generally-received opinion, faid the eldeft of the young gentlemen, *Varro's* life feems to have been, like that of his great contemporaries *Cato* and *Tully,* divided between *literary* and *civil* induftry. If I miftake not,

---

* *De re Ruftica,* lib. i. c. 2.

he

he was entrufted with one of the principal commands in the piratic war; and by his conduct in
that ftation obtained the very diftinguifhed honour
of a *roftral* crown. He commanded afterwards
in *Spain*, in the war between *Pompey* and *Julius
Cæfar*. In his fenatorial character alfo, he feems
to have been much engaged in feveral of the great
political tranfactions of the times.

YOUR obfervation is very true, replied *Crito;*
but perhaps it may be doubted whether it would
not have been better, if,—at leaft during the civil
wars,—he had totally devoted his induftry to the
purfuit of literature. *Varro's* campaign in *Spain*,
to judge of it from the account given in *Cæfar's*
Commentaries, does not feem to add any very
great fplendour to his character. *Varro* feems
himfelf to have been fenfible, that a literary life
was his more proper element. Immediately, if I
remember right, after his *fpanifh* campaign, he
retired from public employments, and gave up
all the remainder of his life to books.

PARDON me, my dear fellow-ftudents, if I
paufe fome moments, to reflect on *Varro's* happinefs in that fphere.

IN his old age, as well as in his youth, *Varro*,
—according to *Erafmus's* expreffion,—*fenfit ftu-*
                                                  diorum

diorum dulcedinem. He had received the greateſt benefits from them in the firſt years of his man-hood, while at the univerſity of *Athens**; and now, in his decline of life, he was protected by them in a great meaſure, from the miſeries of the civil diſtractions. *Illis tempeſtatibus prope ſolus erat in portu. Cum libris in priſtinâ conſuetudine permanſit; & ſtudiorum conſuetudine leniebat dolorem. Ad eam vitam reverſus eſt, quam multi docti homines fortaſſe non rectè, ſed tamen multi, etiam reipublicæ præponendam putaverunt.*

I THINK, ſaid the young nobleman, I remem-ber ſome of thoſe expreſſions in *Tully's* Epiſtles.

THEY are in his epiſtles to *Varro*, replied *Crito*; thoſe epiſtles, which were written ſoon after *Varro's* return from *Spain.* Yeſterday afternoon, when I had laid *Montfaucon* aſide, I read thoſe eight letters: I afterwards employed myſelf, for an hour or two, in turning over ſome leaves of *Varro's* treatiſes *de Linguâ Latinâ,* and *de re Ruſticâ.*

I SHOULD think, ſaid the eldeſt of the young gentlemen, that the opinion of thoſe learned men

---

* *Per omnium honeſtorum artium cultum Varro pueritiam* adoleſcentiamque *tranſegit. Revocabat eum ab illecebris cor-ruptelarum, & lenociniis cupiditatum, præter ipſius bonam inte-gramque naturam, ſtudium ſapientæi.* Vetrannius Maurus.

of whom *Tully* fpeaks, muſt be a very debateable
point. However I ſhall readily own, that there
is ſomething very pleaſing in the idea of a ſtudious retirement. The quiet and ſtillneſs of *Tri-
nity*-college quadrangles, at *Cambridge*, have often
ſtruck me with peculiar pleaſure, on my return
from *London*, after paying ſome weeks diligent
attendance in the gallery of the houſe of commons.
I could wiſh, as we are now entered on the ſubject, that you would favour us with ſome account
of *Varro's* literary labours.

I KNOW not whether it will *ever* be in my
power, replied *Crito*; but I have not yet conſulted ſeveral authors, who are ſaid to have written
ſome account of them. I wiſh I may find ſomething in their writings, which may deſerve your
attention while at *Caſſino*: But I fear, that even
then, I ſhall hardly be able to preſent you with
any thing more, than a collection of teſtimonies
from *Tully, Quintilian, St. Auſtin, Lactantius,*
and, poſſibly, ſome other ancients, relative to
the high literary character of *Varro, in general.*
Any thing *more particular* is not perhaps to be
expected; for I know not whether we can fairly
judge of *Varro's* literary merit from his two treatiſes, which are now extant; one of them being
of the dictionary kind, and very imperfect; the
other being compoſed by him when above four-

ſcore years of age. In regard to his other works, nothing can be ſaid, as they have all long ago pe- riſhed.

YET, let me recollect : There is a reflection, which riſes from this very circumſtance, and de- ſerves the attention of many *learned* members of the republic of letters : a reflection, which ought to humble the proudeſt of their hearts.

IN the whole hiſtory of the literary world, there cannot eaſily perhaps be found any *learned* man, whoſe writings ſeemed more likely to reſiſt the force of time, than *Varro's*. *Varro*, by the uni- verſal teſtimony of ancient authors, was the moſt *learned* perſon, that ever exiſted in the *roman* nation. *Tully* adds, that he was *omnium facile acutiſſimus*. His long life was aſſiduouſly em- ployed in publications; he is ſaid to have been the author of no leſs than five hundred books *.

IN the eightieth year of his age, *Varro* began to compile his three books *de re Ruſticâ*. Let us ſuppoſe, that we now ſee him ſitting down in his

---

* The word *book* is capable of different ſenſes. Thus *Livy* may be ſaid to have written *a book* on the *roman* hiſ- tory; he may be ſaid alſo to have written *one hundred and forty books* on that ſubject. It is in the latter ſenſe, that the number of *Varro's* books is to be underſtood. Even when conſidered in this light, his publications muſt have been of an enormous bulk.

library

library to this employment. At that time, what, probably, were his thoughts?

Properandum eſt. Si eſt homo, ut dicitur, bulla; eó magis ſenex. Annus oƈtogeſimus ádmonet me, ut ſarcinas colligam, antequam proficiſcar e vita. In relation to his corporeal frame indeed, *Varro* muſt have been ſincerely ſenſible, that it was tottering on the brink of the grave, and muſt ſoon fall into duſt and aſhes: But as to his writings, he might have other thoughts. When he ſurveyed with pleaſure the rolls of his five hundred manuſcripts, ranged perhaps in neat order on the ſhelves of his library, he might flatter himſelf, that theſe were as likely to laſt for ever, as the compoſitions of *Tully,* or any other of his contemporary brother authors.

BUT how uncertain are the moſt promiſing hopes of the immortality of any literary performance! *Tully's* works now extant, voluminous as they appear, are but a ſmall part of what he really publiſhed: and as to *Varro's* compoſitions, *not one* of all that vaſt number has eſcaped deſtruction. They have all, except the fragments of his twenty-four books *de Linguâ Latinâ,* long ſince totally periſhed. Scarce even the titles of a tenth part of them are known.

DURING

DURING our refidence at *Florence*, I employed an hour one morning in ftudying that obfcure and imperfect catalogue of the titles of fome
of *Varro's* works, which the learned *Vetrannius
Maurus* has, feemingly with much difficulty,
compiled*.

WHEN I had finifhed that catalogue, I took
a walk to the great duke's gallery. I paffed
through it's three long double rows of ftatues and
bufts: I paffed through it's *Tribuna*, without
attending to the *chef d'œuvres* of fculpture and
painting, which are there collected. I went on
to the fmall room adjoining, in which there is an
object, overlooked, or fhunned perhaps, by many
dilettanti; yet certainly very affecting and inftructive. You muft remember the wax-work of
Caietano Julio: it moft naturally reprefents the
fcene of a burying-vault, in which the gradual

---

* From fome of thefe titles, as well as from other accounts, it fhould feem, that feveral of *Varro's* writings were
of the fatyric kind: confequently the lofs of thefe works
is to be lefs lamented. For the fame reafon we muft greatly
abate our idea of *Varro's* happinefs in his literary labours:
—Happinefs cannot refide in a mind foured with fatyric
malevolence.

But perhaps this may be a miftake; for in thofe works
of *Varro*, which are now extant, no fuch malevolent fpirit
appears. On the contrary, they appear to have been written
from a very benevolent principle: *ut non folum quoad vivam, quid fieri oporteat neceffarios meos moneam, fed etiam poft
mortem.*

progrefs of the diffolution of the human body is exhibited, in feveral fmall figures. The firft corpfe is fwollen, the fecond difcoloured and fpotted, the third full of worms; the laft a bare fkeleton. Among the fculls and bones, which are fcattered on the floor, lies *a torn folio volume* with this infcription,

ET OPERA EORUM SEQUUNTUR ILLOS.

* * *

Such has been, and will be, the fate of numberlefs literary compofitions, even of the beft kind. The learned authors however may have this great confolation; that, though their works certainly perifh, yet their intention in compofing them, if good, will be everlaftingly rewarded, like all other works of charity.

But to what place, continued *Crito*, addreffing himfelf to the young nobleman, fhall we have the honour of attending you, during the remainder of this morning? We are now on the road half way to the *Villa Mattei*. Shall we go thither? I fhould be very glad of your opinion with refpeſt to fome pieces of antique fculpture, which are there preferved.

No

No fooner had *Crito* let fall this hint, than the young nobleman gladly embraced it. He called up his carriage, which was waiting at fome diftance, and told the coachman to drive to the *Villa Mattei, ful Monte Celio.*

WHILE the company were on the way thither, *Crito's* pupil made fome mention of that fecond edition of the Academics, in which dialogue *Varro* is fuppofed converfing with *Tully* and *Atticus.*

ON the mention of *Atticus's* name, the young nobleman took the opportunity of expreffing a regard for his memory. He admired *Atticus's* abilities, judgment, learning, and the purity with which he fpoke the beft foreign language of his time. He admired alfo his prudence; his happinefs in being acquainted with all the great men of his age, and generally efteemed by them; his amiable politenefs, his conftantly living with elegance in high life, yet conftantly declining all offices of ftate, and avoiding all party contefts.

THESE points of *Atticus's* charaĉter, replied *Crito*, feem indeed very pleafing; but I have often heard you wifh, that he had been aĉtuated by a more noble ruling principle. The prefervation of *himfelf* in the moft dangerous times; the

securing

fecuring *his own* eafe; the promoting, if it might
be by fafe methods, *his own* dignity, wealth, and
rank;—thefe feem to have been the principal objects and aim of *Atticus's* wifdom. How muſt
the ancient heroes of this city, the *Curii* and *Fa-
bricii*, have defpifed fo very poor and mean-
fpirited a plan of life!

YET, mean and little as *Atticus's* final object
might be, I fhall readily agree with you, that
many of his actions were very praife-worthy.

SEVERAL inftances of private friendfhip do
great honour to his memory. He was candid:
he was beneficent to every party, *when lowest*: he
was very liberal both to the exiled and diftreffed,
and to their friends and families. Highly amiable
indeed is this behaviour; efpecially, when we
contraſt it with the party-rancour and fury of his
times. And although felf-prefervation might be
Atticus's moſt cogent motive to this political, as
well as charitable conduct; it is very probable,
that feveral fentiments of real humanity and good-
nature were joined and mixed with that motive.
For, as *Middleton* obferves, while the philofophy
of *Atticus* was incompatible with all affections
that did not terminate in himfelf, yet was he frequently influenced, by a goodnefs of nature, to
correct the faultinefs of his principle.

THE

THE converfation now turned on the *epicurean* philofophy. While the company were engaged on that fubject, the coach arrived at the gate of the *Villa Mattei.*

IN that villa are five apartments, each containing feveral valuable antique fculptures. In viewing thefe, the company gave their chief attention to the ftatue of *Livia Augufta;* to the buft of *Cicero,* which is in the fourth apartment; and to the heads of *Portia,* the daughter of *Cato,* and her hufband *Marcus Brutus,* in the third.

THE ftatue of *Livia* is reckoned to be one of the very fineft antique figures now extant: the buft of *Tully* is by the *roman* antiquarians efteemed *il piu bello, e il piu ficuro:* but it was for the fake of feeing the two laft mentioned heads, that *Crito* had propofed coming hither this morning.

THE eldeft of the young gentlemen viewed the countenance of *Marcus Brutus* with peculiar reverence and affection.

CRITO obferved his emotion; and faid, I wifh, dear fir, that you would favour us with your prefent thoughts. The buft before you feems to have made a very deep impreffion on your mind.

How

How can it be otherwise? the young gentle-man ardently replied. From the earlieſt period of my ſtudies at ſchool, the name of *Marcus Brutus* has been dear to me; and ſhall I, while at *Rome*, be cold on this topic? With earneſt impatience have I expeɕted the time, when, in the courſe of your lectures, you ſhould bring us to *the glorious character of this patriotic hero.*

But let me moderate my impetuoſity, and en-deavour to ſpeak in a calmer ſtyle.

Yesterday afternoon I ſet myſelf a kind of ſhort exerciſe on the ſubject: I need not ſay, that I ſhould be glad of your correction of it. My young friends will permit me to read it to you.

Saying this, the young gentleman took from his pocket-book a paper of notes: he caſt his eyes on it for a moment or two, and then thus ad-dreſſed himſelf to *Crito.*

This piece of paper contains only ſome few reflections on the *education* of *Brutus.* I ought to think myſelf much honoured, if after this little ſketch ſhall have undergone proper correction, you will condeſcend to accept it, as a kind of in-troduction to your diſſertation on his character.

Often

OFTEN have I heard you obferve, that the bleffed work of education confifts in the union of two noble arts;—*the improvement of the abilities of the mind,* and the *far more important cultivation of the goodnefs of the heart.* Permit me to confider the education of *Brutus* in each of thefe refpeets. In the *firft* he had a *Tully* for his tutor; in the *fecond,* a *Cato.*

IN the *improvement of the faculties of his mind,* young *Brutus,* my dear friends, did not negleet the ftudy of poetry, hiftory, or any kind of polite literature, though his principal application was given to that of oratory. With regard to the particular ftyle of eloquence in which he excelled, I muft refer you to *Tully's* rhetorical works; in feveral parts of which—as you know better than myfelf—the praifes of young *Brutus* are introduced with great affeetion and refpeet. The dialogue *de Claris Oratoribus* is even infcribed with his name. He had indeed acquired a very early fame at the bar, and was by *Tully* looked upon as the probable fucceffor to his glory in that profeffion. He was bleffed with excellent parts, attended with equal induftry;—*in perennibus ftudiis fe continebat.* His eloquence, befide it's other merits, was accompanied and enriched, as I juft obferved, by much knowledge and learning of various kinds,—*uberrimis Athenarum artibus:*

and

and it was ennobled by that ſtill higher qualifica-
tion, which *Tully*,—happy had it been his own
caſe,—deſcribes as moſt eſſential to an orator.
Summæ eloquentiæ junxit decus omne virtutis.

LET me now, dear ſir, continued the young
gentleman, turning himſelf again to *Crito*, endeavour to conſider thoſe moral philoſophic ſtudies,
by which *the goodneſs of Brutus's heart* was cultivated and improved. If you reflect, that from
his earlieſt youth he appeared moſt excellently
formed by nature to the virtues of gentleneſs and
goodneſs, as well as thoſe of generoſity, fortitude,
ardent patriotiſm, and a ſtrong deſire of always
acting rightly and nobly; you cannot avoid thinking, that *Cato* muſt have been very happy in ſuch
a pupil. On the other hand, *Brutus* certainly
had much more reaſon to eſteem himſelf highly
fortunate in ſuch a philoſophic tutor; a tutor,
whoſe precepts were in ſeveral reſpects excelled
by his practice; and who, both by precept and
example, muſt have been greatly aſſiſtant to his
young ſcholar; although the particular ſyſtem of
moral philoſophy, that of the *platonic* ſect, in
which *Brutus* was chiefly educated, was not the
fame with that, which *Cato* himſelf had ardently,
and as you ſometime ſince obſerved, unfortunately
embraced.

IN

In clofing thefe fhort reflections on the education of *Marcus Brutus*, you, dear fir, I am
fure, will think one obfervation not improperly
added.

BRUTUS was far from confining his ftudious
diligence in any fcience,—much lefs in this of
moral philofophy, the moft important of them all,
—merely to the *time* and the *places* of his education. During the whole continuance of his life
we find him ftill perfevering in this moft noble
kind of induftry: in the midft of the greateft public bufinefs gladly making this beft ufe of every
leifure hour; and for that purpofe frequently de-
nying himfelf the indulgence of all other *meaner*
kinds of refrefhment or reft.

But whither have I been carried by the ftream
of my thoughts on this beloved topic? I have
been impertinently talking a very long time to *you,*
on a fubject, upon which I ought much rather
to have been liftening to your inftructions.

On the contrary, dear fir, replied *Crito,* let
me return you thanks, on my own account, as
well as on that of thefe our two dear friends, for
your kindnefs in communicating to us thefe reflections. I have indeed myfelf attempted to
draw up fome fhort papers relative to the character

of

of *Marcus Brutus;* but they are very imperfect. Some parts of *Brutus's* life, particularly this of his education, I had not sufficiently considered.

THERE are other parts of it, concerning which, after much thinking, I knew not what to say. You will readily guess that I mean *the ides of march*. It seems very difficult to pass a proper judgment on that action. You will pardon me therefore, when you are so kind as to look on my papers, if you find in them no mention of that affair. Yet let me not omit, in justice to his memory, one weighty observation. However divided the public opinion may always have been, in relation to the nature itself of that action, yet has it been unanimously agreed, that the *intent* of *Brutus* in it was certainly most upright and disinterested; full of the most sincere patriotism and ardent desire of restoring liberty to his country, which indeed was his only view.

SURELY, dear sir, replied the eldest of the young gentlemen, we may say of him, with still more propriety than was said of his great ancestor, whom we just now saw in the first apartment of this villa*,

---

* The statue of *Junius Brutus* stands in the first room of the *Villa Mattei*, near the door. See p. 50. of the first volume.

Utcunque

Utcunque ferent ea facta minores,
Vicit amor patriæ*.

WHILE we fhudder at the idea of *Marcus Bru-*
tus ftabbing his friend and benefactor, it is but
juftice to remember, that he did it upon the fame
principles, to which, at the breaking out of the
civil war, he had facrificed the moft juft filial re-
fentment, by joining *Pompey.* Without entering
into the difcuffion of fuch actions, let me join
with you in lamenting the fate of thofe, who are
thrown into fo diftracting a fcene; where they
muft not only ftruggle againft general corruption
and depravity of manners, but where is a much
greater misfortune—they cannot form to themfelves any plan of conduct, which their own hearts
wholly approve, or exercife one virtue, but at
the expenfe of another: In fhort, where they
cannot invariably purfue the nobleft of all objects,
without facrificing the moft amiable fentiments of
humanity.

THANK God, replied *Crito,* thofe fcenes happen very feldom: But, let us quit the fubject.
While I was thinking early this morning in what
place I could beft converfe with you on *Brutus's*
character, I recollected that room in the *Spada*
palace, where the noble coloffus of *Pompey* ftands

* VIRG. *Æn.* vi. 822.

that

that coloffus, which with great probability is thought to be the identical ftatue, at the *bafis* of which,

That all the while ran blood, great Cæfar fell *.

But it would have been impoffible to have conversed in that room on *Brutus's* charaĝer, without having our imaginations totally abforpt by an aĝ, from the perpetration of which I could moft earneftly wifh to *withdraw* your thoughts.

AT the entrance of *this* villa, I endeavoured for the fame reafon, to divert your attention from that noble ftatue of *Julius Cæfar*, which ftands in the garden, on the outfide of the houfe.

LET us fix our minds upon other parts of the life of *Brutus*. There are feveral, faid he, cafting a look of compaffionate benignity on the buft of *Portia*—which are very pleafing; whether we confider him in his *domeftic*, or in his *civic* charaĝer.

* *Pompeii ftatuam contra Theatri ejus regiam marmoreo Jano fuppofuit tranflatam e Curia, in quâ C. Cæfar erat occifus.*
Suetonius, in Aug. cap. 31.
See *Donato*, p. 29. See alfo Abbate *Venuti*, v. ii. p. 84. *Narro Flamminio Vacca, che il bel coloffo alto* xv. *palmi che fi ammira nel palazzo Spada rapprefentante Pompeo fu ritrovato nel vicolo de' Leutari non molto lontano da quefto Teatro, non effendovi di mezzo, che campo di Fiore; potrebbe effere la medefima ftatua rammentata da Suetonio qua Angufto trasferita.*

IN

IN relation to his *civic* character, several months ago, while we were in the *Milanese*, I had the pleasure of compiling some short papers, descriptive of *Brutus's* amiable behaviour, during his provincial government of *Gallia Cisalpina*, and also while he resided in *Asia Minor*. In each of those countries he nobly exemplified the practicability of doing much good to the public, in the worst of times.

IT was in the midst of the miseries of a civil war, continued *Crito*, sitting down, and taking out his roll of papers;—it was about the very time when *Cato* was slaying himself in despair at *Utica*, that *Brutus* accepted the provincial government of *Lombardy*, to the great advantage and happiness of that large and populous country. In those times of license and confusion, the *roman* provinces suffered, if possible, still more than usual, under the violence and avarice of their governors. In the happy province of *Brutus* alone, no insolence or rapine was then seen in the governor, or permitted by him in any of his inferiour officers. Such indeed is said to have been the mildness of *Brutus's* gracious administration in *Lombardy*, as fully to make that country amends even for all her former calamities.

THE

THE ftatue of *Brutus* was erected at *Milan,* moft likely in grateful memory of his good government:—I mean that brazen ftatue, which *Auguftus,* feveral years afterwards, in the latter probably, and better part of his life, much admired, and commanded ftill to be carefully preferved there: thus, generoufly, though a perfonal enemy, maintaining the honour of *Brutus;* and applauding the *milanefe* for their gratitude to a great benefactor.

I COULD wifh, faid the young nobleman, that I had made fome inquiry among the antiquaries at *Milan* relative to that ftatue; though moft probably it has been loft and melted down long ago, in fome of the many devaftations and conflagrations, which that rich city has fuffered. Excufe, my dear fir, this interruption.

THE moft amiable and *univerfally* admired part of *Brutus's* life, faid *Crito,* is his conduct in *Afia,* during the interval between the death of *Julius Cæfar,* and the battle of *Philippi.*

HIGHLY noble indeed does that fcene of provincial government appear, efpecially if we compare it with the tyrannical oppreffion of the fame country by the luxurious, rapacious, and cruel *Anthony.*

BRUTUS had been always in poffeffion of the moft defirable kind of reputation : he was every where generally efteemed by the people, beloved by his friends, and admired by all good men : he was hated by none, not even by his enemies. This univerfal good name he had defervedly acquired by his extraordinary mildefs; a mildnefs, never ruffled by any ill-natured paffion, or corrupted or weakened by any voluptuoufnefs and vicious luxury : a mildnefs accompanied with generofity, with difinterefted integrity, inviolable uprightnefs, magnanimous zeal, and inflexible fteadinefs in whatever he believed juft and honeft. But all thefe his virtues fhone forth in *Afia with even more than ufual* fplendour.

For, though *Brutus* was then deeply engaged in the midft of military preparations, both by fea and land, for fuccouring as foon as poffible his diftreffed countrymen in *Italy*, yet did he give great attention to the affairs of the *afiatics.*

By a proper combination of juftice and mercy, *even then* did *Brutus* revive in that country the happy memory of thofe great bleffings, which the government of *Rutilius* and of *Scævola*, had conferred on it, in former times of peace.

IT is true, that, as this was an era of general confufion, *Afia Minor* was not free from many calamities of war, occafioned particularly by the frenzy of the *lycians.* But even amidft the difmal procefs of war, the goodnefs and humanity of *Brutus* were indefatigably exerted on every poffible occafion. Even in the dreadful deftruction of the city of *Xanthus,* the mercy of a *Brutus* as eminently diftinguifhed itfelf, as that of a *Titus* is faid to have done, in the fimilar horrours of the fiege of *Jerufalem.*

ALL the other provinces of that part of *Afia* found him gracious and merciful to them, even beyond their expectations. He entirely gained their hearts, and fully eftablifhed the love of his government among them by peace and clemency. At the fame time he was, for their fakes,—in exact imitation of *Scævola*—moft bravely and juftly fevere on their *roman* oppreffors. He publicly on this account difgraced and condemned fome, who were the great affiftants and affociates of his own party; and who had born, even at *Rome,* the higheft offices of the ftate.

MANY indeed, and memorable were the acts of juftice, which *Brutus* was conftantly performing throughout the whole of *this* his *afiatic* expe-

dition:

dition : his juſtice was diligent alike in diſpenſing puniſhments and rewards.

In ſome inſtances his conduct was ſtill more exalted, and deſerves perhaps a more venerable, certainly a more *amiable* name, than even that of juſtice itſelf. His contemporary *romans* were highly pleaſed with the puniſhment of *Theodotus,* the murderer of *Pompey* the Great. Yet ſurely, you, my dear young friends, will receive far more noble pleaſure in recollecting, that *Brutus,* about the very ſame time, fully pardoned *Gillius,* who had even attempted to be *his* murtherer.

CRITO now roſe from his chair, and approached the buſt of *Brutus,* with almoſt as much reſpect and regard as were expreſſed a quarter of an hour before by the eldeſt of the young gentlemen. His pupil roſe with him, and, melting at the recital of the laſt-mentioned act of humanity, even embraced the buſt, and preſſed his lips on the cold marble.

From *Aſia,* continued *Crito, Brutus* marched to *Thrace.* In *Thrace,* ſome ſhort time before, he had been very ſerviceable to the *roman* cauſe; having, though in the midſt of a civil war, generouſly recovered to the *romans* their poſſeſſion of

the

the province of *Sadales,* and fuppreffed the incur-
fions of the barbarous *beffi.* From the coafts of
Thrace he now approached to meet his fate at
Philippi: he approached with fortitude and chear-
fulnefs; ftill continuing the moft abundant generofity to his foldiers, and love to his friends; but
above all things, moft earneftly longing to fee the
end, however fatal to himfelf, of the miferies
of this deftructive civil war.

On the fields of *Philippi,* in both engagements,
Brutus at the head of fome few legions only, bore
down every thing before him, and was very near
obtaining a total victory. According to *Plutarch,*
he performed every thing that was poffible for an
expert general, or a valiant foldier, to achieve.
But let me not pretend to fpeak of his military
talents: let me rather defire your attention to
fome of his noble fentiments, as expreffed in two
or three lines, which I have tranfcribed from
Plutarch.

Saying this, *Crito* placed his roll of papers on
the table of inlaid *oriental* gems, that adorns the
apartment, in which the company were then converfing.

Εμβαλων την δεξιαν εκαϛω μαλα Φαιδρ☉ ηδεοϑαι μεν
εφη μεγαλην ηδονην οτι των φιλων αυτον ȣδεις εψευσατο·
——εαυτȣν

εαυτον δε των νενικηκοτων μακαριωτερον νομιζειν, ȣκ εχθες ȣδε πρωην μονον, αλλα και νυν, απολιποντα δοξαν αρετης, ην ȣθ'οπλοις ουδε χρημασιν απολειψȣσῖν οι κεκρατηκοτες· ως μη δοκειν οτι δικαιȣς ανδρας αδικοι, και κακοι χρηςους απολεσαντες, ȣ προσηκοντως αρχȣσιν.— Δεηθεις δε και παρεκαλεσας σωζειν εαυτους, ανεχωρησεν απωτερω.

THE young gentlemen, one after another, read this extract: the converſation for ſome minutes dwelt on it's contents, and afterwards imperceptibly wandered to other topics. The inlaid work of the table firſt drew their attention; then the other pieces of furniture in the apartment; particularly the plan of *Conſtantinople*, which hangs on the wall *. Looking on that plan, they began to talk of their intended travels to the *Levant.*

IF from *Greece* and *Macedon*, ſaid the eldeſt of the young gentlemen, we ſhall be able to go *by land* to *Conſtantinople*, we muſt I believe *neceſſarily* paſs by *Philippi*. Probably we ſhall find ſome tradition ſtill remaining among the natives, relative to the great battles fought there. Perhaps too, in the neighbouring marſhes or plain, we may be ſhown ſome diſtinct places, where, from the peaſants having ploughed up human bones,

---

* In the third apartment of the *Villa Mattei*, is a very curious inlaid table of *oriental* gems; the plan of *Conſtantinople* curiouſly drawn with a pen; valuable buſts of *Brutus* and *Portia* in a group, &c. See *Keyſler's* Travels.

and

and many rufty bits of armour, it is conjectured,
that the army of *Caffius* or of *Brutus* was engaged.
Our imagination will fupply many other circumftances. On *that* part of the field we fhall recollect with ardour the virtues of *Lucilius* and *Meffala. Here*, perhaps, fhall we fay, young *Cato,*
rufhing on the enemy, exclaimed *,

> *I am the fon of Marcus Cato ;*
> *A foe to tyrants, and my country's friend.*

There probably, under that rock, by the fide of
that brook, *Brutus,* the laft hero of the *roman*
republic, expired. Why is not a grove of laurel
planted on the fpot ?

THE young nobleman fmiled with great good-
nature at his friend's patriotic enthufiafm. *Crito's*
pupil then repeated feveral other lines from *Shak-
fpeare;* adding his wifhes, that this tragedy had not
been called *Julius Cæfar,* but had born a more
proper, as well as a more honourable title, that
of *Brutus.*

CRITO, in the mean time, ftood meditating in
filence on the idea, which the ardent imagination

---

* Αγωνιζομεν⊙ υπερ της ελευθεριας, και ꭒτε φυγειν ꭒτε λαθειν αξιω-
σας, αλλα προκαλꭒμεν⊙. τꭒς πολεμιꭒς, εμπροσθεν εαυτον εμ᷉νιζων,
συνεξορμων τε τꭒς συμμενοντας, επεσε, θαυμα της αρετης τοις εναντιοις
παρασχων. *Plutarchi Cato Minor, in fine.*

of the eldest of his young fellow-students had sug-
gested.

FOLLOWING that train of thought, It is true,
said he, we shall all be deeply affected in viewing the place where *Brutus* expired. But unwillingly am I obliged to remind you, that, amidst
the heroisms which adorned his last hours, there
appeared in him some very great defects of moral
character.

PLUTARCH with concern mentions one of
them. There were two others, on which I wish
I were able to offer you some suitable reflections.

BRUTUS, continued *Crito*, resuming his seat,
had, as you observed, happily imbibed in his early
education, and when arrived to years of maturity
had always firmly held fast, the noble doctrine of
Plato and *Pythagoras**; that suicide, on any occasion, was a very mean, as well as a highly irre-
ligious action. Wearied however by affliction
and labour, he himself sunk down to the same dismal and desperate deed. He gave no reason,
which in truth, it was impossible to give; or did
he offer any excuse, for so dire an act, but only
the seeming extremity of his affairs: an excuse,

* See *Plato's Phædo*; and *Cicero de Senectute*, p. 73.

which

which he had by no means allowed in the cafe of *Cato*, whom he always on this account highly blamed.

A DUE confideration of the perpetual mutability of all human affairs is one of the many fupports, which reafon offers againſt fuch defpair. It is impoffible for any perfon ever to be certain, that his condition is really and abfolutely defperate. Perhaps, even at the very time when his circumftances appear to him the moſt extreme, a confiderable change of fortune may be drawing near.

HAD the ftoic *Cato*, in his laft ftudies at *Utica*, fufficiently attended to that doctrine in the Phædo, which is declarative againſt fuicide; and had he prudently retired, as the other fenators did, from the untenable poſt of that *african* city; he would have found in the *neighbouring* country of *Spain* the power of his patriot friends rifing with fuch ftrength, as to be able foon after, even without the affiſtance of *Cato's* name, to reduce *Cæfar* to the greateft extremities.

HAD the *epicurean Caffius* with-held his furious hand from felf-deftruction only fome few *minutes* longer, he would have been made happy with the intelligence of *Brutus's* victory, and *Octavius's* defeat.

defeat. This hafty defpair of *Caffius* is indeed ftrangely contrary to the behaviour of *former ro-man* generals, who in times of the *greateft* dif-trefs thought it their duty, *nunquam defperare de republicâ;* as well as to his own noble conduct in the *parthian* war, after the total defeat of the great army of *Craffus*.

It feems indeed aftonifhing, faid the eldeft of the young gentlemen, that two fuch generals as *Caffius*, and *Pompey* the Great, fhould give up their whole caufe on the ill fuccefs of *one* battle only; though each of them, even after that de-feat, ftill continued in poffeffion of great forces; as well as of a country behind them, which was full of refources; larger, and much richer, than one half of the prefent dominions of the vaft *turkifh* empire. How different has been the behaviour of the king of *Pruffia* in the prefent war*!

Had *Brutus*, continued *Crito*, after his dif-comfiture, adhered with proper perfeverance to this *platonic* and truly *focratic* article of philofo-phy, I mean the abhorrence of fuicide; had he with patience, and fortitude, and proper refig-nation, born the prefent trouble, *only till the next morning;* he would then have heard, that his

* The reader fhould recollect, that this refers to the year 1761.

camp

camp with fourteen thoufand foldiers in it was ftill fafe. Pardon the folly, my dear friends, of thus pretending to talk on military affairs ; but, if I be not much miftaken, fome of *Brutus's* land forces offered to make head, under *Meffala*, againft the triumvirs, even after the death of *Brutus*. However this may be, yet certainly, had *Brutus* deferred the fatal ftroke, and made a retreat, he would foon have been informed of the great victory lately gained by his *naval* forces : a victory; which would have made him mafter of all the neighbouring feas, fo that his fleet, in conjunction with the *ficilian* maritime power, would very probably have carried all before it, in every part of that important element. But *Brutus*,—how inferiour to the heroic chriftian *Alfred*, when in much lower circumftances of diftrefs !—*Brutus* defpaired; and with him therefore at once fell, as you obferve, the republic of *Rome*, and the liberty of his country.

BUT it grows late in the morning : had we not better be walking down to your coach at the garden-gate ?

FROM the porch of the *Villa Mattei* down to it's garden-gate is a narrow walk, on each fide of which are ranged near forty antique funeral urns.

THE

THE company ftopped for fome minutes to read two or three of the infcriptions on them; when the eldeft of the young gentlemen, turning round to *Crito*, afked him, what was the *other* unhappy circumftance, which attended *Brutus's* dying hour!

His fad fpeech, replied *Crito*, which difco-vered fuch unfteadinefs, weaknefs, and defpon-dency of mind. I mean thofe *greek* verfes, Ω τλημον, κ. τ. λ.—which *Brutus* then repeated, and which his friend *Volumnius* was probably afhamed to remember. Totally inconfiftent were they with thofe noble lines, which you juft now read from *Plutarch*. They were indeed, to give them their true name, a very falfe accufation againft virtue: an accufation, highly fhocking in any mouth; but peculiarly unworthy the dying lips of a *Brutus*.

In relation to this fubject, permit me to recol-lect fome paffages in a fermon, which was preached fome time ago in one of the churches of *St. Giu-feppe*, here at *Rome*. The preacher was compar-ing the moral lives and characters of the ancient and modern *romans :* in fome points he fharply re-prehended his audience for their inferiority to their pagan anceftors; in other articles he ardent-ly congratulated them on their fuperiour happinefs. Towards the clofe of his difcourfe, he had occa-fion to fpeak of the piety, joy, faith, and hope, which

which ought to attend and furround a death-bed, enlivening and enlightening all it's gloom. In contraſt with that happy ſcene, he mentioned the above diſpirited ſpeech, which in the moment of dejeȼtion fell unawares from the lips of *Marcus Brutus.* Then turning round, and fixing his eyes on a piȼture which hung over one of the altars, " O my dear brethren, ſaid he, what an opportu-"-nity is now open to us, for pouring forth, if we " were worthy and able, a full ſtream, a torrent " of ſacred eloquence! O my dear brethren, every " day many thouſand chriſtians die in poor cot-" tages, after having paſſed a life full of pain, la-" bour, and want : *many, many* of them die in a " temper of heart, thank God, infinitely ſuperiour " to that of the expiring *Brutus,*—however highly " celebrated for his learning, abilities, and great-" neſs of mind. But it is no wonder. *Brutus* " wanted in his laſt hour that firm ſupport of the " cauſe of virtue,—the ſure and ſtedfaſt hope of " everlaſting life ; that holy faith and hope, which " warms the dying breaſt of every good chriſtian; " and which has enflamed with celeſtial ardour " the departing ſouls of eminently good men.

" LET the freethinker, the partial admirer of " the exaggerated idea of heathen virtue, com-" pare this mean ſpeech of *Marcus Brutus,* with the

" the bleffed raptures of thofe happy, thrice-happy
" fervants and faints of the true God."

Such were the fentiments expreffed in a *roman*
fermon. Pardon me for troubling you with the
recital of them; but indeed they feemed to me
fo very appofite to the fubject, on which we are
now talking, that I thought it much better to endeavour to repeat them to you, than to offer you
any of my own reflections.

SIMILAR reflections would perhaps have naturally arifen in my mind; but I fhould have been
far lefs " worthy and able" to exprefs them, than
this *roman* preacher.

BESIDES I fhould at prefent have declined
launching out into fuch meditations. We fhall
foon have a much more proper opportunity, a
much ftronger call for them. We fhall be foon
drawing near thofe times, in which the heroes of
chriftianity, the primitive martyrs, will begin to
appear. Their virtue was ftrong, was ardent to
the laft moment : never, in any misfortunes of
life, or at their laft hour in any pains of death,
were they fuffered, like *Brutus*, in any manner or
degree to fall away. They looked not for the rewards of virtue in a tranfitory life : they were not
difap-

disappointed at meeting what is called misfortune here; or in finding it continued to the last moments of their existence in *this* world.

> *The world recedes; it disappears:*
> *Heav'n opens on their eyes; their ears*
> *With sounds seraphic ring.*

I FORGET the next line, said *Crito,* and laid his head on one of the stone coffins.

> *O grave! where is thy victory?*
> *O death! where is thy sting?*

*　　*　　*

AFTER the company had been seated some minutes in the carriage, the coachman drove homewards by the same way he came: and being now arrived near those ruins, which in *Noli's* map of *Rome* are marked by the name of the *Curia Hostilia**, *Crito* turned to the eldest of the young gentlemen, and observed: Is it not something singular, that at the battle of *Philippi* there should appear, among the principal leaders of the republican party, two persons, descended from families remarkably famous for their bravery in the same cause *five hundred years* before? I mean the two

* See p. 69. of the first volume.

perfons

perfons of whom you were juft now fpeaking with honour;—*Meffala*, who was lineally defcended from the great *Valerius Publicola;* and *Marcus Brutus*, defcended from the family, if not from the perfon, of *Junius Brutus*.

HAPPY families! I am fure you will always efteem them fuch. Happy, no lefs than honourable, in being thus faithful to the fupport of public liberty, from it's firft rife to it's lateft fall.

MAY I always, replied the worthy youth, continue to be of that opinion! But I muft own, that juft then my thoughts were engaged on *another* fubject.

ABOUT a fortnight ago you were lamenting to us the murder of the *Gracchi*. You had then great reafon to be fhocked at the profpect of the enfuing public miferies; *the very heavy and long-lived confequence of faction and civil difcord*. Through what fcenes of calamity indeed have we fince paffed! *Marius—Sylla—Cæfar—Mark Anthony.* I could almoft wifh you to recapitulate the whole horrid hiftory.

BY no means, anfwered *Crito*. Your thoughts may be much better engaged. But, if you choofe to dwell for fome few moments on that topic, let

us

us take a *more confined* view of thofe public miferies; for inftance, from the fatal hour when *Julius Cæfar* paffed the *Rubicon*, to the battle of
Philippi. During thofe nine or ten years, what
an *Iliad* of evils have we feen! Civil war had
been conftantly ravaging fome one or more of the
roman provinces. May nothing fimilar ever happen to *Great Britain!* But I cannot help obferving, that the civil wars of the *romans* were then
become as extenfive, as even thofe conquefts, of
which they had fo recently vaunted.

NOR was the ftorm appeafed by all that heavy
fhower of blood, which fell on the fields of *Philippi*. Difcord raged—with fome fhort intervals
of a deceitful calm,—for twelve years longer : and
during thofe twelve years, not only *Afia* and *Afric*,
but even *Italy* herfelf felt much diftrefs.

GREAT tracts of her moft fertile regions were
given up as a prey to the legionary foldiers. With
what a melancholy accent did you, my dear pupil,
repeat fome lines of the Bucolics, one evening
while we were walking on the beautiful banks of
the *Po*, near *Cremona!*

Impius hæc tam culta novalia miles habebit?
Barbarus has fegetes? En quo difcordia cives
Perduxit miferos!—Veteres migrate coloni*.

* VIRGIL : *Ecl.* i. 71. and ix. 4.

Other parts of *Italy*, during the fame twelve years, were laid wafte by flaughter and famine.

PERHAPS, faid *Crito's* pupil, it was at *this* time, that *Horace* petitioned *Apollo* to avert from *Italy* *bellum lachrymofum, miferamque famem.* May fuch plagues be always indeed averted from this country; but may they alfo be averted from thofe other nations, which *Horace* mentions in the next verfe.

Hic bellum lachrymofum, hic miferam famem,
Peftemque a populo, & principe Cæfare, in
    Perfas, atque Britannos,
        Veftrâ motus aget prece *.

I thank GOD, however, that inftead of *Horace's* ill-judged and ill-natured wifh taking effect, the corn of *England* now feeds great part of *Italy.*

A.C. 40   THE *Perufina fames* is, I fuppofe, what you are chiefly alluding to, faid the young nobleman, When I was at *Perugia*, I was indeed greatly fhocked in reading the difmal hiftory of the fiege and furrender of that city.

NOT only *Perugia*, anfwered *Crito*, but many other cities of *Italy*, even *Rome* itfelf, fuffered

---

* HORAT. lib. i, od. 21.

much

much mifery of the fame kind, though in an inferiour degree. The fupplies of corn, that ufually came by fea, were cut off. *The fea alfo*, for feveral years, was the bloody theatre of this tragic civil war.

BESIDE other great mifchiefs, the coafts of *Naples* and *Sicily* faw, in the fea-fights and fhipwrecks of *Octavius's* and *Pompey's* fleets, a renewed image of the calamities of the firft *punic* war. In the laft engagement off *Meffina*, if I remember right, each fleet confifted of above three hundred fail; while near two hundred thoufand men ftood in arms on the fhore.

A.C. 36

I COULD wifh, faid the eldeft of the young gentlemen, that there were extant a good and impartial account of the life of *Sextus Pompeius.* Much difhonour has been caft upon his memory by feveral *cæfarean* writers; and yet fome, at leaft, of his actions feem very noble and heroic. But pray, dear fir, inform us, which is the character, that *you* would choofe principally to recommend to us, in our ftudy of the *roman* hiftory, during thofe twelve years.

THE character of OCTAVIA, replied *Crito.*

IF

IF you pleafe, faid the young nobleman, haftily catching at that name, I will order my coachman to ftop at the portico of *Octavia.* We *muft* pafs by it, or near it, in our way home.

CRITO gladly confenting, the young nobleman leaned out of the window, and told his conductor to drive to the church of *St. Angelo* in *Pefcaria.*

*   *   *

AUGUSTUS CÆSAR erected this portico in honour of his fifter *Octavia.* About one hundred and ten years afterwards, being damaged by fire, it was repaired by the emperor *Titus;* and again in the following century, by the emperor *Severus.* *Severus's* name is ftill legible on the front of the building. Some ftately columns are remaining, both in the front and behind it.

THE church of *St. Angelo* in *Pefcaria* takes up, at prefent, the fouth-eaft fide of this portico. The remaining fpace is chiefly occupied by feveral fifhmongers fhops.

WHEN the coach ftopped here, the fifh-market was over, and the fhops empty: the company confequently were able to furvey the place at their leifure,

leifure, and to converfe without interruption. Their converfation turned fometimes on the amiable charaƈter of *Oƈavia*, fometimes on the ancient plan and ornaments of this ftately fabric, which was, in *Ovid's* time,

—*Externo marmore dives opus.*

SOME months ago, faid the young nobleman, when we made our firft tour of the *roman* antiquities, I liftened with earneft attention to our antiquarian in this place. He told me, that the portico before us * was anciently ornamented with many of the fineft paintings from the *grecian* fchools, and many fculptures from the hands of *Phidias, Polycles,* and *Praxiteles.* The idea of a ftruƈture thus richly adorned gave me great pleafure. Here, I imagined, ftood the *Venus* of *Phidias;* and there, before that column, the *Thefpian Cupid.* Such were the ideas, with which my mind was *then* filled. But, fince the progrefs we have made in our prefent courfe of *Roman* Converfations, I begin to have *other* thoughts. I am, by your affiftance, every day learning to confider thefe great *roman* objeƈts with the eye of a philofopher, or a patriot, rather than with that of a mere artift.

* See abbate *Venuti's Roman* Antiquities, vol. ii. p. 89. See alfo *Donato,* p. 98, *Pliny,* lib. xxxvi. c. 5, and *Montfaucon's* Journey to *Italy,* c. 19.

HAD

HAD it been in my power to reftore this ancient fabric to it's former fplendour by a wifh, I fhould certainly *then* have rejoiced to fee the *Venus,* the *Juno,* and the figures of other heathen deities, which once ftood within thefe walls, reftored to their ancient places. But exquifite as their fculp-ture might be, I do not know whether, *in my pre-fent difpofition of mind,* I fhould not rather wifh that their places were filled by the ftatues, how-ever moderately executed, of fome *roman* female charaƈters, which once really exifted, and were truly meritorious: fuch as *Herfilia, Veturia, Vo-lumnia, Valeria Bufa,* the two matrons of the *roman* charity, and *Portia* the wife of *Brutus.* The whole portico might be appropriated *to fe-male merit;* and *Oƈtavia's* ftatue would of courfe have claimed the principal place.

Prima locum fanƈtas heroidas inter haberes: ⁎
Prima bonis animi confpiciere tui.

ON the bafis of the ftatue fome of her amiable aƈtions might have been reprefented in bas-relief. But let me not pretend to talk on the fubjeƈt. I know very little of the *roman* hiftory; and fhould not have ventured to mention the name of *Oc-tavia,* if I had not been charmed with her moft lovely charaƈter, as delineated in the lately pub-lifhed Dialogues of the Dead. That new pam-phlet

phlet fortunately came in our laſt packet from *London.*

WHEN we were making our firſt tour of theſe *roman* antiquities, ſaid *Crito*, no perſon in this company, except my pupil, knew of the work in which I was engaged;—I mean the compilation of theſe *roman* charaĉters. After viſiting this portico, I employed myſelf for ſome days in colleĉting ſeveral particulars of *Oĉavia's* life. But, refleĉting that my pupil was able to deſcribe theſe particulars in a much more agreeable manner than myſelf, I gave him my paper of memorandums, and deſired him to try his poetic genius on the ſubjeĉt. In a week he brought me a copy of *Engliſh* verſes, in which indeed were moſt amiably deſcribed the virtues, as well as the beauties of *Oĉavia:* her ready charity to the diſtreſſed, in the times of the proſcription; her earneſt deſire of being afterwards the inſtrument of public peace and concord; her patient kindneſs to an unworthy huſband; her love to the children which he had hy thoſe vile women *Fulvia* and *Cleopatra;* and laſtly, the overflowing maternal love which ſhe ſhowed to her own good ſon *Marcellus,* as well as to the reſt of her young family. I could wiſh you would perſuade my pupil to communicate this charming copy of verſes to you. He compoſed

N 4

feveral of them, as he told me, in this portico, and the reft in the *Aldrobandine* gardens *.

THE two young gentlemen now earneftly defired *Crito's* pupil to favour them with a fight of the verfes; but could not prevail, as he affured them with truth, that he had not a copy by him.

THE cafe was this. In compofing thofe verfes, his thoughts had often wandered to a young lady † in *England;* the beauties of whofe face and mind he had mixed in this poem with thofe of *Octavia,* in the fame manner as *Rubens* is faid to have drawn one of the graces partly from his own wife.

WHEN he had finifhed this fhort poem,—a kind of ode, drawn up in the manner of that fecond chorus, which Mr. *Pope* defigned for the tragedy of *Brutus;* he prefixed to it fome verfes in another metre, as a dedication of it to the dear object of his efteem; and then fent the *only* copy he had of it to her. He had often heard her admire

---

* The villa *Aldrobandina* is near the church of *St. Dominico,* on *Monte Quirinale.* It's noble buildings and charming gardens claim the preference to moft. It's greateft rarity is a fummer-houfe, in which is an old frefco painting, that, according to *Fred. Zuccaro,* was dug up in 1607 on *Monte Efquilino,* near the place fuppofed to have been anciently the garden of *Mæcenas.* It is an elegant piece, and reprefents a *roman* wedding, &c. *Keyfler's* Travels.

† See the conclufion of the thirteenth day's converfation, vol. i. p. 542.

Octavia's

Octavia's character in *Shakspeare's Anthony* and *Cleopatra*, and was therefore in hopes she would kindly receive on such a subject a poetic love-letter from him.

CRITO having hinted this love-affair to the eldest of the young gentlemen, the conversation now became very chearful and gay. *Crito* himself partook, and greatly contributed to increase it's gaiety. He rejoiced in the thoughts of his pupil's marriage, almost as much as a father could do in that of a beloved son. In this conversation the minutes flew away with unperceived rapidity; till by the striking of the neighbouring church clock they were reminded, that it was high time to return to their lodgings.

In their way thither they passed by *Monte Citorio*, under the pavement of which, *seventy feet deep*, lies buried the amphitheatre of *Statilius Taurus* *.

They dined at the young nobleman's apartments. At dinner the conversation turned on the battle of *Actium*, and the conquest of *Egypt*. As soon as the cloth was removed, their noble host

---

* He was commander in chief of *Augustus's* land-forces, at the time of the battle of *Actium*; and built this amphitheatre in the following year.

produced

produced from his cabinet feveral intaglias, ca-
meos, and other pieces of *vertù*, relative to *Cleopatra.* *Crito's* pupil entertained the company
afterwards with the adventures of *Marcus* and
Barbula *.

In the afternoon the young gentlemen, according to appointment, went with the *french* marquis
to fee the *Colonna* palace, and paffed an hour with
great pleafure in it's noble gallery. They had
often feen it before, but were very glad of this
opportunity of attending their *parifian* friend
thither.

The breadth of that gallery is about thirty-
eight feet; it's length near two hundred and fifty,
not including the elevated part at the upper end,
which makes an addition of about twenty more.
It's height is proportionably noble.

The pavement is of *ficilian* jafper, and other
rich marbles; and the walls are adorned with many
large and *capital* paintings.

To thefe pictures the *french* and *englifh* noblemen gave their chief attention; they frequently,
however, with the reft of the company, looked
up to the painting, with which the whole cieling

* See *Appian*, lib. 4.

is

is covered, and which reprefents the fea-fight of
Lepanto.

IT is remarkable, that this great naval engagement happened nearly in the fame part of the
Ionian gulph as the battle of *Actium.*

A PRINCE of the *Colonna* family commanded
the *roman* part of the combined chriftian fleet.
On the other fide came on the great *turk:*

Victor, ab auroræ populis, & littore rubro;
Ægyptum, virefque Orientis, & ultima fecum
  Bactra vehens *.

*   *   *

While the young gentlemen were thus agreeably amufed, *Crito* was at home, enjoying a much
more exalted, and in all refpects a far fuperiour
happinefs. Saturday afternoon and evening he
generally referved free from all common bufinefs
or ftudy; confidering thofe hours as a proper
time of preparation for the devotions of the following day. But on *this faturday* eve he
had the felicity of experiencing, in a peculiar manner, the benefit of that pious practice.

* VIRG. *Æn.* viii. 686.

Full of joy and gratitude, for the numberlefs unmerited bleffings daily poured down upon him from heaven, he was in his clofet on his knees endeavouring to offer thanks and praife for them.

Whilst in that humble pofture, it occurred to his mind, that on this day he had finifhed the third part of his intended courfe of lectures. However contemptible thefe his labours might *very juftly* appear, in the fight of men of genius and learning, yet he thought he had great reafon to be thankful, that neither himfelf nor his young fellow travellers had been paffing their time *in a worfe manner,* vicioufly, or idly. He might perhaps have employed his time at *Rome much better.* But imperfect as all his defigns and works might be, yet he thought himfelf bound with all humility to be thankful for what had been good in them, however fmall the portion.

In confpectu mifericordiæ Tuæ *cum odore fuavitatis afcendat!*

Such were *Crito's* devotions on *faturday* night. But on *funday* evening his piety was much more fervent. Thinking on the fourth, the far more important part of his work, he proftrated himfelf on the floor; *he wept,* he prayed with earneftnefs, that he might be duly *directed* in the execution of

it;

it; that his weak mind might be endued with a strength in some degree suitable to such an undertaking; and, above all, that his most unutterable unworthiness for so sacred an employment might be most MERCIFULLY pardoned.

ROMAN

ROMAN CONVERSATIONS.

Book IV.

CHAP. I.

NINETEENTH DAY'S CONVERSATION.

AMONG the pictures which I have bought for my father in *Italy*, faid the young nobleman, —as he was walking in the church of *Santa Martina Dei Monti*, with his beloved *englifh* friends, on *monday*, *june* 15,—I have not yet had the good fortune to procure above two or three fmall landfcapes. I am thinking to fupply this deficiency, by defiring our ingenious friend, the *irifh* painter, to employ part of this fummer in drawing fome views of the romantic environs of *Frefcati*, *Albano*, *Tivoli*, and *Nemi*.

In fpeaking thefe words, the young nobleman felt at his heart a pleafure, which no profufion of expence, in mere *vertù*, ever afforded.

THE

THE cafe was this. Befide the thought of pleafing his father by fuch a prefent, he had another *good-motive* to this defign. The laft time he had feen the *irifh* painter, he obferved, that he looked very pale and faint: the heats of *Rome* having, in his prefent weak ftate of convalefcency, almoft overcome him. The worthy, noble youth imagined, that fome cool country air would be the beft kind of medicinal cordial for fuch an indifpofition. With that view he contrived this commiffion for the landfcapes; and that very afternoon intended fending his *roman valet de place* to hire fome proper lodging, for the young *irifhman*, at *Genfano*, a remarkably pleafant village, anciently called *Cynthianum*, and near the lake of *Nemi*, about fixteen miles diftant from *Rome*. It was propofed, that the painter fhould ftay there three weeks, or a month, and then remove, for about the fame fpace of time, to *Albano*. He was to leave *Albano* about the latter end of *auguft*, and to pafs the whole months of *feptember* and *october* at *Frefcati* and *Tivoli*; thofe country towns being very wholefome in the autumn, at which feafon *Genfano* becomes ufually damp and aguifh.

CRITO was made quite happy by this frefh inftance of the young nobleman's benevolence; and, in talking further on the fubject, he defired,—to

ufe

ufe his own humble expreffion,—that he might *accompany* the *valet de place* to *Genfano*.

YOUR fervant, faid he, fhall come back to you to-morrow morning, with fome news relative to the lodgings: but I muft defire you not to ex-pect me till *friday* next. I fhould be very glad *to make*, according to the *italian* phrafe, a *retreat* in that charming village, for two or three days. The prefent fultrinefs of the weather, joined to the ideas fuggefted by *thefe* beautiful landfcapes, makes me long for fome quiet country retire-ment*.

IN fuch weather as this, replied *Crito's* pupil, even a hermit's grove or cavern would not be a difagreeable habitation.

—O quis me gelidis fub montibus Hæmi
Siftat, & ingenti ramorum protegat umbra ?†

* 'The walls of the church of *Santa Martina Dei Monti* are covered with noble landfcapes, the works of *Pouffin* and other celebrated mafters.

In thefe large rural paintings, the hiftories of fome her-mits are introduced; but the human figures bear fo fmall a proportion to the fize of the trees, rocks, lakes and ftreams, that on entering the church, it feems to be furnifhed with mere reprefentations only of rural nature, and of it's vege-table or animal productions.

† *Virgil*, Georg. ii. 488.

THE young nobleman obferved, that there is fomething peculiarly pleafing, during the heats of fummer, in the ornaments of this church. Thefe fine marble columns, intermingled with the verdant fhades of this fylvan fcenery, breathe a very refrefhing coolnefs. Does not the whole ftructure feem to be defigned as a kind of rich *rural* temple?

IN fome refpects, replied *Crito,* after a paufe, this fabric may be confidered as a temple peculiarly adapted to folemn meditations on *natural* religion. Thefe rural reprefentations are indeed uncommon: but in fome degree they feem to be no unfuitable ornaments for a place, dedicated to the adoration of the Great CREATOR.

PROPER paintings certainly, as well as proper mufic, may fometimes have very great and good effects on a tender, devout mind: but the effects will be ftill greater and better, where painting and mufic can both operate together.—How happy fhould we be to hear the *Benedicite Domino omnia opera ejus,* or the 103d pfalm, now chaunted to the organ in this church!

Afcendunt montes, & defcendunt campi,
In locum, quem fundâfti eis.—
Quàm magnificata funt opera tua, Domine!
Omnia in fapientiâ fecifti.

DURING

DURING the chaunt of thefe hymns, you, my dear pupil, would often turn your eyes to the beautiful and majeftic works of the creation, which are reprefented on thefe walls.

PERHAPS, for a while, you would imagine yourfelf with *Adam,* in his terreftrial Paradife.

> *About me round I faw*
> *Hills, dales, and fhady woods, and funny plains,*
> *And liquid lapfe of murmuring ftreams.——*
> *Ye hills and dales, ye rivers, woods and plains,——*
> *Tell me, how I may know him, how adore,*
> *From whom I have, that thus I move and live*.*

THE young nobleman now fixed his eyes in filence, for fome moments, on one of *Pouffin's* landfcapes. He then turned round towards the altar; and, the church being at that time totally empty of other company,—he fung, in a low but manly voice, that favourite air from *Metaftafio's* Paffion Oratorio:

> *Dovunque il guardo giro,*
> *Immenfo Dio, ti vedo.*
> *Nell' opre tue t'ammiro,*
> *Ti riconofco in me.*

---

* MILTON, P. L. Book viii. 261. 270, 280.

La

La terra, il mar, le sfere,
Parlan del tuo potere:
Tu sei per tutto ; & noi
Tutti viviamo in te.

* * *

THE company now retired from the church, and walked to their lodgings.

ON the way *Crito* renewed his requeſt to his pupil, and the other young gentlemen, that they would permit him to make the excurſion he had talked of, to *Genſano.*

THEY all knew how much he ſometimes enjoyed his ſtudies in a rural ſolitude, and therefore gladly conſented to his propoſal.

HOWEVER, ſaid the young nobleman, we will not ſuffer the charms of the country to keep you too long from us. We will come and make you a viſit at *Genſano* on *friday* morning. We ſhall bring our landſcape painter in the coach with us, and take you back.

EVERY thing being thus ſettled, *Crito* left town immediately after dinner: he went in his pupil's
                                                chaiſe

chaife, and arrived at *Genfano* before it was quite dark.

*   *   *

As foon as he was gone, the young nobleman propofed to his two friends, that out of refpeft to *Crito*,—and indeed in confequence of a hint which he dropped to day at table,—they fhould, during his abfence, prepare themfelves for the enfuing lectures, by ftudying, feparately, the hiftory of *Auguftus's* reign.

You, dear fir, faid he, turning to *Crito's* pupil, will be able to employ two or three days very agreeably, in the contemplation of the *fciences*, as well as of the *belles-lettres*, which flourifhed here in that peaceful age.

You, my worthy patriotic friend, will have bufinefs enough, in unravelling the *civil* government of the firft *roman* emperor, and the great *political* events and confequences of his reign.

The more trifling amufement,—that of the confideration of the *fine arts*, which then adorned *Rome*,—will fall to my fhare.

On *thurfday*, if you pleafe, we will meet at breakfaft, and compare notes.

O 3

*   *   *

ON *thurſday* morning very early,—for the heat of the *roman* climate naturally inclines moſt perſons to early riſing,—*Crito's* pupil was viſited by his two friends.

WHILE they were drinking a diſh of chocolate together, he aſked them ſeveral queſtions, relative to the politics and *vertù* of *Auguſtus's* court; and received from their anſwers much inſtruction and pleaſure.

WHEN the chocolate was removed, the young nobleman took up a *Horace,* that lay on the ſettee; and addreſſing himſelf to *Crito's* pupil, I could wiſh, ſaid he, that ſome properly-qualified *engliſh* traveller, while making the tour of *Italy,* would amuſe himſelf with executing that deſign, which I remember to have heard you propoſe.

I MEAN, the collection of proper materials for *A new edition of Horace's Odes, accompanied with a traveller's notes.* Several illuſtrations might doubtleſs with much eaſe and pleaſure be collected, from a view of the face of this country, from an experience of it's climate, and an obſervation of the cuſtoms and manners of it's inhabitants :—

tants :—illuftrations, never perhaps to be expected from the labour or genius of any of our *tra-
montane literati*, who have not had the happinefs
of feeing thefe fouthern parts of *Europe.*

I HAVE been thinking, that fuch an edition
might be very properly adorned ; not only, as
you propofed, with fome neatly-engraved maps
of the *Campagna di Roma*, and other parts of
modern *Italy;* but alfo with fome fmall landfcapes, placed as head or tail-pieces to feveral of
the odes.

LET me give one inftance only of what I mean.
The odes, which are defcriptive of the environs of
Tibur, might be very pleafingly illuminated by
fome views, in miniature, of the real country near
Tivoli; and the prefent remains of *Mæcenas's*
ftately villa there.

I AM fure, when we were at *Tivoli*, viewing
it's thick woods of olives, the romantic figure of
it's hills, and the feveral beautiful ftreams which
defcend in picturefque cafcades down their fides,
through thofe fields, which once were covered
with the pompous gardens of *Mæcenas*, or *Plan-
cus;* we could not help recollecting feveral expreffions in *Horace*, which feemed very appofite:
fuch as

Et

Et præceps Anio, & Tiburni lucus; & uda
Mobilibus pomaria rivis*.

THE young nobleman now opened the *Horace,* and read to the company feveral ftanzas in two or three different odes: he finifhed with fome lines in the xviith ode of the firft book.

Velox amœnum fæpe Lucretilem
Mutat Lycœo Faunus.———
———fiftulá
Valles, & Ufticæ cubantis
Lævia perfonuere faxa.

IT would have been fortunate, faid *Crito's* pu_pil, if, when we were at *Tivoli,* we had thought of extending our excurfion to the *Uftican* valley. *Horace's* fmall but elegant farm-houfe was moft probably fituate among the *Sabine* mountains, about ten miles above *Tivoli.* His river *Digentia* is, as I have heard, now called the *Licenza:* and his neighbouring market-towns, *Mandela* and *Varia,* are known by the half-corrupted names of *Bardela,* and *Vico Varo.* What pleafure would it have afforded us, could we, with any degree of probability, have traced out the fpot of his *ferme ornée!*

---

* CARM. lib. i. od. 7.

HORACE,

HORACE, replied the eldeſt of the young gentlemen, though he kept the higheſt company, yet loved a middle ſtation in life, and knew it's value. This ſeems to *you*, I am ſure, to have been one of the moſt amiable features in his cha-racter.

By the joint favour of the prince and miniſter, *Horace*, doubtlefs, might have accumulated a much larger fortune, and riſen to ſome very con-ſiderable office in public life: but he had viewed things with too piercing and judicious an eye.

> *Cur valle permutem Sabinâ*
> *Divitias operoſiores?* *

I REMEMBER your good tutor making ſome excellent reflections on this ſubject a few years ago, before we left *England.* It was on that day, when we went to ſee the poor *porch-houſe* at *Chertſey*, which in the laſt century was the hum-ble ſcene of *Cowley's* retirement.

AMONG other obſervations, I remember he then took notice, that, though *Horace* was far in-feriour to *Cowley*, in his general moral character; as far indeed, as he was ſuperiour in point of poe-tical ability; yet ſtill, their turns of mind were

* Lib. iii. od. i. 47.

in

in fome refpects very fimilar: The *language of their hearts* was on feveral topics, almoft equally amiable.

Our valued friend then dwelt with pleafure on the moderation, and other amiable qualities of *Horace.* However much, faid he, we ought to abhor his vices, yet furely we are bound to exprefs a due refpect for thefe his virtues.

Such were at that time fome of your amiable tutor's fentiments. But *à propos:* our noble young friend would be glad, if you would go with us this morning, to fee the place of *Mæcenas's* gardens: thofe we mean, that belonged to his *houfe in town;* and to which *Auguftus* frequently loved to retire, whenever a fit of ficknefs prevented him from continuing his application to public bufinefs.

I shall be very glad of the pleafure of attending you thither, replied *Crito's* pupil; for, if I be not miftaken, *Virgil's* houfe was built clofely adjoining to thofe gardens of *Mæcenas.*

He now rofe from his chair, and taking from the fhelf in his clofet the firft volume of *Dodfley's* mifcellaneous poems, turned to the " *Ruins of Rome,*"

written

written by the author of *Grongar-hill*. He then read to his friends the following lines.

Suffice it, now, th' Esquilian mount to reach
With weary wing; and seek the sacred rests
Of Virgil's *humble tenement: a low*
Plain wall remains; a little sun-gilt heap,
Grotesque and wild: the gourd and olive brown
Weave the light roof; the gourd and olive fan
Their am'rous foliage: mingling with the vine,
Who drops her purple clusters thro' the green.—
Here oft the meek good man, the lofty bard,
Fram'd the celestial song; or social walk'd
With Horace, *and the ruler of the world.*
Happy Augustus!——

BUT let me not trouble you too long. Your carriage is at the door. I wish your *roman* servant, who is a tolerable antiquarian, may be able to conduct us to that spot, where *Virgil's* tenement is supposed to have stood.

*　　*　　*

WHILE the company were in the coach, their conversation dwelt on the characters of the two great poets of the *augustan* age. *Crito's* pupil remarked, with visible pleasure, that *Virgil* was at least as conspicuous as *Horace*, for the love of philosophy, of poetry, and rural life.

UPON

UPON coming to the *Efquiline* hill, they found themfelves much puzzled as to the fituation of *Mæcenas's* gardens. *Montfaucon*, with many other antiquarians, places thofe gardens between the church of *Santa Martina Dei Monti*, and the *Aggere Tarquinio*. The abbate *Venuti*, perhaps with more probability, thinks they lay near the church of *St. Pietro ad Vincula*, on the fpot, which was afterwards in a great degree covered with that vaft fabric, the baths of *Titus*.

IF, faid *Crito's* pupil, we cannot with any certitude fix upon the fituation of *Mæcenas's* gardens, I am afraid we ftand much lefs chance of being able to difcover the place of *Virgil's* houfe. Yet certainly there muft be fome tradition kept up at *Rome* concerning it. I have fome recollection of our feeing, in a manufcript at the *Collegio Romano*, an account of *an altar to the Mufes*, which was dug up from among it's ruins.

IT would be fome fatisfaction, faid the young nobleman, if we knew in what mufæum that altar was preferved. We would willingly attend you this morning to the furtheft part of *Rome*, on purpofe to give you the opportunity, and the pleafure, of feeing it. You would, I am fure, *in imagination*, pour fome libations on it.

BUT,

But, as we are totally ignorant of what is become of that altar to the mufes, let us in fome manner fupply the deficiency, by making a vifit this morning to the ruins of the temple of the *Palatine Apollo*. We are not at prefent far diftant from them; and it is yet very early in the day.

* * *

In the large and romantic gardens of the *englifh* college, on the fouthern fummit of the *Palatine* hill, ftands a group of *ftately* ruins, intermingled with feveral fmall groves of lofty cypreffes. It is by far the greateft work of antiquity now to be feen on any part of that hill.

According to common tradition, thefe are the remains of the famous *temple* and *library* of the *Palatine Apollo*. *Marliano* confirms this tradition. But other antiquarians are of opinion, that they feem rather to be the ruins of that *Hemicyclium*, in which were performed the mufical games, in honour of the fame poetic deity.

The young reader of thefe papers, whofe lively imagination is oft enraptured with poetical enthufiafm, and whofe genius breathes it's fire, is defired to think, what would be *his* ideas, while afcending to the feat of the *Palatine Apollo!*

LET him imagine, that the ideas of *his three young countrymen* could not but be of a nature somewhat similar.

THEY ascended the hill, and for some time continued to indulge their thoughts in all the luxuriancy of poetic fancy. They would however have been soon satiated with this delicious entertainment, even with this nectar and ambrosia, if *Crito's* pupil had not kept up their appetite, by taking out his pocket *Virgil,* and reading to them, for about half an hour, some passages of their favourite bard.

THOSE, with which he concluded, were the descriptions of the temples of *Apollo,* at *Cuma,* and at *Delos,* as given in the sixth and third book of the Æneid. He closed the volume as soon as he had rehearsed the following lines:

——*tremere omnia visa repente,*
Liminaque, laurusque Dei ; totusque moveri
Mons circum, & mugire adytis cortina reclusis*.

THEN, suddenly rising from the mossy bricks on which he was sitting, he took two or three short turns by himself in the cypress walk : sometimes looking up, in silent contemplation, to the

* Æn. iii. 90.

ruins

ruins of the adjoining temple and *Hemicyclium*, the tops of which appeared to peculiar advantage, amidft the waving heads of the cyprefles; fometimes looking down into the vaft vaults and fubterranean arches, which, where the ground has given way, difcover themfelves to a great depth.

Is it not very probable, faid he, turning to his companions, that *Milton*, during his ftay at *Rome*, frequently afcended this hill?

PERHAPS he compofed part of his *Penferofo* here.—O that I could now, in his ftyle, invoke the *unfeen genius* of this place to *breathe* to us fome *fweet mufic*,

Above, around, or underneath!

But alas! no genius of this cyprefs grove will deign to liften to *my* invocation; no found of the harp of *Apollo* will anfwer me, from any of the deep recefles of thefe ruins.

THE eldeft of the young gentlemen benevolently fmiled at this poetic enthufiafm. I think, faid he, my dear friend, you are as much affe&ed with the memory of *Virgil* here, as you were laft autumn, when we were rowing in a boat around

the

the lake of *Mantua,* and down the river *Mincio*.*
You will long remember that delightful voyage;—

——— *Tardis ingens ubi flexibus errat*
Mincius, & glaucâ prætexit arundine ripas †.

I WISH, faid the young nobleman, that we
were at prefent in fo cool a fituation. The heat
of the fun, reflected from thefe ruins, begins to
grow intolerable. I am unwilling to quit this
temple; but, fuppofe we were to adjourn, for the
remainder of this morning, acrofs the *Tiber,* to
fome of the fhady apartments in the *Vatican* palace. They are the coolest places we can find in
Rome: and befides, if I be not miftaken, we
fhall fee in them fome things relative to the fubject of our prefent converfation.

THE young gentlemen agreed to this propofal;
walked down the hill to the coach; and getting
into it, bid the driver to fet them down at the
Vatican.

*　*　*

IN

In about half an hour they arrived there. The firſt room they entered was the library. The young nobleman led them immediately to that painting, which repreſents *Virgil* and *Horace* in converſation with *Auguſtus* *.

He then turned round to the librarian, and deſired to be favoured with a ſight of the famous manuſcript of *Virgil.*

This manuſcript is ſuppoſed to have been written in the fourth or fifth century. The young gentleman paſſed ſome time very agreeably, in examining it's charaƈters, and hiſtorical piƈtures: but they thought *Bartoli* had done more than ample juſtice to them in his copper-plates.

From the *Vatican* library the company went up ſtairs into the open galleries, called the *Bible*

---

* See Abbé Richard's Deſcription of the ornaments of the *Vatican* Library. *À gauche on a donné dans differens tableaux une idée des plus anciennes colleƈtions des libres.—Le ſixieme repreſente Ptolomée Philadelphe, accompagné de Demetrius Phalere, ſon Bibliothequaire, & d'Ariſtée, qui arrangent la fameuſe Bibliotheque d'Alexandrie. Dans le ſeptieme, on voit Auguſte, entre Virgile & Horace, ſe promenant dans la bibliotheque, qu'il avoit formée ſur le Mont Palatin, où il avoit fait placer la ſtatue de Varron.* Tom. v. p. 386.

Queſta pittura e d'una mano imitatrice del Baroccio l'inſcrizione dice. Auguſtus Cæſar, Palatinâ Bibliothecâ magnificè ornatâ, viros literarios fovet. Taja, Deſcrittione del Palazzo Vaticano.

of

of Raphael; and thence proceeded to the *Stanzd della Segnatura.*

THAT apartment is, as it were, a noble temple dedicated to the *principal* fciences;—theology, jurifprudence, philofophy, and poetry. The cieling is adorned with four figures, reprefenting.thefe four fciences : under each of which the walls are entirely covered with large pictures, correfpondent to the fame fubjects; all by the hand of *Raphael.* The firft, on entering the room, is that fweet introduction to all fciences, mount *Parnaffus.*

IN this picture, after fome fearch, they found the beautiful, though retired, figure of *Virgil,* clofe by the *Mufes,* on the fummit of the mount ; followed by the principal poets of modern *Italy;* but himfelf modeftly giving place to the majeftic *Homer,* to whofe fong *Clio* is liftening, and *Apollo* himfelf attuning his lyre.

IT is remarkable, that *Raphael,* who, by the flowery *italian* hiftorians, is faid to have lived among all the arts and fciences on mount *Parnaffus,* has here reprefented *his own* figure, clofely attendant on that of *Virgil.* This circumftance occafioned the converfation to be turned to the fimilitude, or, in *Plutarch's* phrafe, the *parallellifm,*

lellifm, of thefe two great charaƈters in the *fifter* arts.

THE young nobleman took this opportunity to inform the company, that he had been lately favoured with a copy of the life of *Raphael,* drawn up by an *englifh* gentleman*, refident at *Rome;* a gentleman, from whom himfelf and all the company had received continual obligations fince their arrival there; and who, as they well knew, was fully a mafter of that noble fubjeƈt. It is needlefs to add, that they were very defirous to hear it; and the young nobleman as willing to read it to them. They fat down near the great piƈture of the fchools of *Athens,* and gave their moft cheerful attention to the following paper.

RAPHAEL D'URBIN.

THERE is hardly a more pleafing or noble objeƈt, efpecially to all real philanthropifts, than to fee a perfon bleffed with a favourable difpofition and genius by nature; and to find alfo every circumftance of his life concur, for the bringing to perfeƈtion what fhe has fo kindly imparted†.

RAPHAEL

---

* Mr. *Jenkins.*

† Περι δε της αγωγης και δη λεκτεον. Καθολου μεν ειπειν ο κατα τεχνων κ, των επιςημων λεγειν ειωθαμεν, ταυτον κ, κατα της αρετης

Φατεον

RAPHAEL D'URBINO ſeems to have been as ſtriking an example of this felicity, as occurs in the hiſtory of an age or nation. He was, doubtleſs, born with the moſt uncommon genius; but was alſo at leaſt equally fortunate, in the firſt and principal bleſſing in life; that is, in having the beſt of fathers: a father, who was moſt deeply convinced, that the proſperity of his ſon totally depended on a good education; and who gave the moſt conſtant attention worthily to execute that great work of a parent's life. For this purpoſe, we ſee him beginning his care of his child, even from the firſt day of his birth; having a regard to the breaſt that was to nouriſh him, which he took care ſhould be that of his moſt tender and loving mother; a woman of the gentleſt diſpoſition. Afterwards, during the firſt years of his ſon's life, he carefully took all opportunities gradually to inſtruct him in every thing, of which

φατιον εςιν· ως εις την παντελη δικαιοπραγιαν τρια δει συνδραμειν, φυσιν, κ̧ λογον, κ̧ εϑ⊙·* καλω δε λογον μεν την μαϑησιν, εϑ⊙· δε την ασκησιν· εισι δε αι μεν αρχαι, της μαϑησεως· αι δε χρησεις, της μελετης· αι δ᾽ ακροτητες, παντων· καθ ὁ δ᾽ αν λειφθη τι τυτων, κατα τυτ᾽ αναγκη χωλην γινεσϑαι την αρετην. Ἡ μεν γαρ φυσις ανευ μαϑησεως τυφλον· η δε μαϑησις διχα φυσεως ελλιπες· η δ᾽ ασκησις χωρις αμφοιν ατελες. Ὡσπερ δ᾽ επι της γεωργιας πρωτον μεν αγαϑην υπαρξαι δει την γην, ειτα δε φυτυργον επιςημονα, ειτα τα σπερματα σπυδαια· (eadem ſimilitudo in Evängelio) τον αυτον τροπον γη μεν εοικεν η φυσις, γεωργω δε ὁ παιδευων, σπερματι δε αἱ των λογων υποϑηκαι, κ̧ τα παραγγελματα——Ευδαιμων μεν υν κ̧ ϑεοφιλης, ει τω ταυτα παντα ϑεων· τις απεδωκεν.

PLUTARCHI de Liberis educandis, c. 2.

ſ●

fo tender an age was capable; and, in particular, he paid the utmoſt regard to the cuſtoms and diſpoſitions of thoſe children, with whom his beloved boy made any acquaintance. During this time young *Raphael* gave every day freſh marks of the ſweeteſt, and moſt amiable temper; joined to which, as if completely to bleſs his good parents, appeared a natural inclination for the ſtudy of painting, the art which his father alſo profeſſed, together with ſufficient proofs of a great genius for it. It was from this motive that his modeſt parent, convinced of his own inability to render him ſuch aſſiſtance as might be neceſſary, made application to *Pietro Perugino*, the moſt eſteemed painter of that age; and had the good fortune to prevail on him, to take this young ſcholar under his care.

THE amiablenefs of *Raphael's* temper, and his promiſing abilities as an artiſt, ſoon gained him the affeſtion of *Pietro Perugino*; whoſe inſtructions he received with ſuch cloſe attention, as in a very ſhort time to imitate his manner ſo well, that it could with great difficulty be diſtinguiſhed which was the maſter. The ſtyle or manner of *Pietro Perugino* was the moſt diligent imitation of nature; mixed indeed with the ſtiffneſs of the preceding ages: but to this he added a degree of gracefulneſs, which to *Raphael* was of the greateſt

impor-

importance, as it gave an opening to that trait of his genius. Thus we find him, in a very early period of life, to have advanced confiderably in his profeffion, by the moft fure and folid princi-ples of that induftry, which, even to a *Raphael*, was neceffary for enabling him afterwards to at-tain with facility the more critical requifites of his art.

HAVING now acquired all the advantage that he could hope from *Perugino*, and hearing of the fame of *Michael Angelo* and *Leonardo da Vinci*, he refolved upon a journey to *Florence*, to fee and ftudy the works of thefe great men.

IN *Michael Angelo* he obferved a greatnefs of ftyle, that was totally oppofite to the drynefs of *Perugino;* and in *Leonardo da Vinci* a roundnefs and force of light and fhadow, never before pro-duced, at leaft fince the revival of the arts. Be-ing fenfible of the excellencies of thefe two great mafters, and knowing how neceffary it was for him to profit by them, he laid afide every other confideration, and determined to beftow his whole attention upon thefe objefts; to which he accordingly applied with all poffible diligence.

DURING this time, as if fortune no lefs than nature had determined *every thing* for the perfec-

tion

tion of this their favourite, *Raphael* made an acquaintance with *fra. Bartholomeo di San Marco,* which foon grew into a ftrict friendfhip. *Bartholomeo* poffeffed the only branch of painting, in which *Raphael* feemed to want any inftructions, namely, that of a perfect knowledge of the quality and application of colours.——But here let us paufe a little, and confider, how wonderful an example is this great man of the important truth, that the fineft genius cannot arrive at it's full glory, without a very induftrious ftudy, or without the help of other men.

HAD it not been for the well-founded principles of diligence, which *Raphael* received from *Pietro Perugino,* it is poffible, that the over-charged outline of *Michael Angelo* might have mifled him to a falfe ftyle of greatnefs. The amiable ftrength of light and fhadow of *Leonardo da Vinci,* which however wanted the truth of colouring, might have been equally dangerous for him, had it not been moft fortunately and effectually prevented, by the friendfhip of *fra. Bartholomeo.*

WHAT a pleafure it is, to fee fuch a feries of fortunate events unite, at a time when probably the greateft genius, that ever was, had the utmoft occafion for every one of them! It was now that a moft favourable occafion offered of dif-

P 4

clofing to the world, in full fplendour, all the ftrength of his talents. The furprizing genius and accomplifhments of this wonderful young man, then about twenty-four years of age, having reached the ears of pope *Julius* the fecond, a great lover of the fine arts, he fent for him, and affigned him immediate employment in the *Vatican*. *Raphael* was now at the crifis of his fortune; and the fuccefs of his firft performance was fo great, that the pope immediately difcharged all the other painters, though fome of the beft artifts of the time, who were employed in adorning that moft famous and fumptuous palace; excepting only *Michael Angelo*, who was then in the principal chapel, carrying on his great work, the picture of the Laft Judgment. The pope ordered alfo, that what thefe painters had already done might be defaced, to make room for the works of *Raphael;* an order, however, which this generous man oppofed to the utmoft of his power: Nay, even contrary to it, he caufed fome of the beft of their works to remain; faying, it was but juft that the world fhould fee, how much he had been beholden to thofe great men who went before him.

GIVE me leave, my dear friends, in reading this paper of Mr. *Jenkins*, to paufe one moment merely to obferve, that fome of the figures on this

very

very cieling are the works of *Pietro Perugino*, thus gratefully preferved by his dear pupil. The two figures in the corner of this great and capital picture of the fchools of *Athens*, under which you are now fitting, are, one of them, the reprefentation of *Raphael* himfelf; and the other, which is here, by *Raphael*, made the *fuperiour* figure, is that of his ever honoured mafter, *Pietro Perugino*.

DURING the courfe of thefe his works in the *Vatican*, pope *Julius* the fecond died. But, as if nothing were to ftop the current of *Raphael's* greatnefs, *Leo* the tenth fucceeded to the chair: a prince, whofe magnificent difpofition led him to patronize all great men, in every art and fcience. He not only employed *Raphael* as a painter; but, finding him likewife an able architect, he gave him the direction of all his fuperb buildings; particularly the ftupendous fabrick of St. *Peter's*.

AT the fame time *Raphael's* favour was folicited by all the great perfonages of *Europe*, who even *prayed* to be made happy with fomething from his excellent hand. Among thefe was *Francis* the firft, then king of *France:* the father of his country; the patron of learning; in fhort, that illuftrious protector of all arts and fciences, in whofe arms *Leonardo da Vinci* had died!

ALL

ALL thefe honours, which in any man of an inferiour difpofition might have enkindled pride or felf-fufficiency, in *Raphael* had a quite contrary effect. As he grew in reputation, we find him increafe in affability and goodnefs towards all around him. Such was the uncommon influence of his amiable temper, that all his difciples, who were very numerous, and every one anxious for his own advancement, lived under his care in the moft perfect harmony with each other: and fo great was his generofity, that he was conftantly ready to part even with the whole of his fortune, to relieve the indigent and miferable. He was indeed a friend and a father to all; and whoever wanted his affiftance might have it at any time, or upon any occafion.

THIS happy difpofition of mind in fo great a man is apparently vifible in all his works: for, as no one had ever a clearer conception for the compofition of them, nor a warmer heart to give the truth of expreffion to each character, fo did he always follow the dictates of his heart, by choofing his fubject at that point of time, which admitted of the execution of the *moft noble and amiable* paffions. Indeed, it is hardly poffible to behold any one paffion expreffed by him, but the mind muft be moft fenfibly affected by it; and the paffions, which he was conftantly moft fond of

expref-

expreffing, were thofe of the higheft degrees of warm and overflowing benevolence of heart, of the moft exalted virtue, and the moft devout piety. Thus did he reprefent, to the view of all fucceeding ages, the moft moving leffons, upon the two great principles of our duty to God, and our duty to man, by a method no way inferiour, either in force or dignity, to that of the greateft hiftorians, orators, or poets.

Happy muft it have proved, had he been equally great in the third effential branch of moral duty, that of felf-government, or temperance! But, as it would be endlefs to recount every particular of the excellence of *Raphael*,—and may thefe bright and good parts of his chara&er never be prefented to us for our inftru&ion and benefit in vain!—fo it is likewife neceffary, to own his failings, in order the better to put us on our guard againft them. Let us never forget, that, in the nobleft fabric, if one principal part be defective, the whole may eafily be ruined.

It is impoffible to be acquainted with fuch a chara&er as *Raphael's*, without conceiving the greateft veneration for it. How melancholy a refle&ion then is it, but at the fame time how *ufeful a leffon*, to think, that fo much worth fhould be loft or leffened to the world, by an imprudent,

or

or a vicious purfuit of pleafure! Such was the cafe with *Raphael*: he was cut off by lafciviouf-nefs, when in the flower of his years; in the fulleft ftrength of his abilities;—in the height of his glory*. Nor had he even that confolation, which many young men, dying at his years, have had; namely, that his end was noble, and therefore im-poffible to be premature.

If *he*, whofe hand is writing this, fhed a tear for fuch an end of fuch a man; how much more reafon to do fo muft *thofe* have had, who were once happy in his acquaintance and friendfhip! They, indeed, were with reafon inconfolable. He was attended to his grave by all of his pro-feffion then in *Rome;* who alike regarded his lofs as that of the moft indulgent parent, the kindeft mafter, and the fincereft friend. Nor was the great crowd of fpectators lefs moved, when the body, according to the cuftom of his country, was expofed to view in the fame place, where his picture of the Transfiguration, his laft and greateft work, then ftood.

*   *   *

* *Raphael* was born on good friday of the year 1483, and died, on his birth-day, in the year 1520; aged only 37!

AFTER

AFTER having been entertained, faid *Crito's* pupil, with fuch a compofition as this, I know not how to venture to trouble you with any of my reflections.

IN attending to it, I could not however help frequently obferving the many fimilar traces, in this character, and in that of *Virgil*. Both were bleffed with great natural talents; in the improvement and perfection of which, both proceeded on the fame *fure and folid foundation, of the greateft induftry*. Both aimed at the utmoft correctnefs, as well as fpirit, in their works. Both gave their attention, with all poffible diligence, to the ftudy of the works of the great men, who had preceded them. Both made themfelves acquainted with many other fciences, befide that which was their principal profeffion*.

EACH of them came to *Rome*, for neither of thefe great *italians* was a native of this city, when a patron of all arts and fciences was on the throne:

---

* *Virgilius, omni curâ, omnique ftudio, fe medicinæ & ma-thematicis tradidit; quibus rebus cum ante alios eruditior peri-tiorque factus effet, fe in urbem contulit, ftatimque Augufti amicitiam nactus,&c.* See his life, faid to have been drawn up by *Donatus*. With what honour and love does *Virgil* fpeak of the firft of thefe his ftudies, in the character of *Iapis!* How ftrongly alfo is his affection for the ftudy of *natural philofophy* expreffed, throughout the whole *Georgics;* particularly towards the conclufion of the fecond book !— *Me vero, primum, &c.*

Each

Each was highly favoured here by the fovereign, and by all the principal men of the ftate. They were indeed the two chief glories of the two *Auguftan* ages of *Rome*.

THEY were equally remarkable in bearing all their great honours with ftill greater modefty, affability, and goodnefs to all around them. Each was, in particular, a kind patron and cordial friend to the other poets and painters of his time: each was confequently beloved by all the contemporaries of his profeffion, while *thefe* were full of rivalfhip and envy among themfelves. Both took all opportunities, in their works, of fhowing their refpeft and gratitude * to their patrons. Both indeed frequently fhowed the fingular goodnefs of their hearts, equal perhaps even to their great abilities of mind, in many parts of their compofitions; and both, in this, as well as in fo many other refpefts, may be attentively ftudied, to the greateft advantage.

*   *   *

FROM the *Vatican* palace, the company returned to their lodgings to dinner.

* *Bucolica fcripta funt in honorem Pollionis, Varii, Galli; quia in diftributione agrorum indemnem fe præftiterunt. Georgica edidit in honorem Mæcenatis. Æneidem autem aggreffus eft, ut Romanæ fimul urbis, & Augufti, originem celebraret.*

AFTER

AFTER dinner the young nobleman very agreeably amufed himfelf for an hour or two with Mr. *Spence's Polymetis.* His attention was firft given to it's fixteenth dialogue, which bears a particular reference to fome of the pictures in the *Vatican* manufcript of *Virgil.* He afterwards turned to the fifth dialogue; the fubject of which is the introduction, improvement, and fall of the arts in *Rome.*

THE eldeft of the young gentlemen laboured without intermiffion, from dinner time till it was dark, in the ftudy of thofe two long fpeeches of *Agrippa* and *Mæcenas*, which fill the fifty-fecond book of *Dion Caffius.*

CRITO'S pupil employed the afternoon in the re-perufal of that treatife of *Plutarch*, which is entitled, Πως δει τον νεον ποιημ̄ατων ακεειν.

SEVERAL paffages in that treatife much moved him. Ουτε γαρ πολιν αι κεκλεισμεναι πυλαι τηρεσιν αναλωτον, αν δια μιας παραδεξηται τ8ς πολεμι8ς· 8τε νεον αι περι τας αλλας ηδονας εγκρατειαι σωζ8σιν, αν γε δια μιας λαθη προεμενΘ αυτον. In reading this period, he could not avoid thinking of the fatal exceffes which *ruined Raphael.*

NOR was he inattentive to fome other obfervations of *Plutarch.* Τοις απο σκηνης λεγομενοις, κ̄ προς
λυραν αδομενοις, κ̄ μελετωμενοις εν διδασκαλειω, ενιοτε
ομολογει τα Πυθαγορε δογματα κ̄ Πλατων©—διο, κ̄
τ8των ενεκα, κ̄ των προειρημενων απαντων, αγαθης δει
τω νεω κυβερνησεως περι την αναγνωσιν, ινα μη προσδια-
βληθεις, αλλα μαλλον προπαιδευθεις, ευμενης κ̄ φιλ© κ̄
οικει© υπο ποιητικης επι Φιλοσοφιαν προπεμπηται—η
μονη τον ανδρειον κ̄ τελειον τοις νεοις περιτιθησι κοσμον. In
peruſing theſe paſſages he wiſhed, that in modern
places of education ſuch care was obſerved, with
reſpeſt to the ſtudy of *Virgil,* and other *latin*
poets, as *Plutarch* preſcribes for the ſtudy of the
greek poets, particularly *Homer.*

IT was now about two and twenty o'clock*.
As *Crito's* pupil ſeldom had occaſion to continue
his ſtudies ſo long as to *fatigue* his mind, he gladly
cloſed the volume of *Plutarch;* and indulged the
poetic meditations, to which his imagination was
now ſtrongly inclined, during a long ſolitary walk
to the church of *St. Onofrio.*

UNDER a flat ſtone, in the pavement of that
church, lies the duſt of *Taſſo:* *Crito's* pupil read
it's ſhort inſcription; and, in reading it, dropt the
noſegay of roſes, which he had in his hand, on the
ſtone; and left it there.

---

* *Four,* in the afternoon.

Do

Da facro cineri flores.——

HE returned to his lodgings from this long walk, fometime after fun-fet. During the following hour or two, he amufed himfelf with reading feveral favourite paffages in the *Georgics* and *Bucolics*. He confidered with pleafure the rural fcenes there defcribed, as the landfcape paintings of *Virgil's* pencil.

IMMEDIATELY, before he retired to his bed-chamber, he compofed his mind by reading thofe defcriptions of happinefs, with which the paftoral of the *Pollio* abounds. The remarkable turn of thought in the following lines feemed to him to be very much in the fpirit of fome facred *oriental* poetry.

Afpice convexo nutantem pondere mundum,
Terrafque, tractufque maris, cælumque profundum:
Afpice, venturo lætentur ut omnia fæclo*.

---

* VIRG. *Ecl,* iv. 50,

CHAP. II.

TWENTIETH DAY'S CONVERSATION.

T H E reader, perhaps, may not be difpleafed to turn his thoughts at prefent from *Rome*, to that delightful country village, to which *Crito* had retired.

CRITO arrived at *Genfano* on *monday* evening. He employed the next day in inquiring after proper lodgings for the young painter, and in giving orders for their being aired, cleaned, and furnifhed. He made diligent inquiry alfo in relation to the medical affiftance, which the young man might want here, in cafe his late diftemper fhould return.

On *wednefday* morning *Crito* refumed his claffic ftudies; having brought with him from *Rome*, in the pockets of his pupil's chaife, feveral octavos and duodecimos, relative to the hiftory of the reign of *Auguftus*.

After fome hours employed in the profecution of thefe ftudies, he took an abftemious dinner,

ner, and in the afternoon walked out into the fields.

At the entrance of the town of *Genfano* are feveral regularly-planted avenues: one of thefe is terminated by a monaftery. From the monaftery a narrow path leads down to the neighbouring beautiful lake *.

Walking along the avenue, *Crito* revolved in his mind what he had juft before been reading upon the fubjeft of *Auguftus*. He reflefted, with fome fatisfaftion, that he was now almoft within fight of that country town, which was for many ages the refidence of that prince's anceftors †. He recollefted what *Suetonius* fays of *Auguftus's* grandfather ‡. May fuch, thought he, be my pupil's happy lot.

Such were *Crito's* refleftions, while walking along the avenue, or fitting under the fhade of

---

* *Profeguendofi fi .entra nelle belliffime ftrade di Genfano* (olim Cynthianum); *lequali hanno piu del giardino, che della ftrada publica, per le fpalliere d'olmi tofati a doppio ordine con ampia larghura. Vi è anche un belliffimo giardino de P. P. cappucini, dal quale fi vede il lago del vicino* Nemi. *Belliffimi fono i paffeggi alla riva di quefto lago, che rende il paefe fruttifero e delixiofo. Il giro del lago è quatro miglia.*
Efchinardi p. 303, 304.

† *Velitræ* is about fix or feven miles diftant from *Genfano*.

‡ *Avus, municipalibus magifteriis contentus, abundante patrimonio tranquilliffimè fenuit.* Suet. *Aug.* in init.

fome

fome of it's elms. But as he paffed by the convent, and entered the woods which hang over the
lake, *other*, and far better thoughts arofe in his
mind.

THE GREAT EVENT, *which came to pafs in
the reign of* Auguftus*, and within the limits of
his dominion, ftrongly attracted *Crito's* attention;
and, by degrees, *totally* engaged both his head
and heart. The hours of the afternoon and evening fled fwiftly away, while his foul continued abforpt as it were in the happy, heavenly contemplation.

NOR was this the cafe only on *wednefday* evening: the whole fucceeding day was employed in
the *fame* manner. All claffical authors were laid
afide. His time at his lodgings was devoted folely
to religious books, written on the fubject of that
GREAT EVENT; and his rural walks were fancti-
fied with fimilar pious meditations.

ON *thurfday* evening, as he ftood on the banks
of the lake, revolving in his mind *that wonderful*
work of DIVINE LOVE, he fearched out a retired place among the bufhes and rocks, where
no eye could behold him. There joyfully knelt
he down on the grafs; and breathing to heaven
fome fervent fighs, he humbly exclaimed,

* See Advertifement, end of chap. iii. of this vol.

Let

Let all the angels of God adore him. Such was the command of the ETERNAL FATHER, *when he brought* HIS SON *into the world: though of the devout spirits of heaven we can scarcely imagine any to have needed such an invitation, or such a command. Oh! what must have been* their *devotions, when they saw the time of his holy incarnation approaching !*

When Thou tookest upon thee to deliver man, Thou didst not abhor the Virgin's womb.

ET HOMO FACTUS EST.

CRITO now rose from the earth, and continued his solitary walk. He ascended from the lake to the upper ground; then, stopping at a small heap of ruins, through which a wild fig-tree had thrust forth it's branches, he sat down there, and for some minutes surveyed the prospect.

ON his left appeared many mountains and hills, formerly productive of spacious olive-gardens, and the richest vineyards. On his right lay extended a vast plain, naturally fruitful, and anciently very populous; though now in a great measure uncultivated, and abandoned.

Q 3

I<small>T</small> fuddenly occurred to *Crito's* imagination, that this part of *Italy*, in it's prefent ftate, might perhaps be juftly confidered, as in feveral refpects very fimilar to the *province of Galilee*, in the condition under which it is defcribed by modern travellers.

W<small>ITH</small> a fwift tranfition of thought he now indulged himfelf in the hope of vifiting that country. —If our *Levant* travels, thought he to himfelf, fhould extend to the *Holy Land*, it will be then fome pleafure to us to compare the prefent condition of *Galilee*, with *Strabo's*, *Pliny's*, and above all, *Jofephus's* defcription of it's ancient populoufnefs, and high degree of cultivation *.

S<small>UCH</small> a comparifon will be the fubject of many melancholy, but pleafing reflections to us, in the intervals of thofe high contemplations and devotions, which are the proper exercife of a traveller's mind, while in thofe regions.—But, with what rapture will my good pupil furvey the mountains and lakes near *Nazareth!* He will love the folitude, he will be pleafed even with the poverty of that facred village †.

CRITO'S

* See *Strabo*, lib. xvi. p. 775.—*Jofephus*, de bello Judaico, lib. iii. cap. iii.—*Pliny*, lib. v. cap. 15.
† See the defcription of *Nazareth* in *Heyman's* Travels. The place, where the Saviour of the world became incarnate,

CRITO'S foul now entered into a calm and grateful meditation on the *happy* virtues of humility, poverty of fpirit, and love of retirement from the world; a meditation, which he was frequently wont to indulge, and which he always intermingled with ardent afpirations to heaven.

BUT let us not dwell any longer on the defcription of a good man's devotions. The celeftial pleafures of piety in a great meafure depend on their being kept concealed. *Soli DEO & angelis ejus nota effe debent, & hominum notitiam devitare.*

ON *friday* morning, about nine o'clock, *Crito* walked out from his lodgings, to the avenue on

carnate, and where he fpent the greater part of his life, is at prefent one of the meaneft in the whole country.

It's fituation is very retired; in a fmall valley at the foot of an hill, furrounded by a chain of mountains.

Thofe mountains, though now bare and uncultivated, would however naturally admit of the fineft improvement from the plantation of olives, figs, and vines: they command an extenfive view of the *fruitful* plain of *Efdraelon*, anciently called the valley of *Jefrael*.

Within two hours journey of *Nazareth* ftands *the moft beautiful of all hills, Mount Tabor:* the lake of *Tiberias* makes part of the profpect from it's fummit.

It may be proper to obferve, that *Galilee* is a very different kind of country from *Judæa*. *Judæa*, particularly the region in the *route* of *Jerufalem*,—from which route moft *europeans* unadvifedly form their ideas of the whole *Terra Sancta*,—is very rocky, and to appearance barren. Whereas *Galilee* is naturally a very beautiful and fertile land; though defolation is at prefent fpread over it, as well as over the neighbouring provinces of *Syria* and *Mefopotamia.*

the

the *roman* road. He fat down there on a bench under one of the trees; and, having a book in his pocket, intended to continue there, till his *englifh* friends, according to their appointment, fhould arrive from *Rome.*

THE book was a *greek* Teftament: the paffage, which on opening that book firft met and gladdened his eye, was the following fhort defcription of piety and beneficence united.

Συνηρχοντο οχλοι πολλοι ακουειν, κ̣ Θεραπευεϑαι υπ' αυτ8 απο των ασθενειων αυτων. Αυτ☉ δε ην υποχωρων εν ταις ερημοις, κ̣ προσευχομεν☉.*

WHILE *Crito* was engaged in this moft happy ftudy, he was joined by an aged father of the neighbouring poor convent. Benignity and humility fhone in his venerable countenance:

His fnowy locks were down his fhoulders fhed,
As hoary froft with fpangles doth attire
The moffy branches of an oak half dead.

His whole appearance, indeed, ftrongly refembled that of "the Hermit Contemplation," as defcribed in *Spenfer's Legend of Holinefs.* He fat down on

* LUKE v. 15, 16.

the

the bench by *Crito*, and by degrees entered into talk with him.

THE reader may, perhaps, some time hence be informed, what was the subject of their discourse. Suffice it at present to take notice only, that their conversation was polite, friendly, loving, and earnest.

WITHIN about an hour the bell of the neighbouring chapel rang: the old man then rose from his seat, and very affectionately took his leave of *Crito*. About the same time *Crito* saw at a distance on the road the coach of his *english* friends; and walked forward to meet them.

HIS pupil with joy saw him coming; and telling the company of it, they ordered the coach to stop. They got out; and after several kind inquiries as to his health, walked with him into the town.

DURING this walk, they informed *Crito*, that they proposed to dine with him to-day at *Genfano:* and after dinner to make a further excursion towards *Laurentum* and *Lavinium*. They intended, they said, to pass a day or two in *that* country, the principal scene of the actions described in the
latter

latter fix books of the Æneid; and fhould be very glad of their tutor's company.

CRITO with thanks declined this propofal: his reafon for fo doing was, partly, becaufe he was unwilling to deprive the young *irifhman* of his feat in the coach during fo agreeable a tour, partly becaufe he was defirous to avail himfelf of the next two or three days, in cultivating a further acquaintance with the good old father, in the convent.

*   *   *

SOME few mornings afterwards the young gentlemen returned to *Genfano;* and thence, taking *Crito* into the coach with them, proceeded to *Rome.*

THEIR converfation, during the firft part of this fhort journey, was on the objects they had been feeing in the neighbourhood of *Lavinium* and *Laurentum.* From thefe it naturally turned to the topic of *Virgil's* poetical and moral character.

THE eldeft of the young gentlemen then informed *Crito* of the entertainment, which he had
lately

lately enjoyed at *Rome*, in hearing *Virgil's* character, compared with that of *Raphael d'Urbin*.

UPON a further explanation of this matter, the
young nobleman promised *Crito*, that, immediately
on their arrival at *Rome*, he would with pleasure
communicate to him Mr. *Jenkins's* paper on the
character of *Raphael*:—but *Crito's* pupil seemed
rather backward in offering to show his tutor the
observations he had made on *Virgil's* character.
He desired further time therefore, to enlarge and
correct those observations.

PERHAPS, said he, during our stay in *Naples*,
I may be able to offer you a poor paper on the
subject, some morning, while we are gathering
fresh laurel branches from his tomb; or when rowing to the arched rocks of that small island, which
is called *his school*. But, at present, I must beg
to be excused.—My worthy friend here, continued
he, turning to the elder of his young companions,
has some papers, that will give you much greater
entertainment. He has been hard at work, I af-
sure you, since you left *Rome*, on the character
of *Agrippa*,

*   *   *

THE coach had now advanced within two or
three miles of *Rome*, when the young nobleman,
looking

looking out at the window, admired the noble effect, which the ancient aqueducts had in the composition of the prospect.

HARDLY any thing indeed can be imagined more striking to a traveller, than the numerous aqueducts, which are still to be seen stretching their long arcades, or bridges, acrofs the *Campania* of *Latium;* and directing their lofty and majestic course to *Rome,* like comets to the centre of the solar system.

IT was at a hilloc on the *Appian* way, just above the church of *Domine quo vadis,* that the company stopped to admire this noble prospect.

CRITO took this opportunity of reminding his young friends, that the most ancient of these aqueducts was the work of *Appius Claudius Crassus,* then cenfor, during the first confulship of the second *Decius:* rather more than three hundred years before the birth of our Saviour. The same person, said he, was the founder of this famous paved road, on which we are now travelling. *Viam munivit, & aquam in urbem duxit, eaque unus perfecit* *.

* Vide *Livii,* lib. ix. c. 29.—*Montfaucon,* tom. iv. part 2. c. 2.—*Hooke,* vol. i. p. 526.

THE

THE fecond aqueduct was built by *Curius Den-
tatus.* *Curius* employed in that work of public
utility all his part of the fpoils taken in the war
with king *Pyrrhus.* But his aqueduct is on the
other fide of *Rome* towards *Tivoli* *.

THE third and moft ufeful of all the aqueducts
was that of the *Aqua Martia.* It was built originally by *Marcius* †, but reftored by *Agrippa;*
who generoufly and juftly left to it the name of
it's firft founder.

THE fourth and fifth of the *roman* aqueducts
were the *Aqua Julia* and the *Aqua Augufta, vulgò
Virginis.* Thefe were, both, *entirely* the works
of *Agrippa;* though that nobly-minded man declined giving his name to either of them. Indeed,
at *Rome,* as well as in all other parts of *Italy,*
Agrippa conftantly endeavoured to hide his beneficence, under the name of his friend, patron, and

* See vol. i. p. 168.
† *Dicantur verâ æftimatione invicta miracula, quæ Q. Marcius rex fecit. Is juffus a fenatu aquarum Appiæ, Anienis,
Tepulæ ductus reficere, novam à nomine fuo appellatam, cuni-
culis per montes actis, intrà præturæ fuæ tempus adduxit. Cla-
riffima aquarum omnium in toto orbe frigoris falubritatifque pal-
mâ præconio urbis Martia eft inter reliqua Deûm munera urbi
tributa.—Amnium omnium comparatione, differentia fuprà dicta
deprenditur, cum quantum Aqua Virgo tactu, tantum præftet
Martia hauftu.* Pliny.
*Martia tota potui totius urbis fervit: reliquæ aquæ aliis ufi-
bus affignantur. Habet longitudinem a capite ad urbem LX milli.
paffuum & DCCCX femis.* Frontinus.

fovereign,

fovereign, *Augustus:* or, which was perhaps
more pleafing to that emperor, to attribute the
honour of the defign to *Augustus's* adoptive father,
Julius.

I AM heartily glad, that we are come to the
times of *Agrippa;* and fhall liften, with very
great pleafure, to your obfervations on his excellent character.

SOME time this afternoon, replied the eldeft of
the young gentlemen, when you are not better
employed, I will fubmit my papers to your correction: in the mean time, let not a thought relative to thofe papers interrupt what you were
going to fay further on the hiftory of thofe aqueducts.

THERE is no occafion, *at prefent,* replied *Crito,*
to trouble you with a long catalogue of the thir-
teen aqueducts, which were built by the fucceffors
of *Augustus.* Let me only obferve to you in general, that fuch works of public utility are certainly the beft channel, in which a fovereign can
difplay his magnificence. King *Ahab* could erect
a houfe of ivory; fo called, I prefume, for the
fame reafon, as *Nero's* palace was called a houfe
of *gold:* but it was the pious *Hezekiah,* who built
an aqueduct, and *brought water into the city.* Let

US

us not, however, at prefent, talk of *Jerufalem*.
Let us rather fix our thoughts on *Rome ;* and, if
you pleafe, profecute our journey thither.

* * *

THE eldeft of the young gentlemen now bade
the coachman drive on; directing him, when he
came to *Rome*, to turn into the *Piazza Navona*.

IN lefs than an hour the company arrived there.
While the carriage was driving flowly round the
great fountain, the young nobleman joined with
Crito's pupil in admiring the auguft idea, with
which *Bernini* muft have been animated, while
forming that magnificent defign. But *Crito*, with
the other young gentleman, obferved, that however juftly the modern *romans* might boaft of
this grand decoration of their city by *Bernini*, they
ought not to forget, that the really ufeful part of
this fountain was originally due to *Agrippa*.

FROM the *Piazzo Navona* the coach proceeded
to the *Fontana di Trevi*. The company here
ftepped out, to enjoy the agreeable, frefh, and
cool air of the place. Under the fhade of one
of the neighbouring fhops they ftood for a confiderable time, to admire the variety of cafcades,
in which *Agrippa's* virgin aqueduct there bufts
forth,

forth, amidſt the artificial rock-work. The young nobleman then turned the attention of the company to the new embelliſhment of that ſuperb *Facciata:*—one of the bas-reliefs, which repreſents *Agrippa,* with his ſoldiers, ſearching for the ſprings of this fountain.

FROM the *Fontana di Trevi* the company walked on to the *Triton* fountain, in the *Piazza Barberini.*

THE deſigns and ornaments of the *modern* fountains in this city, ſaid the young nobleman, are indeed very grand. Yet I much queſtion, whether thoſe of ancient *Rome* were not far ſuperiour. If I rightly recollect, *Agrippa,* in the year of his ædileſhip, built for the uſe of the inhabitants of this city one hundred and thirty reſervoirs of water, and one hundred and five public fountains; in the adorning of which he employed no leſs than *three hundred marble, or braſs, ſtatues,* and *four hundred marble columns.*

BUT let us turn down this ſtreet on our left. By the time we get to our lodgings, I hope, we ſhall find dinner ready. I think we ought to drink to-day a glaſs or two to the glorious memory of *Agrippa:* a glaſs, not of wine, but of what is far more pleaſant in this burning climate, that

that cool and pure water, which ſtill flows from his long-lived munificence; though near eighteen hundred years have elapſed ſince that of the ædile-ſhip. All the houſes in this part of the town, I think, are ſupplied from his aqueducts*.

THE company now walked to their lodgings, and ſat down with pleaſure to dinner. *Crito,* in particular, ſeemed very happy at the thoughts of being returned to *Rome,* and thus ſeated at table again with his dear friends.

DURING dinner-time, the young nobleman introduced the topic of that noble and uſeful work of ſir *Hugh Middleton,* by which *London* and *Weſtminſter* are ſupplied with water; ſubterranean pipes running through almoſt every ſtreet, like the veins through every member of the human body. He compared ſir *Hugh's* benevolence with that of *Agrippa;* though he owned, that, *to outward appearance at leaſt,* the capital of *Britain,* as to it's ſupplies of water, is far inferiour yet, either to ancient or modern *Rome :* as inferiour indeed to *Rome,* as it is ſuperiour to *Paris.*

---

* Τοσουτον δ' εστι το εισαγωγιμον υδωρ δια των υδραγωγειων, ωστε ποταμους δια της πολεως, κ̩ των υπονομων ρειν, απασαν δε οικιαν σχεδον δεξαμενας κ̩ σιφωνας, κ̩ κρουνες εχειν αφθονους, ων πλειστην επιμελειαν εποιησατο Μαρκ Αγριππας πολλοις κ̩ αλλοις αναθημασι κοσμησας την πολιν. *Strabo,* lib. v.

Modern *Rome* has the ſame convenience of plenty of water. See Abbé *Richard's* Travels, vol. vi. p. 225.

BUT let us not wander too much, faid he, from *Agrippa's* character. Where, my dear fir, are we to have the pleafure of reading your paper on that fubject this afternoon?

I SCARCE know, replied the eldeft of the young gentlemen, what place to choofe for that purpofe. *Many* parts of *Rome* were anciently embellifhed with *Agrippa's* public works of various kinds: but I fuppofe you will be glad to vifit that great monument of his memory, which is the moft univerfally celebrated. However, I will wait upon you again in an hour or two, when the air begins to grow cool, and take your directions.

*   *   *

ABOUT fix o'clock in the afternoon, the company went together to the place of the *Septa Julia*, and thence to the ancient fite of *Agrippa's* gardens, and the fmall remains of his baths; obferving, that *Agrippa* finifhed each of thefe works at a great expenfe, and generoufly left them to the public ufe.

THEY next proceeded to the *Pantheon.*

APPROACHING to it, though yet at a confiderable diftance, they faw with pleafure *Agrippa's*
name

name engraven over the portico, in characters now all black with age.

THEY paffed through the ftately portico, and entered the brazen gate.

IF I be not miftaken, faid *Crito*'s pupil, *Virgil*, in his defcription of the building of *Carthage*, feems to have had in his mind, not only the idea of what would be the natural appearance of a new city, in a maritime colony; but alfo the idea of thofe magnificent ftructures, with which *Auguftus* and *Agrippa* were in his time adorning *Rome*.

THE hint of the *alta theatri fundamenta* feems to have been taken from *Marcellus*'s theatre. The principal temple of *Carthage* is embellifhed exact-ly with the fame ornaments as *this Pantheon*.

Ærea cui gradibus furgebant limina, nexæque
Ære trabes, foribus cardo ftridebat ahenis*.

---

* VIRGIL, *Æn.* i. 452. The original brazen gate of the *Pantheon* was carried away by *Genferic:* it's brazen fteps, with many other of it's ornaments, by one of the *conftanti-nopolitan* emperors, in the feventh century: the vaft nails, and other brafs work, of the roof, to the weight of 45,000,250 pounds, by pope *Urban* VIII. The pope indeed employ-ed part of this metal to a very noble purpofe, *viz.* the con-ftruction of the prefent moft magnificent columns and ca-nopy over the tomb of *St. Peter* in the *Vatican.* See ab-bate *Venuti*, vol. ii. p. 73.

YET, perhaps this fancy may have no real foundation. Let us go into the church.—Though we have fo often vifited it, fo venerable a pile ftill ftrikes us with awe.

THE company now advanced to the centre of the *Pantheon*, and looked up to it's roof; while the young nobleman made feveral judicious remarks upon it's architecture.

How pleafing, faid the eldeft of the young gentlemen, turning to *Crito's* pupil, is the kind of light, which flows from that circular aperture! It feems to be fomething half-way between the fplendour of the fun and the foftnefs of the moon. Might not a modern flowery *italian* writer compare this light to the purity and brightnefs of *Agrippa's* character, attempered as it' was and foftened by his modefty?

WE will fit down, if you pleafe, in that recefs on our right, on the wooden bench behind thofe two rich *corinthian* columns. We fhall be there more out of the way of thofe, who are continually coming hither, either from motives of curiofity or devotion.

THE reft of the company now took their feats, while the eldeft of the young gentlemen ftood
leaning

leaning againſt one of the columns. He pauſed for ſome moments in ſilence, and then fluently, without heſitation, or once looking at his paper of notes, delivered his thoughts in the following manner.

* * *

THE charaĉter of *Agrippa*, my dear friends, in one word, ſeems to be this. Very eminent merit; attended with very remarkable modeſty. Let us firſt endeavour to conſider his *military* hiſtory.

AGRIPPA'S eminent merit in this ſphere of aĉtion, is demonſtrated by the ſame proof as that of our *britiſh* general, the duke of *Marlborough:* He was always ſuccefsful*.

AGRIPPA was viĉtorious in the *eaſt:* he was viĉtorious among the moſt warlike nations of the .weſt: in *Hungary* and *Germany;* in *France,* and in *Spain.*

BUT *Agrippa's* military glory was not, like that of all our *modern* commanders, confined to

---

* *Quantas ille res, domi, militiæque, terrâ, marique, quantâque felicitate geſſerit!* Words, equally applicable to *Agrippa,* as to *Pompey.* See Cic. orat. *pro Lege Manil.* xii.

one

one element. If in his campaigns he may, in any particular point, be compared to the duke of *Marlborough*, certainly in his naval victories he may be put on a parallel with the moſt famous commanders at ſea. None of the *britiſh* or *dutch* admirals could ever boaſt of trophies more ſplendid, than the roſtral crown and ſea-green ſtandard of *Agrippa*. He ſubdued the marine power of *Sextus Pompeius;* that ſon of *Neptune*, whoſe fleets were moſt formidable in all the *weſtern* parts of the *Mediterranean*. He had a great ſhare in the victory at *Actium*, over the immenſe combined navies of *Egypt*, and the *Levant*. How eminently diſtinguiſhed is the figure of *Agrippa*, in *Virgil's* picture of the ſea-fight!

———*Ventis, & Diis Agrippa ſecundis*
Arduus, agmen agens; cui, belli inſigne ſuperbum,
Tempora navali fulgent roſtrata coronâ*.

THE word *ſuperbum* in this paſſage was certainly intended to convey the idea of grandeur, not of pride: for *Agrippa's* modeſty was as remarkable in the military world, as his glory. Though in the beginning of *Auguſtus's* reign, *above thirty* other commanders had ſolicited and obtained the honour of a triumph; yet *Agrippa*, from a prin-

---

* ÆN. viii. 682.

ciple

ciple of modesty, as well as of prudence, constantly declined it. He declined *that* honour, which, to a *roman* eye, had always appeared the highest and most desirable object of military pursuit.

PERMIT me to observe, that this modesty of *Agrippa* has been very abundantly rewarded. For, while almost all his contemporary generals and admirals are comparatively sunk into oblivion, the memory of *Agrippa's* military glory still flourishes.

THIS seems the more remarkable; as the works of that great historian, and poet, who particularly recorded *Agrippa's* military history, and whose writings, it might be imagined, would have proved in the long run the most firm supports of his fame, have both long ago perished. — I mean *Livy*, and *Varius.*

OFTEN did I wish last week, that the part of *Livy's* history, which related to *Agrippa*, had been preserved. Often have I heard you, my dear friend,—turning to *Crito's* pupil,—lament the loss of the poems of *Varius;* the *roman Homer.*

Scriberis

Scriberis Vario fortis, & hostium
Victor, Mæonii carminis alite,
Quam rem cunque ferox navibus, aut equis
Miles, te duce, gesserit.

Nos, Agrippa, neque hæc dicere, nec gravem
Peleidæ stomachum, cedere nescii,
Nec cursus duplicis per mare Ulyssei,
Conamur*.

IF *Varius,* in any degree, really resembled *Homer,* particularly in the art of drawing characters, his military character of *Agrippa* may justly be imagined to have contained several particulars, very instructive to the young *roman reader.*

FOR, beside the eminent merit of an able commander, *Agrippa* possessed many military accomplishments, suitable to the character of a poet's hero; and such as a young reader might be animated to the hopes of imitating. *Virtutis erat nobilissimæ; labore, vigiliâ, periculo invictus.*

BUT let us now turn our thoughts to another subject.

---

* HORAT. lib. i. od. 6.

SITTING, as you are at prefent, under the ftately roof of this venerable fabric; a fabric erected
by *Agrippa* for a *religious* purpofe, and for above
thefe laft thoufand years conftantly ufed as a
chriftian church; *you*, my dear fir, faid our
young orator, addreffing himfelf to *Crito*, will
juftly expect, that we fhould endeavour to exercife our little eloquence, not fo much upon
the military achievements of *Agrippa*, as on
that far better topic, his labours in times of
peace.

AGRIPPA, in his high ftation, muft have
had frequent opportunities of being beneficent to
feveral of the nations, who were then fubject to
the *roman* empire. He is faid to have behaved
to them with great equity and goodnefs—But you
are going to fay fomething: let me not prevent
you.

I REMEMBER reading with great pleafure in
Jofephus, replied *Crito*, fome particulars of
Agrippa's juft and true beneficence to the inhabitants of *Afia Minor**; as well as the defcription of his vifit to *Jerufalem†*.

THE

* Προ τας ευεργεσιας υκ εβραδυνετο ο Αγριππας.—Χρης ην κ
μεγαλοψυχ προ το παρεχειν οσα τοις ηξιωκοσιν ωφελιμα, μηδενα
των αλλων ελυπει. Antiq. Judaic. lib. xvi.

† Ηγεν δε εις την πολιν των Ιεροσολυμιτων, υπαντωντ τε τυ δημυ
παντ εν εορτωδει ςολη, κ δεχομενυ τον ανδρα συν ευφημιαις. Αγριππας

THE converſation now dwelt for ſome minutes on that article of the *jewiſh* hiſtory. It afterwards returned to it's former topic; the young nobleman obſerving, that *Agrippa* adorned ſeveral parts of *Europe* with works of great public utility, as well as ſplendour.

I REMEMBER, ſaid he, while in *France*, we were informed, that *Agrippa* was the author of the vaſt deſign of thoſe four great roads, which, from their mutual centre near *Lyons*, were extended to the moſt diſtant parts of the *gallic* provinces. The learned abbé, who gave us this information, added, that ſome remains of theſe roads were ſtill viſible near *Lyons*. You muſt, I think, remember that converſation. It happened ſoon after our firſt arrival from *England* at *Paris*, while we were viewing the church of the *Hôpital des Invalides*. Don't you recollect, with what pleaſure the abbé then digreſſed from this work of *Agrippa*, into a panegyric on the many *modern* public works in *France?* He deſcribed the long and magnificent avenues, planted and paved, which lead from ſeveral quarters, particularly from *Fontainbleau* to *Paris;* then recited a cata-

πας δε τω ΘΕΩ μεν εκατομβην κατεθυσεν, ειςια δε τον δημον.——Απαγγελλεται δε ημιν υπο των εκει Ιεδαιων, ως μεν επειδης της χωρας ευμενης, ως δε απεδωκας τω ΘΕΩ τα τελεια θυματα, τιμων Αυτον επιτελειαις ευχαις, ως δε τον δημον ειςιασας, ή τα παρ᾽ αυτα εκεινα ξενια προσηκω. Ibid.

logue

logue of the splendid structures, with which *Louis le Grand* and *Colbert* adorned the bank of the *Seine;* and told us, that in making the tour of *France*, we should be eye-witnesses of many long canals joining rivers naturally distant; and some joining distant seas.

I VERY well recollect that conversation, replied the eldest of the young gentlemen. Our hearts sympathized with the abbé's public spirit: for, thank God! we have not been educated in the darkness of that narrow and mean policy, which envies and depreciates every noble action achieved by *frenchmen*, or that grudges every blessing vouchsafed by providence to *France*. There is a policy, infinitely more generous, brave, and wise: which knows how to rejoice in the virtues and prosperities of neighbouring nations; although, as in duty bound, it's labours be chiefly directed to the advantage of it's own people.

THE good abbé, I remember, listened with pleasure to the account we gave him, of the improvements which were making in *England;* such as our new bridges, new roads, and other works of peace. I wish we had been able to communicate to him that great plan of inland navigation, which I hear, from *Staffordshire*, is now preparing to be laid before the house of commons: a plan

plan for the junction of the *Severn*, *Trent*, and *Merſey*.

> *Bid harbours open, public ways extend,*
> *Bid temples, worthier of the God, aſcend;*
> *Back to his bounds the ſubjeɛ̌ ſea command,*
> *And roll obedient rivers thro' the land:*
> *Theſe honours* PEACE *to happy Britain brings;*
> *Theſe are* Imperial *works, and worthy* Kings*.

I REMEMBER, ſaid *Crito*, the ſimilar generous ſentiments, which flowed from your lips and heart, while viewing the ruins at *Dunkirk*. As an *engliſhman* you felt glad, that the trade of *London* was ſecured by the diſmantling of *Dunkirk;* but yet, you expreſſed much concern, that a work of ſuch magnificence, and of ſuch utility to the commerce of *France*, and *Flanders*, ſhould be brought to deſolation. You caſt a look of compaſſion on it's long canal, then almoſt choked with ſand; and on it's moles, over which the ſea, at a high tide, was then waſhing. You did not rejoice at the demolition even of it's forts; ſome of which were then in ruins, ſome laid level with the ſands, others buried in the waves. You wiſhed, that the ſecurity of your country could have been effeɛ̌ed by other means. But let us not deviate too much from the ſubjeɛ̌ of our *roman* ſtudies.

* POPE, *Moral Eſſays*, ep. iv. addreſſed to lord *Burlington*.

I F

I F *Agrippa*, continued the eldeſt of the young gentlemen, were beneficent to *France*, he proved, as muſt naturally be imagined, far more ſo to *Italy*.

O F this we ſhall perhaps ſee *one ſpecimen*, in our journey to *Naples*: I mean, that great artificial ſea-port, near *Miſenum*; which, though con-ſtruĉted in time of war, and deſigned as a ſtation for the *italian* fleet, to oppoſe the invaſions of *Sextus Pompeius**; yet certainly proved very uſe-ful to trade and navigation alſo, in the following years of peace.

AGRIPPA'S deſigns were likewiſe very be-neficial in diſperſing the peſtilential vapours, that infeĉted the country round the lake *Averno*. Of his labours, however, between the *Averno* and *Lucrine*, I am afraid, we ſhall find but few traces remaining; as the face of that ſhore is ſaid to be very conſiderably changed, by the inundations of the ſea, and the eruptions of ſubterranean fires.

B U T whatever were the public labours of *Agrippa*, in other parts of *Italy*, *Rome* ſeems to

---

* See *Freinſhem.* book 128. c. 29, 30. and *Suetonius.* A. V. C. 717.—*Miſenum* ſeems to have been the *Plymouth*, as *Antium* was the *Portſmouth*, and *Oſtia* the *Nore*, of ancient *Rome*.

have

have been the place, the improvement and embellifhment of which he had moft at heart.

It is needlefs for me to fpeak on that topic. This morning, this afternoon, this inftant, your own eyes are witneffes of the magnificence, with which he adorned the capital of his country.

Long aqueducts, and numerous fountains; public baths, and public gardens; vaft porticos for the comitia, or affemblies of the people; ftately temples, *particularly his Pantheon;* were the works of *Agrippa*: works, far furpaffing thofe of any other private *roman,* and perhaps unequalled by thofe of any emperor.

O my dear friends! when we fhall be at *Athens,* viewing the grand portico of the temple of *Minerva* in the *Acropolis,* and talking of the times of *Pericles;* fhall we not then recollect *Agrippa,* and his *Pantheon?* *Agrippa* was the *roman Pericles,* in relation to the grandeur of his public ftructures: in other refpects, his character was far fuperiour.

The young nobleman now rofe from his feat; and after fome paufe, How much more honourable to *Agrippa,* faid he, was fuch magnificence, thus difplayed in works of *public utility,* than if he had confined his vaſt expences to the adorning merely his own palace, or villa.

Iꜰ I be not miſtaken, *Agrippa* once propoſed, that the chef d'œuvres of ſculpture and painting then in *Rome* ſhould not be ſuffered to remain any longer in private hands; but, ſatisfaction being made to the owners, ſhould all be removed to ſome of the *public* buildings in this city. *Agrippa* ſet the example of this, as well as propoſed the deſign*.

Tʜᴇ deſign, ſaid *Crito's* pupil, ſeems to have been originally ſuggeſted by *Socrates;* who thought that ſuch a meaſure, in *Athens,* would be a great means of repreſſing *private* luxury and pride; as well as of encouraging the fine arts, and of increaſing the *public* magnificence. If I remember right, it is in the third book of the *Memorabilia.*—But we interrupt our friend.

Wʜᴀᴛ I have further to ſay on this ſubject, replied the eldeſt of the young gentlemen, relates to a circumſtance, which, I am ſure, will give *you* peculiar pleaſure.

* *Extat oratio Agrippæ, de hâc re magnificâ & maxime civium dignâ.* Pʟɪɴʏ.

Tʜɪꜱ

THIS public fpirit of *Agrippa* was attended with the fame *modefty*, that accompanied his military merit. As your tutor obferved this morning, *Agrippa*, in all his ftruſtures, conftantly endeavoured to hide himfelf, under the names of his friends and benefaſtors; and to turn on *them* all the commendation and praife.

BUT *this modefty alfo* has happily failed of it's intended effeſt. *Agrippa's* name is, and will for ever be, moft renowned for thefe works of goodnefs. Some of his works themfelves feem to have met with peculiar favour and mercy, from the rough hand of time. You obferved this morning, that great part of the city is ftill fupplied by his aqueduſt. Is it not alfo fomething remarkable, that this his Pantheon, on the portico of which he was obliged, by *Auguftus*, unwillingly to infcribe his name, fhould ftill fubfift;. far more entire and perfeſt, than any other of all the pompous fabrics, with which this ftately city was ever decorated?

BUT, if you pleafe, we will now ſtep into the portico: You feem tired of *fitting* in this recefs: and we can walk about there more at liberty, than we can in the church.

UNDER

* *. * ·

UNDER the portico of the *Pantheon* arc to this day remaining two great niches: in one of which ſtood anciently the *coloſſal* ſtatue of *Auguſtus;* in the other, that of *Agrippa*.

IF you pleaſe, continued the eldeſt of the young gentlemen, leading his friends to the niche on the left hand, we may *here not improperly* conſider ſome other parts of *Agrippa's* conduct: thoſe I mean, which relate to *Auguſtus*.

As *Auguſtus* lived in the mixed character of a *roman* citizen, and of a *roman* emperor, ſo the behaviour of *Agrippa* to him was proportionately compoſed of the offices, both of a *friend*, and of a *miniſter*.

IF we conſider *Agrippa* in the firſt of theſe points of view, we ſhall find his conduct, according to *Dion Caſſius's* deſcription, to be one of the moſt perfect patterns of affectionate *friendſhip*.

PERMIT me to make a diſtinction here. I commend not *Agrippa's* friendſhip to *Octavius*, but to *Auguſtus*. It was no praiſe to be the friend of the *bloody triumvir*: but it is a great honour to have been ſo to the *wiſe* and *mild emperor*.

CAPABLE as *Agrippa* was to have filled the principal place, he modeftly and wifely chofe the fecond. In that rank he continued to cultivate the favour of *Auguftus*, without meannefs, and without envy. Indeed, their conftant friendfhip confers on each of them equal honour. For it was without diftruft or fufpicion, that *Auguftus* exalted *Agrippa* to the chief honours of the ftate: it was with proper generofity, that *Auguftus* rewarded his merit; making him his colleague in the government, and his intended fucceffor in the empire. It was with lafting gratitude,—how noble a virtue in princes! that on the death of *Agrippa*, *Auguftus* fpoke himfelf the funeral panegyric; placed the urn in his own fepulchre; and continued, ever afterwards, highly to honour his memory.

IF we confider *Agrippa* in the *other* point of view, we fhall find his behaviour that of a moft wife and virtuous *minifter of ftate.*

AGRIPPA aided his fovereign with the beft counfels: and attributed to *Auguftus*, not to *himfelf*, all the honour arifing from them.

AGRIPPA was not lefs beloved by the people, than by the prince.

HE

H E acquired this public favour by the beſt means; without oſtentation; without any ambitious deſign.

H E ſought it with no other intention, than that of ſtrengthening and eſtabliſhing by it the authority of his prince.

O N the other hand, he never made any other uſe of favour with his ſovereign, than that of employing it as an inſtrument for procuring the greateſt benefit and moſt real happineſs to the people.

M Y dear friends, with what philanthropic and patriotic ardour ought we to join our wiſhes, that *Great Britain*, in the preſent and in future centuries, may be often under the guidance of *ſuch* a prime miniſter; the ſupport of the throne,—the bleſſing of the nation!

You were juſt now ſpeaking of *France*, continued the young politician, addreſſing himſelf to his noble companion : I have been thinking, whether or no the illuſtrious pair, whoſe ſtatues once adorned theſe niches, might not be compared, in *ſome* reſpects, to that honeſt prime miniſter, the dùke of *Sully*, and his friend, fellow-ſoldier, and ſovereign, *Henry* the Great; in *others*, to car-

S 2 dinal

dinal *Amboife,* and that father of his people, *Louis* the Twelfth. You may remember what *Mezerai* fays of the cardinal. *Ce miniftre fut juftement aimé de la France, & de fon maitre: parce qu'il les aimoit tous les deux également.*

I wish, faid *Crito,* that at your leifure you would inform me of fome particulars in the life of cardinal *Amboife.* I remember, when in *Normandy,* my going to fee his grand maufoleum in the cathedral at *Rouen;* but I am very little acquainted with his character. In general, I know, it is highly, and I fuppofe juftly, celebrated: yet, if I be not miftaken, there is reafon to wifh, that he had been lefs concerned with the negotiations of *Italy,* and more occupied with the religious bufinefs of his diocefs. Thefe were the fentiments that paffed through my mind, while I ftood leaning on the rails of that altar, which adjoins to his maufoleum.

But let me not at prefent draw off the thoughts of the company from your noble and juft panegyric on *Agrippa.*

I am deeply convinced, replied the worthy youth, that my abilities are very inadequate to the tafk. It is perhaps a very ridiculous vanity in me, at the age of one or two and twenty, to be talking

talking of *Agrippa's* minifterial merit. I fhall
have reafon to be happy, if I may be able to think
properly on the fubject twenty years hence. But
furely I ought to thank *you* for your condefcenfion, who have been fo patiently liftening to me;
though what I have had to fay, deferves to be
confidered in no better light, than that of a fchool-
boy's declamation.

OFTEN did I wifh, laft week, for the abilities
of fome of my father's parliamentary friends, while
I was reading, and endeavouring to underftand,
a long train of argument difcuffed by *Agrippa* and
Mæcenas; I mean, on *that* important debate in
the *roman* cabinet-council, which was to determine whether *Auguftus* fhould retain, or refign,
the imperial power.

IN this debate *Agrippa*, you know, according
to his ufual magnanimity and ardent fenfe of that
glory, which is acquired by great and heroic
actions, ftrongly fupported the propofal, which
feemed the moft generous. He advifed *Auguftus*
gradually, and *prudently*, to refign the fupreme
authority, into the hands of it's ancient owners,
the fenate and people of *Rome.* He enforced this
advice, fo directly againft his own private in-
terefts, with all the fpirit of a oman, zealous for
the name of liberty; and with all the fincerity of

a true

a true friend, anxious for the repofe, profperity, and happinefs of *Auguftus.*

MÆCENAS, on the other hand, elegantly, and with great eloquence, difplayed the true condition of the *roman* ftate. It had long fince loft, he faid, and was now become *incapable* of enjoying, the *real* bleffings of liberty. It's provinces groaned under various fucceffive oppreffors: it's capital was filled with fedition and corruption, confufion and anarchy. All the parts of it's great and populous empire were ravaged with bloody and endlefs civil wars. The fhip of the ftate, crowded with a mutinous and wicked crew, without a rudder, without ballaft, was toffed on a boifterous fea by perpetual ftorms:—ftorms, from the rage and wild fury of which a fettled and moderate monarchy alone could open to her a fecure refuge, and a quiet haven.

IN the name of his country, in the name of mankind, *Mæcenas* then conjured *Auguftus* to retain the fovereignty: to retain it from the principle, not of ambition, but of public fpirit: to fupport what was now become the real intereft of *Rome* by his wife and mild government: and to protect, from the return of the moft dreadful calamities, that large part of the human race, which was fubject to her dominion.

O MY

O my dear countrymen, as an *englifhman* I hope, that I fhall always continue to abominate the idea of the extinction of national liberty : yet, let me own, that if I had lived under *Auguftus's* reign, I fhould have been thankful that the times of anarchy were paffed.

Ημων αυτων ενεκα, κ̓ της πολεως, πεισθωμεν τη τυχη τη μοναρχιαν σοι διδ8ση· κ̓ χαριν γε μεγαλην αυτη εχωμεν, οτι μη μονον των κακων των εμφυλιων ανεπαυσεν ημας, αλλα κ̓ την καταϛασιν της πολιτειας επι σοι πεποιηται.

To the truth and force of thefe arguments *Agrippa* fubmitted. He then, immediately on the determination of this grand debate, began to contrive how he might, by the moft indefatigable application, render the prefent form of govern‐ ment as beneficial to the public as poffible.

But let me not trouble you with a repetition of *Agrippa's* good actions. Let me rather haften to clofe this declamation. And in what manner can I better conclude it, than with the words of *Dion Caffius?*

Αγριππας, των καθ᾽ εαυτον ανθρωπων, διαφανως αριϛ☾.

The

*　　*　　*

THE converſation now turned to other topics. The portico of the *Pantheon* is ſupported by ſixteen columns; which are four feet and a half in diameter, and nine and thirty feet in height, without meaſuring either the capital or the baſe.

THE young nobleman obſerved to the company, that each of theſe lofty pillars was formed out of *one ſingle* block of *egyptian* granite.

ALL architects agree, ſaid he, that this portico was *not* built at the ſame time with the temple, but added to it afterwards. Perhaps the temple might be built by *Agrippa*, before the battle of *Actium;* and the portico added ſoon after the conqueſt of *Egypt.* Perhaps theſe ſtately columns were *then* brought from *Alexandria.* Their materials certainly are *egyptian.* They were probably worked by ſome *greek* artiſts reſident in that country.

IN relation indeed to many of the embelliſhments, which *Italy* received under the reign of *Auguſtus,* and the miniſtry of *Agrippa,* it may be thought, and poſſibly with reaſon, that they were in a great meaſure owing to the circumſtance of

Egypt's

Egypt's being *at that time* united to the roman empire.

HISTORY informs us, that when *Auguſtus* landed at *Alexandria,* he was ſtruck with the remarkable beauty and ſplendour of that city; and expreſſed great veneration for it's founder. It was then, in all probability, that he conceived the noble deſign of embelliſhing *Rome* after a ſimilar manner; that is, of making *Rome* in ſome reſpeĉts a ſecond *Alexandria.*

IT is obſervable in regard to *Agrippa,* that this portico is ſupported by pillars, not unworthy to have made part of the moſt pompous colonnades in the palace of *Cleopatra.* It is remarkable alſo, that his great ſubterranean reſervoir of water at *Miſeno,* which to this day, it is ſaid, ſubſiſts intire, and is called the *Piſcina mirabilis,* is exactly of the ſame kind with thoſe, which, according to modern travellers, are ſtill remaining at *Alexandria.*

I AM very much of your opinion, replied the eldeſt of the young gentlemen. But *the ancient ſovereigns of Memphis, and of Thebes,* as well as the founder and other more modern princes of *Alexandria,* were authors of ſeveral works of national utility, and ſtupendous magnificence; which ſeem feem to have caught the attention, and excited the admiration of *Auguſtus*.

WHILE *Auguſtus* was in *Egypt*, he began to employ his foldiers in clearſing and repairing the old canals, and in cutting new ones. Moſt of the ancient canals were the work of the *kings of Thebes and Memphis.*

AUGUSTUS, on his return to *Italy,* imitated, as you obferve, in this country, the grandeur of *Egypt.* But it was the grandeur, not of the *Pto-lomies* only, but alfo of *Menes* and *Oſymanduas.* Witneſs his mauſoleum, his *Palatine* library, his temples, and other public ſtructures.

AUGUSTUS likewiſe adorned *Rome* with the obeliſks, thoſe moſt noble ſpecimens of the *primeval* wealth and arts of *Egypt.*

SEVERAL of the *roman* emperors followed *Auguſtus's* example. They imported ſo many obeliſks, granite columns, and ſtatues, as almoſt to metamorphoſe *Rome* into an *egyptian* city.

ON *wedneſday* morning I paſſed ſome hours in turning over *Pocock's* and *Norden's* defcriptions of *Egypt.* I afterwards walked to the *Villa Negroni,* and fat down on that hilloc, which is adorned

with

with the coloffal ftatue of *Rome*, in the character
of *Minerva*. Several aged cyprefles encircle that
mount. I fat down, and viewed from between
the cyprefles in folemn profpect the defolated ftate
of the *Viminal* and *Efquiline* hills. At a diftance
on my left I faw a great obelifk rifing among the
vineyards, near the *Lateran* cathedral. By the
gate of the *Negroni* garden I faw another *egyptian*
obelifk, which once ftood by the maufoleum of
Auguftus, but is now placed before the northern
front of *Santa Maria Maggiore*. Thefe objects
inclined me then to imagine myfelf in the neighbourhood of fome ruined cities in *Thebais; Cop-
tos*, for inftance, or *Tentyra*, or *Syene*.

But, if a profpect of part of *Rome*, *even at this
time*, bear a kind of *egyptian* air; how much
greater muft the fimilitude have been, in thofe
ages, when every ftreet in *Rome* contained fomething that was *egyptian*?

That, replied the young nobleman, is ftill in
fome degree the cafe. The only difference feems
to be this : Under the *roman* emperors, thofe *egyptian* monuments, which adorned the ftreets of *Rome*,
were as entire, as when they ftood on the banks
of the *Nile;* but at prefent, many of them are
broken or buried.

What

WHAT numbers, for example, of *egyptian* anti-quities have been found under the *Dominican* convent, behind this *Pantheon!* In the piazza before it you fee a fmall *egyptian* obelifk, front-ing this portico. But let us not attend to little objeɛts. There are at prefent, in this *Campo Marzo,* three *great* obelifks, which *Auguſtus* brought from that country. One of them is bu-ried near the church of *St. Roch:* the fecond lies above ground clofe to the church of *St. Lorenzo:* the third is fet up at the *Porta del Popolo.*

I AM very glad, faid *Crito's* pupil, that the converfation has turned on this topic. I wifh you would permit your coach, which I fee is waiting for you in this piazza, to carry us now to the obelifk at the *Porta del Popolo.* I have a particular reafon for defiring this favour.

THE young nobleman, and the reft of the com-pany, readily agreed to the propofal.

IN their way from the *Pantheon* to the *Porta del Popolo* the converfation turned upon their in-tended travels to the *Levant.* They were talking of vifiting *Alexandria, Grand Cairo,* and *Luxor;* when, the coach entering the piazza *del Popolo,* their attention was recalled to the magnificence of *Rome.*

THERE

*   *   *

THERE is not perhaps a city in the world, the entrance of which is defigned with more magnificence, than that of *Rome*, by the *Porta del Popolo.* The gate is of the architecture of *Michael Angelo* and *Vignola:* it leads into a piazza, where the two famous *twin-churches* appear in front. Between and on each fide of thefe churches are *three* ftraight level ftreets. The ftreet on the right leads to the *Ripetta* of the *Tiber.* That in the middle is above a mile in length, runs through the midft of the *Campus Martius,* and is terminated by the buildings on the *Capitoline* hill. The ftreet on the left leads to the grand ftair-cafe in the piazzo *di Spagna:* it was intended by *Sixtus Quintus* to have been joined to his long *Strada Felice,* and thus continued quite to the *Amphitheatrum Caftrenfe;* forming one continued ftraight ftreet, of more than two *englifh* miles and an half in length.

IN the midft of the piazza *del Popolo* rifes an *egyptian* obelifk : with the view of which all thefe three ftreets nobly terminate.

THE fhaft of this obelifk was originally one folid mafs of granite. It is eighty-two feet in height,

height, and it's fides are richly covered with hieroglyphics.

It's granite bafis is between twenty and thirty feet high. The infcription engraven on it is to this effect: *Imperator Auguflus Cæfar*, *Egypto in poteflatem populi Romani redactâ*, *Soli donum dedit.*

The company now left their carriage and walked up to the obelifk.—While they were ftanding by the fountain, which flows from it's bafis, *Crito's* pupil prefented a fheet of paper to his tutor. I have been lately compiling an exercife, faid he, to be fubmitted to your correction. It is drawn up in the manner of a vifion. I hope you will excufe my folly in the attempt.

CRITO received the paper with thanks; caft his eye with pleafure over fome part of it's contents; and then returning it to his pupil, defired him to read it to the company.

*   *   *

Some few nights ago, faid his worthy pupil, I dreamt that I was with three of my friends; from whom, indeed, the thoughts of my heart, whether fleeping or waking, are hardly ever divided; and that

that we were ſtanding together in this very place. On a ſudden, we ſaw a female figure before us ; ſuch a figure as we have often obſerved in an‐ cient ſculptures or paintings, repreſenting the *Dea Roma.* She was ſitting by this fountain.

SHE appeared ; but not, as in the times of *Virgil* and *Auguſtus,* enthroned like the tower‐ crowned *Cybele ;*

———*Qualis Berecynthia mater,*——
Læta Deûm partu, centum complexa nepotes,
Omnes cælicolas, omnes ſupera alta tenentes : *

She appeared, as in the *gothic* ages ; proſtrate on the ground ; deſpoiled of all her ornaments ; and weeping over her dying children, her *ſciences* and her *arts.*

IN vain was ſhe endeavouring, like the *Medi‐ cean Niobé,* to ſave from the deſtroyers ſome one of *theſe,* her numerous and beauteous offspring. Some one of theſe, ſhe ſaid, may be ſtill a con‐ ſolation to me, amidſt the ruin of all my wealth and power.

————————ΙΚΕΤΕΥΩ ΤΕ ΣΕ
Μη μου το τεκνον εκ χερων απο σπασης;,

* ÆNEID. vi. 784.

Μηδε

Μη δε κλαυητε· των τεθνηκοτων αλις.
Ταυτη γεγηθα, καπιληθομαι κακων·
Ηδ᾽ αντι πολλων εςι μοι παραψυχη*.

We ſtood for ſome time lamenting over her;
when we heard behind us a ſound, as if of the
ſtring of a harp. I thought at firſt that it had
been the harp of *Spencer* †; but, on turning round,
we perceived to our great ſurprize, that the ſound
proceeded from within the ſhaft of the obeliſk;
the top of which ſeemed juſt at that time to be
illuminated and gilt by the riſing ſun. This ſound
was ſucceeded by a voice, which ſeemed alſo to
proceed from within the ſame obeliſk; but which
was far more clear and diſtinct, than what ever
was feigned to iſſue from the ſtatue of *Memnon* ‡.

"Lament not," it ſaid, " the fall of *Rome*, that
" proud, but now humbled city : lament not her,
" though once the patroneſs of learning. Even
" *Thebes* is fallen, that far more glorious city; the
" ſeat of the great *Hermes*, and the *original*
" ſource of all ſcience to mankind.

---

* See the *Hecuba* of *Euripides.*
† Vide *Spencer's* Poem on the Ruins of *Rome,* and of
Time.
‡ The ſtatue of *Memnon*, which is ſtill remaining near
Thebes, is fabulouſly ſaid to have ſpoken every morning, as
ſoon as the rays of the riſing ſun ſtruck on it's head. *Strabo*,
who pretends that he heard it, ſays, the ſound was like that
of the ſtring of an harp.

" Yet,

" YET bewail not the fall either of *Thebes* or
" *Rome*. Lift up your eyes to a view of the hif-
" tory of the whole world in general: and then
" fall proſtrate before HIM, whoſe awful name
" was, in our language, concealed, under that of
" the *divine and immortal* OSIRIS. Thankfully
" adore His Providence; by which ſcience has
" not been always partially confined to one or two
" countries, but has in various ages been appoint-
" ed to viſit and bleſs various regions: and thus,
" perhaps, before the conſummation of all things,
" will have viſited and illuminated in it's turn
" every country on the face of the earth. Even
" as that moſt glorious emblem of knowledge, the
" Sun, to whom, and to philoſophic literature,
" this obeliſk, *of which I am the Genius*, ſtands
" confecrated, has, before the completion of it's
" annual courſe, diſtributed an equal quantity of
" light to the nations of every climate; from the
" equator to both the poles.

" O THAT it were permitted me to remove the
" veil that covers the face of the great *Iſis;* or
" to explain to you certain fragments of the wif-
" dom of *Egypt!*

" BUT I, it is true, am the inferiour and junior
" one of all the *genii*, who preſide over the great
" obeliſks at *Rome*. Much more properly might

VOL. II.   T   " I refer

" I refer you for fuch inftruction to the *genius* of
" the *Lateran*, or *Rameffean* obelifk, which is
" coeval with the fall of *Troy;* or to the elder.
" *genius* of the *Vatican*, the work of the fon of
" *Sefoftris :* or, rather, to that obelifk, which is
" by far the moft noble and ancient of us all; I.
" mean my fellow-traveller, and now near neigh-
" bour in this *Campus Martius*, the obelifk of
" the great *Sefoftris* himfelf.

" As for my own age, I cannot pretend to any
" great antiquity, being hardly more than twenty-
" four hundred years old; which is equal to be-
" tween feventy and eighty of your tranfitory ge-
" nerations. Yet, fhort as my experience hath
" been, my hiftory may be inftructive, at leaft
" to you, O ye children of yefterday!

" I WAS born in the dregs of time: in the
" laft age of the long *egyptian* hiftory. If my
" memory fail me not, it was in the reign of
" *Pfammiticus* or *Amafis*, nearly coeval with
" fome of the firft kings of *Rome*, that I came
" out of our common mother's womb, the ancient
" cavern of the granite rock of *Syene*.

" I WAS formed into my prefent fhape by di-
" rection of the inhabitants of the neighbouring
" facred ifland; the ifland of *Philæ*, famous for
" the

" the fepulchral temple of the great *Ifis*. As foon
" as my fides were adorned with thefe facred cha-
" racters, that ftill remain fo frefh, I was float-
" ed down the *Nile* from the cataracts to thofe
" level meadows of *Heliopolis*, which are at pre-
" fent the fuburbs of *Grand Cairo*. At *Helio-*
" *polis* I ftood no more than fix or feven centu-
" ries, being removed thence to *Rome*, where
" I have been now fcarce eighteen hundred
" years.

" HAVING been originally confecrated to phi-
" lofophic literature, it has been my chief plea-
" fure to contemplate the variations, the rife, and
" the decline of fcience, in the various places
" and various ages of my life.

" IN my firft voyage from *Syene* to *Heliopolis*,
" I remember, that, in paffing by *Thebes* and
" *Memphis*, I heard much complaint of the de-
" cline of wifdom and virtue in *Egypt;* and many
" prognoftications, too foon fatally verified, were
" announced, portentous of the fpeedy fall of
" that great ftate: that ftate, which, in the glory
" of the antiquity of it's hiftory, in the glory of
" it's univerfal reputation for wifdom and learn-
" ing, and particularly, it's peculiar honour in
" the invention of all arts and fciences, was far

T 2   fuperiour

" fuperiour to any other country, which the fun
" ever faw.

Χαιρε, Χαιρε, Αιγυπ7Ⓖ, η Ͽρεψασα με*.

" On my arrival at *Heliopolis,* I was vifited
" and attentively viewed by the learned men of
" feveral foreign regions, who were then travel-
" ling in *Egypt.*

" Those travellers, who were come from the
" *Euphrates,* and were natives of the *Eaft,* fpoke
" as the *egyptians* did of the decline of literature
" in their countries. Whereas other ftrangers,
" from the *North and Weft,* three particularly I
" remember, whofe names were *Thales, Solon,*
" and *Pythagoras,* joyfully expreffed their hopes,
" that fcience was arifing in *Greece* and it's colo-
" nies. It was at that time, indeed, that the
" *ionians* began to have accefs into *Egypt;* and
" thence derived their philofophy, aftronomy,
" and geometry.

" The fame obfervation I heard in fucceeding
" ages ftill more and more confirmed, by the con-
" verfation of feveral *grecians;* who, during the

---

* Vide Epitaphium Ifidis, apud Diodorum Siculum.

" *perfian*

" *perſian* government, viſited the banks of the
" *Nile:* particularly *Herodotus* and *Hippocrates,*
" *Eudoxus* and *Plato.* How often did this laſt
" great man walk round my baſis, meaſure my
" ſeveral proportions, and diligently ſtudy all the
" philoſophical inſcriptions on my ſides!

" THE viſits of theſe illuſtrious *grecians* were
" my greateſt comfort during the firſt three cen-
" turies of my life; moſt part of which time was
" paſſed under the *perſian* government. How fre-
" quently did I then wiſh for ſome *athenian*
" Εκατοντορ☉, or ſome vaſter veſſel, *ſuch* as were
" afterwards ſeen in *Egypt,* under the reigns of
" the *grecian* kings, to remove me to their
" country, then the moſt glorious ſeat of ſcience;
" and to place me in the grove of *Academus;* or
" before the temple of the goddeſs of Wiſdom, in
" the *Acropolis;* or in ſome other *ſacred* or *philo-*
" *ſophic* part of that famous city of the *egyptian*
" *Cecrops!*

" UNEXPECTEDLY, a great revolution hap-
" pened, in learning as well as in empire. *Egypt*
" was delivered from it's *perſian* tyrants, the ſuc-
" ceſſors of the accurſed *Cambyſes;* and *Greece*
" was torn in pieces by the ſucceſſors of *Alexander*
" the Great. All it's arts and ſciences fled then

" for

" for refuge, as it's gods did formerly, during
" the wars of the *Titans,*

" *Cæruleum in gremium, latebrofaque flumina*
" *Nili ＊.*

" *EGYPT,* their original parent, became now
" their proteƈtrefs; -and the *Ptolomies,* in patro-
" nizing learning, began to rival the glories of
" our ancient *thebaic* and *memphitic* fovereigns.

" With what pleafure did I then frequently
" fee, on the banks of the *Nile,* the poetical *Ara-*
" *tus, Theocritus,* and *Callimachus;* and thofe
" far more exalted charaƈters, *Conon, Euclid,*
" and *Archimedes!* But above all, *Demetrius*
" *Phalereus;* the real author of the mufeum and
" library of *Alexandria,* which dignified *Egypt*
" almoft as much as that of *Ofymanduas.* Happy
" *Alexandria!* if thy princes had joined virtue
" to their love of fcience; and confequently had
" given ftability to the happinefs of themfelves,
" and of their people.

" Why fhould I relate what I faw, during the
" next five hundred years? Carried away captive

＊ Virg. *Æn,* viii, 713.

" from

" from my native country, I had at leaſt the ſatis-
" faction of entering *Rome* in the *Auguſtan* age,
" when all the ſciences were here moſt flouriſhing.

" I soon found however, that human great-
" neſs is equally ſhort and tranſitory, in all parts
" of the earth : within ſome very few ages, know-
" ledge declined, and power expired, *here* alſo.

" But why ſhould I repeat, what is the ſubject
" of much melancholy meditation to all travellers,
" who view here the *mingled ruin* of the arts of
" *Egypt, Greece,* and *Rome;* and ſometimes drop
" a tear on the broken coloſſal ſtatues of the *Tiber*
" and the *Nile,* which, not without reaſon, are
" joined together, both on the *Vatican* and *Capi-*
" *toline* hills?

" The ſtorms, which laid waſte the *roman*
" empire, came firſt from the north. I remember
" the dreadful thunderings and blackneſs, with
" which they approached this country, and
" threatened it's deſolation! The land before
" them was then beautiful, beautiful as the land
" of *Egypt:* behind them, a howling wilderneſs!

" Soon the tempeſt became general. *Alaric*
" burſt from the north. Not forty years after-
" wards came *Genſeric,* the revenger of old
" *Carthage,*

" *Carthage,* from the fouth. In the following
" century, *Totilas* made a frefh irruption from
" the north.

" How different were thofe days of terrour and
" of darknefs, from the calm and benign feafons
" which fhone upon this city in the *Auguftan*
" age!

" In thofe repeated hurricanes, or *typhóns,* all
" we, the *egyptian* obelifks at *Rome,* excepting
" the fortunate *Vatican,* bowed our venerable
" heads to the duft: like a grove of tall *thebaic*
" palms, torn up by whirlwinds, driving from the
" deferts of *Lybia* or *Æthiopia.*

" We lay buried, and, with us, all the arts
" and fciences of the weft, for near a thoufand
" years."

Some confufion now rofe in my ideas, according to the ufual incoherency of dreams. The
figure of the *Dea Roma* was vanifhed from our
fight. The *genius* of the obelifk feemed, however, to be ftill continuing his hiftory.

" During the long thoufand years of my in-
" terment, the chief remains of the learning of
" *Europe* were preferved in it's native fpot, the
" dominions

" dominions of *Greece.* It was alſo ſome conſo-
" lation to me in my grave to be informed, for
" the race of the *Genii* communicate and receive
" information by many methods inexplicable to
" human ears, that, under the *arabian caliphs,*
" the learning of *Aſia* and of *Africa* was then re-
" viving in it's native ſeats; the banks of the
" *Euphrates,* and of my beloved *Nile.*

" BUT the violence of the *turkiſh* arms drove
" them all again weſtward.

" ON the revival of arts and ſciences in the weſt,
" many of the *egyptian* obeliſks at *Rome,* aroſe
" again from the duſt, as if become the *taliſ-*
" *mans* of ſcience for renovated *Italy.*

" WE were then re-placed by *Sixtus Quintus.*
" At that time I thought the *Auguſtan* age was in
" ſome meaſure returned hither. I ſaw that pope
" imitate *Agrippa* in the uſeful work of his foun-
" tains and aqueducts, and in the noble ſtructure
" of the dome of *St. Peter's,* built nearly with the
" ſame dimenſions as thoſe of the *Pantheon.* I ſaw
" him imitate *Auguſtus,* in adorning this city with
" various embelliſhments; and in forming that
" great repoſitory of literature at the *Vatican,*
" which is almoſt as famous in modern times,

" as

" as were the *Palatine* or *Alexandrian* in former
" ages.

" BUT now again I begin to hear of the de-
" cline of fcience in *Italy*. Science is faid to be
" far more flourifhing on the other fide of the
" *Alps*, in fome of your weftern regions of
" *Europe:* nay, it is faid to be likely to travel
" ftill further weftward; even to the diftant
" countries beyond the *Atlantic* ocean, which
" I fuppofe are the fame with thofe famous great
" iflands, about which I remember to have heard
" the priefts of *Sais* difcourfing with *Plato.*

" PERHAPS, by fome future generation, I fhall
" be removed from my prefent bafis; and em-
" barked on a voyage to the fhores of that weftern
" world; to adorn the ftreets of fome ftately
" city, the foundations of which are not yet laid.

" SOME of the defcendants of your great
" grand-children may perhaps fee me there. But
" your eyes, O ye prefent youthful generation,
" will foon be clofed. Your bones, with the
" coffins which fhall contain them, will be foon
" reduced to duft. Oh, how fhort do the days
" of man appear to me! The time of your ex-
" iftence is as nothing."———

THE

THE *genius* of the obelifk proceeded to fome further reflections on the brevity of human life. But I am not able properly to repeat them to the company. From *my* lips they would found merely like common-place reflections. As fpoken by the *obelifk*, you may imagine they had a much more powerful effect.

CRITO'S pupil now rolled up his paper; and to prevent any compliments from his friends, who he knew would be *partial* in his favour, propofed to ftep into the carriage again.

THE young nobleman told the coachman to drive to the church of *St. Lorenzo.*

IN their way to that part of the *Campus Martius,* the eldeft of the young gentlemen converfed much with his noble friend, on the fucceffive rife and fall of many feats of fcience, *Thebes, Memphis, Alexandria, Babylon, Athens,* and *Rome:* not without beftowing on his own country the fond, patriotic wifh, *Efto perpetua!* Words worthy to be the dying fpeech of every good man.

HE was repeating them with an emphatic warmth, when the coach ftopped. *Crito* then led the company into a fmall back area, where they faw that famous obelifk, to which, as to an eternal

nal monument, the great *Sefoſtris*, in ſome meaſure, configned the hiſtory of his glory; inſcribing
upon it the extent of his empire, and the number
of his tributary nations. They ſaw it, over-
turned; broken in ſeveral fragments; half covered with filth and rubbiſh; *omni inquinatum
contumelia*;* and proportionately, in as low a
ſtate of ruin and humiliation, as the glory of it's
founder was ever exalted: that proud and inſo-
lent man, who ſo arrogantly ſtyled himſelf *king of
kings,* and *lord of lords!*

Two of it's ſides are intirely maimed and obli-
terated by fire; injuries repeatedly received in
the times of *Cambyſes, Totilas,* and *Robert* of
Normandy. On the other two ſides, and on it's
top, are ſeveral inſcriptions and figures, which
may juſtly be thought the moſt ancient ſculptures
now extant in the whole world†. They are of
ſuch excellent workmanſhip, as plainly to demon-
ſtrate, that the *greek* and *roman* art of ſculpture
was founded on the primeval arts of *Egypt.* Theſe

---

* PHÆDR. I. ii. 21.

† The extreme antiquity of this obeliſk will appear to
the reader in a ſtronger light, when he recollects, that it
was hewn into it's preſent ſhape before any of the pyramids
were built. From *Pliny's* account, this obeliſk was the
work of *Sefoſtris:* and according to all the *greek* hiſtorians,
Sefoſtris was prior in antiquity to *Cheops, Cephren,* or any
of the builders of the pyramids,

figures

figures and infcriptions have been, for many centuries paft, utterly unintelligible.

THE fame fate attends all the other monuments
in *Upper Egypt.* For though their materials and
fabric feem capable of an eternal duration, yet
owing to this defeft, they have not been able to
preferve with *certainty* even the *names* of moft of
their founders. —Thefe were the refleftions of
the young nobleman.

PERHAPS, added he, the time may come, when
the *latin* infcription, which *Auguſtus* has engraved
on the bafis, and which feems as frefh as if the
fculptor had finifhed it but laft week, will be
found as unintelligible as thefe hieroglyphic charafters*.

WHILE the young nobleman was expreffing
thefe fentiments, *Crito* ftood for fome time in
filence, fixing his eyes on the vaft ruins of the
fhaft of the obelifk.

Is not this, faid he, *a ſtrong emblem of the vanity of the greateſt human grandeur?* Such is become the monument and memorial of the proudeft

* This infcription is to the fame effeft as that on the bafis
of the obelifk at *Porta del Popolo,* mentioned in p. 270. of
this volume.

of kings. How awful is this fpectacle! and how inftructive, not only to the philofophic moralift, but even to the moft humble and mortified faint!

Oh, fons of earth! attempt ye ftill to rife
By mountains pil'd on mountains to the fkies?
Heav'n ftill, with laughter, the vain toil furveys,
And buries madmen in the heaps they raife*.

BUT what,—continued he, after another fhort but folemn paufe,—what has become of the *empire* of *Egypt* itfelf?

RUINED, like this *obelifk*; and fallen, never to rife again.

AN example for ever to mankind, that no excellence of fituation, for *Egypt* was almoft as well fituate as any *ifland;* no degree of populoufnefs or power, of wealth or fcience, is able to fecure a nation from ruin and perpetual fervitude; whenever the people, as was the cafe in the decline of *Egypt,* fhall for the love of luxury quit the love of virtue; whenever it's governors fhall think wifdom to be confiftent with felf-intereft and pride: thus defpifing GOD, and injuring mankind; inftead of labouring with joy to be the be-

---

* POPE's *Effay on Man.* ep. iv.

nefactors of their fellow-creatures, and the dutiful fervants of their great and common Creator.

Saying this, *Crito* looked with his ufual kindnefs on his pupil, and repeated to him the following moft poetic lines of the *hebrew* prophet; leaving him to judge, which of the *great modern* cities of the world might moft fuitably bear their application.

Art thou better than the populous city of Ammon?
She that was feated among the waters?
The river of Egypt *was her defence:*
The fea was her dominion and riches.
Lybia *and* Africa *were her helpers:*
Æthiopia *and* Egypt *were her infinite ftrength.*
Yet even fhe went into captivity:
Even fhe was deftroyed utterly *.

O my dear pupil, though I am no prophet, let me contemplate, in imagination, the *probable* hiftory of future ages.

Two thoufand years hence, fome foreigners will perhaps be going up the *Thames,* in fearch of antiquities; in the fame manner as *Norden* lately went up the *Nile.*

* See Nahum, iii. 8—10.

SAILING

SAILING by the ruins of *Greenwich*, they will look to *Flamstead's* hill; they will recollect the name of *Newton*, and of other ancient *english* aftronomers: *How is this ifland degenerated!* they will perhaps add. *It has not at prefent one fchool of mathematics, or of natural philofophy, in any of it's provinces.*

ROWING then along the wide-fpread defolation of *London**, they will pafs through fome arches of it's broken bridges, ftanding in the middle of the ftream. On the graffy fhore, they will view, with admiration, the ftill remaining portico of *St. Paul's*, and perhaps one of the towers of *Weftminfter* Abbey. They will land there; and be fhown the pool of water, where *Weftminfter* Hall, and the Parliament Houfes ftood. They will inquire in vain for *St. James's* palace. On fearching for it in a wrong place, they will accidentally difcover the portico of *St. Martin's*, then again *in the Fields:* they will find it's columns, half buried in the earth.

IF they continue their voyage up the *Thames*, they will pafs clofe by the once elegant fituation of the brick palace at *Hampton-Court*, without

---

* Londinium,—*copiâ negotiatorum, et commeatuum, maximè celebre.* See *Tacit.* Annal. lib. xiv. c. 33.

knowing

knowing it. Advanced fome leagues farther, they will fee from their boat the ftately remains of *Windfor* caftle: but perhaps they will not venture to land, for fear of falling into the hands of the wild inhabitants of the neighbouring woods. The fame fear will damp their defire, and defign, of venturing fo far as to the much-celebrated, but little known, ruins of *Oxford*.

AND do you really think, replied the eldeft of the young gentlemen, that the *englifh* can ever grow as wild as the *arabs*, or the *nubians*?

IT is by no means impoffible, replied *Crito*. Length of time, and a variety of events, may gradually produce fuch a change. The *englifh* nation, two thoufand years hence, *may* very poffibly be in the fame ftate of favage barbarifm, in which it is faid to *have been* two thoufand years ago:

Rurfus & in veterem fato revoluta figuram *.

BUT let us think of retiring to our lodgings. The fun is fet, and the dangerous evening damps of this country begin to make themfelves felt.

* VIRGIL, *Æn.* vi. 449.

Let us take care, what care we can, of thefe our frail bodies. Notwithftanding all our care, they will foon be diffolved, as you my dear pupil, have reminded us, into their original duft.

CHAP.

CHAP. III.

TWENTY-FIRST DAY'S CONVERSATION.

Cedes coemptis faltibus ; & domo,
Villaque, flavus quam Tiberis lavit,
　Cedes, & extructis in altum
　　Divitiis potietur hæres.
Divefne prifco natus ab Inacho
Nil intereft, an pauper, & infimâ
　De gente fub dio morêris,
　　Victima nil miferantis Orci.
Omnes eodem cogimur ; omnium
Verfatur urna ; feriùs ocyùs
　Sors exitura.

　　　　　　HORAT. *Carm.* lib ii. od. 3.

THE maufoleum of *Auguftus* was built in the *Campus Martius;* fronting, though at fome dif-tance, the *Pantheon* of *Agrippa.* It was of a circular fhape, and nearly of the fame fize with that noble temple.

THE walls, though not the roof, of this mau-foleum are ftill remaining. The circular fpace

U 2

within

within the walls is one hundred and feventy feet
in diameter, and at prefent forms a garden, filled
with orange trees and other fragrant evergreens.

In this garden *Crito* was fitting with his pupil
on the morning of *june* 19th, and attending to him
as he read the above lines of *Horace;* when, feeing the two other young gentlemen enter the gate,
he rofe to meet them.

Before the company began their ufual morning lecture, they took feveral turns together,
around and acrofs the garden.

After fome agreeable talk on various fubjects,
Crito's pupil led their attention to the beauty of
the flowers and fhrubs among which they were
walking.—Thefe, faid he, are at prefent the only
ornaments remaining of this imperial maufoleum.
Perhaps fome of thefe plants may be the defcendants of thofe, which flourifhed here in the time
of *Strabo**.   Such chearfully-looking plants and
flowers feem, indeed, no improper embellifhments
for the manfions of death.

I have often thought, while walking in the
neat church-yard belonging to my father's village,

---

* Αξιολογωτατον το Μαυσολειον καλημενον, επι κρηπιδ☉ λευκολιζ☉
πρ☉ τω ποταμω χωμα, αχρι κορυφης τοις αειθελεσι των δενδρων κατ-
εζιφες.   Lib. v. p. 236.

that

that it is right to take fuch methods of abating the gloominefs of the grave, and of foftening it's natural horrours.

THESE fragrant myrtles, thefe fhining-leaved laurels, may be confidered, as if planted here on purpofe to ftand *emblems of the memory of the departed.* They may be confidered alfo, as reprefenting the *immortality* of the foul.

I COULD wifh, my dear pupil, replied *Crito*, that among your poetic works at *Rome*, you would favour me with an ode to *Euthanafia;* or, if you have a mind to exprefs that idea by another phrafe, the *Genius of good death.*

WITH regard to mortality in general, *Horace* will fuggeft to you feveral elegant reflections; though I do not fuppofe, you will choofe to follow his train of thought, in the inferences which he ufually draws from thofe reflections.

YOU may find other claffical affiftance. *Virgil* fometimes confidered death in a much better light than *Horace:* for, notwithftanding *Horace's* many focial virtues, *Virgil* was, certainly, a much better man. You will recollect, I am fure, with pleafure, thofe lines of the fourth Æneid, in which

Iris

Iris is defcribed, as engaged in the benign and gracious office of the genius of death.

Tum Juno omnipotens, longum miferata dolorem,
Difficilefque obitus, Irim demifit Olympo,
Quæ luctantem animam, nexofque refolveret artus.—
Ergo Iris, croceis per cælum rofcida pennis,
Mille trahens varios adverfo fole colores,
Devolat, & fuprà caput aftitit : Hunc ego Diti
Sacrum juffa fero, teque ifto corpore folvo *.

You will wifh, for the fake of greater pro-priety in this paffage, that *Dido's* life had been more virtuous, and her death in particular much more holy. In fuch a cafe, this beautiful defcrip-tion of *Iris* would have anfwered your ideas of a guardian angel, defcending from heaven, to re-leafe a foul ftruggling in the laft agonies of mor-tality, and to difengage her from the incumbrances of duft.

INDEED, when you contemplate thofe confo-lations and overflowing joys, that make the hour of death moft fweet to *good* men; you will difdain, I fhould apprehend, to draw up your ode in the mean ftyle of heathen poetry. You will much more gladly follow the foaring ideas of fome chriftian writers : you will dedicate your ode,

* ÆNEID iv. 693.

not

not to the *Genius,* but to the *Angel of good death.*

You will paint that angel defcending, in radiant fplendour, to vifit the couch of the expiring faint. You will place around that couch Charity, Hope, and true Faith, with her victorious crofs :

> —— *ea fola voluptas,*
> *Solamenque mali.*
>
> ÆNEID. iii. 66o.

You will perhaps attempt to defcribe the departing fpirit, as juft freed from the flefh, and following this blelfed company in their re-afcent to heaven. You may form fome happy and pious ideas, fitted for the purpofe, from that picture, which our noble young friend lately taught us to admire in the *Capitoline* gallery ; the *Anima Beata* of *Guido* *.

I SHOULD be very glad, replied the modeft youth, to obey your commands. But the fubject

---

* *Le delfein de la figure eft de la plus grande correction. Sur fon vifage brille cette ferenité, cette douce fatisfaction, que l'on doit éprouver aux approches d'un bonheur inalterable.—C'eft une des compofitions les plus fçavantes du* Guide—*l'action en eft très-fimple, & en même tems très-poëtique.*
Abbe Richard, vol. vi. p. 27.

is

is too good, and too great. I cannot venture upon it. Such an ode would be a very proper conclufion and crown to the labours of a pious gray-headed poet; whofe long life has been fpent in following the dictates of true faith and charity, and in looking forward to it's end with devout hope. But I am neither worthy nor capable of the grand employment. It is much better to be filent, than to talk of fo important a topic in a trifling and improper manner, as I certainly fhould.

THE company now fat down near a fpreading orange-tree. They admired it's beauty. The eldeft of the young gentlemen began to make a comparifon between this *plant*, the branches of which were loaded at once with the productions of *all* the feafons in the year, buds, flowers, and fruit; and this maufoleum, which has the honour of containing the remains of many worthies, who died young, middled-aged, and old, in all the various feafons of human life.

HAPPY is it for you, my dear young friends, replied *Crito*, that there are none of thefe productions, whether on the tree, or gathered, fweeter than the *bud*. *Marcellus's* virtue, both in life and death, was full as fweet and lovely as even that of *Agrippa* himfelf.

MARCELLUS.

*   *   *

MARCELLUS.

Nor love thy life, nor hate: But what thou liv'ft,
Live well: How long or fhort, permit to heav'n.
MILTON, *P. L.* b. xi. l. 553.

MARCELLUS, nephew and fon-in-law of *Auguftus*, and his declared fucceffor in the impe-rial throne of *Rome*, was fuddenly removed by death, from all this poffeffion and profpeƈt of grandeur. He was cropped in the very flower of his youth, when fcarce twenty years of age.

YET had he made fo good an ufe of his time, as to have then already gained the affeƈtion and efteem of mankind, to a very confiderable de-gree.

FOR, during the age of *Auguftus*, which was certainly in fome refpeƈts a very fplendid epoch of the *roman* hiftory, although feveral truly great charaƈters appeared; of whom fome, and in par-ticular, *Agrippa*, may more juftly demand our *admiration;* yet none of them has been regarded, cither in that or in fucceeding times, with fuch
gencral

general *love,* as the memory of this amiable young man.

AMOR ERAT POPULI ROMANI.

In a courfe of reflection upon the amiable character and immature fate of *Marcellus,* I have often, faid the young nobleman, recollected prince *Henry,* elder brother of *Charles* the Firft.—Excufe the intrufion, which yourfelf occafioned: pray proceed.

In meditating on the character of *Marcellus,* replied *Crito,* I alfo have often recollected fome modern characters: particularly one of a young nobleman of my acquaintance. May his life be much longer than that of *Marcellus:* but may he continue to refemble him in every other particular!

MARCELLUS'S perfon was naturally very beautiful: it was improved in gracefulnefs as well as ftrength, by his perfection in all youthful exercifes: but his mind was ftill more great and noble. *Animo alacer erat: ingenio potens.*

These qualifications however, whether of *body* or of *underftanding,* were but trifling, in comparifon

parifon with thofe of his *heart. Adolefcens patiens erat laboris; voluptatibus alienus: frugalitatis & continentiæ in illis, aut annis, aut opibus, non mediocriter admirandus.*

ALL his actions were full of wifdom, of courage, of modefty, of affability, of kindnefs.

THERE was nothing, indeed, kind or good, which the fubjects of *Auguftus* did not hope, from the government of *Marcellus.* *Fortunæ erat, in quam alebatur, capax.*

No wonder, that his bier was followed by fuch *general* lamentations.

Mater Octavia nullum finem, per omne vitæ fuæ tempus, flendi gemendique fecit. Lugubrem veftem nunquam depofuit. Intenta in unam rem (memoriam fcilicet cariffimi filii) & toto animo affixa, talis per omnem vitam fuit, qualis in funere.

BUT *Auguftus* fuffered by this great lofs in a double capacity; as a relation, and as a *roman.*

In Marcellum enim Auguftus incumbere cœperat; in Marcellum onus imperii reclinare. Laturus enim erat Marcellus quantumcunque illi avunculus imponere, &, ut ita dicam, inædificare voluiffet.

voluiffet. Bene enim legerat nulli ceffura ponderi fundamenta.

THIS eulogium was drawn by the pen of *Seneca**, many years after the death of *Marcellus;* at a time, when no temptation could poffibly exift, for any court-flattery to his memory. It greatly confirms the truth of many paffages, which we find in the poets of the *Auguftan age*, relative to *Marcellus's* merit.

I REMEMBER feveral of the kind in the works of *Horace*. Perhaps there may be fome alfo in *Ovid*. *Virgil*, as my pupil thinks, feems to have fhadowed out the amiable charaĉter of *Marcellus*, under thofe of *Pallas* and *Euryalus*. However that may be, he certainly introduces a very ftriking and noble panegyric on his memory, in thofe famous verfes of the fixth Æneid. They feem, indeed, to have breathed no lefs the fpirit of fincere grief, than of the fweeteft poetry.

THE deep forrow of *Auguftus* feems juftly depiĉted by the language of *Anchifes*, in the lines that follow:

——————— *Manibus date lilia plenis:*
Purpureos fpargam flores, animamque nepotis

* Confol, ad Martiam.

His

*His faltem accumulem donis, & fungar inani
Munere*.*

AUGUSTUS honoured *Marcellus's* memory
with the moſt ſolemn funeral rites. He himſelf
ſpoke the funeral oration ; *non quidem ſolitâ ſuâ
promptâ ac profluenti eloquentiâ†*; for, doubtleſs,
it was interrupted by frequent ſighs and groans,
riſing no leſs from the ſurrounding multitude, than
from the orator's own breaſt.

AUGUSTUS then, with his own hands, placed
the urn in *this* mauſoleum. He had erected this
beautiful ſtructure for the reception of the urns of
his family, and friends. He in particular had
declared, that he would not, even after his death,
be ſeparated from thoſe two perſons, *Agrippa* and
Marcellus, whom in his life-time he had ſo highly
eſteemed, and ſo tenderly loved‡.

*   *   *

THE eldeſt of the young gentlemen now fixed
his eyes on the ground, and ſeemed, for a while,
abſorpt in a train of recollection.

---

* ÆNEID vi. v. 883.
† *Tacit.* Annal. lib. xiii. c. 3.
‡ See *Dio.* p. 541.

PARDON me, faid he, for interrupting you, by
the introduction of a topic, in fome meafure foreign to your prefent difcourfe. *Voltaire*, in that
part of his *Henriade*, where he defcribes the fpirit
of *St. Lewis* fhowing to *Henry* the Fourth the
yet unborn heroes and worthies of the *french* nation, has clofely imitated the paffage you have
quoted from *Virgil*, and very properly applied
it to that amiable young prince, the duke of *Burgundy.*

Quel eſt ce jeune prince, en qui la majeſté
Sur ſon viſage aimable èclate ſans fierté?
D'un œil d'indifference il regarde le trone.
Ciel! quelle nuit foudaine à mes yeux l'environne!
La Mort autour de lui vole ſans s'arrêter:
Il tombe aux pieds du trone, étant pret d'y monter.
O mon fils! des françois vous voyez le plus juſte:
Les cieux le formeront de votre ſang auguſte.
Grand Dieu! ne faites-vous que montrer aux hu-
mains
Cette fleur paſſagere, ouvrage de vos mains?
Hélas! que n'eût point fait cette âme vertueuſe?
La France, fous ſon regne, eût été trop heureuſe.
Il eût entretenu l'abondance & la paix:
Mon fils! Il eut compté ſes jours par ſes bienfaits.
Il eût aimé ſon peuple. O jours remplis d'alarmes!
O combien les françois vont repandre de larmes,
Quand

Quand fous la même tombe ils verront réunis
Et l'époux & la femme, & la mere & le fils*!

WHILST I was at *Paris* I took frequent morning airings in my chaife, towards *Vincennes* and *St. Denis:* and in thofe excurfions read over thefe lines of *Voltaire* fo often, as to imprint them thoroughly on my memory.

LOUIS le Grand is faid to have been, in feveral refpects, a fecond *Auguflus.* They were both examples, indeed, of the vanity and weaknefs of the greateft human grandeur. *Louis* ftrongly refembled *Auguflus* in his family misfortunes, at that melancholy time efpecially, when fo many funeral cars clofely followed each other along the avenue to *St. Denis;* bearing the beloved duke of *Burgundy,* and many others of the royal family.

PERMIT me, faid *Crito,* to read to you, from my paper of notes, fome elegant verfes of *Albinovanus,* relative to thefe misfortunes of *Auguflus.* Far am I from recommending his poem in general to your perufal, for the flattery of fome parts of it is even impious, but only fome extracts from it. They feem to have been compofed by *Albinovanus, on this very fpot,* where we are now converfing.

---

* LA HENRIADE, *Chant* vii. v. 399, &c.

Condidit

Condidit Agrippam quo te, Marcelle, fepulchro,
  Et cepit generos jam locus ifte duos.
Vix pofito Agrippâ tumuli bene janua claufa eft,
  Perficit officium funeris ecce foror.
Ecce ter ante datis jactura noviffima, Drufus
  A magno lacrymas Cæfare quartus habet.
Claudite jam, Parcæ, nimiùm referata fepulchra!
  Claudite! plus jufto jam domus ifta patet.

CRITO'S pupil now rofe from his feat, and took a fhort turn by himfelf in the garden.

THE company followed him. How eagerly, my dear friends, faid he have we heretofore furveyed together the fepulchres of our *englifh* princes, in *Weftminfter Abbey!* How filently have we ftood by the monument of *Edward's* royal confort; or walked over the duft of that excellent queen *Matilda,* who lies near *Edward* the Confeffor's tomb; though without any gravestone to mark the place! Surely not lefs pleafing is the melancholy, which now overfpreads the mind, while thus we are recollecting the amiable characters of feveral perfons *here* interred: I mean thofe eminently virtuous princes, whofe names you juft now mentioned; and who fleep under the orange-trees, and beds of flowers, among which we are now walking. Let us not furvey this garden with a carelefs eye, or tread

it

it inattentively. Who knows, but under thefe dew-befprinkled violets, the good *Octavia* may be repofing? if fo,

> *Gentle lady, may thy grave*
> *Peace and honour ever have!*

You remember, my dear friend, the defcription of that beautiful myrtle, which is faid to have flourifhed from the tomb of *Ariftonous** : perhaps, in fome of *thefe* myrtles, the afhes of *Agrippa* may really vegetate.

Look again at that fweet half-opened rofe, to which you were juft now fmelling without cropping it : may it not have fixed it's root in the urn of a *Drufus*, or a *Germanicus*?

CRITO'S pupil now took out of his pocket a fmall volume of *englifh* poems, and read to the company the following lines :

---

* See the charming adventures of *Ariftonous*, which are generally printed at the end of thofe of *Telemachus*.

Une mirthe, d'une verdure & d'une odeur exquife, naquit au milieu du tombeau ; & éleva fa tête touffue, pour couvrir les deux urnes de fes rameaux, & de fon ombre. Chacun s'écria, qu' Ariftonous, en recompenfe de fa vertu, avoit été changé par les Dieux en un arbre fi beau. Sophronime prit foin de l' arrofer lui-même, & de l' honorer comme une divinité. Cet arbre, loin de vieillir, fe renouvelle de dix ans en dix ans ; & les Dieux ont voulu faire voir par cette merveille, que la vertu, qui jette un fi doux parfum dans la mémoire des hommes, ne meurt jamais.

Perhaps, unknowing of the bloom it gives,
In yon fair fcyon of Apollo's *tree*
  The facred duft of young Marcellus *lives!*
Pluck not the leaf: 'twere facrilege to wound
  Th' ideal memory of fo fweet a fhade.
In thefe fad feats an early grave he found,
  And the firft rites to gloomy Dis *convey'd.*
Oh, loft too foon! Yet why lament a fate,
  By thoufands envy'd, and by heav'n approv'd*?

Such lamentations are indeed very improper; as I remember my parents mutually agreed, fome years ago, when beginning to recover from their deep affliction, on the death of my younger brother. " Man," faid my father, fitting near the good youth's picture, " Man, fhort fighted as he is at beft, ought ever to adore with reverence and thankfulnefs, the wife and gracious difpofals of Providence. We fee, indeed, frequently removed from this world, in early youth, thofe perfons, who feemed likely to do much good, and to enjoy great happinefs amongft us. Yet, let us not complain. We are certain, that good perfons are much happier in the other world than in this; and we may be confident, that GOD will never want inftruments of his beneficence here

---

* *Unde fcis an diutiùs illi vivere expedierit? An illi hâc morte confultum?* SENECA, ad Martiam.

below."

below." In faying thefe words, my dear father kindly took me and my little fifter in his arms.

CRITO now caft a look of affectionate tender- nefs on his pupil: How much more pleafing, faid he, are your ideas, than thofe on which I was ruminating?

I was imagining, *that I faw Auguftus* bear the urn of *Marcellus* into this maufoleum.

WITH what earneftnefs muft *Auguftus then* have fecretly wifhed, that he had lived, and that he had died, like *Marcellus!* How deeply, in the bitter- nefs of confcience, muft he then have reflected on the great difference of his own youthful years, from thofe of his happy nephew?

THE extreme wickednefs of *Auguftus's* youth muft always have been a very heavy burthen on his mind. It is true, there were fome allevia- tions of this confcious weight: for it is allowed, that, during the laft forty years of his life, he was diligent, and fuccefsful, in doing good.

SEVERAL political writers imagine, that the whole life of *Auguftus* was ruled by one mean principle, the fcheme of obtaining and fecuring to himfelf the fovereign authority: that the crimes

of

of his youth were perpetrated to obtain this power; and that the good works of his later years were performed merely to fecure himfelf in it. But an ecclefiaftic can fcarcely be of that opinion: he cannot think it poffible, that any man, engaged in a long courfe of beneficence, though perhaps he might enter on that courfe not from the beft motives, fhould be able to avoid being at length captivated by a *fincere* love of virtue, and converted to it from his *heart.*

WITH pleafure let us recolleƈt fome of the many inftances of beneficence, with which the years of *Auguftus's* manhood and old age were adorned.

HE encouraged *population*, that firft work of a good government. *Neceffe eft enim, ut nafcantur homines, priufquàm felices fiant.*

HE was ambitious to fupport the general *peace* of mankind. *Janum quater claufit.*

HE wifely placed the glory of his government in works of beneficence. Through how many cities have we travelled, which were built by *Auguftus!* How often have we met with the remains of his other public ftruƈtures! Let us recolleƈt what were our fentiments on this fubjeƈt, when at

Treves,

Treves or *Augsburg;* when at *Autun* or *Turin;* and since our arrival in *Italy*, while travelling along the sea coast near *Rimini* and *Pesaro.*

IN these great works of national utility, *Augustus* seems to have imitated the generosity and public spirit of his noble friend and counsellor, *Agrippa.*

I REMEMBER, said the young nobleman, some of the reflections, with which you favoured us in visiting *Augustus's* bridge at *Narni.* You there compared *Angustus*, in those works, to a late emperor of *China.*

THAT *chinese* emperor, replied *Crito*, was in several respects a very worthy prince: he was a protector of the christians*. But let us at present confine ourselves to *Augustus.*

MUCH of the felicity enjoyed by mankind, in this part of the world, during the reign of *Augustus*, is doubtless to be attributed to his benefi-

---

* The emperor *Cambi*, who died in 1722, in his last testament congratulated himself on the vast sums he had expended during his reign in making new canals, new dykes, new roads, and other public works. In looking over his accounts he had found, to his great joy, that the whole sums he had expended on his own palace, did not amount to the *hundredth* part of what he had laid out in works of utility to his subjects.

Political Annals of abbé *St. Pierre*, 1725,

cent government. It conveyed many bleffings to the inhabitants of this city, and of the country at large; and probably, alfo, to all the provinces and allies of the *roman* empire.

LET me with particular pleafure obferve, that *Augustus* enacted feveral laws, tending to the *reformation of manners:* that he very diligently and mercifully himfelf adminiftered *juftice:* and that he was alfo very careful for the fecurity of public *plenty;* according to that boafted maxim of *venetian* policy: *Giuftitia fempre in palazzo, e pane in piazza.*

THAT *Augustus* greatly promoted *literature,* is perhaps, comparatively, but a *trifling* confideration. For as, in private life, it will be much more laudable for you, my dear pupil, to be daily employed in giving bread to the poor families of your neighbourhood, than to be amufing yourfelf in your library, by the profecution of any learned or elegant compofition; fo, amidft the occupations of a prince, the fupport of public plenty is ten thoufand times more ufeful, and more truly honourable, than the patronage of learning.

ON entering this garden about half an hour ago, faid the young nobleman, I ftopped for fome moments to look at the antique ftatue of

Plenty,

Plenty, with her coruncopiæ, which ſtands by the door. My political friend, who was with me, thought that ſtatue very fortunately and properly placed at the entrance of *Auguſtus's* mauſoleum.

I REMEMBER very well, ſaid the eldeſt of the young gentlemen, turning to *Crito's* pupil, the *venetian* proverb, which your good tutor men‧tions. I thought frequently of it during our voyage from *Venice* to *Pola*.

How pleaſantly, replied *Crito's* pupil, did we paſs our time at *Pola!* We ſat down, I remember, between the four columns of the portico of that temple, which is inſcribed *ROMÆ & Auguſto Cæſari, Patri Patriæ*. You there employed an hour in peruſing, not without tears of pleaſure, the account given by *Suetonius* of the many teſ‑timonies of ardent affection, which *Auguſtus* re‑ceived from his grateful people. The inhabitants of *Rome*, the buſy multitudes which then ſwarmed in the cities of *Italy*, and over every part of her fruitful hills and plains, all united in the love of their ſovereign. The other ſubjects of the *roman* empire, ſettled in the various parts of *Europe*, *Aſia*, and *Africa*, all joined their juſtly-merited thanks for his goodneſs, *in bene gerendâ, per ter‑rarum orbem, republicâ*.

THE

THE *navigators of the Mediterranean*, replied the eldeſt of the young gentlemen, *were not leſs ſenſible of the general happineſs.* As the whole circuit of it's ſhores was then ſubjeƈt to *Rome*, and as the whole *roman* empire was then united in peace under *Auguſtus*, commerce conſequently had in general no enemy to fear. The fleets ſtationed by *Auguſtus* at *Frejus*, *Miſeno*, and *Ravenna*, were always ready to ſuppreſs any unforeſeen troubles.

THE greateſt branch of the *roman* commerce was that with *Egypt**. *Auguſtus* ſeems to have given peculiar attention to it's cultivation and improvement. I think *Suetonius* ſays, that *Auguſtus*, in the laſt year of his reign, viſited the ſea-coaſt at *Baiæ* and *Puteoli.* He went thither, perhaps, with ſome ſmall expeƈtation, that the waters might be of ſervice to a conſtitution naturally weak ; and then particularly enfeebled by a diſorder, which, together with the weight of years, was ſinking him to his grave. During his reſidence there, he muſt have found great amuſement in viewing the *Lucrine* port, and the haven near *Miſeno*, the works of his departed friend, *Agrippa;* works, in which indeed they were *both* engaged, during very troubleſome times. But

* See the late edition of *Harris's* voyages, book i. chap. 2, ſeƈtions 8, 9, 10.

while

while *Augustus* was thus amusing himself, a large ship from *Alexandria* came into the harbour with full sails*.

THE crew, hearing that their emperor was then in that port, gladly seized this opportunity of expressing their loyalty and gratitude to him, under whose mild and wise government peace and commerce had long flourished. *Per illum se vivere: per illum navigare; libertate atque fortunis per illum frui.*

WITH what pleasure must *Augustus* have listened to those acclamations! With what sparkling eyes must he have seen the mariners hanging garlands of flowers on the prow, on the poup, on all the masts, and yard-arms of their vessel; while the smooth haven of *Baiæ* echoed to the sound of their harps and flutes! From the deck a cloud of incense arose to heaven; offered for the preservation of their sovereign's life, and for the long continuance of his benign reign.

PARDON me for troubling you with the repetition of this story. Indeed, whenever I recol-

---

* In relation to the appearance of the *alexandrian* ships, when entering the harbour of *Baiæ*, see *Seneca's* Epist. 77. *Gratus illarum (navium alexandrinarum) Campaniæ aspectus est; omnis in pilis Puteolorum turba consistit, &c.*

lect

left it, I am fenfible of frefh pleafure. As an *englifhman,* I find myfelf always peculiarly inter-efted in the fentiments of the fea-faring part of mankind.

The firft time I read this ftory was about two years ago, when I was at *Margate,* in the ifle of *Thanet;* attending my father, who was advifed by his phyficians to bathe there.

I REMEMBER I then heartily wifhed, that his majefty, our late good old king, *George* II, had been at that time defired by his phyficians to vifit the fame place.

If fuch had been the cafe, his majefty would perhaps have made ufe of that opportunity to vifit the grand newly-erected pier, on the neighbouring fhore of *Ramfgate.* He certainly would have taken frequent airings on the cliffs between *Margate* and the *North Foreland;* and furveyed from them the wide-extended mouth of his *Thames.* Perhaps fome large fleet of *englifh* merchantmen might have then arrived from *Afia* or *America.* Hearing that their good old king was on that coaft, they would have fpread all their colours to the wind, founded their trumpets, and fired their guns. The crews would have faluted their fove-reign with repeated cheers. Cheerful indeed

had

had been that found: the applaufes of a grateful people would have been far more cordial
to his royal breaft, than any medicinal prefcrip-
tion.

BUT let me not longer interrupt you, continued he, turning to *Crito*. You were fpeaking
of the goodnefs of *Auguftus*. I fhould be forry,
if I have hindered my friends from liftening to any
of your obfervations on fo pleafing a topic.

THE topic is indeed very pleafing, replied *Crito*,
after a fhort paufe; yet I muft add, that on fully
confidering the whole hiftory of *Auguftus*, there
neceffarily rifes one reflection; which is far from
being equally agreeable, though it feems highly
important and inftructive.

THAT part of *Auguftus's* life, which is generally confidered as it's *good* part, comprehends, as
was juft now obferved, about forty years: a
fpace of time equal to the whole rational and active life of the generality of mankind.

THE powers of *Auguftus* for doing good far
exceeded thofe of the greateft fovereigns in modern *Europe.*

By

By a courfe of wife beneficence, *fo long* and *fo powerfully* exerted, it is natural to imagine, that *Auguftus* muft have acquired a very fplendid name; a real and folid kind of glory *.

YET, furely, *Auguftus* ought never to have entertained any hopes, that the horrid crimes of his youth, however atoned for in the fight of heaven, could even by thefe means be totally effaced from the memory of men. Succeeding generations have looked, and will always look, on the hiftory of his life, with hatred and deteftation, though mixed indeed with admiration, and with pity.

THIS is a melancholy reflection. The fame, alas! is the cafe in private ftations. The crimes of youth fometimes continue as an indelible ftain, throughout life: the beft conduct in manhood and old age will not be fufficient wholly to regain the favour of mankind. Yet let not fuch perfons be too deeply difpirited. Let them lay afide indeed all claims to reputation and honour; but let them fervently, and without ceafing, pray, that their penitence may at length be favourably accepted by the moft gracious and moft merciful of all Beings.

* In relation to *Auguftus's* clemency, fee *Seneca*, *Lipfius's* edition, p. 194, 196.

CRITO

CRITO now turned his eyes fuffufed with tears towards his young companions. Happy, faid he, are you, my dear friends, who have it in your power to begin your lives in the beft courfe of complete virtue; and thus to lay the moft folid, and ample foundation, for the comfort, happinefs, and fplendour, *without a flaw*, of whatever may be the remainder of your days: whether, by the mercy of heaven, you fhall be removed foon to a better ftate; or whether you may have it in your power, by a long life here, to add daily to the happinefs of others, and to your own virtues.

ON the whole, what fhould be your higheft wifh? Firft, that your youth may continue to be as virtuous as the youth of *Marcellus*; and then, that you may either add to it the goodnefs of the middle and latter years of *Auguftus*; or elfe, die foon. May you die early, rather than do any thing to ftain your glory, and degrade your virtue!

Death, if it fin and forrow thus prevent,
Is the next bleffing to a life well fpent.

Μη δητα, μη δητ᾽, Ω Θεων αγνον σεβας,
Ιδοιμι ταυτην ημεραν· αλλ᾽ εκ βροτων

Bαινη

Βαιην αφαντ℗ προσθεν, η τοιχνδ᾽ ιδεw
Κηλιδ᾽ εμαυτω συμφορας αφιγμενην *.

*   *   *

THE company now walked out of the maufoleum; and ftepping into their carriage, bid the
coachman take them to *Marcellus's* theatre.

THE prefent ftate of the theatre of *Marcellus*
is fo very well known, to all perfons who have
read any travels to *Rome,* or looked over a collection of prints reprefenting it's antiquities, that
it is needlefs to infert here any defcription of that
grand ftructure.

SUFFICE it to obferve, that the young nobleman and the reft of the company, in viewing it,
frequently admired the beauty of it's architecture;
but much more frequently thought of the merits
of the virtuous prince, in whofe honour it was
erected.

*   *   *

CRITO taking out his watch, and finding it
yet but early in the day, propofed taking this

* SOPHOCL. *Œdip. Tyr.* ver. 849.

oppor-

opportunity to vifit the arch of *Drufus*. It is fituate, faid he, in a very remote part of *Rome:* but we are now half way on our road thither.

THE company readily agreed to the propofal; and proceeded on their morning ramble towards that arch, paffing under the weftern fide of mount *Palatine*.

THEY looked up with admiration to the pompous ruins of the imperial palace.

OF how much forrow, faid *Crito*, was this *Palatine* hill the feat, in *Auguftus's* time! How was the higheft degree of human grandeur then embittered, by the moft heart-felt difappointment and grief! Under the repetition of how many domeftic misfortunes did *Auguftus there* groan! You remember the flattering lines of *Albinovanus*.

Cæfaris adde domum: quæ certè funeris expers,
    Debuit humanis altior effe malis.
Ille vigil, fummâ facer ille locatus in arce
    Res hominum ex tuto cernere dignus erat.
Nec fleri ipfe fuis, nec quenquam flere fuorum;
    Nec quæ nos patimur vulgus & ipfe pati.

Was this the cafe? Ah! no. Even his moft fevere enemies might have pitied him, while crying out,

A/3'

Αιϑ᾿ οϕελον τ᾿ αγονϴ τ᾿ εμεναι, αγαμϴ τ᾿ απολεσϑαι *.

BESIDE all other forrow, he faw his fifter, the excellent *Octavia*, die of long grief for the lofs of her beloved *Marcellus:* he faw his wife *Livia* burying her only good fon, *Drufus; Drufus,* who, next to *Marcellus,* is generally defcribed to be one of the moft amiable youths of his time, and the moft defervedly regretted by his family and country: *Tiberius,* in the mean time, furviving *Drufus, for the punifhment of his country,* in the fame manner as *Julia, for that of her family,* furvived both *Marcellus* and *Agrippa.*

AT fome diftance from mount *Palatine,* between the *Cælian* and *Aventine* hills, ftands the arch of *Drufus.* It's top is overgrown with mofs and fhrubs, but it's fides are ftill adorned with two rich marble columns.

THE young nobleman, in viewing this monument of the memory of *Drufus*†, recollected what he had heard and feen, relative to the faid *roman* prince, in his paffage through *Lorrain* and *France;* particularly at *Metz* and *Lyons.* At *Metz,* faid he,

---

* *Hom.* Il. Γ. ver. 40. See alfo *Sueton.* in *Augufi.* 65.
† *Primum fuiffe Drufum, cui mortuo arcus dicatus fit, obfervat* Norifius, Cenotaph. Pifan. p. 412. fq. See *Reimar's* edit. of *Dion Caff.* p. 772. This arch is reprefented on fome of the medals of *Drufus.*

I think

I think there are feveral beautiful remains of antiquity, which are afcribed to him : but it was at
Lyons, that *Drufus,* by his moft engaging behaviour,
eftablifhed peace and tranquillity through all the
extenfive regions of the *gauls.* It was at *Lyons,*
then the capital and metropolis of that country,
that he erefted the famous monument of the
concord of fixty *gallic* ftates, and of his own
dutiful refpeft to his father *Auguftus;* I mean
the altar and temple, built near the conflux of the
Saone and *Rhone**.

CRITO'S pupil, who had taken the route of
Holland and the *Low Countries,* recollefted the
noble monument *there* remaining of *Drufus's* wifdom, and greatnefs of mind; namely, the canal †,

---

* Of that ftrufture there are to this day remaining two
ftately columns of *egyptian* granite. They may be feen in
the church of *D'Enay,* which ftands near the point of the
conflux; and probably on the very fpot where the ancient
altar of *Auguftus* was placed. Thefe two granite columns
feem to be of the fame fort and fize with thofe of *Agrippa's*
portico, at the *Pantheon:* but they are now fawn in funder,
and divided into four pillars, which fupport the fmall
dome of that church. As to their original form, pofition,
and ufe, feveral medals may be confulted.

† This canal extended from *Ifeloort* to *Doefburg,* anciently called *Drufus's Burgh.* It joined the *Rhine* to
the *Iffel,* as well as to many of the *batavian* lakes; and
through them to the northern *German* ocean. It is not improbable that *Peter* the Great, while in *Holland,* might attentively confider this great work; and thence take
the hint of feveral fimilar, and ftill more noble defigns, for
uniting the rivers, lakes, and feas, in his own vaft dominions.

which this adoptive fon of *Auguſtus,* with a truly imperial defign, and in the fpirit of the ancient wifdom of *Egypt,* cut through part of *Holland,* that beautiful *European Delta.*

THE eldeſt of the young gentlemen, who had paſſed fome time in *Germany,* particularly in the provinces on the *Rhine,* with pleafure added, that *above fifty german* towns, which now cover the banks of that great river, all owe their foundation to the wifdom of *Drufus.* They derive their origin, faid he, from the feveral ſtations, which *Drufus* prudently chofe for his encampments, in thofe then wild and uncultivated regions. Such was the origin of *Straſburg;* fuch of *Mentz.* I remember feeing at *Mentz* the ruins of an ancient trophy, or cenotaph*, erected to the honour of *Drufus.* It ſtands on the higheſt fpot of ground in the citadel, exactly fronting the conflux of the *Rhine* and *Main.* With great fatisfaction I thence viewed the profpect of that beautiful country, which is now the garden of *Germany,* watered by thofe two noble rivers: a profpect, I fuppofe, in fome meafure analogous to that, which you, my noble friend, have feen from the hills at *Lyons.*

---

* Ελαβε (Δρυσ&) τιμην κινοταφιυ προ- αυτω τω Ρηνω.

Dio Caſſius, lib. 55. p. 772.

How

How happy is it, dear fir, continued he, turning to *Crito*, when the defolating operations of war are thus mixed and tempered with the works of peace : when, by the benevolence of Providence, fo much good is produced, even in the midft, and fpringing, as it were, out of the greateft evils! May fuch be the confolatory confequences of our prefent *north-american* wars! May the *britifh* generals in the *New World* become there the founders of as many cities, as *Alexander*, or his imitator *Seleucus**; as *Auguftus*, or this his noble imitator *Drufus*, have been in the Old!

BUT why am *I* thus talking? I am fure, my dear fir, that you have fome paper on the character of *Drufus*, with which you intend to favour us : and where better than in this place?

I HAVE indeed a very fhort paper of notes on the fubject, replied *Crito*; and I have brought you hither, I own, upon that account. But though this triumphal arch of *Drufus* be a proper object for awakening our curiofity, in relation to his hiftory; yet the fpot is by no means convenient for a ftudious lecture. You fee it ftands on a great public road.

---

* *Seleucus* built no lefs than forty cities in *Afia.*

IF

IF you pleafe, let us retire to your lodgings. We will return thither by the way of the temple of *Minerva Medica*. We fhall have time enough before dinner for making that tour.

* * *

THE company now turned down from the great road into the folitary rural lanes of the *Cælian* hill. They paffed by the ruins of that great aqueduct, which was built by a fon of *Drufus*. They then croffed over to the *Efquiline* hill, and ftopped at the door of a vineyard.

THE name of the vineyard is *Galuzza;* being, moft probably, a corruption and confufion of the names of *Caius* and *Lucius*, the fons of *Agrippa*, and grandfons of *Auguftus;* to whofe memory *Auguftus here* erected a bafilica, and a temple.

THIS temple, like feveral other buildings of the *auguftan* age,—as the *Pantheon*, the *Maufoleum*, and the *Hemicyclium* of the *Palatine Apollo*, —is in the form of a rotunda*. It's mofs-grown

---

* It is a decagon. It's circuit on the outfide is two hundred and twenty-five feet. In the walls between each angle are broad and deep niches for ftatues. Here was found that ftatue, which at prefent makes a principal ornament of the *Ginftiniani* gallery; the ftatue of *Minerva*, with a ferpent at her feet.

walls

walls and lofty roof are ſtill remaining, though much ſhattered in many places.

THE company entered this vineyard. In paſſing through one of it's walks, they looked down into the ſepulchral vaults of the *Arruntian* family : they then proceeded to the temple. In the centre of the temple they found a large fountain, by the ſide of which they ſat down.

CRITO, in a penſive poſture, for a few moments reflected on the common lot of mortality, and on the vanity of all human grandeur. If I remember right, ſaid he, *Auguſtus,* within the ſhort ſpace of eighteen months, was deprived of *Caius* and *Lucius;* thoſe two young princes, to whom, after the death of *Marcellus,* he looked as the ſupport of his family, and whom he had brought up to ſucceed him in the imperial power.—Sorrow upon Sorrow!—Perhaps *Auguſtus* might build this temple as a kind of medicinal lenitive to his grief: for here *Minerva* was honoured, as another *Hygeïa;* graciouſly preſiding over the health of that part of the human nature, which, though not indeed ſubject to mortality, is yet, from the earlieſt childhood, continually liable to various pains, and dreadful maladies. Frequently is the goddeſs of *Wiſdom* on this account, intitled *Minerva Medica;* and repreſented with the attributes

of

of *Æfculapius* *; the ferpent, and the wand; bleffing mankind with the *medicinâ mentis*, as he did
with that of the body.

CRITO now opened a pocket-volume of *Tully*,
and read to his friends the introduction to the
third book of the *Tufculan* queftions : *De ægri-
tudine lenienda* †.

THE converfation afterwards returned to it's
original fubject. The young nobleman took notice of the picturefque appearance of this ruined
temple; and then fpoke of the ftatues of *Caius*
and *Lucius*, which reprefent them with the attributes of *Caflor* and *Pollux* ‡.

THE eldeft of the young gentlemen commended
Auguflus's care in the education of the young
princes of the family. For though *Caius* and *Lucius* died very young, I muft prefume, faid he, that
they had received much inftruction from *Auguflus.*
He was, indeed, very unhappy in *Tiberius* and
Julia; yet, how glorious were the fruits of his

---

* See the plate of the temple and figure of *Minerva Medica*, in *Mountfaucon's* Journey to *Italy*, C. 8

† *Quidnam effe, Brute, caufæ putem, cur, cùm conftemus ex
animo & corpore, corporis curandi tuendique caufâ quæfita fit
ars, ejus atque utilitas, deorum immortalium inventioni confe-
crata : animi autem medicina, nec tam defiderata, &c.*

‡ Thefe ftatues were found near the theatre of *Marcellus*,
and are now placed on the afcent to the *Capitol.*

paternal

paternal care in *Marcellus*, *Drusus*, and *Germanicus !* What imperial palace ever, in one reign, produced three such young princes?

M A Y a similar education for ever bless all the royal youth of *Europe!* But why do I form *so imperfect* a wish, on so great an occasion? May they be blessed with a *far better* education: even with those instructions, which the goddess of this temple is said, under the shape of *Mentor,* to have herself bestowed on the youthful heir of a *grecian* kingdom; and which a *Fenelon* has copied so excellently, for the benefit of all the princes and people of *Europe ;* though his amiable pupil, the duke of *Burgundy,* died equally young with *Drusus* and *Germanicus.*

I A M sure, dear sir, added he, turning to *Crito,* you must often have thought on that noble work with great pleasure, during your last journey through *France :* especially, while you were visiting the archi-episcopal church of *Cambray ;* or when seated by some of the shady fountains in the gardens of *Marli.*

CRITO listened with glowing satisfaction to these sentiments expressed by his young friend. He then turned round to his pupil, and desired to borrow for some moments his pocket *Horace.* He

Y 4

opened

opened it at the fourth book, and read the following lines.

> *Fortes creantur fortibus & bonis—*
> *Doctrina fed vim promovet infitam ;*
> *Rectique mores pectora roborant ;*
>   *Utcunque defecere mores,*
>   *Dedecorant benè nata culpæ *.*

AFTER *Marcellus's* death, continued *Crito,*
Drufus and *Tiberius,* the two princely brothers of
whom *Horace* here fpeaks, were educated together
in the palace, and under the eye of *Augustus.*
Germanicus, the fon of *Drufus,* had afterwards, as
you obferve, the fame happinefs.

DURING the life of *Augustus,* thefe three princes, though the character of *Tiberius* feems always
to have been the loweft of the three, were, in general, regarded by the public with very great
efteem. The *romans,* ftill more than their enemies,

> *Senfêre, quid mens ritè, quid indoles*
> *Nutrita fauftis fub penetralibus*
>   *Possit ; quid Augusti paternus*
>   *In pueros animus Nerones †.*

* *Carm.* Lib. IV. Od. 4.
† Ib. ver. 25.

BUT

BUT let us, at prefent, confine our thoughts to *Drufus*.

HE feems to have been bleffed with a very ex-cellent natural difpofition, as well as with a good education.

Adolefcens erat tot tantarumque virtutum, quantas natura mortalis recipit, aut induftria perficit. Cujus ingenium, utrum bellicis magis operibus, an civilibus fuffecerit artibus, in incerto eft : morum certè dulcedo, & adverfus amicos omnes, æqua & par fui æftimatio inimitabilis fuiffe, dicitur.

IN this panegyric of *Velleius Paterculus* we muft certainly make fome confiderable allowances for the exaggeration of court flattery : but I ap-prehend it, in the main, to be founded on truth. The teftimonies alfo of other ancient writers feem to confirm it. It is, I fuppofe, from thefe writers, that the authors of the Modern Univerfal Hiftory have extracted a very fplendid character of this hero.

DRUSUS was a man of an unblemifhed character; of a probity, which was proof againft all temptations; of great honour, open-hearted, and an enemy to all manner of deceit or diffimulation. He was no way
inferiour,

inferiour, either in courage or conduct, to the moft experienced commanders of his age; and had nothing in view, in all his expeditions, but the glory of the roman *name, and the public welfare.* By the laft expreffions the authors probably mean *the welfare of the* roman *ftate.*

THE character of *Drufus*, faid the eldeft of the young gentlemen, feems to refemble that of our illuftrious prince of *Wales*, fon of our great *Edward* the Third. I think you have feen his monument at *Canterbury;* and you cannot but recollect his military trophies at *Windfor.*

HE certainly refembled *Drufus*, replied *Crito*, in feveral exalted virtues: but particularly in thofe moft amiable of them all, filial refpect and love. To virtues of this kind may you ever continue to give your principal attention!

IT is true, that in *military* affairs *Drufus*, after the deceafe of *Agrippa*, was the greateft character of the times. His campaigns in *Germany* gave full proof, both of his conduct, and of his courage. You muft have noticed, I am fure, many coins of *Auguftus*, which, in honour of the victories of *Drufus*, are adorned with military trophies, and with the infcription " *De Germanis.*"

BUT

BUT, in what manner fhall *we* fpeak of thofe victories?

DRUSUS'S army, in his laft campaigns, paffed the *Rhine* and *Wefer*, and ravaged the whole country even to the banks of the *Elbe.*—Pitiable *Germany !*—how often are thy fair provinces ex-pofed to the ravages of war! Thy plains, from the banks of the *Rhine* to the *Elbe*, are even *now* fmoking with blood. With what horrour, my dear pupil, did we, laft fpring, pafs over feveral fields of carnage, in *Weftphalia*, *Heffe*, and the do-minions of *Brunfwick !*

BUT *Drufus*, being commander of the *roman* army in that bloody expedition, incurred the deepeft malediction of the *german* nations. On *his* head their heavieft curfes fell. Permit me to read to you fome few lines, which I have extracted from *Barre's* Hiftory of *Germany. Tandis qu'à Rome* Drufus *étoit regretté, comme un prince d'un merite diftingué; brave, vertueux, plein de bonté, digne de remplacer* Augufte*; en Germanie, les cattes, les fueves, les cherufques, fe rejouiffoient de fa mort. Ils avoient éprouvé, de la part de ce prince,* [or rather from the *roman* army under his command] *des cruautés inouies; ce qui rendit fa mémoire fi deteftable parmi eux, que lorfqu'ils vou-*
loient

loient du mal à quelqu'un, ils souhaitoient, qu'il tombat entre les mains d'un autre Drusus *.

I REMEMBER that, when we afterwards came from the northern parts of *Germany* into the *Palatinate*, I passed some days, at *Manheim*, in reading the dismal history of the destruction in that country, done by order of *Lewis* the Fourteenth, and by the army under the command of marshal *Turenne:* a name, which, on this occasion, I grieve to repeat. I then thought, that a parallel might be drawn, between the *german* expedition of *Drusus*, and this sad part of the military history of *Turenne*. Both must have been hated in *Germany*, for executing the orders of their sovereigns : while both were, justly, beloved at home, for their own virtues †.

CRITO now paused for some moments; and then, resuming his discourse, recited those well-known verses of *Addison:*

* Histoire d'Allemagne, vol. i. p. 146. quarto edition. Pere *Barre* refers, on this head, to *Crusius ;* Ann. Suev. lib. ii. p. 2. & 45.

† " *A military profession is very dangerous to persons desirous of leading a life of goodness.*" Such was the famous reflection of marshal *Turenne*, made by him on his death-bed ; probably while recollecting the dreadful ruin of the *Palatinate.*

" Men may *live* fools ; but fools they cannot *die !*"

Should

Should he go further, numbers will be wanting
To form new battles, and support his crimes.
Ye Gods! what havock does ambition make
Among your works*!

WOULD I were now endued with the thoughts
and the language of an *Addifon,* or of a *Fenelon;*
duly to lament the difmal effects and confequences
of the pride of monarchs, difmal to the world in
general, and ten-fold more difmal, often, to themfelves!

LEWIS lived long enough to fee the *Palatinate*
revenged at *Blenheim.* *Augustus* lived to behold
and feel the heavy punifhment, which the *Neme-
fis* of *Germany* poured down upon the legions of
Varus. Permit me to read to you a fhort extract
from *Dion Cassius.*

Τοτε δε μαθων ο Αυγϗϛ℗ τα τω Ουαρω συμβεβηκοτα,
πενθ℗ μεγα εποιησατο, επι τοις απολωλοσι, κ̣ επι τω
περι των γερμανιων δεει· τοτε μεγιϛον, οτι κ̣ επι την
Ιταλιαν, την τε Ρωμην αυτην, ορμησειν σΦας προσεδοκησε.

SUCH, indeed, was at laft the cafe.

LET us reflect, my dear and noble friend, for
a few moments, on the ftately magnificence in

* CATO, *Scene* I.

which

which *Rome* appeared, towards the clofe of *Auguſtus's* reign: when the buildings we háve this day viſited; his imperial mauſoleum, the theatre of *Marcellus*, the triumphal arch of *Druſus*, and *this* temple, were all in their full fplendour. Then let us aſk ourſelves, What was the mighty power, that could be able to deſtroy this proud city?——— The warlike defcendants of thofe very *german* nations, whofe lands were invaded and ravaged by *Druſus's* army.

PLEASE to recolleĉt, my dear pupil, the viſion which appeared to *Æneas:* the viſion of thofe future *roman* generals, who were to puniſh *Greece* for it's ancient cruelties to *Troy:*

> *Ille*
> *Viĉtor aget currum, eæfis infignis achivis;*
> *Eruet ille Argos, agamemnoniafque Mycenas*
> *Ultus avos Trojæ*.*

In the fame manner, you may imagine that *german* prophetefs, who, on the banks of the *Elbe,* drove back the *roman* army by her execrations. You may imagine her, I fay, on one hand, denouncing fpeedy death to *Druſus,* and loading with curfes the whole family of the *Cæfars;* in the fame ſtyle, perhaps, as the *britiſh druid* curfed

---

* ÆNEID, vi. 837.

the

the Plantagenei family: * on the other hand, turning to the feveral nations of *Germany*, and prophecying their future victories. " The defcendants of *this* chief of the *bructeri* fhall fubdue *Mentz* and *Lyons*, and expel the *romans* from all the provinces of *Gaul*. The pofterity of *that* chief of the *quadi* fhall take ample revenge on *Rome* herfelf; fhall fire *Mount Palatine*, fhall deface *Drufus's* triumphal arch, fhall overthrow the maufoleum of *Auguflus*, and trample indignantly on his afhes."

IT feems very obfervable, faid the young nobleman, that, in digging among the ruins of *this* temple, feveral of it's ftatues and ornaments have been found broken and battered ; and among them lay fome old *german* hatchets, probably the inftruments of their demolition †.

BUT enough of *Germany*, faid *Crito :* I fhould not, perhaps, have proceeded fo far in this kind of digreffion, had I not confidered you, my dear fellow-travellers, as in a manner peculiarly concerned in the hiftory of ancient *Germany*. Your illuftrious families, it is very likely, are all defcended from fome *german* origin. Your *faxon*

* See *Gray's* Ode : *Ruin feize thee, &c.*
† See abbé *Richard's* Voyage d'Italie.

ancestors

anceſtors came into *England* from thoſe provinces, which are waſhed by the *Weſer,* and by the *Elbe.*

LET us now turn our thoughts again to *Druſus;* and conſider him, not amidſt the horrours of war, but in a far more amiable light; in his *domeſtic* and *civic* character.

Occidit, exemplum juvenis venerabile morum :
Maximus ille armis : maximus ille togá.

LIKE his dear *Antonia,* the worthy daughter of the virtuous and beautiful *Octavia, Druſus* united to a graceful body a ſtill more lovely mind. He is ſaid to have been poſſeſſed of all the qualities, which are fitted to produce either eſteem or affection. He was generous; he was popular:—

IF I be not miſtaken, ſaid the eldeſt of the young gentlemen, *Druſus* had deeply imbibed the doctrines of civil liberty. In caſe he had ſurvived and ſucceeded *Auguſtus,* it was generally expected, that he would have reſtored the *roman* republic *.—Credebatur, ſi rerum potitus foret, libertatem redditurus.*

* See *Tacit.* Ann. lib. i. c. 33.

IT

IT *was* fo reported, faid *Crito*, but I know not with what truth: much lefs can I pretend to judge, whether or no a defign like this would have been *really* expedient. I fhould rather imagine, that *Drufus's* good fenfe, and good intentions, would in that cafe have directed him to *another* work; to a plan and fyftem of policy, lefs fplendid perhaps, but in reality far more beneficial for the public.

BUT, however this may be, it is certain, that *Drufus* was generally beloved at *Rome*. *Magna ejus erat apud populum romanum memoria.* His character was refpected highly, to ufe a modern expreffion, both by the country and the court-party.

NOR let us liften to the vulgar calumnies thrown out againft *Auguftus* *. Wicked as courts fometimes may really be, yet I do not believe they are ever nearly fo bad as they are reported: and I am confident, that you, dear fir, from your natural generofity of heart, and from a ftrong fenfe of political duty, will often turn your ears, with horrour and deteftation, from many villainous

---

* *Difplicere regnantibus civilia filiorum ingenia; neque ob aliud interceptos, quàm quia populum romanum æquo jure complecti redditâ libertate agitaverint.*—*Hos vulgi fermones, &c.*
                                    Tacit. Ann. lib. ii. c. 82.

lies, fuggefted againft government with equal falfhood and malice.

AUGUSTUS feems not only to have been totally innocent of this villainous accufation, but to have been really and deeply afflicted at the death of *Drufus.*

I cannot but think, that the grief and affection of *Auguftus* towards this his amiable adopted fon muft have been fincere, while he was compofing the hiftory of his life. He even fpoke the funeral oration over his corpfe.

In that oration, *Auguftus* declared, with tears, that all he wifhed for the glory of his then furviving children was this—that they might live to refemble *Drufus.*

He added, in the ftyle of a *roman* orator, that all he defired *for himfelf* was, that he might die like this hero, in the fervice of his country; in the midft of his triumphs.

The emperor afterwards took the urn, bore it into his maufoleum, and placed it there; probably near that of *Marcellus.*

*   *   *

THE folemn entry of *Drufus's* corpfe into *Rome**; the deep and mournful filence, with which his urn was depofited in the tomb; thefe, my dear friends, are fubjeƈts of meditation, far more edifying, far more pleafing, than the defcription of any ovation, or triumph.

YET, pleafing as is the idea, let me refrain myfelf from enlarging on the fubjeƈt.—There is, however, one circumftance relative to it, on which I could be glad if you would, for fome moments, indulge your imaginations.

THE hiftorian, *Livy*, was at the time of *Drufus's* burial about fifty years of age. It is highly probable, that he was then refident at *Rome*, and prefent at the funeral folemnity. Let me defire you to confider, what were moft probably *his* thoughts on that occafion.

Is it not likely, that he meditated upon it with much application of mind? If we examine the epitome, or contents of his hiftory, we fhall find, that the aƈtions of *Drufus* conftitute the principal argument of the five laft books; and that the conclufion of his whole work is *Drufus's* death.

---

* *Accedebat, ad hanc mortem Drufi, ingens civium provinciarumque & totius Italiæ defiderium : per quam effufis in officium lugubre municipiis, coloniifque, ufque in urbem duƈtum erat funus, triumpho fimillimum.* Seneca, Confol ad Martiam.

Corpus

Corpus Romam perveƐum, & in C. Julii * *tu-mulo conditum. Laudatus eƒt a Cæƒare Auguƒto vitrico; & ƒupremis ejus plures honores additi.*

THE great and noble work of *Livy's roman* hiƒ-tory thus cloƒing with the funeral of *Drufus,* it is not to be doubted, that the writer exerted the full ƒtrength of his genius on this mournful occaƒion; particularly by delineating the characƐer of *Drufus* in a ƒtyle ƒuitable to the hero's merit, and worthy of his own pen. If the concluƒion of *Livy's* labours were yet extant, I ƒhould probably with much pleaƒure have preƒented to you an extraƐ from it this morning, while you were ƒtanding under the ƒhade of *Drufus's* arch.

How does this refleƐion recall our repeated wiƒhes, that the hiƒtory of *Livy* had been found at *Conƒtantinople* entire!

PARDON me for this reverie, ƒaid the young nobleman; but I cannot help imagining, that, if the learned world be ever to rejoice in ƒuch a dif-covery, that diƒcovery will moƒt likely be made in *Italy;* probably within the precinƐs of *Rome.* Perhaps on ƒome fortunate day, a cheƒt may be

---

* Auguƒti *eƒt intelligendum.* Nam, inquit Dio, ɛς το τɐ Αυγɤσɐ μνημɛιν κατɛτɛϑη. Seg. Vide *Livii,* edit. *oxon.* vol. vi. p. 175.

found

found deeply buried in the ruins of this city : a cheſt containing the works of *Livy*, in great meaſure perfeſt, together with ſome other ancient authors. This conjeſture will not ſeem *totally abſurd* to thoſe perſons, who have been eye-witneſſes of the ſurpriſing depth of ſoil, to which the ruins of this ancient city extend. They extend, in ſeveral places, ſo low down as twenty feet; in the *Cælian* hill to near ſeventy. Among theſe ruins, and particularly among thoſe on *Mount Palatine*, ſeveral arched vaults have been frequently diſcovered by accident, at different periods of time. Many curious paintings, and many chef-d'œuvres of antique ſculpture, have been found in theſe ſubterranean receſſes. Is it not poſſible, that ſome of them may contain a far more precious treaſure?

I could wiſh, ſaid *Crito's* pupil, that the goddeſs of this temple would, with her ſnaky-wreathed wand, kindly point out to us the ſpot, where we might dig for that treaſure?

I remember, replied the eldeſt of the young gentlemen, with a ſmile, that, when we viſited the mines in *Germany*, we heard much of the crooked haſelſtick. Might it not be wiſhed, that there was ſome ſuch divining rod for the diſcovery of the gold mines of literature? But perhaps the

wand

wand of *Minerva Medica* might be full as fure a guide.

THE converfation now fhifted to various topics; when the young nobleman, taking out his watch, was furprifed to find it fo late. We muft make hafte home, faid he, or we fhall lofe our dinner. Befides, our fervants and horfes have been a long while ftanding expofed to the fcorching fun. Let us have pity on them, and return to our lodgings. We fhall have made, this morning, almoft the whole tour of *Rome.*

*   *   *

IN the way home, *Crito* mentioned a fcheme, which he had heard propofed among fome travellers; and which he thought might poffibly be productive of many important difcoveries. He wifhed this fcheme at fome time or other might be brought to effect; as it feemed conducive to the advancement of charity and policy, no lefs than of *literature* and *vertù* *.

THE

---

* The ftreets of *Rome* fwarm with poor, who are fed indeed at the gates of the convents; but live in a great meafure deftitute both of lodging and clothes. Several of thefe miferable wretches might, by induftry, if they could get employment, provide for themfelves better; and many of them feem very well able to work.

If a fubfcription of 200l. or 300l. were raifed, and permiffion

THE young gentlemen ftrongly approved the idea of this propofal; and ardently wifhed it could be begun during their ftay in *Rome*, as they would gladly have fubfcribed to it.

THE fubfcription, I apprehend, faid *Crito,* would without much difficulty be raifed among *englifh* travellers: but the *whole* management of the money muft be entrufted to *roman* hands. Happy, if a *roman* of proper dignity would undertake it.

CRITO'S pupil now amufed his friends with fome pleafing conjectures with refpect to the writers of antiquity, whofe works might by thefe means be poffibly recovered. If, faid he, the royal mafter of the *Farnefe* gardens, the king of *Naples*, would give permiffion for the ruins

miffion obtained from the government, *under proper reftric-tions*, for digging; it is almoft certain, that, before that fum was expended, it would be in a great degree reimburfed by the fale of the mere bricks and tiles, that would be turned up.

But it is highly probable, that many things of value alfo might be difcovered, the fale of which would thoroughly indemnify the fubfcribers; and thus, the charity might be continued, for feveral years, by fuch a circulation of expending and receiving.

If any thing of *very extraordinary* note were found, it would by no means be proper to have it expofed to fale, and exported from *Rome*. The truftees of the charity might prefent it gratis to the *roman* government; to be depofited, if an article of vertù, in the *Capitoline Mufæum;* if of literature, in the *Vatican Library*.

of

of the *Palatine* library to be thoroughly examined, it is not impoffible that *Varius*, and fome other eminent authors of the *auguftan* age, might be brought to light. Perhaps too their works might be found in a much better condition, than the fcorched and pulverized manufcripts at *Herculaneum*.

BUT, among all the literary produ&ions of the *auguftan* age, none would be fo acceptable to the public as a perfe& *Livy*. Indeed, the lofs, which *Livy's* hiftory has fuffered, is much more generally lamented, than that of any other *roman* or *greek* compofition: which feems fomewhat extraordinary; for, notwithftanding the real high merit of *Livy*, there certainly have been feveral other writers, who deferve to be at leaft equally regretted.

THE converfation now turned on the works of *Livy*. It dwelt on that fubje& for a confiderable time; both while the company were in the coach, and while they were feated together at dinner.

*   *   *

AFTER dinner the young gentlemen dreffed, and went out to make fome vifits. *Crito* retired

to

to his apartment, to put his papers and books in order.

HAVING now paffed through all the feries of ages contained in *Livy's* hiftory, he laid thófe volumes, together with *Freinfhemius's* Supplement, afide; not without fome fentiments of refpeɛt and gratitude for the refpeɛtive authors. In putting away the laft volume, he had the curiofity to fee in what manner *Freinfhemius* concluded the long and laborious work of his Supplement.

THE laft paragraph of that work is as follows:

Præfenti labori meo, in his temporibus aɛtifque, finem facio, circà quæ Livianam etiam hifloricam defiiffe indicio Epitomarum deprehenditur; toto animo verfus in majoris & conflantioris imperii auɛtorem dominumque JESUM CHRISTUM: quem fub hofce annos,—de natali enim ejus, haud levibus argumentis, inter doɛtos difputatur—hominem natum fuus afpexit potiùs quàm agnovit orbis. Hujus beneficio, fiquid utiliter elaboravi, debere me totum profiteor; eumque fuppliciter oro, ut porrò, mentem eam mihi fervet, omnia de quibus hic fcripfi, regna, viɛtorias, triumphos nullo modo digna reputantem; ob quæ Illius fanɛtiffima feɛta, aut quidquid ea facere, ac pati jubet, ullâ ex parte negligatur.

CRITO

CRITO, after perufing thefe fentences with deep attention, retired to his clofet for a quarter of an hour: he afterwards took a folitary walk, it being now late in the afternoon, along the fhady fide of the *Strado felice.* The ftreets of *Rome* are not indeed improper places for ftudy and contemplation, fome of them being as *quiet* and *ftill* as any college quadrangles.

ARRIVED at the ftately northern front of the bafilica of *Santa Maria Maggiore*, *Crito* ftood for fome minutes admiring it. He then turned his eyes to the *egyptian* obelifk, which is erected before it; and which was removed hither from the maufoleum of *Auguftus.*

CRITO perufed the infcriptions on it's bafis. He then went up the flight of fteps into the church: he turned fhort on his left hand by the four *porphyry* pillars, which fupport the canopy over the high altar; and entered the chapel, which adorns it's *northern* fide.

ADVER-

ADVERTISEMENT;

TO THE

READER.

I T feems highly proper, at this time, to break the thread of thefe fuppofed ROMAN CONVERSATIONS.

YOU are now arrived at the important æra of the GREATEST EVENT, that ever ennobled the hiftory of the world.

WHAT *that event* was, the author is by no means worthy to fay. Senfible of his extreme demerit, he can only refer you to the fecond chapter of the gofpel of St. LUKE; particularly to it's firft twenty verfes. See alfo the firft chapter of that gofpel, from the twenty-fixth to the thirty-eighth verfe; and the gofpel of St. JOHN, the firft chapter, and fourteenth verfe.

Magnus, ab integro, Sæclorum nafcitur ORDO!
VIRGIL, *Pollio.* Ecl. iv. 5.

CHAP.

C H A P. IV.

TWENTY-SECOND DAY'S CONVERSATION.

—

IT feems to have been a very defirable event for the welfare of the *roman* ftate, if *Auguftus*, in the beft part of his reign, had, with the advice of his council, defigned *a wife plan of future legiflation;* if, during that time of general tranquillity, he had fettled *a folid form of government; a proper diftribution of the civil power, between the prince, the fenate, and the people;* and *a regular, hereditary fucceffion to the imperial authority.* Such a work would have been far more laudable than any fcheme, for reftoring the anarchy of the late republic.

SUCCEEDING generations would then have had the greateft reafon to honour and to blefs the memory of *Auguftus.* Such a form of government would, in all probability, have prevented many of thofe miferies, which foon after the death of *Auguftus* began to fall on the *roman* people, on the fenatorial families, and on his imperial fucceffors themfelves. The want of fuch a fet-

tled

tled form of government was indeed feverely felt, fo long as the *roman* empire continued to exift.

BUT perhaps, notwithftanding the beauty and general utility of fuch a legiflative plan, and it's remarkable congeniality, in feveral particulars, with the old *roman* conftitution, *Augustus* might not find himfelf hardy enough to venture upon it. It might poffibly give fome difturbance to the prefent public calm, or rather public *lethargy*: and therefore it might be dropped, like feveral other noble defigns for the public good; which are continually loft, in all ages and countries, by the exceffive caution of government, or rather it's timidity, *movendi compofita.*

PERHAPS, alfo, neither *Augustus*, nor any of his council, was endued with fufficient ftrength of political wifdom. A mixed diftribution of civil power is continually before our eyes in *England:* but there is a very wide difference between feeing and admiring a complicated machine, and the being able to have invented it. Not one of all the moft celebrated *legiflators* of antiquity appears to have arrived at the perfect comprehenfion of fo great an idea; though feveral, both at *Rome* and in *Greece*, feem to have made very confiderable approaches towards it.

SUCH

SUCH were the fentiments expreffed by the el-deft of the young gentlemen to his three friends, as they fat round his table to-day after breakfaft. He then took up *Tacitus's* Annals, which lay among fome other political books on the table, and proceeded as follows.

TACITUS feems to have almoft formed the complete idea of fuch a plan; but, at the fame time, to have confidered it as ideal only; and to have thought, that no real fabric of government could ever be built, or ftand long, on fuch foun-dations.

Cunctas nationes & urbes, populus, aut primores, aut finguli regunt. Delecta ex his & conftituta reipublicæ forma, laudari facilius, quàm evenire; vel fi evenit, haud diuturna effe poteft*.

THANK GOD, fuch a fyftem of government has really exifted in *Great Britain*, allowing fome confiderable and effential variations, for now above ten centuries.

PROBABLY, faid the young nobleman, the *ro-man* empire was of too great an extent for fo happy a plan of government. Several political

* Annal. lib. iv. c. 33.

writers

writers are, I believe, of opinion, that democracy, ariftocracy, or limited monarchy, is beft fuited for ftates of a moderate fize: but that vaft and enormous empires demand an abfolute fovereign.

MAY not another reafon be given for it? faid *Crito.* Did *Rome deferve* fuch happinefs? Let us recollect the long and black catalogue of her former crimes: let us *now* re-confider the miferies of thofe many nations, whom fhe had invaded, enflaved, extirpated. Did *fhe* deferve fo eminent a political bleffing? Ah! no. Other things are prepared for her. *Her* people alfo fhall be enflaved: *Rome* fhall groan under the moft abfolute defpotifm, the moft bloody tyranny. The firft fucceffor of *Auguftus,* fhall be a *Tiberius.*

Poft hunc caftrenfis caligæ cognomine Cæfar
Succedet fævo fævior ingenio:
Cædibus inceftifque dehinc maculofus, & omni
Crimine pollutum qui fuperabit avum.

I forget what the poet fays of *Claudius,* and *Nero:* but I think we may affert, with confidence, that as no ftate was ever vifited with a feries of *fuch* oppreffors, fo will it be difficult to find any people, whofe wickednefs more deferved fuch a punifhment.

• *TACITUS*

TACITUS fays, that *Sejanus* acquired his great power, *non tam folertiâ, quàm Deûm irâ in rem romanam* *. The fame obfervation may be made in relation to moft of the twelve *Cæfars.*

·PROVIDENCE *caſt upon the* romans *the furioufneſs of it's wrath, by fending theſe evil angels among them.* PSAL. lxxviii. v. 49.

*   *   *

BUT let me correct my afperity in the application. The *romans* were indeed very bad; yet in the midſt of their punifhment, many mercies and bleffings were vouchfafed to them. Their tyrants were, in general, very execrable; but yet there was not one of them, of whom it might not be juftly faid, that he had fometimes performed fomething that was good.

I REMEMBER, faid *Crito's* pupil, a great abfurdity, of which I was guilty when at the univerfity. In reading *Tacitus's* Annals, I met with feveral particulars of the life of *Tiberius,* which were very laudable; feveral actions of generofity and fortitude, which feemed not unworthy the character even of the beft of princes. In *Velleius's* encomium, alfo, I thought I found much

* TACIT. *Annal.* lib. iv. c. i.

truth, as well as much falsehood and flattery. I employed myself, for a week, in collecting all these laudable parts of *Tiberius's* history into one paper, omitting whatever was of a contrary nature. That paper I lately found in my *porte-feuille;* and will communicate it to you, if I think of it, when you are at *Puteoli,* viewing the antique marble in the market place *.

I INTENDED to pursue the same scheme with respect to the reigns of *Caligula, Claudius,* and *Nero.* But the absurdity of the design became in the process so very glaring; the evil, which I could scarce avoid reading, especially if I took up *Suetonius,* so infinitely outweighed the good, and appeared of so very heinous and horrid a nature; that, before I had finished the life of *Tiberius,* I cast aside the paper, incomplete and incorrect, into my *porte-feuille.* Perhaps I ought rather to have flung it, with indignation, into the fire.

WHEN I afterwards mentioned the affair to you, my dear tutor, you kindly told me, that from my week's exercise I might at least draw two useful lessons for my own conduct. First, that some

* The pedestal of that statue of *Tiberius,* which was erected by fourteen cities of *Asia,* in gratitude for his beneficence to them, when laid desolate by an earthquake. See *Painter's* Letters from *Italy,* letter 73.

tranfient

tranfient acts of generofity are far from being fufficient, to denominate a perfon truly charitable.
The difpofitions to charity muft, by frequent acts,
be wrought into his very frame; and become the
firm, permanent, habitual affections of his foul.
Secondly, much lefs is a tranfient practice of *one*
virtue, for inftance, that virtue to which youth is
moft eafily difpofed, *erogandæ per honefta pecuniæ,*
fufficient to juftify a young man in an high opinion of himfelf; particularly if he neglect other
not lefs noble or ufeful branches of virtue. The
moft difficult, but perhaps the moft important part
of his duty is, properly to govern thofe paffions,
which eafily lead, firft to venial offences, then to
more vitious excefs; and which, if not timely
prevented, will thence gradually drag down his
foul to the depth of criminal horrours. Many
young men, who were at firft well principled,
have been by imperceptible degrees fo corrupted,
as to have too much reafon, at leaft, to cry out
with *Phædra;*

Why was I born with fuch a fenfe of virtue,
So great abhorrence of the fmalleft crime:
And yet a flave to fuch impetuous guilt? *

THESE were the inftructions, with which, I
well remember, you, my kind tutor, favoured

---

* See SMITH's *Phædra* and *Hippolitus,* act i. fc. 3.

me,

me, while at the univerfity. But let me not, by talking any longer on this fubject, prevent you from beginning the lecture, with which you intend to favour us this morning.

* * *

YESTERDAY, faid *Crito,* we concluded our review of that long feries of the generations of *Rome,* whofe actions were the fubject of *Livy's* hiftory. This morning we are to begin the thread of *Tacitus's* Annals. Much reafon have I to wifh, that I were *in any degree* capable of converfing properly with you on thofe topics, which a *Livy* or a *Tacitus* thought worthy of their labours.

THIS firft volume of *Tacitus* comprehends the two and twenty years of *Tiberius's* reign. Notwithftanding the general wretchednefs of thofe times, yet a catalogue might be extracted from it of *feveral* good men, whofe names *Tacitus* here mentions with honour. But the *chief* hero of this volume is *Germanicus.* If you pleafe, we will allot this morning to *his* memory.

YOUR coach fhall carry us, if you have no objection, to the *Barberini* palace. We will vifit the apartment which is adorned with *Pouffin's*
picture

picture of the death of *Germanicus;* and, either in that apartment of the *Barberini* palace, or in one of the chambers of the *Capitoline* mufeum, profecute our ufual morning's ftudy.

WE fhall gladly attend you, replied the young nobleman, to that picture. Often, fince I came to *Rome,* I have reflected with pleafure, that in thefe my lodgings * *Pouffin* lived, thought, and laboured. Perhaps it was in this very room, where we are now fitting, that *Pouffin* conceived the idea, and executed the defign, of that noble painting of *Germanicus's* death.

* * *

THE *Barberini* palace contains ten noble apartments; each of which confifts of feveral rooms, furnifhed with great abundance of ftatues and paintings.

IN the eighth room of the prince's fummerapartment, is that famous picture of the death of *Germanicus,* by *Nicolo Pouffin;* for which, it is faid, the great duke offered no lefs a price than 15000 crowns, or 3750l. fterling.

* Next door to the *french* convent, on *Monte de Trinità.*

THE company employed near an hour in studying this picture: they afterwards proceeded to
the *Capitol.*

* * *

IN paffing through the fecond room of the *Capitoline* mufeum, the company ftopped for fome
time, to admire the recumbent thoughtful ftatue
of *Agrippina.* They then went on to the *imperial chamber.*

THE imperial chamber is called by that title,
on account of the antique bufts which it contains,
reprefenting moft of the *roman* emperors, empreffes, *Cæfars,* and confuls of the imperial blood.
Thefe bufts are ranged round the room, in two
rows, and are difpofed in a regular chronological
feries *.

HOW grand is this affemblage! faid the young
nobleman. This congrefs of almoft all the great

---

* *Videfi in primo luogo collocato il busto di Giulio Cefare di
alabaftro a righe. Siegue quello di Augufto. Indi una tefta di
Marcello suo nepote. Altra poi di Tiberio, e un busto del mede-
mo. Di bianchiffimo marmo eal busto del suo fratello Drufo fatte
certamente in quel tempi, come ei manifefta l'eccollenza del lavoro. Alla finiftra di effo vedefi la ftimabiliffima tefta della di
lui moglie Antonia detta minore. La tefta di Germanico loro
figliuolo viene appreffo. Poi quella della di lui moglie Agrippina, molto ftimabile pel lavoro, &c.*
Mufeo Capitolino, p. 47.

families

families who were honoured with the imperial crown of *Rome,* during the three centuries of it's greateft fplendour!

IT is, indeed, a very majeftic affembly, replied the eldeft of the young gentlemen. But the awe which we feel on firft entering the room, very confiderably abates, when we confider the *difference* of the charaĉters of thefe perfonages.

SEVERAL of them, I grant, faid he, had noble and exalted minds;—pointing to the bufts of *Germanicus* and *Agrippina* on the upper row, near the window : but, in how many other of thefe breafts did the greateft meannefs and mifery lurk !

I AM afraid we fhall too frequently find by our own experience, in all the courts, and in all the auguft affemblies of the prefent age, a fimilar ftrange mixture of company.

BUT, to confider it, continued he, turning to *Crito's* pupil, in a calm view, as one of your philofophers in the next room * might do ; how ill-forted does this company appear! *Agrippa, Marcellus, Drufus,* and *Germanicus ; Titus,*

---

* The philofophic chamber in the *Capitoline Mufæum,* mentioned page 56 of this vol. is the room next adjoining to this imperial chamber.

Nerva.

Nerva, and thefe feveral bufts of *Marcus Aure-lius;* mixed with thofe of *Tiberius, Caligula, Claudius, Nero, Domitian,* and that moft ill-looking *Caracalla* in that corner*!

DOES not this ftrange mixture of company put you in mind of that part of the fculpture, on *Æneas's* fhield; in which *Virgil* has placed fome of the worft, as well as fome of the beft of the *roman* characters, clofely, and therefore inftruc-tively, contrafted together?

———— *Te, Catilina, minaci*
Pendentem fcopulo, furiarumque ora trementem:
Secretofque pios, his dantem jura Catonem †.

HAPPY would it be, faid *Crito,* after having fixed his eyes in filence for fome moments on the floor, if in the future courfe of your lives you could dwell and converfe *only with the good.* Such a bleffing would, in fome meafure, turn earth into heaven.

I REMEMBER, about the middle of the firft *november* that I paffed on the continent, I heard

---

* *Alla fierezza del volto, al terribile fopraciglio, ed alla minacciofa voltata di tefta facil cofa é il riconofcere Caracalla effigiato in un bufto di porfido con la tefta di marmo,*
Mufeo Capitolino, p. 51.

† ÆNEID. viii. 668.

at

at *Amiens* an anthem; the words of which gave me great pleafure. *Juſtum deduxit dominus per vias rectas, & oſtendit illi regnum* DEI. *O beatum virum, cujus anima Paradiſum poſſidet; unde exultant angeli, lætantur archangeli, chorus ſanctorum proclamat, turba virginum invitat; mane nobiſcum in æternum!* Certainly, no little part of the perpetually increaſing felicity and holineſs of the celeſtial kingdom muſt be derived from the unmixed ſociety, the eternal communion of it's ſaints.

HAPPY is the man, whoſe lot on earth, in ſome degree, reſembles theirs!

BUT woe is me, who am conſtrained to dwell with Meſech, *and to have my habitation among the tents of* Kedar **!*

LET us endeavour, my dear friends, to avoid, as much as poſſible, all bad connexions. It is the duty of eminently virtuous perſons, to condeſcend to the converſation, and to endeavour the amendment of the wicked. But our principles of piety are as yet far too weak; let us not venture upon contagion. When we are forced among bad perſons, let us recollect, how dange-

---

* PSAL. CXX. 4.

rous a place this world is. So long as we continue in this life, we ftand between heaven and
hell ; and out of every one of us, there will grow,
either an angel, or what G o d of his infinite mercy
for ever prevent, a devil.

But let us turn our thoughts to lefs weighty
fubjects. Let us refume our claffic ftudies.

This affembly of the imperial families of *Rome*
fhows us virtue, and vice, both placed in the
higheft ftations.

May the bufts of *Tiberius,* and of thofe other
tyrants, revive in your hearts the abhorrence of
their characters: but may the amiable looks of
Germanicus, and of thefe other princes, whofe
hiftories are adorned with many illuftrious marks
of wifdom and goodnefs, increafe and inflame
your noble emulation, your ardent defire of making by imitation their virtues your own; fo far,
at leaft, as your different ftations and fpheres of
action feem to allow.

I have brought a paper for your perufal here,
on the back of which I find a reference to the
beginning of *Demetrius's* life in *Plutarch,* and
alfo fome lines quoted from one of his treatifes.—
Επιλο-

Επιλογιζεσθαι δι' αμφοτερων, οπως τα μεν Φυλαττομενοι,
βελτιϗς ωμεν αυτων, τα δε μιμϗμενοι, μη χειρονες *.

THIS paper contains a kind of contraſt, between the characters of *Germanicus* and *Tiberius*.

EVERY day of my life ought I to grow more
and more deeply convinced of my infinite un-
worthineſs, to have any concern in the great work
of education. May that bleſſed work flouriſh in
other hands! Yet, as I have paſſed much time in
ſtudying the ſubject, however unprofitably, allow
me to mention ſome of the opinions of the authors
whom I have conſulted.

IT is the opinion of ſeveral learned writers,
that the moſt likely mean of preſerving and increaſing the love of virtue in young perſons is,
to place before their eyes continually, and on all
ſides, the nobleſt and brighteſt examples, that have
exiſted ſince the foundation of the world. Perhaps the next beſt method, for the ſame purpoſe,
is to ſhow to them ſometimes, but not often, the
extreme baſeneſs and horrour of an oppoſite character †.

* See *Plutarch's* treatiſe, *De capiendâ ex inimico utilitate,*
at the concluſion.
† See, eſpecially, HORACE, *Sat.* lib. i. ſat. 4.
——————*Inſuevit pater optimus hoc me,*
Ut fugerem exemplis vitiorum quæque notando, &c.

FOR,

FOR, as no one can refuſe his thankſgivings to heaven, for the glory and happineſs of virtue to which he has been called, and which has been exemplified to him in the numerous examples of the wiſe and good; all, in a long ſeries, through many ages, ardently imitating the excellencies of their predeceſſors: ſo, on the other hand, no perſon can help fearing for himſelf, when he ſees the blackneſs, darkneſs, deep infamy, extreme wretchedneſs, and horrid miſery of vice.

PERHAPS ſome of thoſe, who lye in that gulph of vice, were once walking in the ſhining paths of virtue. Alas! *quam mutati ſunt in deterius.* Such ſeems to have been, in a remarkable manner, the ſad caſe of *Tiberius.*

BUT let me not indulge myſelf to an extreme of loquacity. I ſhall ſufficiently exerciſe your patience by the peruſal of this paper.

GERMANICUS.

THERE is not, perhaps, any part of the *roman* hiſtory, which ſhows more ſtrongly the miſery of degenerating from a good education, and of loſing the virtuous reputation gained in our youth,

youth, than the contraſt between the charaćters of *Germanicus* and *Tiberius.*

THEY both began their lives on the ſame exalted theatre of human grandeur; the *palace* of the *roman* empire. Both were educated by *Auguſtus*, at that time in the height of his goodneſs and wiſdom. Both were poſſeſſed of great natural genius and abilities of mind. Both, in their early manhood, aćted virtuouſly and nobly. But *Tiberius* ſuffered himſelf to grow *gradually* corrupt in heart, and to degenerate from the glorious beginning of his career. His aćtions of virtue and goodneſs became daily fewer and fewer: his heart grew worſe and worſe. *Morum enim tempora illi diverſa. Egregius vitâ, famâque, quoad privatus, vel in imperiis ſub Auguſto fuit: fingens virtutes, donec ſuperfuit Germanicus: inter bona, malaque mixtus, incolumi matre: poſteâ in ſcelera omnia, & dedecora prorumpens*[*]. Thus did he, *gradually*, become the moſt deſpicable, the moſt hated, the moſt accurſed of charaćters: his long life, and exalted ſtation, only adding to the weight of infamy and miſery on his head.

THE name of *Germanicus* has been now, for more than ſeventeen centuries, and will probably continue, as long as the *roman* hiſtory remains,

---

[*] TACIT. *Annal.* lib. vi. c. ult.

beloved

beloved and reverenced. *Ingenium illi contiget, in utroque eloquentiæ ac doctrinæ studio præcellens;* and that in poetry too, as well as oratory. *Multa reliquit studiorum monumenta;* particularly a tranſlation of *Aratus,* with aſtronomical notes. But, what is of infinitely more conſequence, *fortitudinem habuit egregiam; benevolentiam ſingularem: conciliandæque hominum gratiæ, ac promerendi amoris, mirum & efficax studium* *.

HE continued always to keep his heart, with all diligence, *in the conſtant habit of intending and aiming at the beſt deſigns:* he conſequently was both in mind and countenance, and in all his words and actions, open, generous, and noble. *Tiberius,* on the contrary, as the neceſſary conſequence of his wickedneſs, is ſaid to have always had diſſimulation in his countenance, inſincerity and darkneſs in his ſpeech, and malevolence in his heart. For, in proportion as he himſelf loſt all title to real glory, he became moſt meanly envious of others; ſo that all the honours, which *they* acquired, offended him.

GERMANICUS was compaſſionate to the unhappy, and kind even to his rivals. He was faithful and brave himſelf in the ſervice of his country. He honoured all the living and dead

* Vid. SUETON, in *Calig.* 2.

who

who had been fo. *Sicubi clarorum virorum fepul-chra cognofceret, inferias manibus dabat. Cæforum Varianorum præfertim reliquias colligere & tumulo condere primus aggreffus eft.* I recollect with pleafure *your* fentiments upon the fubject, my good pupil. On your journey through *Weftphalia*, in the neighbourhood of *Paderborn*, you vifited *that* fpot.

IF I be not miftaken, replied *Crito's* pupil, turning the converfation, and pointing to the bufts of *Trajan* *, *that* emperor acted in the fame noble and generous manner. In a *french* hiftory of his life, which I lately read, it is remarked, that *Trajan fit elever un autel, en memoire de ceux qui étoient tués dans les combats ; & y fonda des facrifices annuels.* But pray proceed to the other parts of *Germanicus's* character.

AT the hazard of his own life, continued *Crito*, *Germanicus* was loyal to *Tiberius*, his adoptive father; although he was in continual danger of deftruction from his malice, and almoft fure of obtaining the imperial power, had he been inclined to wreft it from the poffeffor. *Legiones impera-*

---

* *Amendue i bufti di Trajano fono di un perfetto lavoro, & fomigliantiffimi con le medaglie, amendue di marmo bianco, ed il primo e tutto di un pezzo.* Mufeo Capitolino, p. 49.

torem

torem Tiberium recufantes, & fibi fummum im-
perium deferentes compefcuit; incertùm majore
conftantiâ an pietate. Thefe legions were the
army on the *Rhine; robur imperii, & vi fuâ*
cunƈta traƈturum. How different was this noble
fpirit of *Germanicus*, from that *ignavia*, of which
Velleius Paterculus fo injurioufly accufes him!

BUT, to proceed in the contraft between his
charaƈter, and that of *Tiberius.* *Tiberius*, by
degrees, came to have fcarce any objeƈt, but that
of mean felf-love, and falfe ambition; to have
no affeƈtion for any perfon; to be fufpicious and
fearful of all. And yet,—wretched fruit of fuch
a temper!—this tyrant was continually admitting
the worft of men to his fociety and favour; and
continually bufied in the horrid work of per-
fecuting and murdering his near relations, as
well as the moft innocent and worthy of his
fubjeƈts.

GERMANICUS was always inclined to benignity and goodnefs; mild and forgiving to his
flanderers; fupporting affronts with true magnanimity and patience; and with the greateft generofity faving the lives, even of his moft determined enemies. *Tiberius*, on the contrary, grew
more hard-hearted and cruel; and became infti-
gated

gated by fuch mean malevolence towards all his fellow-creatures, as at laft, in the bitternefs of his malice, to repeat that diabolical line,

$$\text{Εμε Θανοντ©⸱, γαια μιγθητω πυρι.}$$

A sentiment, the wickednefs of which could be imitated only by himfelf, or by a *Nero* *. But let us haften from a train of thought fo truly dreadful. From fuch a hell, *Libera nos, Domine!*

This laft expreffion of *Crito* was occafioned by the accidental circumftance, that happened while he was yet fpeaking. The monks of *Ara Cœli* were at that inftant croffing the *Capitoline* area in proceffion, finging the litany. Their chaunt was heard diftinctly in the mufeum. The company went to the balcony in the *Sala Grande*, to fee the proceffion; and then, at the defire of the young nobleman, walked down the ftone ftair-cafe.

*   *   *

At the bottom of the ftair-cafe is a fmall paved court, adorned with a fountain. In the midft of

---

* *Nero's* fentiment was, if poffible, ftill more infernal : *Repetente enim quodam hoc carmen : immò, inquit* Εμε ζωντ©⸱. *Shakfpeare* has placed the fame horrid wifh in the mouth of a fimilar tyrant, *Macbeth.*

I wifh the ftate of the world were now undone!

this fountain is placed a coloſſal antique ſtatue, repreſenting, if we may truſt common opinion, the river *Rhine.* This ſtatue is generally known by the name of *Marforio ;* probably on account of it's having been once a principal ornament of the adjoining *forum,* and temple of *Mars* *.

PERHAPS, ſaid the young nobleman, this ſtatue may bear ſome relation to the hiſtory of *Germani-cus.* Pere *Bougeant* ſays, that *Germanicus adorned the temple of* Mars *the revenger*†, *with the ornaments of his triumph, and the ſpoils of* Germany. Poſſibly this figure of the *Rhine* might be then placed there. I know not on what authority pere *Bougeant's* hiſtory is founded; but I think *Tacitus* ſpeaks of a triumphal arch, built within a ſtone's caſt of this forum, expreſsly on account of theſe *german* victories‡. Is it not probable, that the *romans* might then have placed this ſtatue of the *Rhine* before the temple of their idols, as a per-

manent

---

* The forum of *Auguſtus* ſtood nearly adjoining to the *Capitol:* in the middle of this forum was the temple of *Mars* the revenger.

  See *Donati's Roman* Antiquities, book ii. ch. 22.

† Hiſtoire d'Allemagne, livre ii. p. 205. *Germanicus mit pied à terre, quitta ſa robe triumphale, & ſacrifia à Jupiter pluſieurs taureaux blancs : il porta enſuite au temple de Mars le vengeur les ornemens du triomphe, & les depouilles des germains.*

‡ *Fine anni dicatur arcus, propter ædem Saturni, ob recepta ſigna, cum Varo amiſſa, ductu Germanici, auſpiciis Tiberii.*

Annal. lib. ii. c. 41.

.On

manent emblem of their victories, after having dragged it, as it were captive, through their ftreets? It feems a confirmation of this conjecture, that *Tacitus*, in defcribing the triumph of *Germanicus*, fays exprefsly, *Vecta fimulacra fluminum* *.

Such indeed, faid the eldeft of the young gentlemen, was, on many occafions, the haughty pride of the *romans*. But with refpect to *Germany*, their boafts of victory were not only arrogant, but alfo void of foundation. Often did they pretend to triumph over *Germany:* whereas, in fact, this mighty river, the *Rhine*, was the impaffable boundary, the *ne plus ultrà* of the *roman* empire.

On the foundations of this temple of *Saturn*, adjoining to the forum of *Auguftus*, the church of St. *Adrian* in *Campo vaccino* now ftands. Clofe by which church, this ftatue of the *Rhine* lay on the ground, neglected, during many of the middle ages. It has been but lately removed to the *Capitol*.

At the diftance of fome few yards from the church of St. *Adrian*, is a triumphal arch, infcribed to *Severus;* probably built on the very fpot of *Germanicus's* or *Tiberius's* triumphal arch; and, poffibly, compofed in a great meafure of it's materials. It might even be imagined, without any very *great* appearance of abfurdity, that it is the fame identical arch, without any other alteration than that of the infcription. The fculptures on it feem very applicable to the hiftory of *Germanicus's* campaigns: particularly the naval expeditions, and the reliefs of the four river-gods *foprà gli archi collaterali;* two of which may perhaps reprefent the *Elbe* and *Rhine*, and the other two, which are younger, and without beards, the *Ems* and *Wefer*.

* *Tacit.* Annal. lib. ii. c. 41.

It

IT is true, that *Germanicus*, and his father *Dru-sus*, extended the ravages of war acrofs it's ftreams; and made the banks of the *Ems*, the *Wefer*, and the *Elbe*, the theatre of fome of their campaigns. One of their officers, I think, even paffed the *Elbe* * ; yet thefe campaigns, bloody and deftructive as they were, produced no fettled conquefts. After much flaughter and toil, after many viciffitudes of defeat and victory, the *romans* found themfelves obliged to fall back again to the *Rhine.*

THE *Rhine* continued, ever afterwards, the limit of their dominion. This is generally attributed to the wife policy and ftate-maxims of fome of the emperors. But there were manifeftly other reafons for it. *Rome* was able, and therefore willing, to extend her dominion in the weft, beyond the great boundary of the ocean; and to penetrate even to the *filures* and *brigantes:* but fhe was never able to fubdue the warlike inhabitants of *Weftphalia* and *Hanover.* I recollect *Florus's* obfervation on this fubject. *Imperium, quod non fleterat in littore oceani, ftabat in ripâ fluminis Rheni:* it might be added, *femper ftetit.* How much muft fome of our *faxon* anceftors have exulted in this thought!

* L. Domitius exercitu flumen Albim tranfcendit, longiùs pe-netratâ Germaniâ, quam quifquam priorum.

Tacit. Annal. lib. iv. c. 44.
THE

THE converfation now was changed, for fome minutes, into a panegyric on the heroifm and fortitude of the *german* nations. It foon, however, returned to the charaĉter of *Germanicus*.

I REMEMBER, continued the eldeſt of the young gentlemen, that, when at *Cologne*, I employed a long afternoon, in the ftudy of thofe campaigns of *Germanicus*, which are defcribed in *Tacitus's* Annals.

IN the morning, I had been for feveral hours walking about that old city, and viewing with much pleafure the magazine of antique *roman* arms in the *ſtadt-houſe**, and the bas-reliefs of the head of *Germanicus* on the walls of fome of the public buildings. After ːdinner I went up into my chamber, the windows of which commanded an extenfive profpeĉt acrofs the *Rhine;* I fat down in the window feat, and turned over feveral parts of the firſt two books of *Tacitus*.

SOMETIMES I caſt my eyes acrofs the river, and imagined I faw *Agrippina* ſtanding at the foot of the bridge: fometimes I looked up the ſtream towards *Bonn,* and recolleĉted *Germanicus's* fide-

* *Pococke* obferves, that thefe arms are very fimilar to thofe, which he had feen in an old *roman* arfenal, at *Beer,* on the *Euphrates.*

lity

lity there to *Tiberius :* at other times I looked down the ftream, and thought of *Germanicus's* laborious campaigns in *Friefland* and *Embden.*

IN reading the hiftory of thefe campaigns, I met with feveral paffages, which, from a want of prac- tice in the ftyle of *Tacitus,* and from my extreme ignorance in the art of war, ancient as well as mo- dern, I could not underftand. The obfcurity was increafed by the great changes, which fince *Tacitus's* time have happened, in the countries near the mouths of the *Rhine.*

IF you pleafe, faid *Crito,* we will at prefent turn our thoughts from *Germanicus's* military hif- tory. His warlike achievements gained him in- deed great reputation at *Rome;* yet we muft own, that, as in the military hiftory of *Drufus, Scipio,* and other *roman* heroes, fo likewife in this of *Ger- manicus,* there are many things, that are really the objefts of horrour, not of admiration.—*Quin- quaginta millium fpatium, ferro flammifque per- vaftavit: non fexus, non ætas, miferationem at- tulit*. — Infifterent cædibus; nil opus captivis; folam internecionem gentis finem bello foret†.*

SHUTTING our eyes to thefe fcenes of warlike cruelty, the perpetual difgrace of *roman* heroifm;

* Annalium. lib. i. c. 51.
† Annal. lib. ii. c. 21.

let

let us contemplate *Germanicus* in another, and far more pleafing light.

So faying, *Crito* turned from the figure of the *Rhine*, and walked into the adjoining portico.

* * *

AT the end of the portico, fronting the ftair-cafe, is a room called the *Canopus*. It is adorned with about a dozen *egyptian* fculptures, executed in a manner remarkably elegant.

THE company paffed a quarter of an hour in that room; during which time their converfation naturally fell upon the hiftory of *Egypt*.

IN the middle of the fame portico, fronting the gate, ftand two *egyptian* ftatues, of a much larger fize, and to all appearance of much greater anti-quity. One of them bears on it's head a kind of *corona turrita ;* holds in it's right hand the roll of a book, and in it's left a palm-branch : feveral hieroglyphic charaĉters are engraved on it's fide.

THE ftudy of the *egyptian* hiftory, faid *Crito*, would be a very amufing employment to perfons refident at *Rome*, were there at prefent in this city any *coptite* or *abyffinian* prieft, capable of

explaining

explaining the hieroglyphic language ; in the fame manner as the learned *Hermapion*, whofe book on that fubject is mentioned by *Ammianus Marcellinus**. If fuch were the cafe, perhaps we might find, from thefe hieroglyphic characters, that the perfon reprefented by this ftatue was the moft glorious, the moft beneficent of conquerors, the *royal Ofiris: Ofiris*, the builder of cities; the patron of agriculture, of learning, and of all the arts of peace.

My pupil's vifion of the genius of the obelifk, has turned my thoughts, fince I heard it, to the hiftory of *Egypt*. One morning, in the latter end of laft week, I took up the firft book of *Diodorus Siculus;* and read, with much pleafure, the account of *king Ofiris's* expeditions.

That account feems, at firft view, a mere romance ; but perhaps *you*, dear fir, continued *Crito*, turning to the eldeft of his young friends, might have been able to extract from it fome important doctrines of *true* political wifdom.

If we fuppofe the prince of a civilized country to have any concerns with favage and barbarous nations, what better or wifer plan of policy can

* See *Ammianus Marcellinus's* Hiftory of *Conftantius.* Book 17.

he

he lay down for himfelf, than the grand outlines of *Ofiris's* conduct? To become, not fo much the formidable enemy, as the real friend of barbarians; not to invade, and confequently *force* them to learn the *arts* of war, but to communicate to them the far happier arts of peace; to introduce among them the bleffings of civilized life; to inftruct them in agriculture; to enlighten their minds with ufeful knowledge, and blefs them with the pureft doctrines of piety and morality.

HAPPY would it have been for the *roman* empire, if *Auguftus* and his fucceffors had followed, far as they were able, this wholefome plan of po_licy, in regard to the *german* nations. Happy would it have been, if *Germanicus* had been fent to the banks of the *Wefer* and *Elbe*, not in the character of a dreadful *roman* general, a fevere, though excellent mafter in the art of war;* but rather in a character fimilar to that of *Ofiris's* lieutenant, *Triptolemus.*

How rejoiced would *Germanicus* have been, in an employment fo fuitable to the goodnefs of his heart! With what pleafure would he have inftructed the barbarians, to till their foil, to drain

* *Diriguntur acies, non, ut olim apud germanos, vagis incurfibus, aut dijectas per catervas : quippe longâ adverfus nos militiâ infueverant fequi figna, fubfidiis firmari, dicta imperatorum accipere.* Tacit. Ann. lib. ii. c. 45.

their

their marſhes, and to clear thoſe vaſt foreſts, with which *Germany* was then covered!

HAD ſuch a plan of policy been followed, it is probable the *germans* would have been much more happy : for thus they might have partaken the benefits of a civilized life, without being corrupted or enſlaved by luxury : and it is alſo very probable, that *Rome* would never have been deſtroyed by the inundations of the *german* nations. Againſt their fiercenefs, the plough would have been a much better weapon, than the *roman* ſword.

IN faɛt, we find the dreadful inundations of the north never to have ceaſed, till agriculture, civilization, and other ſciences were introduced into that quarter. While the northern nations depended on hunting for their ſubſiſtence, they perpetually found their vaſt regions too narrow for their numbers : but, upon applying themſelves to agriculture, they found the ſame extent of country amply capable of ſupporting them, even had their multitudes been increaſed an hundred fold.

* * *

THE converſation now imperceptibly wandered to the account given by *Tacitus* of *Germanicus's* travels

travels into *Egypt*; and of his voyage up the *Nile*, from the town of *Canopus*, to the great city of *Osiris*, the hundred-gated *Thebes* *.

I REMEMBER, faid *Crito's* pupil, that, while reading in *England* this part of *Tacitus*, I frequently confulted *Pococke's* travels into the *Eaſt*, and *Norden's* late voyage on the *Nile* from the ruins of *Alexandria* up to thofe of *Luxor* and *Carnac*. Since our arrival at *Rome*, I vainly pleafe myfelf with the fancy of having here met with a memorial of *Germanicus's* vifit to *Thebes*. On the *Lateran* obelifk, which, if I be not miftaken, was originally a *principal* ornament of that great *egyptian* metropolis, I think I difcovered one day, when the fun fhone remarkably favourable on that part, feveral *roman* charafters; being the firft five or fix letters of *Germanicus's* name, engraven fideways among, or rather acrofs, the hieroglyphics. Allowing me to indulge this fancy, it is probable, that thefe letters might be thus engraved by *Germanicus's* order, while at *Thebes*, as a memorial of his journey thither; in the fame manner as, according to *Pococke* and *Norden*, many other *roman* and *greek* names are infcribed on the feet of *Memnon's* ſtatue.

* Annal. lib. ii. c. 60.

But

BUT I muſt not trouble you any longer with a conjecture, which, if not wholly void of foundation, certainly is but trifling. Let me rather defire my tutor to continue his delineation of the characters of *Germanicus* and *Tiberius*.

* * *

IN order to place in a ſtronger light the comparifon of thefe characters, replied *Crito*, it may not be an improper method to confider *Germanicus*, as we are now doing, during his travels through thofe parts of the world, which were at that time moſt famous, either for the ancient, or for the actual merit of their inhabitants.

GERMANICUS travelled with the greateſt continual pleaſure, becaufe with continued innocence; and with a fixed intention to learn, and practiſe goodneſs, in every place.

GERMANICUS, according to the doctrine of *Pythagoras*, a doctrine, my dear pupil, worthy the notice of every young traveller to *Italy*, Μɑσɑς Σειρηνων ηδιɛς ηγειτο.

GERMANICUS, in vifiting and examining the venerable antiquities of *Greece*, *Aſia*, and *Egypt*,

Egypt, fatisfied a very laudable curiofity: it might have been wifhed, however, that, before he went into *Egypt,* he had not forgotten to afk *Tiberius's* permiffion for making that tour.

GERMANICUS refpeƐted the inhabitants of thofe celebrated countries, for the fake of their anceftors. And, being invefted with a great fhare in the government, he conftantly, in fome degree like the great and good *Ofiris,* made it his bufinefs, in all countries through which he paffed, to take that opportunity of eftablifhing the public tranquillity, order, and plenty; appeafing, to his utmoft, all difcords, and relieving every oppref- fion, whether foreign or domeftic*.

——————— Φιλ☉ δ'ην ανϑρωποισι,
Παντας γαρ Φιλεεσκεν.

In contraft with this affability and beneficence of *Germanicus,* let us confider *Tiberius,* the ab- folute monarch of the vaft *roman* empire, ab- fconding even from *Rome.* Moft part of the latter end of his reign he paffed in a fmall ifland, about two hundred miles diftant from this city.

---

* *Provincias, internis certaminibus, aut magiftratuum injuriis feffas, refovebat.* Annal. lib. ii. c. 54. *Levavit apertis horreis pretia frugum.* Ibid. c. 59. *Alexandriam adiit, propter im- menfam ac. repentinam famem.* Sueton. in Tiberio, c. 52.

During

During the laft eleven years of his life, he never
once entered his own palace; never fet foot in
the *roman* forum; never afcended the *Capitoline*
hill : *gravatus afpeflum civium.*

IF one of the humble lay-brothers of the adjoining convent of *Ara Cæli* were now to over-
hear this part of our converfations, he would
probably, by his charity, be induced to pleafe
himfelf with the imagination, that *Tiberius*, in his
old age, might have chofen that retreat, from
penitential motives. Many a true penitent, he
might fay, has retired from the pomps of the world,
to rocky deferts, and folitary iflands, there to give
himfelf up to fuch religious compunction, as produced amendment of life : thus, after many years
of bitter forrow, lightening the load of the heart;
and chearing it gradually with fome humble hopes
of mercy; fome gleaming ray, at leaft, of true
felicity.

FAR otherwife, alas! with *Tiberius* : *his* purpofes of retirement had nothing holy in them. It
was originally owing partly to the artifice of his
prime minifter; partly to his own *worldly* fenfe of
confcious fhame: *Pudore fcelerum, & libidinum.*
At *Rome* he fometimes could not avoid hearing
voces illas, veras & graves, & probra, quibus

per

per occultum lacerabatur. Sometimes he was even reproached to his face for the vileſt actions.

IN chooſing the *place of his ſolitude, Tiberius* ſhowed no ſymptoms of a heart touched with any penitential ſenſe of it's crimes *. Innocence might have properly delighted itſelf in a retreat like *Capreæ:* but a true penitent would never have been curious in ſelecting ſo delightful a ſpot, or have thought himſelf worthy of ſuch an habitation.

" AND yet," our monk might add, " although pleaſantneſs of ſituation is a circumſtance by no means ſuitable to the juſt idea of a penitential retirement, it is neverthelefs poſſible, that *Tiberius* might employ his time well there. I know little of his hiſtory, notwithſtanding my bare feet every day tread this hill, which, as I have heard, was once a principal part of the city. Such kind of hiſtory is not indeed our ſtudy; which chiefly regards the piety of thoſe happy men, who have conſecrated by their retirements the deſerts of *Scete,* and dignified the mountains of *Alverno* and *Chartreuſe.* Pray inform me, what were

---

* *Inſula in Favonium obverſa, & aperto circum pelago peramæna; proſpectabatque pulcherrimum ſinum, antequam Veſuvius mons ardeſcens faciem loci verteret.*

Tacit, Annal. lib. iv. c. 67.

Tiberius's

Tiberius's frame of mind, and manner of life in his folitude?"—Let me anticipate your reply:

"*Malum otium,—luxus,—libido,—fævitia.*"

" Were thefe worft of devils the conftant poffeffors of his foul?"

" THEY feem to have been fo; except when, at intervals, confcience, arifing in all her blackeft terrours, aftonifhed him, overwhelmed him, almoft drove him mad. *Non enim illum fortuna, non folitudines protegebant, quin tormenta pectoris, fuafque ipfe pœnas fateretur. Ad fenatum enim his verbis orfus eft epiftolam,* " *Quid fcribam vobis,* " *patres confcripti, hoc tempore, aut quomodo* " *fcribam, aut quid omninò non fcribam, Di me,* " *Deæque pejus perdant, quàm perire quotidie* " *fentio, fi fcio.*" *Adeo facinora atque flagitia fua ipfi quoque in fupplicium verterant. Neque fruftrà præftantiffimus fapientiæ firmare folitus eft, fi recludantur tyrannorum mentes, poffe afpici laniatus & ictus; quando, ut corpora verberibus, ita fævitiâ, libidine, malis confultis, animus dilaceretur**."

BUT why, continued *Crito,* fhould I *imagine* myfelf talking on this fubject with one of the in-

* TACIT, *Annal.* lib. vi. c. 6.

habitants

habitants of the adjoining convent? It is with *you*, my fellow travellers, that I am *really* conversing.

You will foon, from the key and mole of *Naples*, behold that unhappy ifland, which is become eternally infamous by the perpetrations of it's diabolical inhabitant, *Tiberius*. You will fee it in every airing you take towards the fuburbs of *Paufilypo*, or *Maddalena:* but never will you have any defire to make a nearer approach to it, or to fet your feet on it's contaminated fhore.

Effugimus fcopulos Ithacæ, Laertia regna;
Et terram altricim fævi execramur Ulyffis*.

In the fame environs of *Naples*, you will perhaps fee other terrific objects: I mean, the horrours of the neighbouring volcanoes, which frequently burft forth in roaring rivers of liquid fire, in clouds of darknefs, and fhowers of flaming brimftone.

These horrours you will obferve with awe, if an eruption of mount *Vefuvius* fhould happen while you are at *Naples*. At all other times, your eyes will be charmed with the ferenity and fweet-

---

ÆNEID iii. 272.

nefs of the landfcapes, the truly *elyſian* fields, on the *neapolitan* coaſt; that coaſt, which in general, according to the proverb, *e un pezzo di ciel, caduto in terra* *. A young poet, indeed, after filling his mind with the ideas of *Pindar* or *Virgil*, might reprefent that coaſt as an emblem of the regions of the bleſſed: but never, I believe, did any man, of the plaineſt education, look upon *Veſuvius*, during an eruption, without almoſt inſtantaneouſly confidering it as an emblem, or rather as a viſible type, of hell.

Yet, alas! how great the difference! The conflagration of that hill, however horrid, is not an unquenchable flame; *that* is not an *everlaſting fire.*

No wonder, that guilty minds ſhould deeply feel the prefentiments of their future, unſpeakable mifery.

I remember, faid *Crito's* pupil, a paſſage in *Plutarch*, very applicable to your prefent topic†.

But

---

* "A *patch* of Heaven, dropped down upon the earth."

† Ουτ۞ μακαρι۞ εν αγορα νομιζεται,
Επαν δ᾽ ανοιξη τας θυρας, τρισαθλι۞.

‖ εαυτη κακια αει σινοικεσα τοις σπλαγχνοις, κ᾽ προςπεφυκυια νυκτωρ κ᾽ καθ᾽ ημεραν,
Εισι ατερ δαλε, κ᾽ ωμω γηραι δωκε.

Κα.

But there is no occafion to quote learned writers, for thofe fentiments, which are moft loudly ex-preffed by the voice of univerfal nature. The illi-terate and the learned, the rich and the poor, the high and low, are all alike expofed to the irrefifti-ble influence of confcience. With what attention, my dear young friends, have we often obferved in *England* a large audience, compofed of the moft different ranks and kinds of men; all, in deep filence, liftening to thofe fcenes of *Shak-fpeare*, in which the terrours of confcience are exemplified! I mean, particularly, the conclu-fion of the tragedies of *Richard* the Third, and *Macbeth.*

Cold fearful drops ſtand on my trembling fleſh.
O coward confcience, how doſt thou afflict me!
Oh, the affliction of thofe terrible dreams,
That ſhake us nightly! Better be with the dead,
Than on fuch torture of the mind to lie.
Oh! full of fcorpions is my mind.—I'm fill'd with
horrour!

In this refpect, the caftle of *Dunfinane* feems ftrongly to have refembled the palace of *Tiberius* in *Capreæ.*

Καὶ γαρ ὁ καθευδων, τȣ ΣΩΜΑΤΟΣ ὑπν@ εϛι κ̀ ἀναπαυσις, της δε ψυχης πλοιαι κ̀ ονειροι κ̀ ταραχαι δια δεισιδαιμονιαν. Πȣ τοινυν το ἡδυ της κακιας εϛιν, ει μηδαμȣ το αμεριμνον, μηδ' αταραξια, μηδε ἡσυχια. Plutarch, Περι αρετης και κακιας.

Iɴ

* * *.

I F you pleafe, faid *Crito*, we will refume our
claffical ftudies. My *own* confcience alfo preffes
too hard, to enable me to continue thefe moral
reflections. May Heaven have mercy on us all!

SPEAKING thefe words, *Crito* turned round,
and with a flow and penfive ftep walked acrofs
the *Capitoline* area, to the oppofite building, the
Palazzo Dei Confervatori.

IN the court of this building, on the left hand,
againft the wall, ftands a large ftone urn; on which
is the following infcription, in characters very
deeply cut:

OSSA
AGRIPPINÆ, M. AGRIPPÆ, DIVI AUGUSTI
NEPTIS, UXORIS GERMANICI, &c.

THE young gentlemen, after having for fome
time furveyed this fepulchral urn with melancholy pleafure, gave their attention to *Crito ;* who
with a down-caft look proceeded as follows.

I F we confider the domeftic life of *Germanicus,*
we fhall find him in that, as well as in other parts
of his character, infinitely more refpectable, and
infinitely more happy, than *Tiberius.*

TIBERIUS

TIBERIUS was, indeed, in his earlier years, a good brother; the temper of *Drusus* being perhaps irresistibly amiable: but he afterwards became an enemy to all his family; he was a bad son; and a cruel husband, to a wicked wife.

GERMANICUS, on the contrary, seems to have practised many of the virtues, and to have enjoyed many of the felicities of a family-life. He began by being a good brother, and a good son; and afterwards, in the usual progress of such a character, became a good father.

But let me desire you, at present, to consider him in his *conjugal* station.

The dignity and happiness of *Germanicus* were both very considerably increased, by his marriage with *Agrippina*.

The character of *Agrippina* would have been far more amiable, if to her many other virtues she had added a greater degree of meekness and humility; if she had been less sensible of the high quality of her family, and of her own real merit. But, standing as we now are before *that* urn, which probably for many centuries contained her ashes, let us do justice, and pay due tribute to her very respectable memory, by owning, that,

C c 3

among

among the matrons of heathen *Rome, Agrippina,* notwithstanding every defect, was one of the brightest examples of conjugal virtue.

SHE attained that dignity of character, partly by her own native goodness; partly by the aid and influence of her beloved husband's example.

CRITO now paused for some moments, to wipe away the tears that stood in his eyes, and which really hindered him from reading his paper of notes.

IN her arms, continued *Crito* with a sigh, *Germanicus* expired. With her alone had he passed through life from his earliest years: for he enjoyed the *great happiness* of *marrying early;* and of thus soon blessing both himself and his parents, with the sight of no less than six of his children.

O MY noble young friend! *You* who so frequently inquire after proper subjects in the *roman* story, on which you may employ some of the painters, whether *english* or *italian,* now in this city; what subject can you find, either more pleasing, or more instructive, than the scene of *Augustus,* placed on his imperial seat, and enacting the *laws against celibacy,* which at that time, in a manner much more destructive than
any

civil war, was wafting and extirpating the greateſt families in *Rome* *? Seated in that ſtate, and per-haps on *this very hill,* he directed, that his great grand-children, the offspring of *Germanicus,* ſhould be brought into his preſence. He then, in fight of the whole ſenate, took up ſome of theſe little ones in his arms; others he placed on the knees of the young prince their father; and, with the happy and amiable pride of a parent, ſhowed to the aſſembly all theſe, *his treaſures;* inviting the young nobility of *Rome* to be ſenſible of ſuch happineſs, and haſten to follow the example of his *Germanicus. Ne gravarentur imitari juvenis exemplum* †.

Such was *Germanicus,* when he had ſcarcely completed his twenty-fourth year. — Compare with this charming ſpectacle ſome parts of the character of *Tiberius.*

But, indeed, the contraſt now grows far too diſmal and horrid for deſcription, either by pen

* The young reader is *moſt earneſtly* referred on this oc-caſion, to the beginning of the fifty-ſixth book of *Dio Caſſius,* p. 573—578. He is deſired alſo to conſult Univerſal Hiſ-tory, vol. xiv. p. 20.—*Tacit.* lib. iii. c. 25, and *Freinſhem.* lib. lix. c. 53, with it's note.
Auguſtus libros totos, & ſenatui recitavit, & populo notos per edictum ſæpe fecit : ut orationes Q. Metelli, de prole augendâ, & Rutilii de modo ædificiorum; quo magis perſuaderet utram-que rem, non à ſe primo animadverſam, ſed antiquis jam tunc curæ fuiſſe. Sueton. Auguſtus, 89.
† Sueton. in *Auguſt.* 34.

or

or pencil. It's horrours are greatly augmented by the confideration, that *Tiberius's* enormous wickednefs was continued to his old age. For, as I before obferved, he feems never to have attempted to wafh away, with bitter tears, the black and difmal crimes, of which he had been guilty.

No wonder, that fo foon as the death of this vileft of tyrants was publicly known, the univerfal hatred and deteftation of his memory fhould break forth, with the greateft indignation and fury. No wonder, that, in all the ftreets which furround this hill, the populace fhould be crying out, with the loudeft clamours; fome, that his vile corpfe, as unworthy of fepulture, fhould be caft into the river; *Tiberius in Tiberim:* others, that it fhould with all ignominy be dragged from the palace-gates to the *public gibbet;* or expofed, like the bodies of other *far lefs guilty* malefactors, on the *Scalæ Gemoniæ* *.

But let us not think any longer on this hateful fubject.

As a relief from the difhonourable conclufion of *Tiberius's* infamous exiftence, let us turn our eyes again to the hiftory of *Germanicus.*

* Sueton, *Vita Tiberii.* c. 74.

With

With what pleafure, my dear fellow-travellers, did you, while at *Lyons*, vifit the pleafant hill, and furvey the magnificent profpeƈt, of *Antiquaille & Forviere* *; the place where *Germanicus*, though I know not on what authority, is faid to have been *born!* With what affeƈtion alfo did you yefterday vifit the place of his *fepulture*, in the *Campo Marzo!* From his cradle indeed to his grave, the charaƈter of *Germanicus* was almoft ever amiable, as well as refpeƈtable.

Virtuum fruƈlum uberrimum tulit: maximè probatus & dileƈus a fuis: dileƈlus etiam ab omnibus, in vitâ; & multò magis in morte, & poft mortem †.

His reputation was fo great, as to have gained him multitudes of friends and admirers, even in countries which he had never feen. *Flebant Germanicum, etiam ignoti.*

Much ftronger, probably, were the love and veneration of thofe, who had really felt and been made happy by his goodnefs. The provincials of whom he had been governor; the allies of the *roman* empire, to whom he had been a very bene-

---

* Perhaps a corruption of the words *Antiquum palatium fori veteris.*

† Sueton. in Vit. *Calig.* 4.

volent general and commander; even the enemies of *Rome*, to whom, after the horrours of the campaign were paſſed, he had been a merciful conqueror;—all theſe cordially joined in honouring the memory, and lamenting the fate, of *Germanicus.*

But with reſpect to *Italy*, and to *Rome*, the ſincere and zealous affection born to *Germanicus* while alive, and the general grief, deſolation, and even deſpair, which attended, and long followed his departure; *theſe* were, in all reſpects, ſo *very great*, as far to exceed any power of deſcription: nay, even were the *genius of this place* to inſpire us, whom you, my dear poetic pupil, may ſuppoſe, to be now hovering over and protecting this urn of *Agrippina.*

> *Quis deſiderio ſit pudor, aut modus,*
> *Tam chari capitis?·Præcipe lugubres*
>   *Cantus, Melpomene! cui liquidam pater*
>   *Vocem cum cithará dedit* *.

If, my dear fellow-travellers, continued *Crito*, after a pauſe, if in our *Levant* travels, we ſhould ever pitch our tent amidſt the ruins of *Antioch;* ſhall we not then, among many other ſubjects of

HORAT. lib. i. od. 24.

meditation,

meditation, recollect the death of *Germanicus*?
Shall we not there bestow some serious thoughts
on the scene of his last hour?

YET, let me observe, that this scene would
have been far more noble, if *Germanicus* had not
even at such a period excited his friends to *revenge* his death. With a trembling voice let me
add, that his virtue would have been far more
perfect, if, like *St. Stephen*, or like some HOLIER
PERSON, who was then living in sacred retirement, in the neighbouring province of *Galilee*, he
had expired, blessing and praying for his murderers.

BUT let us not at present carry our thoughts so
far as to *eastern* travels. In the course of our
short intended tour through the kingdom of *Naples*, we shall see several places, that will strongly
remind us of the death of *Germanicus*.

DURING that tour, you will certainly pass some
days at *Brindisi*. While you, my dear pupil, are
walking in the thick olive groves, with which that
fertile coast is covered, and viewing from them
the two famous *horns* of that spacious haven; will
you not be frequently inclined to recollect *Tacitus's* description of *Agrippina*, landing at *that*
port, with the urn of *Germanicus* in her hands?

and

and muſt not that recollection awaken in your mind ſome ideas of a ſweet poetic melancholy ?

In your return fram *Brindiſi* to the northern parts of *Italy*, particularly at *Terracina*, you will call to mind the great public love, admiration, and grief, which followed the urn of *Germanicus* from *Brunduſium*, through all the provinces of *Italy*, to his grave at *Rome*.

I am the more inclined to believe, that you will be ſtrongly affected with this recollection, as in your journey through *France*, particularly when you were in the neighbourhood of *Straſburgh*, you often re-peruſed, and ſometimes not without tears of pleaſure, the deſcriptions given by the *french* hiſtorians of that public love and veneration, which attended the corpſe of *Turenne*, through all the cities and provinces of that great kingdom, to the royal mauſoleum at *St. Dennis.*

I remember too the pleaſure you expreſſed at the ſimilar public reſpect, which was paid in our own country to the memory of our late youthful hero, general *Wolfe.* What addreſs did any city or county then preſent to the throne of *Great Britain*, in which general *Wolfe's* name was not mentioned, with terms of the greateſt praiſe and love? I remember alſo your deſcription of
that

that eloquence, with which the houfe of commons was then moved to vote, and it was voted *unanimoufly*, That a monument fhould be erected to his memory, at the public charge, in *Weftminfter Abbey.*

BUT through what wanderings of thought have I led you! Permit me to clofe my paper of notes, by defiring you to employ fome of your firft leifure hours, in perufing afrefh *Tacitus's* account of the general grief of *Rome* on the death of *Germanicus.* The great ftrength of fenfe to be found in that hiftorian will make ample amends for your patience, in liftening to whatever may have been the improprieties or follies of my imagination.

IN proof, however, of the utility, that may be derived from the contraft of fuch characters, as thofe which I have this day endeavoured to place before your eyes, let me fubmit to your reflection three or four lines of that great hiftorian.

Exequi infignia per honeftum, aut notabili dedecore. Præcipuum munus annalium reor, ne virtutes fileantur, utque pravis dictis factifque ex pofteritate & infamiâ metus fit *.

* *Tacit.* Annal. lib. iii. c. 65.

CRITO

* * *

CRITO having thus concluded the morning's. lecture, with a ferious countenance folded up his papers, and fat down in filence.

His young friends now entered into a warm debate upon fome particulars, which he had mentioned towards the conclufion of his lecture.

The eldeft of the gentlemen compared the glorious fate of general *Wolfe* to that of *Epaminondas;* and repeated with energy fome expreffions of *Valerius Maximus. Si eum Di immortales victoriis fuis perfrui paffi effent, hofpes gloriofior patriæ mænia non intráffet.*

The young nobleman recollected feveral circumftances relative to the death of marfhal *Turenne.* He lamented *Drufus* alfo, cut down in the flower of his age, during his *german* campaign. He then made fome remarks on the excellence of that marble buft, which they had juft now feen in the *Capitoline* mufeum, and which reprefents *Drufus* in the prime of manhood.

Yet why, faid *Crito's* pupil, fhould the early death of *Drufus* be lamented? *Drufus* certainly
had

had the happinefs, the greateft happinefs, I fuppofe, which a father can feel, of leaving a fon, who excelled him in virtue—a *Germanicus.*

Πατρῷ δ᾽ ογε ϖολλον αμεινων.

Both father, indeed, and fon died young: but neither of their deaths can be reckoned premature. Let us look only on the family of the *Cæfars,* and compare the fhort lives of *Drufus* and *Germanicus,* with thofe of *Caligula* and *Nero,* none of whom furvived the thirtieth year of his age; and furely we fhall not want a proof, that the *height of human glory,* as well as the *depth of infamy,* may be the confequence of the virtues and vices practifed within thefe years.

* * *

The converfation now took fome frefh *detours:* though, amidft the labyrinth of it's feveral wanderings, it ftill recurred to the proper object of this day's ftudy, the hiftory of *Tiberius's* reign.

The eldeft of the young gentlemen fpoke with proper refpect of the hiftorian *Cremutius Cordus;* cheerfully repeating on that occafion a few fentences

tences from *Seneca**. He then proceeded with horrour to fome of the other cruelties of *Tiberius,* and of that infamy of prime minifters, *Sejanus.*

CRITO mentioned, from *Tacitus,* the banifh- ment of fome thoufand jews by *Tiberius* into the marfhes of *Sardinia:*—*fi interirent, vile damnum.* He alfo cited, from *Philo Judæus,* Sejanus's de- fign of extirpating the whole jewifh nation.

CRITO'S pupil, on this occafion, compared *Sejanus* to *Haman;* and following that tract of thought, recollected feveral verfes of *Racine's Efther,* which feemed to him very applicable to the fudden fall of *Sejanus.*

J'ai vu l'Impie adoré fur la terre:
Pareil au cedre il cachoit dans les cieux
Son front audacieux.
Il fembloit à fon gré gouverner le tonnerre;
Il fouloit aux piés fes ennemis vaincus.
Je n'ai fait que paffer; il n'étoit déja plus.—
Miferable! Le Dieu vengeur de l'innocence,
Tout prêt à te juger, tient déja fa balance:
Bientot fon jufte arrêt te fera prononcé.
Tremble. Ton jour approche, & ton regne eft paffé.

---

* See *Seneca's* confolation, addreffed to *Martia,* the daugh- ter of *Cremutius Cordus.*

——*le*

―――― *le Traitre eſt expiré.*
Par le peuple en fureur à moitié dechiré;
On traine, on va donner en ſpectacle funeſte,
De ſon corps tout ſanglant le miſerable reſte *.

*　　*　　*

THE company now went out of the court of the *Palazzo dei conſervatori.* But the fall of *Se-janus* continued to be their topic, while walking down the ſlope of the *Capitoline* hill, towards the forum.

I HAVE lately, ſaid the eldeſt of the young gentlemen, been reading *Dion Caſſius's* account of the grandeur and fall of that infamous court favourite †.

DION'S reflections, on the vanity of all human pride, ſtrike me at preſent very ſtrongly; while oppoſite to us, on the *Palatine* mount, I ſee the ruins of that building, which *Sejanus* entered, full of pride, and big with the expectation of being *that morning* inveſted with the tribunitian power. Cloſe on our right hand is the temple of Concord; in which, on the *afternoon of the ſame day*, *Seja-nus* was unanimouſly condemned to death. About

―――――――――――――――

* The above quotations are thrown together, from *Eſther,* acte iii. ſcenes 5, 8, 9.
† *Dio Caſſius,* book lviii. p. 623 to 630.

one hundred yards on our left is the prifon, in which, *before night,* he was ftrangled*.

In that difmal evening, he faw perhaps, from the grates of his cell, the deftruction of his ftatues in *this* forum; and heard the curfes of the people from all fides upon his memory.

The then-felt *vanity* of his exceffive honours, riches, and ambitious hopes, together with the confcioufnefs of his horrid crimes, muft have greatly embittered the deep diftrefs of his laft hour.

Ergo quid optandum foret, ignoráffe fatendum eft
Sejanum : nam qui nimios optabat honores,
Et nimias pofcebat opes, numerofa parabat
Excelfæ turris tabulata, unde altior effet
Cafus, & impulfæ præceps immane ruinæ†.

CRITO'S pupil repeated fome verfes of *Shak-fpeare,* relative to cardinal *Wolfey.* I have often, added he, thought of thofe verfes in paffing

---

* The antique infcription, *now remaining* on the prifon walls, was engraven in the ædilefhip of *Vibius* and *Cocceius Nerva.* They were confuls about four or five years after *Sejanus's* death. See *Abbate Venuti,* vol. i, p. 58. The *Scalæ Gemoniæ,* where *Sejanus's* body was caft, were fituate in that fhort, crooked, fteep lane, which paffes by the fide of the *Tullian* prifon, and leads up to the *Capitol.*

† JUVENAL. *Sat.* x. 103.

through

through *Leicefter*. We had frefh occafion to recollect them fome weeks ago; when we were fhown the *Palazzo*, built by that cardinal's orders, here, at *Rome*.

I remember, faid *Crito*, that when we were at *Milan*, I met with a paffage in *St. Auftin's* works, which appears very fuitable to the topic on which you are now converfing. It is the reflection of a perfon, who, if I miftake not, was of confiderable rank in the court of the *roman* emperor, predeceffor to *Theodofius*.

" With all the pains we take, what doth our " ambition afpire to? What is it we feek, and " propofe to ourfelves?

" Can we have any greater hopes at court, than " to arrive at the favour of the emperor? *Per* " *quot pericula pervenitur ad illud* grandius *peri-* " *culum? Et quamdiu iftud erit?*

" *Amicus autem DEI, fi voluero, ecce, nunc fio.*"

The converfation now dwelt, for a confiderable time, on the outward fplendour, but frequent real mifery, of a minifterial or court life.

OUR young nobleman, during the difcuffion, communicated to his friends feveral very important reflections, which he had heard from his father on thefe fubjects.

* * *

THE company returned to their lodgings about dinner-time; but *Crito* made fome excufe for not dining with them. He retired to his clofet, and it being *faturday* afternoon, applied himfelf, as ufual, to fome private ftudies.

THE object of his meditation was a character, remarkably contrary to the wickednefs of this world; contrary as light is to darknefs: the character of the auftere, pure, and holy *St. John* the Baptift.

IT was about the time of *Sejanus's* death, that *St. John came preaching in* Judæa *the baptifm of repentance, for the remiffion of fins.*

CRITO paffed fome moments in confidering this holy character, compared with thofe, which are generally found in *king's houfes:* but he foon quitted that kind of thought, and began to apply the weighty doctrine of penitence *home* to *his own* heart.

WHY

Why fhould he look for faults among other men? He found enow in the recorded memorial of his own actions.

In deep compunction of mind he *thought there-on, and wept.* He applied himfelf afrefh to the ftudy of the Baptift's life: he afterwards took up the poetical tranflation of the *Pfalter*, lately pub-lifhed at *Arezzo*, by *Peter Roffi;* and perufed two or three of the penitential pfalms.

He perufed alfo fome part of the copy of verfes prefixed to the work; in which the author thus addreffes himfelf to the *hebrew* pfalmift.

—— *Canendi fpiritum mihi impetra,*
Tuo refufus qui calebat pectore;
Tuis ut inftem proximus veftigiis,
Tuofque fenfus, et verenda intelligam
Tuis repofta verfibus myfteria.——
Id fi negetur, et frequenti crimine
Cæcata, mens fpectare non tam altùm poteft;
Placare læfi me doce iram Numinis
Tua æmulantem exempla; et illas intimo
E corde ductas ac falubres lacrymas,
Quibus juventæ tu piafti improvidæ
Errata, et æquum leniifti judicem.
Id fi impetráro, multò erit jucundius,
Quàm fi tua æmuler canendo carmina.

C H A P. V.

. TWENTY-THIRD DAY'S CONVERSATION.

IN the account of yefterday's tranfactions, no notice was taken of the manner in which the young gentlemen employed their afternoon.

THEY vifited the Capitol, with the intention of recollecting in that place part of the morning's lecture. They paffed fome time there, converfing on the conclufion of *Tiberius's* wicked reign; and afterwards defcended into the *Campo Vaccino.*

IN that part of the *roman forum,* which lies between the *Capitoline* and *Palatine* hills, there ftands a fingle marble column, of the *corinthian* order, fluted, and about fifty feet in height.

IT is the opinion of fome antiquarians, faid the young nobleman, that this column made part of that bridge, which the fucceffor of *Tiberius* built acrofs the *forum.* It may, with more probability perhaps, be fuppofed to have made part of fome of thofe temples, or porticos, over which that bridge was carried.

I HAVE

I HAVE often thought, that such a bridge, thus joining the *Capitoline* and *Palatine* hills, might be of real and considerable convenience to the public. It probably saved much time, and many a wearisome step, to the industrious inhabitants of this part of *Rome;* which, in the time of *Caligula*, was the most populous, or at least the most frequented.

BUT, alas! far different was the motive of *Caligula.* His design, in the erection of that bridge, was not beneficence to his subjects; but the indulgence of his own most absurd, and impious pride.

IN the temple of *Castor* and *Pollux*, which stood near those three columns of *Jupiter Stator*, *Caligula* frequently seated himself, between the statues of the *Dioscuri;* and from their temple he built the bridge to the Capitol, merely that he might, with more convenience and ease to himself, go often to receive the same horrid adoration in the temple of *Jupiter Capitolinus.*

As to *Jupiter*, replied *Crito's* pupil, if we consider the history of that king of *Crete*, as given by the poets, we shall not find his character to have been much better than that of *Caligula.*

BUT

BUT the inhabitants of the *grecian* and *roman* world, fuch was the extreme abfurdity of paganifm, connected with the word *Jupiter* a very different idea; even that of the Great Creator and Preferver of the univerfe; the Moft Beneficent; the Moft Holy. Now, if we confider the affair in this light, horrid indeed was the wickednefs of *Caligula*, in daring to affume fuch a name.

I RECOLLECT reading fometime ago, with my tutor, the account given by *Jofephus* and *Philo* of *Caligula's* attempt to profane even the temple of *Jerufalem*, by erecting his own ftatue in it.

To what *incredible* degrees of *madnefs* may human pride fometimes extend!

A *babylonian* monarch, if I remember rightly, could fo far yield to the flattery of his courtiers, as to forbid his fubjects offering *any petition*, to *any god or man*, but himfelf. This *roman* emperor was impious enough to claim even DIVINE honours; though he was in reality one of the vileft monfters, that ever difgraced humanity.

O MY dear friends, what a place of horrour was then *that Palatine* mount!

Cur

Cur non apertæ tum fuerunt cælorum cataractæ?
Cur non rupti erant fontes abyſſi magni? *

SURELY, no antediluvian wickednefs could be greater, than that of *Caligula's* court.

AT leaft, why did not the *Tiber* then fwell, with a ten-fold abundance of torrents, to wafh away that *Palatine* hilloc, and drown all the *roman campagna* in a broad afphaltic lake; while the *tufculan* and *fabine* mountains poured forth on it their fulphurous materials, by the eruption of an hundred volcanoes?

BUT why fhould fuch expreffions fall from my lips? Notwithftanding the unutterable abominations of the imperial palace, and great corruption of the public manners, there were doubtlefs, even during this reign, multitudes in *Rome* of a very different character. Of it's meaner inhabitants feveral thoufands, probably, lived in the faithful practice of the duties of their ftations, according to the light of nature. Many, in all likelihood, were the virtuous perfons, then engaged in agriculture, commerce, or trade; many honeft men were to be found in the profeffions. Some alfo, who were bleffed by Providence with a more independent fortune, and who, from the kindnefs

* Vid. Lib. *Genef.* cap. vii. 15.

of

of their parents, had received a more ornamented education, paffed their days happily in ftudious privacy; mafters of their own time, and difpofing it to the beft purpofes, meditation, and works of beneficence. From the vain occupations of this vaft city, from the falfe pleafures, honours, and riches around them, *Recepere fe ad tranquilliora, tutiora, majora. Tenuit illos, in hoc genere vitæ, multum bonarum artium, amor virtutum atque ufus, cupiditatum oblivio, vivendi atque moriendi fcientia, alta rerum quies**.

In all probability there were alfo, even in the higher conditions of life, feveral, who lived in the practice of much moral virtue.

There was one eminent example of merit, replied the eldeft of the young gentlemen, even in the family of *Caligula:* I mean his father-in-law, the wife and good *M. Silanus.* But he could not live there long : he was one of the many perfons, who perifhed by that tyrant's cruelty and ingratitude. *Caianæ cladis erat magna portio.*

Your temper, my dear friend, is meeknefs itfelf: χρυσιον ωιον. I ufe this expreffion in the

* See *Seneca de brevitate vitæ :* a treatife written, according to *Lipfius,* within *fome few days* after the death of *Caligula. Modò, intrà* paucos illos dies, *quibus Caius Cæfar periit, &c.*

fame

fame good fenfe in which *Dion* underftood it.
But it is no difhonour to fuch a temper, that it
can kindle itfelf into a proper indignation at the
thoughts of that moft horrid impiety, that moft
abominable wickednefs, that moft bloody defpotifm, which reigned day and night in the court of
Caligula.

*Hoc ifti belluæ quotidianum eft : ad hæc vivit,
ad hæc vigilat, ad hæc lucubrat* *.

EVEN if we were to confine our thoughts to
the laft article, I mean the *political* confiderations,
moft odious, furely, ought to be the name, and
moft execrable the memory, of that fupreme magiftrate, who could wifh, " that it were in his
power to bid the *axe* fall on the neck of his whole
people !"

LET us think no longer on his detefted reign.
Let us rather reflect with fatisfaction, that we are
at prefent only fome few fteps diftant from *that
place*, where this tyrant received his due punifhment from the hand of *Chærea;—Chærea, the third
Brutus.*

BUT it becomes me immediately to correct that
verbum ardens. Caligula deferved a more fevere

* *Seneca de irâ*, lib. iii, c. 18.

fate thán either *Tarquin*, or *Julius Cæfar*: but *Chærea* ftained his glory, by the murder of *Cæfonia*, and her infant daughter: a crime, of which, certainly, neither *Junius* nor *Marcus Brutus* would on any account have been guilty.

I REMEMBER, in my more youthful years, that, on reading the hiftory of *Caligula*'s death, I felt much regret at the thought, that fuch an opportunity for reftoring the republic had offered itfelf in vain. For in vain was it, that the walls of the parliament-houfe on *that Capitoline* hill then echoed with the cry of liberty. The people crowded to the gates; not as anciently, to applaud the confcript fathers for their zeal in their country's freedom; not, as in other times, to vent their jealous murmurs, at fome fuppofed infringement of the popular privileges; but, to demand. the immediate nomination of a new defpot.

WHILE at the univerfity, I was not a little heated with democratic notions, and confequently felt myfelf highly fhocked at this aftonifhing inftance of *roman* degeneracy. But, as my admiration of *republican* liberty in particular is fince that time very much cooled, though my zeal for liberty in general will I hope always burn with due fervour and flame; fo likewife is my indignation againft the *romans*, for their behaviour on

this

this occafion, fomewhat abated. The *roman* people had too much reafon to remember the bloody hiftory of the former civil wars. They had equal reafon to fear, that the diffentions in the fenate, and the difobedience of the army, might foon, if a new emperor were not immediately elected, produce a renewal of the fame calamities; calamities which after much confufion and anarchy, much mifery and blood-fhed, would certainly terminate as the former had done, in the eftablifhment only of a new abfolute mafter.

BESIDES, there was another motive for their conduct: a motive in itfelf inexcufable, but which operated without refiftance. The *origo mali* lay deep in the conftitution of their hearts, but necef-farily fhowed it's virulence by thefe exteriour fymptoms. *Vice* had fo much weakened and enfeebled all the nerves and mufcles, if we may fo fpeak, of the *national roman* mind, as to render it neither worthy, nor fufceptible, of the labours and perils of any kind of liberty.

THE city of *Rome*, replied the young nobleman, was indeed at that time corrupted by vice, in a much more dreadful manner than ever it had been by any peftilence. For, notwithftanding the charitable fuppofitions of our good friend here, certainly the imperial court, the nobility, the peo-ple,

ple, breathed forth infernal contagion on each other.

HORRID as was the character of *Caligula*, yet his crimes would not have been so enormous, had he ruled over a better nation.

MUCH of his wickedness may perhaps be attributed to the infanity of his underftanding: but more to the badnefs of his heart, and to the examples among which he lived.

BUT let us not confine our attention to his enormous crimes. If we could banifh *them* totally from our memory, I might then venture to confider *other* parts of his character in a cooler manner; and apply to them fome reflections, with which I remember your tutor favoured us upon a former occafion.

HE obferved *, that the folly and vice, the pride and cruelty, which fhock us in reading fome parts of the *roman* hiftory, are only the extremes of that abufe, which we *fee* every day made, of lefs degrees of wealth and power.

I REMEMBER alfo my father's obferving to me, that many young men of fortune in our own coun-

* See page 334, of the firft volume.

try, while reading *Caligula's* reign, look on it's contents as almoſt incredible : yet, happy ought they to eſteem themſelves, if in their future life ſome of them do not become really of a very ſimilar character; that is to ſay, ſo far as their inferiour degrees of wealth and power will permit. In a word, though innocent of his enormous crimes, they may yet become *Caligulas* in miniature : bad in domeſtic life; hating their aged relations; living in intimacy with gameſters, jockeys, and ſtage-players; proud; luxurious; fickle; impiouſly ungrateful to heaven for all it's bleſſings; laviſhing their fortunes in various kinds of folly; and then from want oppreſſing their tenants, and other dependants *.

But let us quit this topic. If you incline to take a little tour in the coach this evening, it ſhall carry us round the *Cælian* hill, and thence home by the *Strada Felice.*

CRITO'S pupil, and his other companion, readily conſented to the propoſal of their noble friend.

On ſeveral parts of the *Cælian* hill they obſerved many lofty arches of a ruined aqueduct.

* See *Dio's Caligula,* Χρηματα αφειδεϛατα ανηλισκε, κϳ ρυπαρωτατα ηργυρολογει.

TRAT

THAT aqueduĉt, faid the young nobleman, if I be not miſtaken, was begun in the ſecond year of *Caligula's* reign: for thanks to Providence, *ſome* good is done to mankind even by the worſt of men*. It was finiſhed by *Claudius;* as appears by the inſcription ſtill remaining over the *Porta Maggiore.* As the *Strada Felice* is not very far from that gate, we may, if you pleaſe, tell the coachman to drive thither.

* * *

THE *Porta Maggiore* is a ſtately monument†, erec̈ted by the emperor *Titus,* in memory of the great work of the *Claudian* aqueduĉt. Over it's arches are three inſcriptions, the upper one of which is as follows.

Ti. Claudius Druſi. f. Cæſar Auguſtus Germaⲛicus Pontif. Maxim. Tribunitiâ poteſtate xii. *Coſ.* v. *Imperator* xxvii. *Pater Patriæ, aquas Clau-*

---

* *Quid Nerone pejus?*
Quid thermis melius Neronianis? Mart.
† *Queſt' edificio è uno de' piu belli dell' antica Roma ; ed è di altezza e di groſſezza piu di ogni altro ſingolare. E fabbricato di macigni di travertino congiunti inſieme ſenza calce; ſoſtenuto da quattro grandi archi con colonne alla ruſtica d'ordine Ionico.—Per comprendere di qual magnificenza ſiano gli archi di queſto monumento baſta ſapere che quello, che in oggi forma la porta ha di lunghezza palmi* 49, *e ciaſcun pezzo di travertino è groſſo palmi* 3 *once* 3 *lungo palmi* 9 *once* 5, *e taluno* 2½ *ed è compoſta tutta l'alta, e vaſta arcata di ſoli* 26 *pezzi di pietra.*
Abbate Venuti, v. p. 124, 125.

diam

diam ex fontibus, qui vocantur Cæruleus et Curtius,
a milliar. XXXV. *item Anienem novum, a millia-*
rio LXII. *fuâ impenfâ, in urbem perducendas*
curavit.

THE two infcriptions fubjoined to this are in
honour of *Vefpafian* and *Titus.* Each of thefe
emperors thought it an honour to repair or improve this aqueduft.

IT is obferved, faid the young nobleman, I
think either by *Suetonius* or *Aurelius Viftor,* that
Vefpafian repaired *feveral* of *Claudius's* works,
and alfo completed that temple on *Monte Cælio,*
which was erefted in his honour; but which had
been ungratefully neglefted, or in part demolifh-
ed, by *Nero.*

As to the temple, it would have been certainly
much better, if *Vefpafian* had left it in it's ruins.
The aqueduft, on the other hand, as a work of
public benefit, had a juft claim both upon him,
and all future emperors, for it's fupport.

THE water conveyed to *Rome* by this aqueduft
was of great convenience to the inhabitants; efpecially to thofe, who then in great numbers dwelt
on the fummit of her feven hills. It was alfo in it's
nature almoft equally good with the *Aqua Martia;*

VOL. II. E e and

and confequently, it feems to have been well worth the expenfe and labour of it's conveyance; though exclufive of it's long fubterranean channel, and of it's upper canal, it is carried *upon arches,* in different places, through a fpace of near ten miles. The new river, from the *Anio,* which is joined to the *Aqua Claudia,* is alfo carried about feven miles upon arches; feveral of which are one hundred feet in height.

IT feems very ftrange, faid *Crito's* pupil, that a reign liketh at of *Claudius* fhould be ennobled by fo fplendid and fo ufeful a work.

CLAUDIUS'S mind was generally buried in the deepeft ftupidity, fadly increafed by gluttony and other vices: and yet it muft have been furprifingly illuminated at times, by fome lucid interval of good fenfe, or by fome brighter ray of benevolence.

SUETONIUS obferves of *Claudius,* with refpect to his behaviour when feated on the tribunals of juftice, *Mirâ animi varietate fuit; modo circumfpectus, & fagax; modo inconfultus, ac præceps; nonnunquam frivolus, amentique fimilis.* The fame obfervation is doubtlefs applicable to many other parts of *Claudius's* hiftory.

IT

IT fhould feem probable, indeed, at firft fight, that the actions of wife benevolence, with which *Claudius's* reign is adorned; actions numerous, and fome of which required a vigorous and a continued exertion of reafoning; are to be afcribed to the virtues and abilities of his miniftry—more efpecially as his reign was a reign of favourites. But, on the contrary, hiftory affures us, that *Claudius's* miniftry was in general compofed of perfons much more wicked than himfelf: perfons, whofe whole attention feems to have been given to works of various vices; but, peculiarly, of rapacity, pride, and bloody revenge. Such, at leaft, was the character of his empreffes, *Meffalina* and *Agrippina;* and perhaps alfo of his two head fervants, *Narciffus* and *Pallas.* In a word, it was a court fit only for the education of a *Nero.*

DION feems to impute moft of the crimes of this reign to the prevailing influence of the courtiers: and to leave the merit of all the laudable acts and benevolent defigns in it to the emperor himfelf. The emperor, however, was fenfible only by fits; and, what appears ftill more contradictory, he was frequently very cruel. *Claudius* was cruel, not only from a falfe notion of juftice, or from a cowardly care of felf-prefervation, or laftly from a fhamefully ftupid fubmiffion to the will of his miniftry; but alfo,

accord-

according to *Suetonius*, from a real delight in the moſt ſhocking aĉts of inhumanity*.

IN what manner, then, can we account for this paradox? Certainly we cannot do it in a better manner, than by conſidering it, according to the hint which you juſt now gave us, as one of the many proofs, that there is an over-ruling Providence: a Providence, which originally created light out of darkneſs; and which, both in public and in private affairs, ſometimes condeſcends to draw good out of evil; to employ the hands even of the wicked, and the counſels of madmen or fools, as inſtruments in performing ſome of it's all-wiſe and all-gracious deſigns, for the benefit of mankind.

* * *

THE company now ſtept into their carriage. In their way home, the young nobleman took notice, that *Claudius's* reign was ennobled by another work, ſtill more beneficial to this vaſt city.

---

* *Sævum & ſanguinarium naturâ fuiſſe, magnis minimiſque apparuit rebus. —Beſtiariis, meridianiſque, adeô delectabatur, ut etiam primâ luce ad ſpectaculum deſcenderet; & meridie, di-miſſo ad prandium populo, perſederet. Præterque deſtinatos, etiam levi ſubitâque de cauſâ, quoſdam committeret: de fabro-rum quoque, ac miniſtrorum, atque id genus numero, ſi αυτοματον, vel pegma, vel quid tale aliud parum ceſſiſſet.*
SUETONIUS, in *Claud.* 34.

I MEAN

I MEAN, faid he, the very ufeful fea-port, which this emperor conftructed on that branch of the *Tiber*, which lies fome few miles north-weft of *Oftia*.

I WISH, that, when we were on our laft excurfion to *Oftia**, we had taken that opportunity of viewing it's remains, if any. I hope, however, we may revifit the place, before we take a final leave of *Rome*. We will carry thither fome prints and plans, as well as fome antique medals, which have a reference to that celebrated haven. Thofe medals and plans will be of the more ufe to us, as I am afraid we muft not flatter ourfelves, that we fhall find many traces remaining, either of it's ornamental, or of it's more fubftantial parts. According to the defcription given us of *Fiumicino*, the winds and waves have totally changed the face of that fhore.

————— *notiffima famâ ;*
Nunc tantum finus, & ftatio malefida carinis †.

BUT, however deeply the *moles* and the *pharos* of *Claudius's* haven may be now buried in the fands, pleafing it is to confider, that it's fplendour, in fome manner, ftill exifts in that mode of

* See vol. i. p. 29.
† VIRG. *Æn.* ii. 21.

reprefen-

reprefentation, by which, alone, the grandeur of ancient *Rome* is efpecially preferved; I mean, in her hiftory, and by her coins.

DION CASSIUS'S defcription of the grandeur and public utility of this fea-port is happily ftill remaining *. When I come to my lodgings, I will compare it with what *Dionyfius* has told us of the haven of king *Ancus*.

IF I rightly recolleft, faid the eldeft of the young gentlemen, not only *Vefpafian* and *Titus*, but the emperor *Trajan* alfo, among his many glorious labours for the benefit of this country, thought it an honour, to repair fome of the works of *Claudius*.

VERY great, and heavy indeed, is the contempt generally caft upon the memory of *Claudius:* and equally exceffive, perhaps, is the veneration paid

---

* The great famine, which raged at *Rome* in the reign of *Claudius*, prompted him to undertake the conftruftion of a large and convenient haven, at the mouth of the *Tiber*. This vaft work he happily completed, although *Cæfar* the diftator, if fome miftake have not crept into *Suetonius*, had many years before attempted it in vain. It was an undertaking, fays *Dion Caffius*, worthy the grandeur of the *roman* empire. But the fucceffors of *Claudius* were not able to maintain it; fo that, foon after his death, it was choked up with fand, and became quite ufelefs.
See Univerfal Hiftory, vol. xiv. p. 329,

to

to the name of *Trajan*, his more fortunate fucceffor.

I⊤ might hardly be imagined, that *Trajan* was,
in any refpe&, an imitator of *Claudius:* and yet,
in feveral inftances, he certainly followed *Claudius's* defigns: in none however more manifeftly,
than in the reparation of that haven: for *Trajan,*
if I be rightly informed, repaired that fea-port,
as well as thofe of *Civita-Vecchia* and *Ancona.*

TRAJAN is faid alfo to have profecuted another proje& of *Claudius;* namely, that of draining the *Fucine* lake.

I HAVE often wifhed, replied the young nobleman, that fome ingenious traveller, after having
paffed a year or two in making the common tour
of *Italy,* would allow himfelf another year: not
for the extenfion of his travels into the *Levant;*
but to vifit thofe provinces of the *tufcan, ecclefiaftic,* or *neapolitan* ftate, that lie out of the beaten
track of travellers; but which, probably, contain
many curious remains of antiquity.

I⊤ paffing through the *Abruzzo,* for inftance,
I prefume he could not fail of finding fome very
confiderable remains of that work you mention, at the *Fucine* lake; which employed thirty-

E e 4   thoufand

thoufand labourers conftantly, during eleven years of *Claudius's* reign.

WHAT would be your fentiments, my dear friend, in viewing that lake, and the channel of it's *emiffario?* Should I ever attend you thither, *my* thoughts might poffibly be employed in forming an idea of that magnificent, but bloody fpectacle, which *Claudius* exhibited on it's waves; while all the hills 'around it were covered with the inhabitants of that part of *Italy*, like the fides of a vaft amphitheatre. *Your* mind, however, would be bufy in a *much more noble* contemplation, the real public utility of the *work* itfelf.

I AM confident you are of opinion with me, that this attempt of *Claudius*, though it failed of fuccefs, deferves to be mentioned in the *roman* hiftory with peculiar honour.

THE fecurity of fo ample a fupply of water to the current of the *Tiber** was, furely, a defign very favourable to the improvement of the inland navigation of *Italy*.

THE addition alfo of fome thoufand acres of fertile foil to the territory was a no lefs important

* *Dion* fo confiders it: *Tacitus* feems to refer the improvement to the *Liris*.

Vid. TACIT. *Annal.* lib. xii. c. 56.

object.

objeɛt. The fpace of ground, covered and fwal-
lowed up, as it were, by that lake, muſt have
given bread to the inhabitants of many new towns,
had not the fcheme of draining it failed ; firſt, by
the negligence or avarice of *Claudius's* miniſtry ;
and afterwards, by the envy of a *Nero.*

I REMEMBER, my dear friend, fome of your
obfervations on a fimilar topic, when we were
croſſing the *Beemſter,* in *North Holland*.* It
was fome few days after we had been feeing *Corbulo's* canal, from *Leyden* and *Delft,* to *Maeſlandt
Sluys.*

THE draining of lakes, the opening of havens,
and the building of aqueduɛts, are indeed, faid
Crito's pupil, works of great public utility : but
I own myfelf much more pleafed with fome *other*
aɛtions of *Claudius's* reign.

---

* " There is, in *North Holland,* an eſſay made of the poſſi-
bility of draining great lakes; by one, about two leagues
broad, having been made firm land, within thefe forty
years.

" This makes that part of the country called *Beemſter ;* being now the richeſt foil of the province, lying upon a dead
flat divided with canals, and the ways through it diſtinguiſhed with ranges of trees ; which make the pleafanteſt fummer landfcape of any country I have feen of that fort.

" There is one very great lake of freſh water, ſtill remaining in the province of *Holland,* by the name of *Harlem Meer;*
which might, they fay, be eafily drained, and would thereby make a mighty addition of land.—Much difcourfe has
there been about fuch an attempt, &c."

Sir *William Temple's* Account of *Holland.*

WHEN

WHEN I confider the vaft multitudes that then inhabited this extenfive metropolis, I cannot help admiring, and even loving the memory of *Claudius*, for the conftant and anxious care he took, in fupplying them with bread, during feveral years of fcarcity and famine. *Ad fubvehendos etiam hyberno tempore commeatus, nihil non excogitavit.* A ftrange expreffion *this* of *Suetonius*, if *Claudius*, as is commonly imagined, were really funk in *continual* ftupidity.

WITH much greater veneration ought we to recollect *Claudius's* philanthropic defign of extending the privileges of this city to many of the nations, that were fubject to her dominion.

I SPEAK this in reference, not merely to his kindnefs towards the people of *Ilium, Rhodes, Cos,* and *Byzantium:* for *Claudius* was very generous in granting *roman* privileges to the natives of many other lefs celebrated countries. A generofity, which, though much abufed in many particular cafes, and fometimes practifed with great levity, yet certainly, in general, was highly laudable.

THIS intention of *Claudius* is fhamefully ridiculed, by the author of that fatyrical treatife, commonly known by the title of the Αποκολοκυντωσις.

I cannot

I can fcarce imagine *Seneca* to have been really
the author of that piece; at leaft of fome paffages,
which we now find in it: for they are moft contradictory, both to the contents of that oration,
which he himfelf compofed, to be fpoken by *Nero*
at *Claudius's* funeral*; and to the epiftle, which,
fome years before, he infcribed to *Polybius.*
Permit me to repeat my hopes, that fome critic
may arife, who fhall be able to refcue *Seneca*
from the difhonour of having fitten down to write
fo very meanly-fpirited a fatire †.

It is granted, that the ftupidity and wickednefs
of *Claudius* were *at times* exceffive: but they
both certainly had their intervals. His defign
to grant the *civic franchifes,* of which we are now
fpeaking, was furely replete with humanity and
true political wifdom: it would have done very
great honour to the reign of an *Antoninus Pius,* or
a *Marcus Aurelius.*

---

* See *Tacitus,* Annal. lib. xiii. c. 3.

† Poifon and murder, domeftic and civil treafon, are no
jefts: *capitalia crimina ludis.* See the epigrams prefixed to
the *Confolatio ad Helviam.* It is faid by *Dion,* that *Seneca*
compofed a fatire on the memory of *Claudius,* called the
Αποκολοκυντωσις. But *Dion* was no friend to *Seneca;* and it does
not appear *certain,* that the treatife we now have under that
name is the work alluded to.—*De titulo libri inter eruditos
non convenit. Beatus Rhenanus, qui reperiffe & primus typis
publicâffe dicitur, ludum de morte Claudii Cæfaris appelláffe,
potiùs quam fic inveniffe, creditur. Junius, & omnes jam,
paffim, Claudii Cæfaris* Αποκολοκυντωσιν, *Dione præeunte nun-
cupatum vadunt.* See *Fromondus's* Preface to the Αποκ.
Lipfius's edition.

J REMEM-

I REMEMBER reading, with great pleafure, in the eleventh book of *Tacitus*, a fpeech of *Claudius* from the throne, concerning the admiffion of fome *gallic* nobles to feats in the *roman* fenate. In the courfe of the debate, thofe very fenators, who oppofed the bill, did not objeƐt to granting the privileges of *roman* citizenfhip to the provincial inhabitants fo admitted.

IF I be not miftaken, continued *Crito's* pupil, *even our countrymen* are reckoned among the nations, to whom *Claudius* intended that favour:— *Conftituerat omnes, græcos, gallos, hifpanos, britannos, togatos videre.* Whether or not the fatyrift had any real foundation for this, probably much exaggerated, affertion, I cannot tell: but it fhould *feem* probable, from a paffage in *Dion,* if I underftand it right, that the conditions offered by *Claudius* to the *britons* bore at leaft a mild and favourable appearance *. ·

HOWEVER this might be, furely fo flattering a propofal could have but little weight with the *britons;* in whofe breafts a love of liberty, and

---

† Ταυτα μεν δη δια τα Βρεταννικα επραχ9η, ϗ ΙΝΑ ΓΕ ΑΛΛΟΙ ΡΑΟΝ ΕΣ ΟΜΟΛΟΓΙΑΝ ΙΩΣΙΝ, εψηφισ9η, τας συμβασεις απασας, εσας αν ο Κλαυδι℗, η ϗ οι |αντιϛρατηγοι αυτϧ, ϖρ℗ τινας ϖοιησωνται, κυριας, ως ϗ ϖρ℗ την βϧλην τον τε δημον, ειναι.

Dio Caffius, lib. lx.

a warm

a warm zeal for their country's true welfare, have, I truſt, always glowed. The privileges of *roman* citizenſhip might be ſome comfort, ſome conſiderable relief indeed to nations, already ſunk under the *roman* yoke: but by the unconquered inhabitants of our iſland it never could be eſteemed as any thing in the balance againſt the invaluable privileges of their own native freedom.

MANY thanks to you, dear ſir, replied the eldeſt of the young gentlemen, for that noble ſentiment. The glorious ſpirit of national liberty, which you expreſs, beats, I am ſure, through every pulſe, and pants in every breaſt of this company.

I HAD ſome intention to take a copy, this afternoon, of the inſcription on that antique marble, which is preſerved in the wall of the *Barberini* terrace. But, fired as we are at preſent by your generous feelings, how could we bear to fix our eyes on ſuch an objeſt*!

* The inſcription on this marble, which perhaps originally ſtood over *Caludius's* triumphal arch, in the *Via lata*, is as follows:

TI. CLAUDIO CÆS.
  AUGUSTO
Pontifici Max. Tr. p.   [1]
Coſ. V. Imp. 16. *P. P.*
Senatus Popul. Q. R. Quòd
Reges Britanniæ, Abſque ullâ
Jaſturâ domuerit, Genteſque Barbaras,
Primus indicio, ſubegerit.

         THEN

THEN, after a paufe of fome minutes, during which he feemed deeply abforpt in thought, there is not, continued he, any part of *Tacitus's* works, the lofs of which, as *englifhmen*, we have more reafon to regret, than thofe books of his Annals, that contained the commencement and the firft events of the *britifh* wars, during *Claudius's* reign. *Dion's* hiftory alfo, in it's prefent curtailed condition, is by far too concife on that fubject.

CLAUDIUS is faid to have been in *Britain* little more than a fortnight. Probably he went over merely to accept the honour of the furrender of *Maldon,* in *Effex. Suetonius* agrees with the *Barberini* marble, in faying, that there was no bloodfhed, at leaft among the *roman* legions, on that occafion : yet, according to *Dion,* there was a battle. In all probability, no more, either of battle, or of fiege occurred, than what was barely deemed fufficient, to qualify the emperor for the honour of a triumph; and entitle him to treat the people with a fhow of the fiege of *Maldon,* or of *Colchefter,* as reprefented in the *Campo Marzo*.* The invafion of *Britain* was indeed, fo far as *Claudius* himfelf was concerned in it, little more than a vain pageantry : but as

---

* *Edidit et in campo Martio expugnationem direptionemque oppidi, ad imaginem bellicam, & deditionem Britanniæ regum, præfeditque paludatus.* Suetonius, in Vit. Claud. 21.

refpecting

rcfpecting *Plautius, Vefpafian,* and his other lieu-
tenants, it was a very ferious, a very long, and
difficult labour.

TACITUS'S account of the firft eight years of
that war is unhappily loft. During thofe eight
years, that part of our ifland which lies neareft the
continent, that is, the whole tract, from the fhores
of the *britifh* channel, to the banks of the *Severn,
Avon,* and *Nen,* fecms to have been flowly and
gradually fubdued by the *roman* armies : not
without much refiftance from our brave iflanders;
not, as our *Shakfpeare* would phrafe it, without
grinning, like lions, on the pikes of their hunters.
Often then, in our hills and woods, was heard
the conflict of war : often did our filver ftreams
run purple with *britifh* blood ; fhed from *thofe
hardy, naked breafts,* which, in the glorious caufe
of a country's liberty, *flept before targes of
proof.*

SUETONIUS, fpeaking of *Vefpafian,* obferves,
that *in Britanniâ tricies cum hofte conflixit.* It
fecms very improbable, that *Vefpafian* could be
prefent at *all* the engagements in thefe *britifh* wars.
It is moft likely, that, befide thefe *thirty* battles,
there were many other bloody fields of conteft,
which he never faw.

I N

In thinking on this subject, my dear friends, what must be the emotion and the ardour of an *english* heart? Never did I hear the last act of *Shakspeare's Cymbeline* performed at *Drury-Lane*, without feeling myself much and strongly agitated. If a *fable* could so transport me, what ought to be the effect of real *history?*

Mr. *PITT**, in the heat of one of his most noble orations, dared to compare the magnanimity of *british* liberty to the description of the war-horse, so inimitably given us in the book of *Job†.* ——O for a style so animated! O for an equal thunder of eloquence!

PARDON

* The late earl of *Chatham.*

† See Chap. xxxix. ver. 19,—25. Thus finely para-phrased by Dr. YOUNG.

> *Survey the warlike horse! didst thou invest*
> *With thunder, his robust distended chest?*
> *No sense of fear his dauntless soul allays;*
> *'Tis dreadful to behold his nostrils blaze:*
> *To paw the vale he proudly takes delight,*
> *And triumphs in the fullness of his might.*
> *High-rais'd, he snuffs the battle from afar,*
> *And burns to plunge amidst the raging war;*
> *And mocks at death, and throws his foam around,*
> *And in a storm of fury shakes the ground.*
> *How does his firm, his rising heart advance*
> *Full on the brandish'd sword and shaken lance!*
> *While his fix'd eye-balls meet the dazzling shield,*
> *Gaze, and return the lightning of the field.*
> *He sinks the sense of pain in generous pride,*
> *Nor feels the shaft that trembles in his side:*
> *But neighs to the shrill trumpet's dreadful blast,*
> *Till death; and when he groans, he groans his last!*

" There

PARDON me, my dear friends, for this rapture. But how can I avoid wiſhing for the abilities of ſuch an orator, while I am on ſuch a topic? And why ſhould we not think the courage of our iſlanders to have exerted itſelf as nobly, in this war of ſelf-preſervation againſt the *romans*, as ever ſince, on any other call?

FOR, let us conſider not only the many engagements, or, in other words, the *activity* of this war, but it's *duration* alſo.

FROM the time of the *roman* invaſion in *Claudius's* reign, to the entire reduction of our iſland under *Domitian*, was a ſpace of *above forty* years. I have been with pleaſure calculating, that it was *ſo long* before the *roman* power, though then at it's height, could conquer *Britain*. The *britons*, probably, would never have been ſubdued by all the force of this mighty empire, had they been but as much accuſtomed to the *roman* art military, as the contemporary *germans* were; or if they had

---

" There is an excellent critique on the above celebrated deſcription, in the *Guardian.* See Vol. II. In this glowing paſſage, our vulgar tranſlation has much more ſpirit than the *Septuagint;* always taking the original in the moſt poetical and exalted ſenſe; ſo that moſt commentators, even on the hebrew itſelf, fall beneath it." See the paraphraſe at the cloſe of the *Night-Thoughts.*

been then happily connected and united, under the standard of one prince. *Sed, dum singuli pugnant, universi vincuntur* *. Their struggles indeed were unsuccessful; but their heroisms were highly glorious : *Nulla, tum, in detrectandis periculis, formido.* Of that weakness the *britons* were accused, after they were conquered and corrupted; *Amissa virtute pariter & libertate:* but in those early days, while they were yet free, they were eminently valiant.

O quàm multorum opera egregia in obscuro jacent!

WHO would not wish for a more particular detail of their achievements? But how brief, how defective is this part of our national history! We receive more information as to the affairs of ancient *Britain* from *Tacitus*, than from any other writer; yet surely, that information, though most sensible and authentic, is far from being sufficiently ample, or particular.

OFTEN have I wished, not only that the works of *Tacitus* had come down to us complete; but also that *Tacitus* had composed another history, and that not a concise one, but of a just size, expressly on the subject of the *forty year's war* in *Britain.*

* Vita Agricolæ, c. 12.

IN

IN fuch a work, the patriotic fortitude of *Ca-raƈacus*, of *Galgacus*, and of many other *britifh* heroes, whofe achievements are now loft in ob-livion, would have appeared in due fplendour and dignity: not contraƈted in their proportions, merely to give fpace in the piƈture for the horrid forms of the contemporary wickedneffes of *Rome;* but reprefented in full magnitude. Many fuc-ceffive generations of *britifh* youths would thus have gazed with ardour on the glorious portraits: *Intereà animos ad virtutem vehementiffimè accendi; flammam in peƈtore crefcere; neque priùs fedari, quàm majorum famam atque gloriam adæqua-verint*.*

INDEED, dear fir, replied *Crito's* pupil, I have fometimes framed the fame kind of wifh. Such a work would have been highly valuable, not only on that important account which you mention, but for feveral other, lefs weighty rea-fons.

THE *ftudent of* englifh *hiftory, whatever were his time of life, or temper of mind,* would pro-bably confider fuch a book, as one of the moft favourite volumes in his library.

_____
* Vid. SALLUST. *Bel. Jug.* c. iv. and vol. i. p. 450.

THE

THE *antiquarian* would certainly find in it materials for a much more accurate defcription of
the rivers and hills in ancient *Britain,* and of the
boundaries of her feveral nations, than any he
can now colleƈt, from all the authors who have
written on the fubjeƈt. With great fatisfaƈtion
he would learn thence the exaƈt courfe of
many of her public ways, and the true fituation
and origin of many of her cities. But his greateft
feaft would be in thofe digreffions, which we may
fuppofe to have treated of religious doƈtrines,
of the fciences, and perhaps of the feats of learning belonging to the *druids.*

VESPASIAN, if I miftake not, conquered
the ifle of *Wight,* and feveral other *britifh* prin-
cipalities, which probably lay between that ifland
and the territory of the *dobuni.* This territory,
I think, comprehended the counties of *Oxford*
and *Glocefter.* I have been told there is a place
in *Wiltfhire,* not far from *Stonehenge,* ftill called
by the name of *Vefpafian's camp.* The difciples
of Dr. *Stukeley,* therefore, in a clear and ample
hiftory of *Vefpafian's* campaigns, would reafon-
ably expeƈt to find fome defcription of the *druidical* temples at *Stonehenge* and *Abury,* as they
appeared in thofe times, when their barbarous
grandeur was probably ftill entire.

I REMEMBER going, laſt *april* twelvemonth, to the vaſt amphitheatrical temple of *Abury**, in company with my tutor, and there liſtening to ſome of his opinions reſpecting the doctrine of the *druids*. Several of their tenets he admired and revered ; particularly thoſe capital articles of their belief, the immortality of the ſoul, and the certainty of that future ſtate, in which charity, as well as patriotic fortitude, are to be rewarded †: articles, which, very much to the honour of our parts of *Europe,* were firmly and ardently retained by our *britiſh* anceſtors ; while, at the ſame time, the corrupted inhabitants of *Greece* and *Rome* ſeem to have been endeavouring, by luxury and ſophiſtry, to extinguiſh in their breaſts every ſpark of that noble and bleſſed hope, which is kindled by the breath of nature in the hearts of all mankind, even of the moſt rude and wild.

ON the other hand, it was *with much averſion* my tutor mentioned ſome of the bad rites, and as it were *north-american* doctrines of the *druids*. He pitied their ſuperſtitions ; but he abominated the cruel ſacrificing of their captives : and on this laſt account, he expreſſed ſtrongly his joy, that

---

* The circumference of the mound of that amphitheatre is not leſs than eighteen hundred yards.

† Compare *Seneca* with *Lucan*, lib. i. v. 442.

the

the *romans*, by the abolition of druidifm, had cleared a way for the future progrefs of chrif-tianity.

BEFORE my good friend had thus turned my attention to fo ferious a train of thought, I was employed in another manner. I was hammering out a copy of verfes. Cold indeed, or rather totally dead, muft have been my imagination, had it not been *then* fufceptible of fome poetic ideas: *then,* while I was treading the foft turf of *Abury*, amidft the circles of thofe mofs-grown ftones; or mufing in that long meadow, which leads from the temple to the filver fprings of the *Kennet,* and the verdant pyramid of *Silbury.*

IN the centre of that pyramid moft probably refts the duft of a *britifh* king; the brave pro-tector of his people in war, and the munificent founder of religious edifices. The temple of *Abury* was in all likelihood his work. Often has his name been repeated in the fongs of *britifh* poets; though it is now totally unknown, or but uncertainly gueffed at. Often around that hill, in the folemn ceremony of annual affemblies,

Vos quoque, qui fortes animas, belloque peremptas
Laudibus in longum vates demittitis ævum,
                                        Plurima

Plurima fecuri fudiſtis carmina bardi :
Et vos barbaricos ritus, moremque ſiniſtrum
Sacrorum druidæ poſitis repetiſtis ab armis *.

BUT let me not wander too much my dear ſir, from the ſubjeᛐ, on which you were ſpeaking. Your indulgence will pardon the digreſſion.

I CANNOT but be of opinion, that the *hiſtory* of *Britain, during thoſe forty years*, would have furniſhed very rich and abundant matter for *poetic* imagery: even the mixture of barbariſm in it would have been of no diſſervice to the muſe.

IF ſuch a hiſtory had been extant, the adventures of it's heroes and heroines would have found celebrity from the harps of *Shakſpeare, Spenſer*, and *Milton*, arrayed in peculiar ſweetneſs. All the *epic, lyric*, and *tragic* muſes of modern *Britain* might have ſeleᛐed thence their favourite themes: they would probably have conſidered that epocha with as much love and reſpeᛐ, as was rendered by the muſes of *Greece* and *Rome* to the inexhauſtible ſtory of the wars and fall of *Troy.*

EVEN the *politician* would not diſdain to pay a deep attention to the contents of ſuch a work from

* LUCAN. *Pharſal.* Lib. I. 447.

the

the hand of *Tacitus.* For, however barbarous *Britain* might then be in her national manners, in her few laws, and rough form of government; yet, furely, many important propofitions and ufeful maxims might be deduced from a judicious and faithful defcription of them.

THE hiftory of our anceftors, even of thofe who are moft remote from our own times and cuftoms, will always be found to contain fomething inftructive to their pofterity. Such I remember was the reflection you made, when reading to me, at *Hanover, Tacitus's* effay *De Moribus Germanorum;* and tracing out, from it, the origin of the manners and government of our *anglo-faxon* fathers: a reflection, certainly, not inapplicable to our *britifh* anceftors alfo, and to the hiftory of our ifland in *their* times.

LET us judge of the utility of their hiftory in general from one article, of which we have fome knowledge: I mean the all-fupporting article of population. *Britain,* though deftitute of *manu-factures,* and of *commerce,* and probably but little inftructed in the *art* of agriculture, yet feems, in the times of *Claudius,* and of his fucceffor, to have been at leaft as full of people as at prefent. According to that fhort account of *britifh* affairs which we *now* find in *Tacitus,* the number of flain,

in

in the defeat of one *britiſh* army, and in the
deſtruction of two *britiſh* cities, amounted to
leſs than one hundred and fifty thouſand*!—
Cæſar alſo ſays in his commentaries, that *Britain*
was, in his time, abundantly inhabited:—*Hominum eſt* infinita multitudo; *creberrima edificia;
pecoris magnus numerus* †. I ſhould be glad to
ſee theſe facts, if true, rationally accounted for.
Such a diſcuſſion would certainly lead you to
ſome very important reflections.

BUT I forget, that I am all this while interrupting you. You were ſpeaking of the progreſs
of the *roman* arms in the conqueſt of our iſland.

INDEED, dear ſir, replied the eldeſt of the
young gentlemen, I had much rather follow *your*
train of ideas, than return to my former unpleaf-
ing topic.

IT is true, that the progreſs of the *roman* arms
in the weſtern or eaſtern frontiers of the empire
is a much more manly object of thought, than

---

* Annal. lib. xiv. c. 33. 37. *Boadicea's* army, according
to *Dion Caſſius*, confiſted of 120,000 in the beginning of her
inſurrection: it afterwards increaſed to 230,000. But in
this almoſt incredible multitude, it is probable, that even
the women and children, who flocked in great throngs to
the camp, are to be reckoned. Even if ſo, the number is
aſtoniſhing.

† CÆS. *de Bello Gal.* Lib. v. c. 12.

the degenerate manners of the contemporary *fenate* and *people of Rome,* if they merit the being called by *that* name, or the vile arcana of the court of the *Cæfars.* It is true, that the labours of *Corbulo,* and other *roman* generals, who commanded with honour in the reign of *Claudius,* are fufficiently noble, to recall to our minds the hiftory of fome of the moft celebrated heroes in the *roman* republic *. It is obferved, if I be not miftaken, by the noble author of the *Spirit of Laws,* that the military virtues of this city furvived all the reft. But what was the objeĉt of thefe *virtues,* as they are *moft improperly* called ?—the invafion, the flaughter, the plunder, the enflaving of innocent nations. Such, at leaft, was the cafe in *Britain.*

THE firft commander in chief of that *britifh* invafion, was *Plautius.*

IN our late journey to *Tivoli,* I ftood for fome minutes on the *Ponte Lucano,* viewing that ad-

---

* The charaĉter of *Corbulo* feems, in feveral particulars, to bear a refemblance to that of *Scipio Africanus.*

Ομοια γαρ τοις πρωτοις Ρωμαιων, 8χ οτι τω γενει λαμπρ☉, η τω σωματι ισχυρ☉ αλλα κ̀ τη ψυχη αρτιϕρων ην· κ̀ πολυ μεν το ανδρειον, πολυ δε κ̀ το δικαιον, τοτε πιςον εις παντας, κ̀ τ8ς οικει8ς, κ̀ τ8ς πολεμι8ς ειχεν. *Dio.* lib. lxii. c. 19.

Mixed with thefe great qualities, there were unhappily fome ingredients of vanity and oftentation; and what is much more to be lamented, a confiderable degree of that *roman* ambition, which was not fufficiently fparing of human blood.

joining

joining maffy tower, which is the maufoleum of the *Plautian family**. My thoughts, at that time, were engaged on the hiftory of this *Plautius*, of whom we are now fpeaking ; and my fentiments in regard to him were very fluctuating.   I could not but feel fome refpect for the memory of his military merit; but I felt much more horrour in recollecting, that he was the deftroyer of my country. Perhaps around that tower, during his funeral folemnity, much *britifh* blood was fhed in fport, juft as it had been here, in the *circus* or *forum*, at the time of his ovation †.   Such were the horrid

* See vol. i. p. 169.

† Πλαυτι⌐ απο τ⌐ Ὑρεταννικ⌐ πολεμ⌐, ως κⱼ καλως αυτον χειρισας κⱼ κατορθωσας, κⱼ επηνεθη υπο τ⌐ Κλαυδι⌐, κⱼ εθριαμβευσε· κⱼ κατα την οπλομαχιαν πολλοι κⱼ των ξενων απελευθερων, κⱼ οι αιχμαλωτοι οι Βρεταννοι εμαχεσαντο· κⱼ πολλ⌐ς οσ⌐ς κⱼ εν τ⌐τω ειδει της θεας ανηλισκε, κⱼ εν τ⌐τω εσεμνυνετο.

Dio Caffius. lib. lx.

If *Plautius's* wife, *Pomponia Græcina*, were really, as fome writers think, a chriftian, with what horrour muft fhe have looked on this fcene of pride and wanton cruelty ; and with what heart-felt grief reflect, that her hufband was concerned in it !

It feems very obfervable, that in the reign of *Claudius*, eloquence, and other polite literature flourifhed much in *Rome*.   Five centuries afterwards, all the arts and fciences of the *roman* empire were perifhing, under the cold influence of northern ignorance ; yet, even under thefe great difadvantages, chriftianity was able to render the hearts of the *roman* people much more humane than formerly. Many inftances might be produced of this fact.   It may be fufficient in this note, juft to hint the contraft, between the cruelty of *Plautius* to his *britifh* prifoners, and the charitable fentiments of *Gregory* the Great, when feeing in the *roman forum* fome poor captives of the fame country.

cruelties

cruelties of *Rome*, even in thofe ages, which are thought to have been the moſt civilized and polite. For, although the *romans* did not then, fo frequently as formerly, murder their captive kings, in cold blood, after a triumph; yet they feem to have continued as inhuman as ever to the common race of mankind.

THE next *roman* general, who ravaged *Britain,* was *Oſtorius.* He laid our country waſte, almoſt to the fhores of the *iriſh* fea. From the concife account of his campaigns in *Tacitus,* we are led highly to eſtimate his activity, and other military virtues; but, at the fame time, to form a very exalted idea of *britiſh* valour.

I HAVE often regretted, that, when we paſſed through *Ludlow,* we did not know how near we were to *Brampton-Brian,* and *Caer-Caradock:*— the places where *Caractacus* ſtruggled for *britiſh* liberty, againſt the legions of *Oſtorius.*

WITH what poetic pleafure would you have walked amid thofe venerable oaks, which *Camden* I think defcribes, as in his time fhading *Brampton-Brian;* and which, perhaps, may have vegetated there, in a conſtant fucceſſion, ever fince the *druidical* ages!

WITH what patriotic raptures fhould we all have viewed the river near *Caer-Caradock;* and thofe rocks, on which *Caractacus* ftood, encouraging his fellow-countrymen to the combat*!

IN that battle much valour was exerted on both fides. . The *britons* were in a very ftrong fituation; but the *romans* had the much greater advantage of numbers, and proper arms ; and, above all, the irrefiftible weight of excellent difcipline.

YET, though defeated in that bloody field, the brave *filures* ftill continued the war. They continued their oppofition with fuch fpirit, and by degrees with fuch fuccefs, that *Oftorius* at length funk under it. Vexation and difappointment, added to the other cares and fatigues of his unfuccefsful expedition, broke his heart. He died in *Britain.* Perhaps his bones ftill lie there, interred under fome lofty barrow, or pile of ftones, on our coafts ; in the fame manner as the corpfe of *Ajax* was buried on the fhore of *Troy.* May they remain undifturbed!

---

* *Enimvero Caractacus, huc illuc volitans, illum diem, illam aciem teftabatur, aut recuperandæ libertatis, aut fervitutis æternæ initium fore. Vocabatque nomina majorum, qui dictatorem Cæfarem pepuliffent; quorum virtute vacui à fecuribus & tributis, intemerata conjugum & liberorum corpora retinerent.*

Tacit. Annal, lib, xii. c. 34.

BUT

BUT what muſt have been the ſentiments of *Caractacus,* when, during his captivity, he heard that his *ſilures,* though threatened with extirpation, were ſtill in arms? With what ardour muſt he have wiſhed to be then among them, on the banks of the *Severn,* or the *Wye,* hazarding his life again for the deliverance of his country?

IF you, my dear friend, continued he, turning to *Crito's* pupil, were to exert your mind in ſome poetic effuſion on the noble indignation of a *Caractacus,* thus obliged to lie idle, at *ſuch* a time; would not the fire of his patriotic heroiſm appear to you equal, at leaſt, to that of any the more ancient warriors, deſcribed by the epic or dramatic poets of *Greece* or *Rome?*

I OUGHT to be duly ſenſible, replied *Crito's* pupil, that my mind is not ſtrong enough, to form a proper idea of *Caractacus,* on ſuch an occaſion. But were I endeavouring to repreſent his captive daughter, or any of her virgin train, as weeping on the ſhore of *Dover,* while the *roman* fleet was bending it's ſails for the voyage, I certainly ſhould take your hint of conſulting ſome of the *greek* tragedians. Probably I ſhould have immediate recourſe to that beautiful chorus, in the *Hecuba* of *Euripides,* ver. 443.

Αυϛϰ

Αυρα ποντιας αυρα,
Ατε ποντοπορυς κομιζεις
Θοας ακοτυς επ' οιδμα λιμνας,
Ποι με ταν μελεαν πορευσεις;
Τω δυλοσυνῷ πρῷ οικον
Κτηθεισ' αφιξομαι.

BUT why do I prefume to talk on this fubject? The ftory of *Caractacus* has already been treated *incomparably* better by Mr. *Mafon.*

IN one particular, Mr. *Mafon* has, in my opinion, very much *improved* upon the original: I mean, by having painted the *druid* character as endued with many graces, borrowed from a better religion. Such, in particular, is the meek doctrine of refignation; which, if I remember right, *his druid* inculcates upon *Caractacus,* both after his defeat, and in his captivity.

I HEARTILY wifh the poet could have thought it proper to add another act to his drama, defcriptive of *Caractacus,* when arrived at *Rome.* With what pleafure fhould we be *now* perufing the fcenes and choruffes of *that* act!

MANY have been the princes of various nations, faid the young nobleman, whofe captivity here at *Rome* we have fincerely pitied, during the courfe of your kind tutor's lectures: but, furely, there

there is none that affects us so nearly, as this of our own magnanimous king, *Caractacus.*

IT will, indeed, exhibit a melancholy object: but let us go visit the place, where our king appeared in fetters. I mean the *Castro Prætorio.* If we turn up the first road on our right, we shall be there in less than half an hour.

*   *   *

Ad portam Viminalem sunt mœnia, ultrà reliquos muros quadrata, quam formam vallo fossâque muni-tam romani usurpabant in castris:— injuria tempo-rum, & hominum incuria multa mutavit. Et verò ibi fuisse castra militum. Prætorianorum cum Onu-phrius de iis agens, & Lipsius tradunt; & commu-niter antiquarii.

THE foregoing lines are from *Donati.* *Eschi-nardi* confirms the same: *Un avanzo di sontuoso edificio scorgesi presso la porta chiusa: non è difficile dalla figura accennar che fosse, e ravvisarvi li linea-menti del Castro Prætorio. Certi tubi quivi trovati dell' aquedotto dell' aqua Martia, nella di cui in-scrizione è nominato il Castro Prætorio, sono testimoni di tal fabrica.* Abbate *Venuti* adds: *Il Signor Piranesi ne da l'intera pianta * avanzi il suo disfa-*

* Tav. xxxix.

cimento,

cimento, laquale egli dice averla rilevata da' fuoi avanzi, & dal profpetto, che fi vede nel baffo relievo dell' Arco di Conftantino, dalle medaglie, & dagli antichi fcrittori.

In this place, which is now a vineyard, belonging to the Novitiate of the jefuits, the young *englifhmen* fat down on the grafs. The eldeft took out a pocket edition of *Tacitus*, and read to his friends the defcription of *Caractacus's* approach to the tribunal of the *roman* empire.

I cannot help imagining, faid the young nobleman, that I now fee really all the fplendour of that *grand* ceremony; for *grand* it muft be called, though every *britifh* heart, then in *Rome*, fighed ready to break on the occafion. Cannot you fancy to yourfelf the *roman* court, *there* feated, in the utmoft magnificence; the *roman* people, innumerable for multitude, *there* fpreading out one wide furface of faces; the prætorian regiments on both fides, drawn out in fquare battalions, doubtlefs with the found of military inftruments, and all the poffible *pride and pomp of war?* The proceffion begins.—Be fo kind as to read thofe lines of *Tacitus* again.

Cæfar, dum fuum decus extollit, addidit gloriam victo. Vocatus quippe, ut ad infigne fpectaculum,

populus. Stetere in armis prætoriæ cohortes, campo qui caftra præjacet. *Tunc, incedentibus regiis
clientelis, phaleræ, torquefque, quæque externis bellis
quæfierat, traducta; mox fratres, & conjux, & filia.
Poftremò, ipfe* CARACTACUS *oftentatus* *.

IT was probably, continued the eldeft of the
young gentlemen, not without fome flattery to
the court and miniftry, that the *roman* fenate compared the captivity of *Caractacus* to that of the
fucceffor of *Alexander* the Great. Indeed, the
form of this part of the proceffion feems copied
from the triumph of *Paulus Æmilius:* but, how
different was the fpirit of our *britifh* prince, from
the timidity of that degenerate king of *Macedonia?*
*At non Caractacus aut vultu demiffo, aut verbis
mifericordiam requirens, ubi tribunali aftitit, in
hunc modum locutus eft* †. I think I never read,
in any of the ancient hiftorians, a fpeech that
feemed more genuine than this, and lefs the invention of the writer.

I AM very much of your opinion, replied *Crito's*
pupil. It is very concife and fenfible; open, generous, and full of that true courage, which, though
not defpifing felf-prefervation, will not fay or do
any thing mean to fecure it.

---

* TACIT. *Annal.* lib. xii. c. 36.   † Ibid.

YET

YET I own myfelf much more pleafed at the furprife, which *Caraetacus* expreffed, in viewing the greatnefs and fplendour of the capital of the *roman* empire; and his aftonifhment at the infatiable and mean voracity of it's inhabitants; who, though poffeffed of the richeft empire in the world, and gorged as it were to the throat with it's luxuries, yet could ftoop fo miferably low, as to deem it an addition of happinefs, that their troops were ravaging the poor provinces of *Wales*, and plundering or deftroying it's humble cottages*.

THE love of our country, for all *England* you know was then *Welch*, will lead us to concur with *Caraetacus* in his aftonifhment at this avarice and ambition of *Rome*. But ought not philanthropy to carry us at leaft one ftep farther? Is not *Britain* at prefent poffeffed of an empire more extenfive, and perhaps almoft as opulent as the *roman?* And is it not highly probable, that in viewing the ftreets and fquares of *London*, feveral *american* chiefs, whofe countries border on our back fettlements, may have vented *their complaints,* in expreffions fomewhat fimilar to thofe of *Caraetacus;* or to thofe, which *Galgacus* ut-

---

* *Caraetacus, barbarorum princeps, captus & Romam duetus, cum veniam a Claudio impetraffet, & dimiffus perluftraffet urbis magnitudinem & fplendorem, " Itane, inquit, vos, quum hae tanta ac talia poffideatis, noftra concupifcitis tuguriola?"*

Zonaras.

tered.

tered, fome years afterwards, at the feet of the *Grampian* mountains? *Si locuples hoftis eft, avari: fi pauper, ambitiofi. Quos non oriens, non occidens fatiaverit. Soli omnium opes atque inopiam pari affectu concupifcunt. Auferre, trucidare, rapere falfis nominibus imperium: atque ubi folitudinem faciunt, pacem appellant*.*

FROM national affairs, let us look down to the private fcenes of rural life. What muft we imagine to be the fentiments of the *englifh* labourer, or poor farmer, in viewing from the door or little window of his hovel, the pompous feat and gardens of his avaricious and oppreffive landlord? But this, certainly, is very feldom the cafe. For one inftance of a cruel landlord, there are, I believe, both in *England* and *Italy*, hundreds, who are kind and beneficent.

CRITO'S pupil, having now turned the converfation to his favourite topics, proceeded to pour forth the fentiments of his heart, ia the fweet eloquence of artlefs good-nature.

FROM thefe humbler topics,. he rofe again, gradually, like the fky-lark, from his beloved neft on the ground. He rofe to themes of a heavenly kind; themes far more fublime than thofe,

* Vid. TACIT. vit. *Agricolæ.* c. 30.

on

on which his young friends had been meditating, whether of military heroifm, or patriotic fortitude.

A RELIGIOUS foul, indeed, notwithftanding it's lowlinefs, foars infinitely higher than the mind of the patriot, or the hero. We may be con-vinced of this by one refleƐion only. Let us con-fider the charaƐer of that man, who, either in the fenate or in the field, nobly fights the battles of his country, without having another objeƐ in view, than the mere *glory* of fuch a conduƐ. How fublime is his objeƐ *generally* efteemed; but how really defpicable is it, in comparifon of the objeƐs of a religious life! Yet let not this obfervation be underftood, as depreciating too much the merit of thefe *englijh* youths. They were both honeft and worthy men; though by no means on a level with their admired friend, *Crito's* pupil.

IF the ftate of his mind, at the clofe of this *fa-turday* evening's converfation, could have been reprefented by any corporeal fimilitude, it would have much refembled that figure, with which *Ra-phael's* pencil has adorned one of the altars in *Bologna*: the figure, I mean, of *St. Cecilia*, treading on the trumpet, and other inftruments both of military and common mufic; but laying

her

her hand on the organ, and casting up her eyes to heaven.

* * *

ABOUT eleven o'clock on *sunday* morning, the young gentlemen called at *Crito's* apartment. They had not however the pleasure of finding him there. His servant informed them, that his master, having risen at day-break, had continued several hours in his closet, and afterwards walked out towards *St. Peter's;* but that he expected him home in about half an hour.

The young gentlemen went into *Crito's* apartment, and sat down at his table; where they saw some books, which he had been studying the preceding evening. These consisted of two or three volumes on religious subjects; *Seneca's* Consolation to *Helvia,* open at the beginning of the ninth chapter; and a short treatise, relative to that science, which most strongly disposes the mind to devotion;—astronomy.

AMONG these books lay a small roll of paper; which, as *Crito's* pupil informed them, was intended for their perusal. They opened it, and cast their eyes over it's first leaf, which was a

kind

kind of introduction to the whole. The contents
of that leaf were as follows.

" My dear friends, when beginning our prefent
courfe of ftudies, we were greatly encouraged in
it by the confideration, that perhaps there never
exifted, on the face of the whole earth, any heathen nation, more celebrated from the practice of
feveral moral virtues, than the *roman.* But we
are now advanced to thofe fad times, the reigns
of *Caligula* and *Claudius,* in which we find the
roman people totally changed; and their annals
become remarkable for hardly any thing elfe, than
the blacknefs and atrocious enormity of their
crimes. How can I defire you to continue your
attention to *their* hiftory?

" WHILE we were compiling the catalogue of
thofe worthies, who crowded this city during her
early republican government, we frequently, at
fhort intervals, turned our thoughts to the contemporary illuftrious characters of *Greece:* in the
fame manner as an aftronomer, though ftudying
nightly the number and magnitude of thofe ftars,
which fill the part of the heavens over his head,
yet fometimes turns his globe, to confider the
conftellations in the other hemifphere. But what
can we do at prefent? Thick and foul clouds now
hang over each country :—pardon me for this al-

legorical

legorical ſtyle : the bright conſtellations of *Greece*
ſeem all extinguiſhed : and *Italy* lies ſunk in midnight gloom; covered with the deep and *palpable
darkneſs* of vice.

" BUT look towards the ſouth-eaſt, and you
will ſee, in the utmoſt edge of the horizon, ſome
ſtreaks, as of the twilight of a riſing morning.
Fix your eyes on this phenomenon. It becomes
more and more diſtinguiſhable.

" IF an angel were now to be looking down on
the *roman* empire, he would ſee it's ſouth-eaſtern
provinces, *Paleſtine* and *Syria*, bright with exceſſive ſplendour.

" THE illumination is extending itſelf over *Cyprus, Aſia Minor, and Greece:* ſome of it's rays
already reach *Rome.* Yet, what is very peculiar,
this ſteady and pure light ſeems to ſhine only on
ſome low and humble roofs ; not on the lofty pin-
nacles of any of the *roman* palaces : over moſt of
theſe the thick cloud is ſtill hanging.

" BUT, in a little time, every part of the city
will be enlightened by this riſing *ſun of righteouſ-
neſs*, in a manner ten millions of times more glorious, than by all the glittering of her old heathen
virtues.

FROM

" FROM *Rome* the light will proceed weftward. But let me not tire you, my dear fellow-ftudents, with the continuation of this allegorical ftyle; a ftyle, in which my thoughts at prefent flow, owing to my having been lately ftudying fome books of this fpecies of natural philofophy. Let me rather, in plain language, beg you to turn your thoughts, from the black crimes of *Caligula's* and *Claudius's* court, to the contemplation of the pure bright-nefs of that Holy Church, which in *Paleftine* and *Syria* was then beginning to be known, by the name of CHRISTIAN.

" A GENERAL view of the hiftory of the Apo-ftolic Church, during the three laft years of *Ti-berius's* life, and throughout the whole reigns of *Caligula* and *Claudius*, will by no means be an improper fubjeft for your meditations to-morrow, that is, *funday morning.*"

AFTER this introduftory leaf followed a trea-tife, compofed by *Crito* fome months ago ; being a kind of meditation on the hiftory of chriftianity, during it's firft twenty years ; which clofed about the end of the reign of *Claudius*. In this treatife there was a confiderable degree of learning, very much humility, and ftill more devotion : a devo-tion, as appeared by the references marked in the

margin,

margin, greatly inflamed by the ſtudy of *St. Chry-ſoſtom.* The whole treatiſe however was ſo ſhort, that the young gentlemen read it through in little more than a quarter of an hour. They had laid it down again, and were beginning to talk of it's contents, when *Crito* entered the room. He ſaluted them with more than ordinary earneſtneſs and affeɛtion.

CRITO'S pupil, in the name of his two friends, returned him thanks for the manuſcript on the table. I believe, replied he, I ought much rather to aſk your pardon, for troubling you with thoſe papers.

Iт would perhaps have been much better, if I had deſired you this morning to conſult, in your ſeveral apartments, that book, from which almoſt every thing on this ſubjeɛt is extraɛted.

Thıs excellent part of eccleſiaſtical hiſtory is in a great meaſure contained in the firſt ſeventeen chapters of the *Aɛts of the Apoſtles.* You muſt however add to theſe chapters part of the 18th; for *Gallio,* the brother of *Seneca,* whom you will find mentioned in the middle of the 18th chapter, was governor of *Achaia,* if I miſtake not, about the end of *Claudius's* reign.

Iɴ

In the beginning of the fame 18th chapter, the *jews* are faid to have been expelled from *Rome* by *Claudius*. Permit me to trouble you with fome few words on that occafion.

SUETONIUS relates the fame fact: adding the moft improbable and moft fhocking reafon for it. *Judæos, impulfore CHRISTO, affiduè tumultuantes, Româ expulit**. That the *jews*, under the cruel and impious oppreffion of the *roman* tyranny, were very inclinable to rife in tumults, feems credible indeed from their hiftory in *Judæa*, during thofe times. But how could Chriftianity, Apoftolical Chriftianity, be a teacher of fedition? Could her doctrines, which inculcate the utmoft patience and charity in private life, and which exprefsly command obedience to all legal authority, as to the will of GOD; and inforce that obedience by the moft awful and tremendous fanctions; could thefe doctrines breathe the rebellious fpirit of mutiny and infurrection?

THE truth, *probably*, was this. The *jews*, from a motive of zeal, raifed fome tumults againft the chriftians, who were at that time chiefly of the fame nation; in the fame manner as they perfecuted them in *Achaia*, and in other countries. *Claudius*, without inquiring into the difference, or

* Vid. Vit. *Claudii*, c. 25.

making

making any diftinction, expelled them both. A conduct fuitable to the pride of the *roman* court, which held the whole *jewifh* nation in the utmoft contempt: as well as to the particular temper of *Claudius*, on which the rumour of a tumult had the greateft effect. *Nulla adeò fufpicio* (fays the fame *Suetonius*), *nullus auctor tam levis extitit, a quo non mediocri fcrupulo injecto ad cavendum ulcifcendumque compelleretur **.

But however this may be, you are furely too well acquainted with hiftory, to be furprifed at feeing innocence fometimes attacked by the groffeft calumnies. You have feen a *Rutilius* banifhed from this fame city, for crimes the moft improbable; the moft contrary to the whole tenour of his life. Similar was the injuftice done to the chriftians in this cafe; and particularly to *St. Peter*, if, as fome writers think, he was one of thofe, who were then expelled from *Rome*.

Give me leave to turn to his firft epiftle. This epiftle is generally thought to have been written by *St. Peter* while at *Rome;* I know not at what period of his life.

But whenever it was written, whether in the reign of *Claudius*, or in that of his fucceffor, it

---

* Vitâ CLAUD. c. 37.

contains

contains doctrines, far different from the spirit of
sedition. Several passages in it, as well as in some
epistles of *St. Paul,* strongly justify the apostolic
church from such calumnies. Permit me to read
to you only the last fourteen verses of the second
chapter.

Do not these verses totally confute the absurd
accusation of christianity, mentioned by *Suetonius?*

In a word, this false accusation of christianity,
together with the sentence of banishment pronounced, in consequence of it, by *Claudius,* may
be considered by us as the preface and introduction to the history, or black decad of those perse-
cutions, and of those scarcely less cruel calumnies,
which the christian church patiently suffered under the *roman* government, during the three following centuries.

But, continued *Crito,* looking on the clock,
the morning wears away. Let us turn our thoughts
to another employment; an employment, however, which is very much connected with the
topic, on which we have been reading and conversing.

The

THE young gentlemen ftaid'about half an hour longer in *Crito's* apartment, and then returned to their feveral lodgings.

* * *

The *Villa Medicis,* moft fortunately for *englifh* travellers, is fituate near that part of *Rome* in which they generally lodge.

THIS *Villa* has the particular honour of having once belonged to that great *Florentine* family, which revived the arts and fciences of antiquity. It's high walls, on the garden-front, are entirely covered with rich baffo-relievos: it's gardens are filled with many other valuable antiquities of *Italy, Greece,* and *Egypt;* and are always free and open for the amufement of the public.

THIS evening, *funday, june* 21, *Crito* was fitting alone in the portico of the *Villa Medicis,* and viewing thence the quiet and folemn afpect of the diftant pine-groves, when he was joined by his pupil, and his two other young friends.

AFTER fome talk on the beauties of this *Villa,* *Crito's* pupil inquired what was to be the place and fubject of to-morrow's lecture.

THE

THE next charaƈter, replied *Crito*, which I intended to propofe to your confideration, in following the order of hiſtory, was *Arria*, the wife of *Pætus*. The place, which, on that occaſion, you would probably have thought moſt proper to have viſited, would have been an apartment of the *Villa Ludoviſi:* I mean that apartment, in which the ſtatues of *Arria* and of her huſband are preſerved; a groupe eſtimated by the author of the *Mercurio Errante* at upwards of twelve thouſand pounds ſterling. After having viſited that apartment, you would perhaps have taken an airing in your coach to the church of *SanƈƚƗa Maria in Scholá Græcâ:* in the walls of which church, you know, ſeveral marble pillars are ſtill to be feen, belonging to that temple of *Pudicitia Patricia*, which anciently ſtood on that ſpot.

EVEN this very portico, in which you are now ſitting, would not be an improper ſcene for the clofe of ſuch a converſation. Theſe ſix coloffal ſtatues of *ſabine* matrons would not fail of reviving in your minds ſome pleaſing ideas, relative to that *female* merit, with which the republic of *Rome* was adorned, during it's moſt incorrupt ages*.

THE

* See Abbé *Richard's* Defcription of the *Villa Medicis*, vol. vi. p. 141,

THE view *from* this portico might alfo fuggeft to your imaginations a very fhocking contraft.

IF I be not miftaken in the topography of ancient *Rome*, which indeed may eafily be the cafe, part of the ground, which lies between this portico and that oppofite pine-grove, was towards the end of the republic covered by the famous gardens of *Lucullus.* During the reign of *Claudius*, thofe gardens were in the poffeffion of *Valerius Afiaticus.* But they were fatal poffeffions. They were coveted by the avaricious and bloody *Meffalina.* For the fake of thofe gardens, fhe plotted a falfe accufation againft *Valerius;* had him tried; and condemned: in a word, fhe murdered him, and then entered on his eftate.

MARK, now, the awful workings of Providence. Scarcely had fome few months paft, when fhe was called to fuffer for all her crimes. Fleeing from the imperial palace, in that day of terrour, fhe wandered about the ftreets and environs of this city: fometimes on foot, deferted by all her train, *id repente folitudinis erat,* fometimes riding,

Sous le portique fix ftatues des fabines. Les dames romaines les honoroient de quelque culte religieux, à la fête appellé Matronalia, le premier de mars. Parmi les differentes caufes qu' Ovide donne à cette fête, la premiere eft, de ce que les fabines, enlevées par les romains, qui les épouferent, arrêterent par leurs larmes la guerre cruelle, qui étoit prête à s'élever entre leurs peres, leurs freres, & leurs époux.

not

not in any of her ufual *proud* carriages, but in a common fcavenger's cart. She wandered about, yet found no foul to pity her. The deformity of her abominations had prevailed over all fentiments of compaffion.

BUT whither at laft did fhe bend her trembling fteps? Or, rather, to what place were they directed, by an influence far fuperiour to the defigns of her own mind?—To *thofe very* gardens of *Afiaticus.*

THITHER was fhe purfued by the minifters of juftice: there was fhe found by the executioner, lying on the cold earth, but herfelf far more chilled by difmay and horrour *: there was her guilty blood actually poured forth.

---

* *Interim Meſſalina Lucullianis in hortis prolatare vitam, componere preces; nonnullâ fpe, & aliquando irâ : tantâ inter extrema fuperbiâ agebat.—Prorupit Narciſſus (e palatio) denuntiatque centurionibus & tribuno qui aderant, exſequi cædem: ita imperatorem jubere. Cuſtos & exactore libertis Evodus datus. Iſque raptim in hortos prægreſſus, reperit fufam humi, aſſidente matre Lepidâ; quæ florenti filiæ haud concors, fupremis ejus neceſſitatibus ad miferationem evicta erat.—Animo per libidines corrupto, nihil honeſtum inerat: lacrymæque & queſtus irriti ducebantur. Cum impetu venientium pulfæ fores : adſtitit tribunus per filentium, at libertus increpans multis ac fervilibus probris. Tunc primùm fortunam fuam introſpexit, ferrumque accepit, quod fruſtrà jugulo ac pectori per trepidationem admovens, ictu tribuni transfigitur.*

Tacit. Annal. lib. xi. in fine.

IF *Afiaticus* had been a good man, would not this hiftory of his gardens have appeared to you very fimilar to that of *Naboth's* vineyard, in the fields of *Jezreel?*

BUT let us take a fhort walk to *that part* of thefe *Medici* gardens, which feems to have bordered upon, or perhaps, to have comprehended part of the ground, once belonging to the gardens of *Afiaticus.*

THE company readily followed *Crito* to the feparate enclofure, on the fouthern fide of the *Villa Medici.* They paffed fome time there, on the mount, in very ferious converfation on the dreadful cataftrophe of that vile woman. They afterwards returned into the more frequented parts of the garden: *Crito,* in the mean time, lamenting the extreme hardnefs, with which vice frequently petrifies the human heart. Notwithftanding the fhocking fate of *Meffalina,* her crime was, foon afterwards, exactly copied by *Claudius's* fecond emprefs, *Agrippina;* I mean, in relation to the gardens of *Statilius Taurus.* But *Agrippina's* crimes alfo will be followed by their punifhment.

WHILE *Crito* purfued this fubject, the company were paffing by the fine ftatue of the dying *Cleopatra.* How wretched, faid *Crito,* fomewhat
changing

changing the difcourfe, muſt *Cleopatra*, that *egyp-tian Agrippina*, even in the midſt of all her pride and luxury, have appeared even in her own eyes! efpecially, when ſhe compared herſelf to fome of the *virtuous* matrons of *Rome:* of *two* in particu-lar, whofe charaɛters were well known in the court of *Alexandria;* namely, firſt *Cornelia*, the wife of *Pompey* the Great; and fecondly, *Oc-tavia!*

THE company now croffed over into the mid-dle ſhady walk: and there, after fome defultory talk on various other fubjeɛts, refumed their former topic in the following manner.

I MUST defire you, faid *Crito*, to excufe me for not having prepared, as was my intention, fome effay on *Arria's* charaɛter, for your perufal to-morrow morning.

GIVE me leave, my dear pupil, to beg the favour of you to relieve me in this particular. A copy of verfes on that fubjeɛt, compofed by your pen, will give your two young friends here almoſt as much pleafure, as if you had been able to fhow them the ode, which your mufe infcribed to the memory of *Oɛtavia*.

I SAY

I say *almoſt*, for though the temper of *Arria's* mind was, in general, very noble and exalted; and though ſeveral of her actions, as *Rollin* obſerves*, were truly laudable; yet I am ſure you will not join in the common admiration of her ſuicide; or approve of her avowed contempt of life, if forced to ſurvive her huſband. This doctrine, however, ſhe inculcated into her daughter's mind, by precepts, as well as by example. In theſe reſpects, *Arria* ſeems to have born much more reſemblance to an *indian* princeſs, while aſcending her huſband's funeral pile, than to the meek-ſpirited *Octavia*. *Octavia's* long-indulged grief, for the death of her ſon *Marcellus*, though at length, indeed, it broke her heart, yet never did it lift her hand to ſelf-deſtruction.

Much leſs ſhould we preſume to compare *Arria*, with any of thoſe female worthies, who are *moſt juſtly* celebrated in the hiſtory of chriſtianity: who loved their huſbands and children with at leaſt as much fidelity, as ever was practiſed on the banks of the *Tiber*, or the *Ganges;* and yet, with due reſignation, ſubmitted that love to the dictates of ſound reaſon, and of true religion.

* See alſo *Pliny's* Epiſtles, book iii. ep. 16.

But

BUT after making fuitable allowances for *Arria's* mifguided conduct in thofe particulars, the reft of her character may certainly furnifh a very pleafingly poetic fubject. So eminent an example of conjugal virtue will be a very agreeable and *proper topic* for *all* your thoughts.

I KNOW not how it may found from *my* lips, yet I think it my duty on this occafion to fay, and to repeat it, That the goodnefs of the remainder of your refpective lives will in a great meafure depend on the union, by which each of you, probably, foon after your return home, may be made happy in the bands of virtuous ' wedded love'. *Juvenes, citò prudentes, citò pii; citò mariti, citò patres; citò omnis officii curiofi**. I thought yefterday of you all, while, talking of *Germanicus,* we expatiated on his early and happy marriage. *Expectant vos etiam jampridem domi tibicines, & Hymenœum qui cantent,*

> *Felices ter & amplius,*
> *Quos irrupta tenet copula; nec malis*
> *Divulfus querimoniis,*
> *Supremâ citius folvet amor die †.*

BUT let me repeat to you fome other verfes on the fubject. They are the compofition of a

---

* *Seneca* ad Martiam.
† HORAT. lib. i. od. 13.

modern

modern *italian* poet*; and feem rather more
fuitable to this day.

> *O te, beatum, qui Deum caſtè colis*
> *Ejuſque ſervas ſemitas!*
> *Tuæ labore quod manus paraverint*
> *Te nutriet fruſtu ubere.*
> *Tibi bene eſt, eritque; cunſtis affluis,*
> *Et ſemper afflues bonis.*
> *Qualis tuis conjunſta vitis mœnibus*
> *Uvis abundat dulcibus;*
> *Sic prole multâ te beabit optima*
> *Uxor, ferens natas pares.*
> *Virentibuſque ſeu novella frondibus*
> *Vigent olivæ germina:*
> *Venuſta menſam ſic tuam circumdabit*
> *Florens corona liberûm.*
> *En! ut bonis ditabitur quamplurimis,*
> *Timere qui novit Deum!*
> *Hæc largiatur, pluraque Ille munera*
> *Tibi, arce ex Sioniâ:*
> *Patriæque perfruare felicis bonis,*
> *Per cunſta vitæ tempora:*
> *Cernas tuorum liberorum filios,*
> *Lætamque pace patriam †.*

THE

---

* Signior *Roſſi* of *Arrezzo-Arretium* in *Tuſcany.*
† Vid. *Pſalm.* DAV. cxxviii. The reader of taſte, on a
due confideration of the beauties exhibited in this fpecimen
of facred poefy, will be ready to own, of the book of Pfalms
in

THE company were by this time arrived at the farther end of the middle walk of the garden; when *Crito*, leaning on the iron rails, paused a while; and then again addreſſed himſelf to his pupil, and his other young companions. May you all, ſaid he, *in ſome few years*, be ſurrounded with a numerous and beautiful young family; but much more long lived, much more the favourites of heaven, than that which here ſurrounds *Niobe*, in this moſt noble of all ſtatuary groups; proba-bly the maſter-piece of the great *Scopas!*

BUT let us now take another turn in this walk: and give me leave again, to expreſs my hopes, that you, my dear pupil, will favour me with a ſhort compoſition on this ſubjeƈt. A copy of ſuch a compoſition, by *you*, will give much more pleaſure to your parents in *England*, than even that which went hence laſt week *.

THE charaƈter of *Arria*, notwithſtanding it's defeƈts, is capable of being ſo repreſented, as to

in general, what the excellent biſhop HORNE ſo empha-tically ſays concerning them. " They preſent religion to us, in the moſt engaging dreſs: communicating truths, which *philoſophy* could never inveſtigate; in a ſtyle, which *poetry* can never equal: while *hiſtory* is made the vehicle of pro-phecy; and *creation* lends all it's charms, to paint the glo-ries of *redemption*." See his Commentary on the *Pſalms*, vol. i. pref. p. 64. 8vo. B.

* See, of this work, book iii. chap. vii. vol. ii. p. 126.

make a very agreeable figure. Some of it's features much refemble thofe of *Panthea,* as painted by *Xenophon.*

WHILE you are indulging your poetical ideas in this ode, I fhall be employing my thoughts on a fubject more fuitable to my years : a fubject, which has filled my mind ever fince fun-rife this morning; and on which I fhall be very happy to converfe with you all, my dear friends, to-morrow, in that folemn pine-grove of the *Villa Borghefe;* and on *tuefday,* in the fpacious and auguft *piazza* of *that* moft fplendid church.

As *Crito* was pronouncing thefe words, he ftretched forth his right hand towards *St. Peter's;* the dome and front of which church appear very diftinctly from the *Medici* gardens.

CRITO remained, for fome little time, quite motionlefs in that attitude, and his mind feemed to be labouring under fome great thought. He was ready to give it utterance, when fuddenly two or three *french* gentlemen, who had been reading the infcription over the chapel, in the northern corner of the garden *, came up to our *englifh* company;

* If I remember right, the infcription alluded to is in honour of a perfon of fortune, who lived in this part of *Rome,* at the time when it was facked by the duke of *Bourbon's*

company; and confequently broke off all further private converfation between them.

---

bon's army. This perfon, fuppofed, from his former very frugal manner of life, to have amaffed great wealth, was then put to the torture by the foldiers, to force him to dif-cover the fources of his opulence. It was difcovered, that he had, indeed, a great treafure; but that treafure was laid up by him, not on earth; but *in heaven:* far out of the reach of fpoilers.

CHAP.

C H A P. VI.

TWENTY-FOURTH DAY'S CONVERSATION.

SCENE. *The apartment of the eldest of the young gentlemen: himself reading a volume of* Tacitus: *a map of* England *lying before him on the table.*

[*Enter his two young friends.*]

ELDEST.

How pleasant is it for travellers, who have been so long abroad as ourselves, to take up now and then such a map as this; and to feast their eyes with the fight of *their own* country!

I HAVE been looking over some parts of *North Wales;* and have recollected many agreeable circumstances, which occurred to us in our tour through that romantic region, the summer before last.

Such has been my amusement since breakfast; though, when I rose this morning, I had another motive for taking this map out of my travelling chest. My reason for it was, that I might by this

help

help be better enabled to underſtand *Tacitus's* account of *Suetonius Paulinus's* campaigns. If I
be not miſtaken, it was not till the *eighteenth* year
of the *britiſh* war, that the *roman* legions pene-
trated into *Caernarvonſhire.* *Paulinus,* ardently
deſirous to complete his conqueſt of this part of
Britain, invaded *Angleſea* alſo; and in that action *ſwam* his cavalry acroſs *this* arm of the ſea.
He ſeems from *this circumſtance* to have been a
very *bold* commander; as, on the other hand, his
conduct, and *perſeverance,* are highly extolled by
Tacitus.

TACITUS hints at a compariſon between *Paulinus's* campaigns in *Britain,* and thoſe of *Corbulo*
in *Armenia.* Indeed, though the hills of *North
Wales,* and even *Snowdon* itſelf, are not to be compared to the mountains of *Ararat;* and though in
this part of the world, during the conteſt between
the *romans* and the *britons,* there was no *third*
nation, of ſuch power and dignity as *Parthia,* to
interfere, and ennoble the ſcene of their campaigns and negotiations: yet, if we confine our
thoughts merely to the native bravery of it's inhabitants, ſurely *Britain* was as difficult a theatre
of war as *Armenia,* or perhaps any region of
Aſia. In ſaying this, I am far from thinking myſelf partial to my country.

BUT

BUT how dreadful is the idea, which now rifes to our minds, if from *Wales* we turn our eyes to the eaſtern ſide of *Britain;* and contemplate the vaſt effuſion of human blood, which *then* ſuddenly burſt forth, almoſt in every field of *Hertford-ſhire* and *Eſſex,* and diſcoloured all the beautiful verdure of the banks of the *Thames!*

CRITO'S PUPIL.

HORRID, indeed, as you obſerve, very horrid were thoſe maſſacres. They blot out the glory of our otherwiſe patriotic heroine, *Boadicea:* they caſt a ſtain of diſhonour on the hiſtory of our nation. It is true, that the *roman* armies, which then oppreſſed *Britain,* were full of inſolence, impiety, cruelty, and inſatiable avarice; but the ſavage revenge of the *britons* is not thereby juſtified.

SOME verſes of *Glover's Boadicea* affeɛted me greatly, when I firſt heard them: and I hope they will long remain freſh on my memory.

Of all the paths, which lead to human bliſs,
The moſt ſecure, and grateful to our ſteps,
With mercy and humanity is mark'd.——
Ah, how much brighter is the wreath of glory,
When interwove with clemency and juſtice!
YOUNG

- YOUNG NOBLEMAN.

IT feems fomewhat extraordinary, that the *ro-man* hiftorians, though they fpeak much of the deftruction of *Camalodunum, Verulam,* and *London,* by the fury of *Boadicea,* yet give us no de-fcription of the fituation of that famous field of battle, where her prodigious army was foon after-wards totally defeated.

AN *englifh* writer, I know not of what repute among the antiquarians, thinks it probable, that this battle might be fought near *Kefton* camp, on *Hayes* and *Bromley Common**. Indeed, it feems not unlikely, that *Paulinus,* on being obliged to abandon *London,* fhould retire to the fouthward of the *Thames,* towards *Kent;* in order that he might, there, more readily receive reinforcements from the continent.

---

* It is not known, that any coins or marks of the *romans* were ever found at *Kefton* camp : but it is perhaps obferva-ble, that the brook, which rifes clofe adjoining to it, is call-ed *Ravernfburn,* which word feems a corruption of *romans bourne.* In like manner, the fame writer obferves, that the *Ravenfbank,* which croffes the low-lands of *Lincolnfhire,* is in old writings, according to Dr. *Stukeley,* termed the *ro-mans bank.* The *roman* camp alfo in *Hertfordfhire* goes by the name of *Ravenfborough Caftle.* I have fomewhere feen another fortification of that name.
See *Salmon's* Survey of *England,* vol. i. p. 92. and 355.

CRITO'S PUPIL.

IT were well, if *Salmon's* conjecture could be *fully* proved. I owe fo much love and gratitude to the environs of *Bromley,* that I ought heartily to wifh for the fuccefs of every hypothefis, which may contribute in any degree to their honour.

ELDEST.

I OWN, for myfelf, that I have more curiofity to know the place where *Boadicea,* according to an extract from *Dion,* fubjoined in the notes to this edition of *Tacitus,* was interred by her faithful, though ruined fubjects. Δεινως αυτην επενθησαν, κ͘ πολυτελως εθαψαν. If we had any tolerably comple account of the *Britannia Romana,* we fhould probably find in it fome defcription of the *place* and *form of her fepulchre.* Often, perhaps, have we feen the fpot; often may our feet unknowingly have trodden upon that turf, under which, in fome future age, her bones may be difcovered; intermingled with the brazen head of her fpear, and fome of the golden ornaments of her royalty.

BUT, continued he, rolling up the map, let us, though with reluctance, withdraw our thoughts totally from *England.* Let us think of *Rome.*

* * *

BREAKFAST being now brought in, the company fat down to it. The converfation afterwards turned on the fubject of *Nero's* reign.

CRITO's PUPIL.

(Taking up Dion Caffius from the table.)

IF I reçollect right, the characteriftics of this reign, according to *Dion,* were thefe three; Ασελγεια, Ωμοτης, Ασχημοσυνη. Like the *foul deities* whom they worfhipped, the wretched people of *Rome* exhibited themfelves

——— *partial, changeful, paffionate, unjuft:*
Whofe attributes were rage, revenge, *and* luft*.

LET us pafs over the firft black article as quick and filently as poffible. As to the other two, I cannot help obferving, that the pride of the *roman* nation, if we may judge from their writers, feems to have been as much hurt by the third article, as by the fecond; though, certainly, there is no comparifon between them. The folly, which *Nero* exhibited on the ftage, might indeed juftly

* POPE. *Effay on Man,* Ep. iii.

render

render him very contemptible; but in how different a manner ought we to think of the *multiplied
horrour* of his murders!

I wish I could properly repeat to you what
my tutor lately advanced on that dreadful fubject.

Some few days ago I attended him to the
Lateran cathedral. His converfation at firft
turned upon feveral ecclefiaftical, and very important topics. Towards the clofe of that converfation, we relaxed our minds with fome lighter
fubjects: it became a *claffic talk*.

He gave me a fhort hiftory of the *fabric* where
we ftood, from the time of *Lateranus, who was
flain by* Nero, to the reign of *Conftantine:* and
thence to the prefent age *.

We afterwards walked from the church to the
back door of the baptiftery: where *the remains*

---

* The hiftory of the *Lateran* cathedral appears *in general* to be this. On the *execution of Lateranus*, his houfe and
gardens were confifcated to the emperor, and feem to have
continued part of the imperial eftate, down to the times of
Conftantine.
Conftantine is fuppofed to have authorifed the chriftians
in *Rome* to make ufe of part of his *Lateran* palace, for the
place of their religious affemblies. It thus became the firft
chriftian church ever opened by the *authority* of a fupreme
magiftrate: and partly, perhaps, for this reafon, it is entitled *Omnium ecclefiarum, in urbe, & in orbe, mater, & caput.*
of

of Lateranus's *stately house* are more visible, than in any other part.

I STOPPED to admire one of the great columns of porphyry †. My tutor took that opportunity to give me some instructions, relative to the excessive magnificence in which the ancient *roman* nobility passed their days; as well as to the instability and vanity of such magnificence.

IN the times, said he, of their prosperity and wealth, what were the *serious thoughts* of the generality of the *roman* noblemen? The rebuilding, or the enlarging, of their villas and palaces; those proud structures, which they had designed as the repositories of their enormous opulence of every kind; and as the scenes of their intended ease and luxury, for many, many years to come.—Αφρων, ταυτη τη νυκτι, την ψυχην σ8 απαιτ8σιν απο σ8. Α δε ητοιμασας, τινι εςαι*;

THE same folly strongly infected even the *reputed* wise men of that generation. They saw the

---

* *Il battisterio, denominato di Constantino, fabbrica de' tempi bassi, fatta con le spoglie della Casa de i Laterani—dietro al battisterio si vedono alcuni maggiori avanzi di questo palazzo —Le colonne di porfido, che sono al battisterio erano di questo palazzo, come quelle che sono nel muro verso la sagrestia, e che sostengono un pezzo di fregio, & di cornice antica.*
See *Abbate Venuti,* part. i. p. 134, 135.
† Div. Luc. c. xii. 20.

vanity of fuch defigns daily exemplified; yet their proud hearts were not converted by the fight. *Tot divitum fubita paupertas,* fays a contemporary writer, *(Seneca,) in oculos incidit: & nobis nunquam in mentem venit,* noftras *quoque opes* æquè *in lubrico pofitas.* That lot, however, which they had fo frequently feen falling on others, fell, at length, in reality upon themfelves.

Temporibus diris igitur, juffuque Neronis,
Longinum, & magnos Senecæ prædivitis hortos
Claufit, et egregias Lateranorum *obfidet* ædes
Tota cohors *.

But let us fit down by the ruins of this pompous portico; and meditate awhile on the fubject.

With refpect to *Lateranus* himfelf, we will not, at prefent, enter into any difcuffion of the lawfulnefs of that intended infurrection, which was defigned to deliver the world from the tyranny of *Nero:* or into any particular examination of that fenator's character; though a very great idea of it is conveyed to us, in fome few concife expreffions of *Tacitus: Lateranum, confulem defignatum, nulla injuria, fed amor reipublicæ fociavit conjurationi*†. How very fimilar

* Juvenal. Sat. X. 15.
† Tacit. *Annal.* lib. xv. 49.

was this motive to that, which influenced *Marcus Brutus!*

LET me rather again defire your attention, my dear pupil, to the *fuddennefs of that ruin,* which fell on *Lateranus,* and his opulent family. According to *Suetonius, Nero* generally gave *but one hour's refpite* to the perfons, whom he ordered to die: immediately after that hour had elapfed, they were forced to put themfelves to death. But with *Lateranus* the refpite was not fo long. Perhaps it might be in this ftately portico, that *Lateranus* was feized. Let me read to you here a line or two of my extraƈts from *Tacitus.*

Proximam necem Plautii Laterani, confulis de-fignati, Nero adjungit; adeò properè, *ut, non compleƈti liberos, non illud breve mortis arbitrium, permitteret. Raptus in locum fervilibus pænis fe-pofitum, manu Statii tribuni trucidatur*.*

MY tutor now paufed for fome moments: then, recolleƈting his thoughts, he proceeded as follows.

RUIN, equally unexpeƈted, and equally de-ftruƈtive, fell at various times on many other ftately edifices, inhabited by the *roman* nobility.

---

* *Annal.* lib. xv. c. 60.

THE history of the extirpation of most of the great senatorial families in *Rome* has often, my dear pupil, led me to a very serious train of thought. How many of the *roman* nobles were slaughtered, in the civil wars of *Marius* and *Sylla*, *Cæsar* and *Pompey*, *Anthony* and *Octavius!* Even when the sword slept, in *Augustus's* reign, we see them continue to perish by other causes. Many were impoverished by luxury and vice. A very remarkable number dropped into their graves, without leaving children to inherit their titles and estates. Vengeance still pursued the remainder of them. In the following reigns; under *Tiberius*, the *roman* house of lords was thinned by the *axe of mock-justice;* they destroyed themselves, by their own votes and decrees: under *Caligula*, they bled by the *sword of the soldiery:* and under *Claudius*, and *Nero*, they perished by *both* these destructive instruments of tyranny united.

THE dispensations of Providence are most just. Let us recollect what our countryman, Mr. *Hooke*, says, of the wickedness of the *roman* senate, in the corrupt and degenerate times of the republic; their avarice, cruelty, perfidy, and pride. Their houses were filled with the spoils of innocent nations. But their crimes shall be punished, even to the third and fourth generation of their children. Four tyrants,—a series of monsters,—such

as

as the world never till then faw, and never fince
has feen, feated on the throne of government, fhall
be appointed to rule over them ; and to dafh them
to pieces, as with the continued ftrokes of a rod
of iron.

NERO was the principal inftrument appointed
to humble and confound the pride of the *roman*
nobility, in *Rome* itfelf; in the fight of all the nations of the earth*; no lefs than to fhed their
blood in almoft every province of the empire.

WHILE he was thus talking to me, my own
heart, too keenly, joined in my tutor's fentiments.

WELL might *Tacitus,* thought I declare upon
this occafion, *Ira illa numinum in res Romanas
fuit:* For, certainly, in the cruelties of a *Nero,*
and a *Poppæa,*

* Εκεινο δειξαι κ̓ αισχιϛον κ̓ δεινοτατον αμα εγενετο, οτι κ̓ ανδρες κ̓
γυναικες ʊχ οπως τʊ ιππικʊ αλλα κ̓ τʊ βʊλευτικʊ αξιωματ⊕-, ες την
ορχηϛραν, κ̓ ες τον ιπποδρομον, τοτε θεατρον, το κυνηγετικον εισηλθον,
ωσπερ οι ατιμοτατοι· εισηλθον οι μεν εθελονται, οι δε ϖανυ ακοντες.——
Και ειδον οι τοτε ανθρωποι τα γενη τα μεγαλα, τʊς Φʊριʊς, τʊς Ορα-
τιʊς, τʊς Φαβιʊς, τʊς Πορκιʊς, τʊς Ουαλεριʊς, τ'αλλα ϖαντα, ὡν τα
τροπαια, ὡν οι ναοι εωρωντο, κατω τε εϛηκοτας, κ̓ τοιαυτα δρωντας, ων
ενια ʊδ'ʹ υπ' αλλων γινομενα εθεωρʊν. Και εδακτυλοδεικτʊν γε αυτʊς
αλληλοις, κ̓ επελεγον Μακεδονες μεν, Ουτ⊕- εϛιν ο τʊ Παυλʊ εκγον⊕-,
Ελληνες δε Ουτ⊕- τʊ Μομμιʊ· Σικελιωται, ιδετε τον Κλαυδιον· Ηπειρω-
ται ιδετε τον Αππιου· Ασιανοι τον Λʊκιον· Ιβηρες τον Πʊπλιον· Καρχη-
δονιοι Αφρικανον.   *Dio Caffius,* lib. lxi.
See alfo *Montefquieu,* Grandeur et Decadence des Romains, the 15th chapter; and that paragraph, which begins
with the words: *C'eft ici qu'il faut fe donner le fpectacle des
chofes humaines, &c.*

Non tibi Tyndaridis facies invifa Lacænæ,
Culpatufve Paris; verum inclementia Divûm
Has evertit opes, fternitque a culmine Trojam *.

But I was recalled from this train of thought by my tutor; who obferved, that, although *Nero* was a proper *inftrument* of vengeance, yet he, himfelf, deferved the greateft of punifhments.

MY tutor then proceeded to fpeak of fome of *Nero's* crimes, particularly his murders, in fuch a ftyle, as to fill me with inexpreffible horrour. He *unfolded* them in fuch a manner, as would almoft

—*harrow up your fouls, freeze your young blood ;*
Make your combin'd and knotted locks to part ;
And each particular hair to ftand an end,
Like quills upon the fretful porcupine †.

SUCH were my tutor's reflections, on viewing the ruins of the palace of *Lateranus.* Let us, now, for a while quit the horrid topic :—or, if the hiftory of *Nero* muft be the principal fubject of our thoughts this day, let us contrive to intermingle with it fome other bufinefs, or amufement, which may ferve frequently to divert and relieve the mind.

* ÆNEID. ii. 601.
† SHAKSPEARE, *Hamlet,* act i, fc. 3.

SUPPOSE

SUPPOSE we take a ride this morning. My tutor has walked out by the *Porta del Popolo* to the *Villa Borghefe.* If you pleafe, we will make a little excurfion into the campagna, and in our return call on him there.

*   *   *

THIS propofal being readily affented to, the young gentlemen ordered their horfes, and rode out from the *Porta Pia.*

THE eldeft pointed to the *Caftro Prætorio,* a little to the right on the high road. *Suetonius,* faid he, informs us, that it was *thence Nero* had the bitter mortification, in the hour of ex-pulfion from his imperial palace, to hear, *ex prox-imis caftris, clamorem militum, & fibi adverfa, & Galbæ profpera ominantium.* It was along this very road, that the tyrant, then, in the laft night of his life, fled away, filled with *fear* and *fhame.* But why do I mention thefe little cir-cumftances? *Extreme,* at that time, furely, muft have been his confufion, and horrour of con-fcience; while the heavens roared in thunders over his head; the lightnings flafhed in his face; and the ground, in an earthquake, tottered be-neath his feet*.

BUT

---

* *Tremore terræ, & fulgure adverfo pavefactus.*
Suetonius, Nero. 48.

See

But I forget, my dear friend: you propofed this ride chiefly as an amufement. Let us talk on fome other topic.

* * *

If you pleafe, faid *Crito's* pupil, we will follow the road that leads towards *Nomentum.*

The company accordingly continued their ride for three or four miles: during which time the converfation varied to many different fubjects.

The pleafantnefs of the weather, and the beauty of the country, the vegetation of which was in this month at it's height, revived at length fome favourite ideas in the breaft of *Crito's* pupil.

As he imagined himfelf to be nearly approaching the fpot of *Seneca's* fuburban villa *, he began

gan

See alfo what *Dion* fays on the occafion.

————φυγειν επεχειρησεν. Προς χωριον τι φαωντⒼ——νυκτος επιϐσης ηλασε* κ̣ αυτȣ ταυτα πραττοντⒼ, ϹεισμⒼ εξαισιⒼ εγενετο, ωϛε κ̣ δοκησιν παρασχειν, οτι ητε γη πασα διαρρηγνυται, κ̣ αι των πεφονευμενων ψυχαι πασαι αμα επ' αυτον αναθορνȣσι.

Obfervatum etiam fuerat, Nero *fic cantâffe;*

Θανειν μ'ανωγει συγ̈αμⒼ, μητηρ, πατηρ.

Perfecto, demum, fcelere, magnitudo ejus intellecta eft.

* *Tacitus* fays, that *Seneca* had a villa about four miles diftant from *Rome.* See Annal. lib. xv. *In fuburbano rure, quartum apud lapidem.* It is fubmitted to the reader's confideration,

gan to fpeak of the virtues, which that philofopher there *really* praƐtifed; not only in his laft hour, but during many preceding years.

CRITO'S pupil now indulged himfelf in one of his moft beloved topics, the happy bufinefs of a country life; a life, which agriculture and gardening, temperance, moderate labour, and moderate ftudy, all contribute to render delightful. Bleffed lot! but rendered far more bleft, when accompanied by conftant daily exercifes of piety and charity.

Of all the profeffions in humble life, I know not, faid he, any, that I fhould prefer to the employment of a gardener, or fmall farmer, when in tolerably eafy circumftances. His mind is kept in vigour; his body in health; his field or garden is full of innocent charms, to delight all his fenfes; and of objeƐts, proper, frequently, to fuggeft to his foul fome moral or *pious* thought.

fideration, whether or no *that* might not be the villa, which belonged to *Seneca*, in *Nomentanâ regione*, of which he fpeaks in his 104th and 110th epiftles; and which is alfo mentioned with particular honour by his contemporary *Columella.* See *De re ruſticâ*, lib. iii. c. 3. *Sed Nomentana regio nunc celeberrimâ famâ eſt illuſtris, & præcipuè quam poſſidet Seneca, vir excellentis ingenii atque doƐtrinæ, cujus in prædiis vinearum jugera ſingula culleos oƐtonos reddidiſſe, plerumque compertum eſt.* But it is to be remembered, that *Seneca* had alfo a villa *in Albano*, and perhaps others.

I REMEMBER my father's obſerving, that in *this laſt* reſpeᔑ the ſentiments of ſome chriſtian writers, who have treated on the ſubjeᔑs of gardening and huſbandry, are certainly far ſuperiour to thoſe of the moſt eminent heathens. But, as to myſelf, I know ſcarce any thing of either. Of the *roman* writers *de re ruſticâ, Columella* is, I think, reckoned the moſt elegant. I am yet but very little acquainted with his works; but intend ſoon to peruſe them. I have been reading, this morning, the introduᔑion to his firſt book. The principal ſubjeᔑ of that introduᔑion is, you know, the contraſt, between the rural induſtry of the ancient *romans,* and the *trifling* manners of their poſterity, in *Columella's* time: that is, in *Nero's* reign. *Luxuriæ deliciiſque noſtris virilis vita diſplicet.*

INDEED, the life of men of fortune, ſaid the young nobleman, is uſually too full of trifling; eſpecially while they are reſident in great cities. But it was, probably, much more ſo, amidſt the immenſe opulence and luxury of *Rome,* and the bad examples of *Nero's* court*.

---

* *Jam vero propria & peculiaria hujus urbis vitia, pæne in utero matris concipi mihi videntur; hiſtrionalis favor, & gladiatorum equorumque ſtudia. Quibus occupatus & obſeſſus animus, quantulum loci bonis artibus relinquit?*

　　　　See the treatiſe on Oratory, uſually publiſhed with *Tacitus's* works: cap. 29.

THE whole life of *Nero* was always trifling, whether at *Rome,* at *Naples,* or in other places. But, in a particular degree, what a tour of folly was his journey to *Greece!* His amufements there were theatrical diverfions; his *ferious* occupation was *fiddling.* With great exactnefs and care he laboured for the prize of mufic; totally neglecting the proper employment of a fovereign, the welfare of his people *.

BUT let me recollect: am not I, though a private perfon, in fome meafure guilty of the fame kind of fault? Am not I now, while on my travels, fquandering away on mufic, vertù, and other *inerti negotio,* thofe days, of which I muft give a ftrict account? Ought not I rather to apply my attention, with all diligence, to the much more important bufinefs of doing, or preparing myfelf to do, as much good, as is really in the power of one in my ftation? fome public, fome private, or at leaft fome domeftic beneficence?—*Ad hæc quærenda natus, æftimare debeo; quàm non multum acceperim temporis, etiam fi illud totum his operibus vindicem.— Quod feneЕta vocatur, paucorum eft circuitus annorum.—Sed nunc, dum calet fanguis, certè vigen-*

---

* Παντα εποιει, ινα τον των κιθαρωδων αγωνα νικησας ηττηθη τον των Καισαρων.——Τις νικη ατοπωτερα, εν ᷢ τον κοτινον, η την δαφνην, η το ζελινον, η την ϖιτυν λαβων, απωλεσε τον ΠΟΛΙΤΙΚΟΝ.

Dio Caffius.

tius

tius ad meliora eundum eſt. Ante ſeneɛtutem curem, ut bene vivam : in ſeneɛtute, ut bene moriar.—Theſe words of *Seneca* ſtruck me ſtrongly, while I was dipping into his works laſt night.—I hope, however, that my turn for the amuſements, of which I have been ſpeaking, has not been remarkably exceſſive; though I am every day more and more ſtrongly convinced, that I ought to correɛt myſelf in them.

WHILE the young nobleman was expreſſing theſe good ſentiments, his two friends looked on him with great regard. His preſent turn of thought ſeemed to favour the patriotic ardour of his elder friend; but in reality it was much nearer allied to the piety, humility, and charity of *Crito's* pupil.

IF I be not miſtaken, replied *Crito's* pupil, *Nero* made the tour of almoſt all the *grecian* cities; except the two principal, *Athens* and *Lacedæmon.* He ſhunned the *athenian* territory, his conſcience not ſuffering him to approach the temple of *Eleuſis.* He ſhunned *Sparta,* for a ſimilar reaſon. I remember *Dion's* words : Διχ τ8ς Λυκ8ργ8 νομ8ς, ως εναντι8ς τη προαιρεσει αυτ8 οντχς.

HAD *Nero* perſevered in his intended voyage to *Egypt,* he would probably, *in like manner,* have

have paffed much time at *Alexandria, Canopus,* and other feats of idlenefs on the *Nile*: but never would he have vifited the facred habitations of thofe *therapeutic* philofophers, whom *Philo* defcribes as then fpread over all *Egypt;* living retired from the world; having difpofed of their fortunes to their relations; praftifing much aufterity; and giving up their time to pious ftudies and meditations.

Such a depravity, and weaknefs of mind, in fome degree, appears by no means in you, my worthy friend: but it does in feveral young travellers, of various nations, who, as my tutor obferved to me, wander through many parts of *Europe*, particularly *Italy;* thinking of fcarcely any thing except diverfions, and the moft trifling kinds of mufic and vertù; and fhunning or flighting thofe places, which are remarkable either for devotion, or aufterity of manners *. Their time is totally employed in the purfuit of pleafure, which flees them; and confequently becomes void, in a great meafure, of dignity, utility, and real happinefs.

* * *

The company now quitted the *Nomentan* road, and turned acrofs the campagna to their left.

---

* *Difcurrunt, & locorum mutationibus inquietantur; ægri animi jaftatione.* *Senec.* Ep. 2.

MUCH was it to be wifhed, faid the eldeft of the young gentlemen, that *Nero*, in his *grecian* tour, had been guided by folly only. But there, as in *Italy*, he was ftained with vices, far exceeding the moft enormous wickednefs of modern ages. Rapine went on his left hand, and Murder on his right *.

IF our travels *fhould* extend to *Greece*, we fhall certainly make it our chief bufinefs, in feveral parts of that country, to recollect the heroifms of it's ancient natives : but I hope we fhall not be fo wholly taken up with their panegyrics, as at *Cenchreæ* to forget the name of *Corbulo*.

IN that *corinthian* port, by the command of *Nero*, *Corbulo* was murdered.

WHILE we are treading on that coaft, and viewing on one fide of the bay the hills of *Attica*, on the other the mountains of the *Peloponnefus*, fhall we not think *Corbulo* happy, at leaft, in this circumftance; that he died, and was buried in that land, which gave birth to, and contained the afhes of fo many heroes ? Shall we not then endeavour, by recollecting the principal events in the *grecian* hiftory, to find fome illuftrious *gre-*

---

* Πασαν Ελλαδα λελατησε.   *Dio Caffius.*
Nunquam inter voluptates, à rapinâ & cæde ceffabat.

cian character fimilar to his? I wifh I were able, even now, when in the fuburbs of *Rome*, to expatiate, with proper dignity of fentiment and language, on the character of *Corbulo*.

AMONG many other particulars, highly to his honour, ought we not to take notice, that it was to be attributed to *Corbulo* alone, that the *roman* army in *Syria* was fo ftrengthened, by newly-revived difcipline, as to ftrike terrour over all the eaft?

IT was to *Corbulo* alone, that *Nero* owed the moft fplendid circumftance of his reign: I mean, the fubmiffion of the royal family of *Parthia*, ftrongly expreffed by *Tiridates's* coming hither, to receive the inveftiture of the kingdom of *Armenia*.

How great, indeed, did the majefty of this imperial city then appear! From the fhores of the *Cafpian*, *Tiridates* came, to pay his homage, and receive his crown. In that very year, it is remarkable, that *Suetonius Paulinus*, the conqueror of the weftern fhores of *Britain*, was invefted with the confulfhip; and, probably, affifted at that pompous ceremony.

BUT what muft have been the thoughts of *Paulinus*, while feeing the fuppliant *parthian* in
the

the *roman forum?* Muſt he not have recollected
the appearance of *Caractacus,* in the *Caſtro Prætorio?* Muſt he not have compared their behaviour? How ſervilely impious was the ſpeech
of the deſcendant of *Arſaces!* How noble that
of the *britiſh* king!

THIS morning, ſaid the young nobleman, I
peruſed *Dion's* relation of the ſurprizing magnificence and incredible profuſion of *Nero's* court,
on account of *Tiridates's* journey and entrance
into *Rome.*

I HAVE ſince been conſidering, what an idea
of *roman* ſplendour muſt have been impreſſed on
the mind of the *parthian* prince. I next recollected the ſentiments uttered by *Hormiſdas,* when
he attended hither the ſon of *Conſtantine* the
Great; and I was, juſt now, doubting, at which
of thoſe times this city appeared in the moſt noble
outward grandeur.

BUT your *much more manly reflections* ought
to draw my attention entirely from ſuch vain
thoughts.

INDEED, under all the glitter of *Nero's* court,
how much of vile and horrid wickedneſs was
there practiſed! The blood of *Barea Soranus,*
the

the imitator of *Scævola* and *Ritilius,* was then
fhedding *.

NOR was it's pomp lefs *tranfitory.* For let us,
after admiring the fplendour of *Nero* in the *forum,*
the *theatre,* and the *circus,* recolleĉt what happened to him only *fome few months after,* *in the
very place to which we are approaching.*

* * *

THE company were now arrived at *Serpentara,*
where the houfe of *Phaon, Nero's* freedman,
ftood; and where *Nero* himfelf, in the moft mean
and miferable manner, breathed his laft.

THEY inquired for the reed-ground, in which
that vile trembling parricide hid his wretched
head. They next looked about for that filthy
puddle, too pure however for his hands, of which
he drank. They wifhed to fee the fituation of
that hovel, in which he expired †.

CRITO'S

---

* Της ζυμπασης αρετης τα ωρωτα αυηχοντες, απεθανον ωστε, οτι
τοιυτοι ησαν. *Dio Caffius.*

*Baream Soranum —eques romanus popofcerat reum ex pro-
confulatu Afiæ ; in quâ offenfiones principis auxit, juftitiâ atque
induftriâ.—Tempus damnationi deleĉtum, quo Tiridates acci-
piendo Armeniæ regno adventabat.*
Tacit. Annal. lib. xvi. c. 23.

† *Offerente Phaonte liberto fuburbanum fuum, inter Sala-
riam & Nomentanam viam, circa quartum milliarium,—inter*

CRITO'S pupil repeated a few *englifh* verfes, in fome degree applicable to the fubject *. He then proceeded to much more important topics. He reflected, properly, on the folly which accompanied *Nero*, even to his laft hour. He confidered alfo, in a very awful manner, the punifhments of the other world ; thofe punifhments, of which the pains and agonies of death are only the

begin-

---

fruticeta & vepres, per arundineti femitam ægre, ad adverfum villæ parietem evafit.—Aquam ex fubjectâ lacunâ potaturus manu haufit.—Quadrupes per anguftias effoffæ cavernæ receptus, in proximam cellam decubuit fuper lectum modicellâ culcitrâ, vetere pallio ftratu inftructum, &c.

Vide *Suetonium.* 48.

Ες καλαμωδιαν τινα τοπον κατεκρυφθη· κ) ενταυθα μεχρι της ημερας υπεμεινεν ερριμμεν⟨ος⟩, οπως ως ηκιϛα διορωτο· κ) παντα μεν τον παροντα, ως κ) εφ’ εαυτον ηκοντα υποπτευων, πασαν δε φωνην ως κ) αναζητησαν αυτον υποτρεμων· ειτε τα κυνιδιον υλαξειν, η κ) ορνιθιον εφθεγξατο, ρωπιον τε κ) κλαδ⟨ος⟩ υπ’ αυρας εσεισθη, δεινως εταραττετο· κ) ουθ’ ησυχαζειν υπ’ αυτων ηδυνατο, ουτ’ αυλαλειν τινι των παροντων, μη κ) ετερ⟨ος⟩ τις ακουση, ετολμα· αλλ’αυτ⟨ος⟩ καθ’ εαυτον τη ψυχη κ) ωδυρνει κ) ωλοφυρετο· ελογιζετο γαρ τα τε αλλα, κ) προσετι οτι πολυανθρωποτατη ποτε θεραπεια γαυρωθεις, μετα τριων εξελευθερων εκυπτιαζε. τοιουτον γαρ δραμα τοτε Δαιμονιου αυτω παρεσκευασεν, ινα μηκετι τους αλλους μητροφονους κ) αλητας, αλλ’ ηδη κ) εαυτον υποκρινηται. Και τοτε μετεγιγνωσκεν εφ’ οις ετετολμηκει· καθαπερ απρακτον τι αυτων ποιησαι δυναμεν⟨ος⟩. Νερων μεν δη τοιαυτα ετραχωδει, κ) το επ⟨ι⟩ εκεινο συνεχως ενενοει,

Οικτρως θανειν μ’ ανωγε σιγαμ⟨ος⟩, πατηρ.

Οψε δ’ην ποτε, επειδη μηδεις αυτον αναζητων ευρατο, μετηλθεν εις το αντρον· κανταυθα κ) εφαγε πεινησας αρτον οποιον ουδε πωποτε εξεβρωκει, κ) επει διψησας υδωρ οποιον ουδε πωποτε πεπωκεν. Εφ’ ω δυσανασχετησας ειπε, τουτο εϛιν εκεινο το ποτον το εμον το απεφθον.

Και ομεν εν τουτοις ην, &c.　　　　　　*Dio.* lib. lxiii.

* See thofe lines of Mr. *Pope*, on the death-bed of *Villiers*, duke of Buckingham :

In

beginning. *Defecit Nero extantibus rigentibufque oculis, ufque ad horrorem, formidinemque vifentium* *.

DISCOURSING earneftly on this dreadful fubject, a fubject, which fo totally abforbed their attention, as to render them unfufceptible of any other ideas, the young gentlemen returned from *Serpentara to Rome.*

NEAR the *Porta Flaminia* hangs a vaft fragment of a ruined wall, commonly known by the name of *Muro Torto.* It is thought to have been part of that maufoleum of the *Domitii,* in which *Nero* was buried †.

In the worft inn's worft room, with mat half hung,
The floors with plaifter, and the walls with dung, &c.

Circumftances of humiliation, like thofe enumerated in the text, would not have had the leaft effect on the mind of a wife and good man, when dying: but they were really *painful* to a *Nero.*

* *Suetonius.* 49.

† Such is the horrour *ftill* remaining at *Rome* of *Nero's* memory, that *to this day* the neighbourhood of his grave is the place appointed for the interment of all public malefactors, who die impenitent. Still greater was the terrour of this place *fome ages paft;* when wailing ghofts were *imagined* frequently to be feen fitting near it, and the cries and fhrieks of hell to be heard from it: an opinion, that gave occafion to the building of the ancient church, which is now ftanding near it. In fo wild an opinion, there was undoubtedly a very great mixture of the *ignorance* and *fuperftition of the times:* but a true philofopher may, notwithftanding, difcover in it's origin fome genuine fuggeftions of reafon and confcience, and the real ftrong voice of nature.

FROM

FROM *Muro Torto* they turned into the *adjoining* entrance of *Villa Borghefe*, and alighted.

* * *

WALKING towards the gardens, they found *Crito*, fitting at the roots of a tall pine : the Annals of *Tacitus*, and the Memorabilia of *Xenophon* lay by him on the grafs. His heart feemed overflowing with the calmeft happinefs; and his countenance, as ferene and bright as the morning itfelf. No wonder; for his mind was then filled with the idea of a *dying Socrates;* with which idea he was comparing the behaviour of *Seneca*, when in the fame circumftances.

HE liftened with pleafure to his pupil's conjefture, as to the fituation of that fuburban villa, on the *Nomentan* road, in which *Seneca* died.

BUT his countenance changed, on the other gentlemen's informing him what had been the fubjeft of their converfation, at *Serpentara*, and *Muro Torto*.

HE rofe from the ground; and while accompanying his young friends through the grove to the villa, he joined his refleftions to their's, and fell into the fame track of thought.

FROM

FROM what has been the ſubjeét of your thoughts this morning at *Serpentara,* ſaid *Crito,* you may in ſome degree conceive, how terrible the pain of ſelf-condemnation muſt be, when a guilty wretch finds himſelf *really* drawing near to his laſt hour.

A BAD conſcience is a very tormenting com-panion, even in times of the greateſt health and proſperity * : but it's pangs, it's confuſion, it's horrours muſt be infinitely more terrifying, at the *near* proſpeét of diſſolution ; of the gates of hell ; the powers of darkneſs ; and the bitter pains of eternal death.

MAY we all, deeply and frequently, meditate on this ! But I hope and pray, that none of this company will ever, ever feel it. O my dear friends ! bleſs GOD that you have, *to appearance,* much time of life before you ; that you have ſtrength to employ yourſelves in many ſuch works of true faith and love, as will not fail to bring you peace at the laſt.

WOULD to GOD it were now in my power to diſplay, or worthily to deſcribe to you, the ex-alted happineſs of a *truly chriſtian* death-bed.

---

* Both *Tiberius* and *Nero* experienced this truth.—*Tibe-rius omnium mortalium triſtiſſimus.*———*Nero nunquam ſceleris concientiam ferre potuit : ſæpe confeſſus exagitari ſe maternâ ſpecie, &c. Sueton. c.* 34.

WITH

WITH a very inferiour degree of earneftnefs, I alfo wifh I could prefent to your thoughts a worthy idea even of *Socrates*, during the laft days of his life.

WHAT I have now to fhow you, is, really, *far inferiour to either of thefe;* yet it is fuch, as very well deferves your attention.

SAYING this, *Crito* entered the villa, and turned on his right hand into the firft apartment, which is adorned with the famous ftatue of *Seneca*. That ftatue reprefents him, finking indeed under the languor of death; but with eyes fo elevated, and with a gefture of countenance, lips, and hands fo very ftriking, as plainly to point out in what manner he paffed his laft moments *.

Noviffimo

---

* A print of this ftatue, taken from a drawing, which *Rubens* brought with him from *Rome* to *Antwerp*, may be feen in the *introduction* to *Lipfius's* edition of *Seneca's* works: together with the following defcription of it. *Imago Senecæ ex Lucelleo marmore fabrefacta, inter cardinalis Borgefii admiranda antiquitatis monumenta cernitur. Vera eft effigies in balneo animam jam exhalantis, & in verbis monitifque aureis deficientis: vividum, acre, igneum aliquid refert. Manus digitofque ita exporrectos vides, ut fapientiæ et conftantiæ præcepta, advocatis fcriptoribus, dictantem, haud obfcurè cum Tacito agnofcas: a quibus nec vicinæ mortis cruciatus, fatis peritè in ipfo vultu ab artifice adumbrati, fapientem prohibebant. Facies parum formofa, nefcio quid africanum præ fe ferat: buccâ hianti, turgentibus labris, naribus diftentis: ut hominem Cordubæ, in Bæticæ provinciæ coloniâ, quæ Africæ* proximè

Noviſſimo quoque momènto, continued he, *ſup-peditante eloquentiâ, advocatis ſcriptoribus, ple-raque tradidit.* How much is it to be regretted, that *Tacitus* did not inſert that diſcourſe in his Annals.

THE reaſonings of ſuch a man, at ſuch a time; that is, of one of the wiſeſt in the philoſophical world, when at it's higheſt ſtate of wiſdom and experience; all that he *then* ſaid, in *that hour of ſincerity,* on the excellence of virtue, on the emptineſs of riches, and on the *real* vanity of all human grandeur, would ſurely form ſome of the moſt proper and ſtriking leſſons of inſtruction, for the minds, not only of the youthful, but of the aged alſo.

A DEEP ſilence enſued. The eyes of all the company continued fixed on thoſe of the ſtatue.

CHAIRS being handed round, they ſat down *oppoſite* to it.

---

proximè adjacet; & parentibus cordubenſibus natum minimè requiras.

Sed & corpus longâ valetudine, multo ſtudio, &, ex Taciti ſententiâ, parvo victu attenuatum paullo attentius conſidera ; quod cum exercitiis durioribus, cultu agri, & foſſione vinearum, firmaſſe ipſum conſtet ; cutis, exhauſto ſucco, laxatæ maciem, & laboribus induratæ firmitatem, venis muſculiſque quos labor maximè attolli: extantibus, ingenioſè & diligenter ſtatuarius effinxit.

WHILE

WHILE they were thus engaged, and entering as it were into the very thoughts of *Seneca; Crito* communicated to them a fheet or two of paper, which contained feveral extracts felected by him, from the moft fenfible and candid authors, both ancient and modern, relative to the *ftyle* and *doctrine* of *Seneca's* writings; as well as to the *hiftory of his life and death.* Thefe extracts were digefted in a manner fo judicious, as to form a regular kind of *treatife* on the fubject.

THAT part of this treatife, which related to the *ftyle* of *Seneca,* was very fhort. The detail of his *doctrines* feemed to be compiled with much more attention. It comprehended many proofs, both of the *remarkable refemblance* which *Seneca's* philofophy bears, in *feveral* of it's features, to the Chriftian morality; and of it's *extreme diffimilitude* to it, in *others* *.

IN the fecond part of *Crito's* paper, *Seneca's actions* and *character* were very fairly ftated. The whole concluded with this candid obfervation, That *Seneca's* failings appear to have much abated, and fome of his virtues to have much increafed, as he more nearly approached his latter end.

* See *Marfollier's* Life of St. *Francis de Sales,* vol. ii. p. 42.

*　　*　　*

AFTER half an hour paſſed in reading this paper, and converſing on it, the company roſe
from their ſeats ; and, with ſome reſpeſt, taking
their leave of *Seneca's* ſtatue, began to employ
their attention upon the other works of ſculpture,
with which that apartment is adorned. From
it they proceeded to the other apartments.
More than two hours were occupied in ſurveying
the great number of ſtatues, buſts, and baſſo-
relievos, with which this country-palace is filled,
in all it's ſaloons and chambers ; and even covered externally, on each of it's four fronts *.

THE young gentlemen being very deſirous to
paſs the remainder of the day amidſt ſuch a profuſion of *vertù*, obtained the *majordomo's* conſent
to it. They dined on ſome cold proviſion,
which one of their ſervants had brought from
Rome ; in a charming grotto, on a table of white

---

* The ſtruſture itſelf is quadrangular. The four ſides
of it are decorated with beautiful antique ſtatues and baſſo-
relievos, curiouſly and appoſitely ranged. But, as the
prodigious variety of them renders it impoſſible to give a
particular account of each piece, I ſhall only mention the
moſt remarkable ; which are the buſt of *Geta, Trajan,* &c.
The whole circumference of the building is 734 palms :
each being nine inches, or a quarter of a royal *Paris* foot.
See *Keyſler's* Travels.

marble

marble of one piece, inlaid with brocatello, twenty palms in length, and eight in breadth *.

AFTER dinner, *Crito's* pupil turned the conversation to the history of the person, who built this sumptuous villa.

IF I be not misinformed, said he, it was cardinal *Scipio :* who in his youth lived in a state of poverty and obscurity, deserted by his own family ; but was charitably received under the protection and patronage of the *Borghese.* Rising afterwards to a very great fortune, he took the name of his benefactor ; and, from a principle of gratitude, erected this splendid fabric ; leaving it to the descendants of that family, to which he had been indebted for his own exaltation.

I AM not acquainted with the other parts of the history of this cardinal : but these circumstances of it, if true, are very amiable.

IT might however be wished, for the cardinal's further honour, that this villa had been somewhat less pompous and rich. Had this country seat been adorned, not with such royal magnificence, but with proper ecclesiastical sim-

* *Keysler.*

plicity,

plicity, humility, and neat rural beauty; the cardinal's behaviour would certainly have been much more truly laudable.   In fuch a cafe, we might perhaps have compared his gratitude to that of *Ariftonous* *.

BUT the afternoon is wearing away.   Shall we take a walk round the garden?   The beauty of it's plantations is furely, at leaft, as pleafing an object, as the fculptured marbles in any of thofe grand apartments.

THE company, after drinking each a glafs of frefh *aqua virgine*, now left the grotto, and made the circuit of the gardens; paffing through a great variety of flower-beds, fountains, and fhades †. They fat down, at the end of their long walk, on a green bank, thickly covered with laurels.

IT now began to draw towards evening, when the converfation took at length a more *claffical* turn.

---

* See the hiftory of *Ariftonous*, generally fubjoined to the Adventures of *Telemachus*.

† *Son circuit eft de trois milles, ou d'une lieue de France.*— *On peut dire que cet endroit eft delicieux, par la beauté de fes plantations, de fes bois, & de fes eaux : il eft peuplé de chevreuils, des daims, de lievres, & de faifans, que l'on y voit en troupes : & par tout, l'utile y eft melé avec l'agréable; avec autant d'ordre, que d'élegance.*

Voyages d'Abbé *Richard*, tome vi. p. 188.

THE

THE eldeſt of the young gentlemen, with a ſhort apology, deſired *Crito* and his young friends to beſtow ſome of their thoughts on the charaĉter of *Thraſeas.*

THRASEAS.

ELDEST.

HE was, perhaps, one of the moſt humane and beſt of men, though he lived in an age of the greateſt wickednefs and cruelty. Under the reign of a *Nero, Thraſeas* equalled, if not ſurpaſſed, the virtues of a *Cato.*

THE condition of the times, indeed, would not ſuffer ſo wiſe a man to attempt imitating *Cato* in his ſtrong ſtruggles for liberty, and in his unyielding reſiſtance to tyranny and uſurpation: for all the ſtrength of *roman* freedom had long ſince periſhed. It's ſpirit alſo, generally ſpeaking, had departed. Nothing but the form of the old conſtitution, it's name, and it's ceremonies, were now ſubſiſting.

YOUNG NOBLEMAN.

SUCH being the ſtate of public affairs, I ſhould be glad to know what were the *peculiar virtues* of this

this *roman* nobleman. For, if I be not miſtaken, *Thraſeas* was a perſon of the higheſt rank and fortune in his country.

ELDEST.

IT might be anſwered, in the firſt place, The moſt exalted and venerable ſanctity of private life; and, in the ſecond place, The moſt undaunted and patient expectation of death. In each of theſe particulars, he was even ſuperiour to *Cato*.

CRITO'S PUPIL.

I CANNOT help thinking, that the behaviour of *Thraſeas*, at his death, was at leaſt equal to that of his great contemporary, *Seneca*. In his life, perhaps *Thraſeas* far excelled him. If I ſay wrong in this, I ſhall gladly receive correction from you and my tutor.

CRITO.

I COULD wiſh, that we had more particulars of the life of *Thraſeas* preſerved to us in hiſtory. But with regard to *Seneca*, as was obſerved this morning, it ſeems but too evident, that ſome parts of his life by no means anſwered to the goodneſs of the reſt. Your friend compares *Thraſeas* to *Cato*.

Why

Why may we not look upon *Seneca* as *a faint image of* Tully? *Seneca's* eloquence was much admired at *Rome.* In faying this, I do not pretend to judge of the literary tafte of his age; but whatever may be the merits or defects of his ftyle, his *fentiments,* furely, are often very noble. Some of *Seneca's* writings are perhaps the moft valuable effufions of moral philofophy in heathen *Rome.*

AND yet *Seneca,* like his illuftrious predeceffor in oratory and philofophy, funk very low, when tried in adverfity; and when in profperity, he grew too fond of riches and honours.

IT muft, alas! be acknowledged, that in *Seneca's* hiftory there are ftains, the memory of which has not been, and cannot be wiped away, either by the many great and real virtues of his life, or by the magnanimity difplayed at his laft hour. Thefe ftains he probably incurred by his extreme confidence in his own virtue, which, as he prefumptuoufly flattered himfelf, was fuperiour to all temptations, whether of profperity, or of adverfity; and by his blind, and even impious pride, which attributed whatever was good in his own breaft to himfelf alone.

I HAVE fometimes inclined to wifh, that the hiftory of *Seneca's* failings had been buried in

utter

utter oblivion: but on more serious thoughts, I am convinced, that it is much better as it is. For, as they may justly be considered to have been a kind of humiliating judgment on *him;* so it is certain, that we may deduce from them some very important instructions for *ourselves.*

But let me not repeat, what I said this morning concerning *Seneca.* As to the character of *Thraseas,* so far perhaps as we *can* judge, from the *short* accounts we have of his life, it appears to have been much more uniformly noble. I do not at present recollect any marks in it of stoical pride, though he was reckoned of that sect of philosophers; or on the other hand, any symptoms of that usual consequence of pride, degeneracy. But I forget myself: I am interrupting you. Pray proceed.

I wish, replied the eldest of the young gentlemen, that I was in the least worthy to speak on such a character. Yet, however unworthy, permit me to add, that *Thraseas,* though he gained a very high reputation, by the virtue which he practised in his *private* life; a life, too, happily extended to an advanced old age; did not omit, to the utmost of his abilities, the doing of those *public* services to his country, which the condition of the times would allow,

HE was, indeed, a fenator: but that office, formerly fo high, was *then* become of little *real* dignity, and invefted with ftill lefs ability of doing good. In this ftation, however, contracted as it was, and fhrunk in it's powers and privileges, did *Thrafeas* frequently difplay an example of great patriotic fortitude, and of found civil wifdom, duly attempered together.

HE formed the plan of feveral falutary laws: he propofed them to the houfe; and by the weight of his wifdom and goodnefs carried them through it. He checked, in fome degree, the oppreffion and rapine of the governors, and *intendants*, of feveral *roman* provinces. He gave fome check alfo, to the tyranny of *Nero* himfelf.

WHILE the majority, and almoft the whole body of the *roman* legiflature, behaved as the moft abject flatterers, and fervile inftruments of the wickednefs of their tyrant; *Thrafeas* alone fupported the true dignity of the fenatorial character*.

WITH the nobleft indignation he refufed to join them in the approbation of their fovereign's crimes. More than once he boldly left his feat,

---

* *Offenfione manifeftâ principis fuetâ animi magnitudine, non receffit Thrafeas a fententiâ.*

when

when fuch matters were under deliberation*; and went out of the fenate-houfe, openly rejoicing, that although *death* might be the confequence of his bold integrity, it was not in the emperor's power to inflict on him, by fuch a punifhment, *any real hurt†*.

WITH a firm and honeſt perfeverance in the fame fentiments, he actually met his death. *Trucidatis tot infignibus viris*, fays Tacitus, *ad poſtremum Nero virtutem ipfam exfcindere concupivit, interfecto Thrafeâ‡*.

IT has been frequently exemplified, by the hiftories of many patriots, that integrity naturally produces courage. Ethic writers have alfo, I think, obferved, that where the faculties of the foul are fraught with various kinds of moral excellence, fortitude will generally be found deeply rooted in the centre of the heart. Such, certainly, was the cafe with *Thrafeas*.

---

* Θρασεας ατε ες το βαλητηριον συνεχως, ως αχ αρεσκομενⓈ τοις ↓ηφιζομενοις, απηντα. *Dio*. lib. lxii.

† ΤοιατⓈ μεν ο Θρασεας εγενετο, χ τατο αει προ εαυτον ελεγε. Ο μεν Νερων αποκτειναι με δυναται, βλαψαι δε ου. *Dio*. lib. lxi.

Somewhat fimilar to this was the anfwer of a celebrated *englifhman;* who, on being told by a great lord of the court, that it was perilous ſtriving with princes; *Indignatio principis mors eſt;* replied, "Is that all, my Lord? Then, in "good faith, the difference between your grace and me is "but this only; that I fhall die to day, and you to-morrow.

‡ *Annal*. xvi. 21.

BUT, let me paufe now for a few moments. Let me defire you to confider the ftate of this great man's family; and to contemplate the virtuous perfons that compofed it; who, probably, owed the greatnefs of their virtues, to a mutual imitation of each other's excellencies.

SURELY, my dear noble friend, there never was a better fubject for a family-picture. How happy would you be, next month, while at *Naples*, if among the antique paintings, which are now difcovering at *Herculaneum*, a good piece fhould be found reprefenting *Thrafeas*, in converfation with his family and friends, on the day of his death!

SUCH a fubject, had the perfons lived in more modern times, would not have been unworthy the pencil even of a *Holbein*.

CANNOT you imagine fuch a compofition as this now before your eyes? The principal figure in it *Thrafeas* himfelf; *venerabili fpecie;* the moft virtuous character of his age and country. On one hand, his fon-in-law, *Helvidius Prifcus;* on the other, his grand-fon, *Pliny* the Younger, and his friend, the famous *Rufticus Arulenus*. In the back ground, the tomb of his mother; the celebrated *Arria*.

BUT

BUT you can much better defign and arrange fuch a *painting* than myfelf. Let me no longer expofe my ignorance, by pretending to talk on fo fine an art. Let *me* think only on the *tableau de l'hiftoire.*

THRASEAS'S wife and fon-in-law, with *Aru-lenus,* and many other friends, attended him in his laft hour. While the fenate was fitting in anxious deliberation, though furrounded with *Nero's* guards, on paffing *Thrafeas's* fentence of death, a fentence, which indeed they did not wade through, *fine fummâ mæftitiâ, ac pavore;* that worthy man was converfing with his friends in his garden: and very probably, with great calmnefs and tranquillity of mind; although he knew, that he fhould never again behold the vegetative beauties of nature, or review the glories of that fetting fun.

POSSIBLY the fituation of *Thrafeas's* garden might not be far diftant from this of the *Villa Borghefe.* At leaft there is no reafon why we may not indulge ourfelves in the fanciful imagination. With that idea, permit me to read to you fome paffages, which I have extracted from *Tacitus.*

Tum

Tum ad Thraſeam in hortis agentem quæſtor conſulis miſſus, veſperaſcente jam die.—Ibi illuſtrium virorum fœminarumque catus agebat, maximè intentus Demetrio philoſopho; cum quo inquirebat de naturâ animæ, & diſſociatione ſpiritûs corporiſque*.—Quando Arulenus offerebat ſe interceſſurum ſenatûs conſulto, (nam plebis tribunus erat;) cohibuit ſpiritus ejus Thraſeas, ne vana, et reo non profitura, interceſſori exitioſa inciperet†.—Conjugem tentantem exemplum Arriæ matris ſequi, monet retinere vitam; how ſuperiour in this to *Seneca!—filiæque communi ſubſidium unicum non adimere.—Flentes amicos, (nuntiatum enim jam erat de condemnatione) faceſſere propere hortatur, non pericula ſua miſcere cum ſorte damnati‡.*

THEN, *progreſſus in porticum,* he met the officers, guards, and executioners. He received his death-warrant, *lætitiæ propior, quia Helvidium, generum ſuum, Italiâ tantùm arceri cognoverat.* For he had feared, left *Helvidius* ſhould have been ſentenced to die with him.

---

* This *Demetrius* is probably the ſame perſon, whoſe praiſes we often find recited in *Seneca. Demetrius* (ſays that writer) *vir meo judicio magnus, etiam ſi maximis comparetur.*—But ſee the hiſtory of his degeneracy from this great character in *Tacitus's* account of the beginning of *Veſpaſian's* reign.

† *Tacit.* Ann. lib. xvi. 26. ‡ Ib. c. 34.

Helvidium,

Helvidium, dehinc, & Demetrium in cubiculum inducit; porrectifque utriufque brachii venis, poftquam cruorem effudit, humum fuper fpargens, propiùs vocato quæftore, " *Libemus, inquit, Jovi Liberatori;*"—the very expreffion of *Seneca**.

" *Specta, juvenis: & omen quidem dii prohibeant; cæterùm, in ea tempora natus es, quibus firmare animum expediet conftantibus exemplis.*"

Poft, lentitudine exitûs graves cruciatus afferente, obverfus in Demetrium†—What a pity it is, that the manufcript of *Tacitus* fhould here break off fo abruptly!

PROBABLY the dying words, which *Thrafeas* addreffed to his philofophical friend, *Demetrius,* were not lefs worthy of attention than the laft difcourfe of *Seneca.*

IN my younger days, I have lamented the great chafms and ruins in the auguft fabric of *Livy's* hiftory. But in my prefent difpofition of mind, were it in my power to reftore intire, either the work of *Livy,* or of *Tacitus,* I know not which I fhould prefer: though certainly a very confiderable part of the times defcribed in *Tacitus's*

---

* *Tacit,* Annal, lib. xv. c. 64.   † Ibid. xvi. 36.

writings

writings was very inferiour, in public virtue, to fome of the epochs contained in the decads of *Livy*.

THE young gentleman then took out of his pocket a fmall edition of *Tacitus;* and read to his friends fome of that fenfible writer's complaints on this head.

HE would probably have added fome further reflections on this fubject; but the cold dew of the evening reminded him, that it was proper to think of returning to their lodgings.

THE company now rofe from their graffy feat, and walked to that garden gate, which opens near the *Porta Penciana.* On their way, *Crito* made feveral fhort, but pertinent obfervations, on the exceffive wickednefs, that prevailed, in government, during moft part of the life of *Thrafeas.*

THE young nobleman recollected the names of *many* contemporary virtuous *romans,* who ended their days in the fame cruel manner, and proceeded to fome very fenfible reflections, on the extreme meannefs of the *roman* fenate, which could, with bafe timidity, confent to condemn to death fuch men; eminent not only for their innocence, but for their active merit.

YET,

YET fuch, faid he, was once the cafe, in *England;* even in the trial of peers. Thankful ought we to be, that our lot has fallen on a better age! thankful to a benign Providence, that the times of extreme perfecution and tyranny fo rarely occur in the hiftory of the world. But the mention juft now made of the name of *Holbein* neceffarily recalls to my memory the hiftory of the *Tudor* family; particularly the reign of *Henry* VIII. Horrid indeed was that defpotic era! It was not only the houfe of peers, which then fuffered in that manner: the fame tyranny prevailed over common juries, in capital trials; the fame tyranny prevailed in acts of attainder, paffed by the whole legiflature. How, *then*, did the parliament of *England* appear? Alas! it fadly refembled that defpicable fenate, which could crouch at the foot-ftool even of a *Tiberius*, or a *Nero*.

IT feems a very confiderable confolation, however, replied *Crito*, that as the annals of *Nero's* reign contain the hiftory of a *Thrafeas;* fo that era of *englifh tyranny*, in like manner, was not deftitute of many virtuous characters; and particularly one, in fome refpects, very fimilar: a character even fuperiour to the moft illuftrious, whether of *Greece* or *Rome*, in their nobleft excellencies. In virtue, and in patriotifm; in con-

tempt

tempt of wealth; in patience, temperance, and even love of poverty! integrity, unmoved by any ambitious profpect or temptation, of honour, or power; intrepidity and magnanimity, un-fhaken by menaces; unappall'd by dangers; or even by death itfelf!

It is almoft fuperfluous to add his name: a name, juftly reverenced by all *englifhmen,* how-ever various in their fentiments, either on politi-cal or religious fubjects. And this is the more extraordinary, as he fuffered on a religious ac-count; and is faid, how truly I cannot tell, to have been himfelf fometimes *cruel* in religious matters. In other refpects, his behaviour was moft amiable, moft refpectable, moft pious. He was the *Ariftides,* the *Phocion,* the *Fabricius,* the *Thrafeas* of *England.*—He was SIR THOMAS MORE.

I HAVE at my lodgings a *fmall* collection of fome of his works; particularly his letters, medi-tations, and devotions, while in the *Tower.* Per-mit me to recommend it for your perufal to-night, after fupper.

THE fummer before laft, I remember, I em-ployed part of an afternoon, in a boat on the *Thames,* reading the life of fir *Thomas More.*
. I took

I took boat at *Chelſea;* and was gently rowed down the river, paſſing between *Lambeth* and *Weſtminſter Hall.* In ſir *Thomas's* life frequent mention is made of each of thoſe three places. On my landing at the *Tower* gate, I recollected ſir *Thomas's* laſt interview there with his daughter. I caſt my eye along the ſide of thoſe ancient walls, and looked up for the grated window of his priſon. In walking over *Tower-Hill*, I ſtopped, with reverence for the ſpot, at that place of execution, whence his innocent, virtuous, pious ſoul took her flight to heaven.

CHAP.

C H A P. VII.

TWENTY-FIFTH DAY'S CONVERSATION.

CRITO, about eight o'clock this morning, on entering the young nobleman's apartment, found his three young friends, as ufual, deeply engaged together in ftudy. He drew a chair, and fat down among them.

THE table was covered with feveral books of antiquities and hiftory, fcattered among which, lay many coins of the upper empire ; and two or three drawers full of a feries of impreffions in wax, taken from antique feals, that bore the royal, and moft of the *principal* republican, heads of *Rome.*

WE have been imagining, faid the young nobleman, that there is fome kind of refemblance between the beginning and ending of the imperial *Cæfarean* family, and thofe of the ancient kings of *Rome.*

JULIUS,

JULIUS, who founded the grandeur of the *Cæfarean* family, feems, not only in the great abilities of his mind, and in the manner and place of his death, but alfo in other particulars *, to bear a ftrong fimilitude to *Romulus*. *Auguſtus*, in the mildnefs and tranquillity of above forty years of his reign, was perhaps, in fome fmall degree, a faint image of the good *Numa*. The hiftory of the *Cæfarean* family ends in a *Nero*, juſt as the feries of *monarchs* clofed with *Tarquin*.

BUT *Nero* greatly furpaffed *Tarquin* in wickednefs : and far diftant, do I believe, you would kindly have endeavoured to turn our thoughts from the hiftory of *his* vile life ; had you not thought, that the memory of thofe *good* men, who fuffered under the cruel tyranny of a *Nero*, juftly claimed much refpeſt from us, during our profecution of this part of our courfe of *roman* ſtudies.

THEY do, *indeed*, deferve much refpeſt, replied *Crito*.

THE eldeſt of the young gentlemen now opened *Dion's* works; and, turning to the fixtieth book, read two or three lines.

* See the INTRODUCTION to this Work, vol. I. p. xxiv.

Tπo

Υπο της συνεχειας των κακων εις τυτο τα πραγματα
προεληλυθει, ως' αρετην μηκετ' αλλο μηδεν, η το γενναιως
αποθανειν, νομιζεσθαι.

A NOBLE philofophic fortitude, faid he, able
to meet death in cool blood, feems to have been
the peculiar turn, which the temper of the old
romans adopted, during the latter reigns of the
Cæfarean family.

THE magnanimity of thefe fuffering heroes,
replied *Crito's* pupil, was perhaps at leaft equally
as laudable, as the military courage of their pro-
genitors. Such, at leaft, we may eafily imagine
to have been the fentiment of a *Seneca*, or of a
Demetrius.

THEIR fortitude, faid *Crito*, was indeed very
remarkable. And although their conduct was
not fo void of defect, but that confiderable objections may be made to it; yet, in general, the
hiftory of their fufferings may prove to *us* a very
ufeful branch of ftudy.

THIS was your topic yefterday evening, as
you were walking out of the gardens of the *Villa
Borghefe.* I have fince been thinking much, and
indeed almoft during the whole night, upon the

subject :

fubjeft: and, in confequence, on rifing this morning, I committed my thoughts to paper.

So faying, *Crito* laid upon the table a fheet or two of paper. Their contents were as follows; their title was

SUFFERING VIRTUE.

* * *

FANNIUS, the friend of *Pliny*, wrote an account of the laft hours of thofe many illuftrious perfons, who fuffered under *Nero* *. It is, probably, much to be lamented, that this work is not now extant.

Such a hiftory, my dear pupil, if elegantly compofed, would have prefented to your view many fcenes of afflicted innocence, defcribed in a mafterly ftyle: fcenes much more real, and confequently much more moving, than any contained in the fineft fet of tragedies, written on the fame favourite fubject of *Suffering Virtue*.

Nor would the effects of fuch a hiftory be lefs, were we to fuppofe it to have been compofed in the plaineft manner; provided it were judicious and faithful. The facts contained in it would

* Vid. *Pliny's* Epiftle to *Maximus,* book v. p. 5.

make

make us afhamed to complain, or be difpirited, at any of the little adverfities, real or imaginary, which may happen to ourfelves: nay, they would, in fome meafure, ferve to prepare *us alfo* for fupporting the greateft trials, if ever we fhould be called to them.

PERMIT me, my dear pupil, to exprefs my idea, in fome lines from *Seneca's* confolation to his mother *Helvia,* blended with a few expref-fions, which I remember to have been ufed by *Tully.*

Fleant & gemant, quorum delicatas mentes longa voluptatum contemplatio enervavit; quâ cum diffluimus, nec apis aculeum ferre poffumus; & ad leviffimarum injuriarum motus collabantur. Nos autem, talium virorum exempla fpeЄtantes, & inter hæc ftudia nutritos, pudeat laborem & calamitatem ægrè ferre.

Feramus vulnera fortunæ, velut veterani; fine ululatu, fine vociferatione. Libera fit noftra virtus; inviolabilis; inconcuffa; adverfùs apparatus terribilium reЄtos oculos teneat. Nihil ex vultu mutet.

TULLY, if I rightly underftand his words, hints to us the beft method of acquiring fortitude. *Vereor, ne non tam* virtutis fiducia *nitendum nobis,*

ad

ad ſpem beatè vivendi, quam vota facienda *vide-antur* *.

BUT let not my pen wander too far from the ſubjeƈt propoſed. It might perhaps be wiſhed, not only that *Fannius's* work had been preſerved ; but that the ſame good fortune had proteƈted thoſe other judicious authors, for ſuch probably there were, whoſe writings deſcribed the ſufferings of *roman* virtue, during *the three preceding reigns :* namely, under the malice of *Tiberius,* the mad-neſs of *Caligula,* and the reiterated ſtupidity of *Claudius.*

WERE thoſe writings ſtill extant, they would probably, on this occaſion, have been lying upon your table ; bound up, in one large volume, to-gether with the work of *Fannius.*

A DISMAL volume! for diſmal, ſurely, were the events of the civil hiſtory of this great and wretched metropolis, from the middle of *Tiberius's* reign, to the end of that of *Nero: an epoch of about forty years !*

I WISH I had been diligent enough, in my late ſtudies of the hiſtory of that period, to have ex-traƈted from the fragments of *Tacitus, Dion,* and

* *Cicero* Tuſc. Quæſt. lib. v. Cap. 1.

ſome

fome other books, a catalogue of the illuftrious
fufferers. The length of that catalogue, and the
fplendour of the names contained in it, would
have been very ftriking and inftructive; even
though I had not endeavoured to fubjoin to it
any particular account, either of their refpective
fufferings, or of their characters.

In truth, the hiftorians of that dreadful epoch
feem to have been fatigued with fo long a feries of
cruelty. The expreffions of *Tacitus* are very
ftriking : *Neque fum ignarus, à plerifque fcrip-*
toribus omiffa multorum pericula & pœnas, dum
copiâ fatifcunt ; aut, quæ ipfis nimia & mæfta
fuerant, ne pari tædio lecturos adficerent, veren-
tur *. For the fake of pofterity, however, it
might have been wifhed, that *Tacitus* himfelf had
been more particular in the characters he gives of
feveral of the fufferers : whofe virtues were in his
time generally known and celebrated in the world ;
but, by his omiffion of them, are now either
partly loft, or wholly buried in oblivion.

Yet let us not at *prefent* indulge ourfelves,
idly, in lamenting either the omiffions of the *ro-*
man hiftorians, or the wide ravages and deftruction of time on their works. We have the lefs
reafon to lament them, becaufe we find in *other*

* Annal. lib. vi. c. 7.

hiſtories *of the ſame* epocha, examples of a much higher merit very fully delineated: examples, far more edifying to us, as to the practice of *virtue* in general; whether, as men of the world, we call that virtue *fortitude;* or, as chriſtians *patience.*

LET us now, my fellow-ſtudents, for the remainder of *this* day, lay aſide all heathen hiſtory: let us lift up our hearts to much higher meditations.

As the heathen annals of *Rome,* in this age, ſufficiently inform us, that *proſperity* is not without many fears and much diſreliſh; even ſo does the hiſtory of chriſtian religion ſhow us in a much ſtronger light, that *virtuous adverſity* is not without many comforts, many hopes; and that felicity of heart, which is infinitely heightened by the aſſured proſpect of a happy immortality, and by the aſſiſtance of GRACE DIVINE.

In cruce robur mentis; ſumma virtutis; perfectio ſanctitatis; gaudium etiam ſpiritûs; & ſupernæ ſuavitatis infuſio*.

O, my dear friends! ye are all ſo prudent and judicious, that I can need no apology for the

---

* Imitatio Chriſti, lib. ii. c. 12. § 4.

freedom I take, in fo often communicating to you
thofe thoughts, with which my own heart is filled;
and from the abundance of which, on every proper occafion, it is fo ready to overflow.

BUT, on the prefent occafion, permit me to
fpeak more at large. Surely I ought not *now* to
confine my pen to fome fhort hint, òr faint allu-
fion, pointing, like a bad compafs, with much
unfteadinefs towards fome religious objeĉt. We
are called, in the ftudies of this day, to fix our
thoughts on fuch an objeĉt, as invariably, and as
intenfely as poffible.

LET us remember, that *the period of forty
years*, of which we were juft now fpeaking, was
the epoch of Suffering Virtue; not with regard to
Rome only, but in refpeĉt of *the whole world.* It
was fo, in the greateft degree; κατ' εξοχην.

DURING that period was imprifoned, and beheaded, that moft juft and holy man, of whofe
feftival this afternoon is the eve: I mean *St.
John* the *Baptift.* Of him, the *Word of Truth*
itfelf faid, That among thofe born of women,
there had not arifen a greater or a brighter charaĉter. *St. John* was great, not in worldly honours, not in the erroneous judgment and foolifh
opinion

opinion of men; but he was great indeed:—
Μεγας ην ενωπιον τε ΘΕΟΥ*.

HE was *a prophet*, and *more than a prophet:*
the worthy harbinger of the world's Redeemer.

HIS fpotlefs innocence, his unparallcled fpirit
of mortification, prayer, and retirement, his zeal
and charity were wonderful: but the foundation
of all his virtues, the crown of all his greatnefs, was fincere humility. The name, which
was given to him from heaven, juftly fignified,
full of grace;—the *gift of* GOD.

OF fuch a life, let us now afk, a life fo holy
and fo pure, what were the comforts, and what
was the conclufion? Little reafon furely has any
pious man, either to complain of the fufferings,
or to love what are called the good things of this
world. With devout refignation let him rather
confider the lot appointed to *St. John* the Baptift.

THE life of *St. John* confifted of about two and
thirty years. They were *thus* paffed.

FROM his infancy, to his thirtieth year, he
lived *in the defert, in great aufterity.* From the
defert he entered on the labours of his public mi-

---

* Divi Luc. cap. i. ver. 15.

niftry;

niftry; which continued for about fifteen months. By the tyranny of *Herod* he was then committed to *prifon;* where, during twelve months, he was *confined,* and at laft *murdered.* Such was *his* lot.

Beatus vir, qui fuffert tentationem; quoniam cum probatus fuerit, accipiet coronam vitæ, quam repromifit DEUS *diligentibus fe*.*

THE hiftory of *St. John* the Baptift may be confidered as one of the greateft examples of Suffering Virtue, that the world had ever feen, fince it's creation. But it is as nothing, in comparifon with that, which I am now going to mention. How ought my feeble hand to tremble, in writing thefe lines !

DURING this fame period of forty years, our Lord and Saviour JESUS CHRIST himfelf—— But let *me* not dare to proceed on that awful fubjeƈt. May you all, my dear, and ever valued young friends, referve it for your more private, and moft folemn thoughts! ,

PROSTRATE, in the devotions of your clofets, may you duly refleƈt, that, *forafmuch as* CHRIST *hath fuffered for us, we ought alfo to arm ourfelves with the fame mind. Let us not think it ftrange,*

* Epift. *St. Jacobi,* cap. i. ver. 12.

if

if we also be called to the same trial. The servant is not greater than his Lord. Let us pray for grace, that with a ready mind we may faithfully take up our cross daily, and follow HIM.

* * *

ON concluding this paper the company separated: each person retiring to his lodgings, impressed with the most solemn meditations.

AT ten o'clock they met again on the terras; where they found the young nobleman's carriage waiting for them. They went into it; and by *Crito's* desire directed the coachman to drive to *St. Paul's.*

THEY passed along the *Corso;* where they stopped, for some time, to visit the church of *Santa Maria in viâ latâ,* and it's subterranean apartments.

THEY afterwards proceeded through the rest of the city and suburbs: then passed within sight of *Monte Testaccio,* and went out of the *Ostian gate.*

TRAVELLING another mile, they arrived at that venerable *Basilica,* which *Constantine* the

Great

Great erected to the memory of *St. Paul;* and which, in the following century, the emperors *Theodoſius* and *Honorius* conſiderably enlarged *.

Iᴛ's dimenſions are very great. It's breadth within the walls exceeds that of the piazza *Navona:* that piazza, which was the ancient *Circus Agonalis,* and which at preſent is the principal *ſquare,* if ſo improper a term may be uſed, of modern *Rome.*

Tʜᴇ moſt remarkable ornament of this ſpacious church conſiſts of ſeveral vaſt pillars of *egyptian* granite; and of four rows of columns, the innermoſt of which are peculiarly ſtately and beautiful, being compoſed of the richeſt *grecian* marbles.

Iᴛ's ancient *moſaics* are alſo curious; but it's roof and pavement are very diſproportionally mean †.

Tʜɪs

---

* At the upper end of this baſilica are to be ſeen the two following verſes, in ancient characters:
    Theodoſius *cœpit, perfecit* Honorius *aulam,*
    Doctoris mundi ſacratam corpore Pᴀᴜʟɪ.
Queſta chieſa fu fondata da Conſtantino—la fabbrico in queſto luogo in un podere di S. Lucina Madrona Romana; in cui vi era anche il ſuo cimeterio di S. S. Martiri, e vi fu ſepolto per la prima volta l'apoſtolo S. Pavlo da Timoteo ſuo diſcepolo: il detto cimeterio e ſotto queſta chieſa, & vi ſi cala dalla appreſſo l' altar maggiore. Mer. Errante.
    See alſo Dr. *Cave's* Life of *St. Paul;* ſect. 2.
    † The pavement is compoſed of innumerable fragments
of

THIS church, being fituate about two miles diftant from the parts of *Rome*, which are *now* inhabited, is but little frequented. Solitude and filence generally reign in all it's chapels, and long ailes.

THE company paffed here an hour with great fatisfaction. The remarkable coolnefs of the place breathed a very agreeable refrefhment around them; their minds were foothed into tranquillity and quiet meditation, by the cooings of the many doves, which were fometimes perched on the roof, fometimes flying among the timbers.

SUCH were the pleafing fenfations of thefe three worthy young men, when their tutor led them to that place, in the middle of the church, where part of the mortal remains of *St. Paul* is faid to

of ancient tomb-ftones, put together without order. The roof is of plain timber. In *Theodofius's* time the roof was all gilt, and is fo defcribed by a contemporary writer:

> *Parte aliá titulum Pauli via fervat Oftienfis,*
>   *Quà ftringit amnis cefpitem finiftrum.*
> *Regia pompa loci eft: princeps bonus has facravit arces,*
>   *Lufitque magnis ambitum talentis.*
> *Bracteolas trabibus fublevit, ut omnis aurulenta*
>   *Lux effet intus, ceu jubar fub ortu.*
> *Subdidit & parias fulvis laquearibus columnas,*
>   *Diftinguit illic quas quaternus ordo.*
> *Tum camuros hyalo infigni varie cucurrit arcus,*
>   *Sic prata vernis floribus renident.*

PRUDENTIUS, in paffione Apoft. Petri, et Pauli, v. 45. Vid. *Corp. Poet.* 1620.

be ftill rcpofing. *Crito* here prefented to them a
paper, containing fome extracts from the conclufion of *St. Chryfoftom's* laft homily on *St. Paul's*
epiftle to the *Romans* *.

As foon as the young gentlemen had perufed
this fhort paper, *Crito*, in a tone of voice expreffive of the greateft humility, yet with a flow of
eloquence far fuperiour to his ufual ftyle; in a
ftyle, indeed, almoft worthy of the fubject; began
to fpeak of thofe particulars in *St. Paul's* character,
which are proper objects, not only of the admiration, but of the imitation alfo of every chriftian.

---

* Εγω κ᾽ την Ρωμην δια τετο φιλω· και τοι γε αυτην και ετερωθεν εχων
επαινειν, κ᾽ απο τε μεγεθες, κ᾽ απο της αρχαιοτητ©., κ᾽ απο τε καλ-
λες, κ᾽ απο τε πληθες, κ᾽ απο της δυναςειας, κ᾽ απο τε πλητε, κ᾽
απο των κατορθωματων των εν πολεμω· αλλα παντα ταυτα αφεις, δια
τετο αυτην μακαριζω, οτι (Παυλ©.) κ᾽ ζων αυτοις εγραφε, κ᾽ ουτως αυτες
εφιλει, κ᾽ παρων αυτοις διελεχθη, κ᾽ τον βιον εκει κατελυσε· διο κ᾽ επι-
σημ©. η πολις εντευθεν μαλλον, η απο των αλλων απαντων—δια ταυτα
θαυμαζω την πολιν, ε δια τον χρυσον τον πολυν, ε δια τες κιονας, ε διχ την
αλλην φαντασιαν.—Τις μοι νυν εδωκε περιχυθηναι τω σωματι Παυλε, κ᾽
προσηλωθηναι τω ταφω, κ᾽ την κονιν ιδειν τε σωματ©. εκεινε;—την
κονιν τε σοματ©.,—δι᾽ ου ελαλει εναντιον βασιλεων, κ᾽ εκ ησχυνετο;—
τυραννες επεσομισε,—την οικεμενην τω ΘΕΩ προσηγαγε·——την κονιν της
καρδιας, η ετω πλατεια ην ως κ᾽ πολεις ολοκληρες δεχεσθαι, κ᾽ δημες,
κ᾽ εθνη—την καρδιαν εκεινην πυρεμενην καθ᾽ εκαςον των απολλυμενων,—
την κεινην ζησασαν ζωην, ε ταυτην την ημετεραν. Ζω γαρ εκετι εγω,
ζη δε εν εμοι, φησιν, ο ΧΡΙΣΤΟΣ.—Εβελομην την κονιν ιδειν των χειρων, των
εν αλυσει,—δι᾽ ων ταυτα τα γραμματα εγραφετο·—την κονιν των ποδων
των περιδραμοντων την οικεμενην, κ᾽ μη καμνοντων, των εν ξυλω δεδεμενων,
ηνικα το δεσμωτηριον εσεισε.——Μη τοινυν θαυμαζωμεν αυτον μονον,—
αλλα κ᾽ μιμωμεθα, ινα καταξιωθωμεν κ᾽ εντευθεν απελθοντες αυτον ιδειν
(εν ερανοις) κ᾽ της απορρητε δοξης μετασχειν· ης γενοιτο παντας ημας
επιτυχειν χαριτι κ᾽ φιλανθρωπια τε Κυριε ημων ΙΗΣΟΥ ΧΡΙΣΤΟΥ, μεθ᾽
ΟΥ τω ΠΑΤΡΙ, αμα τω ΑΓΙΩ ΠΝΕΥΜΑΤΙ δοξα, κρατ©., τιμη, νυν
κ᾽ αει, κ᾽ εις τες αιωνας των αιωνων, Αμην,

He

He fpoke of the piety, and the charity; the humility, the zeal, and the patience of this holy apoftle.

O that in thefe things, faid he, *we could as well become imitators of* St. Paul, *as He was of a far greater perfon* * !

THE young gentlemen now recollected feveral exalted paffages in the writings of this diftinguifhed apoftle, and enumerated many fhining incidents in the hiftory of his life. They were beginning to fpeak more fully on thefe topics, when the converfation was unexpectedly interrupted, by the arrival of fome *italian* and *maltefe* gentlemen, with whom our *englifh* company were acquainted.

THUS accidentally met, the gentlemen converfed together for a few minutes, and then refpectfully feparated. The *maltefe* and *italians* continued in the church; and the *englifh* party, very defirous to purfue the prefent interefting topic, proceeded in their carriage to the neighbouring valley of *Aquæ Salviæ*.

*   *   *

* *Non aliter IPSE intravit.*

THE

THE valley of *Aquæ Salviæ* is a very retired fpot, that feems almoft uninhabited. Not a farmhoufe, no village, or any other building is to be feen here; three chapels only excepted, which ftand in the middle of a green pafture.

IN one of thefe chapels is an exquifite picture of the crucifixion of *St. Peter*, executed by *Guido Rheni*: in another are the figures of the twelve apoftles, from the fchool of *Raphael*.

AFTER the young nobleman, and the reft of this *englifh* company, had paffed a quarter of an hour in admiring thefe paintings, they fat down on a graffy bank, near the porch of the chapel.

PERMIT me, faid *Crito*, to return to the fubject, on which you were juft now fpeaking: I mean the hiftory of *St. Paul.*

IT is remarkable, that many of his writings bear fome relation to *Rome*, or at leaft to *Italy.*

THE epiftle to the *hebrews* was written by him, when in *Italy.* That to the *romans*, as appears by the title, is addreffed to the chriftian inhabitants of this city. The epiftles to the *galatians* and *ephefians*, to the *philippians*, and the *coloffians*, were all compofed by *St. Paul*, while

refident

refident in this metropolis. The fame may be faid of his letter to the beloved, the faithful, the charitable *Philemon;* and of his fecond epiftle to *Timotheus:* which epiftle, indeed, was *St. Paul's* laft work; and according to *St. Chryfoftom,* may juftly be confidered as his laft teftament *.

I THINK, faid the eldeft of the young gentlemen, we were informed this morning, in the *viâ latâ,* that the Acts of the Apoftles were written, or at leaft finifhed, at *Rome,* by *St. Luke,* under the infpection of *St. Paul.*

THAT opinion feems indeed very probable, replied *Crito,* as the book concludes with the account of *St. Paul's* being brought prifoner hither from *Judæa* †.

* See *Tillemont's* Hiftory of *St. Paul;* article 49.
Il n'écrivoit pas fimplement à St. Timothée pour l'appeller auprès de lui; mais pour l'exhorter, tout de nouveau, à s'acquitter de tous les devoirs d'un evêque & d'un docteur, avec un zele digne de tant de graces qu'il avoit recues; & avec un genereux mépris de tous les maux de ce monde; puifque l'efprit du chriftianifme n'eft point un efprit de crainte, mais de courage & d'amour; & que tous ceux qui veulent vivre avec pieté en Jefu Chrift, doivent être perfecutés : comme il le voyoit par fon exemple.

Κακοπαθησον, ως καλ Θ. ϛρατιωτης ΙΗΣΟΥ ΧΡΙΣΤΟΥ.

† Vide *St. Hieronymi* Catal. Vir. Illuftrium c. 7. and Dr. *Cave's* Life of *St. Luke,* p. 181. par. 5. It is faid however by fome, that the *Acts* of the Apoftles were written at *Alexandria* by *St. Luke,* the year after *St. Paul* had left *Rome,* to vifit the farther parts of *Italy.*—Vide Prolegomena *Millii,* p. xiv.

How

How happy would it have been, said *Crito's* pupil, if *St. Luke* had lived long enough to have completed the hiſtory of *St. Paul* by the addition of a ſecond book of the Acts *?

WITH regard to the ſacred writings, replied *Crito*, there is no doubt, but that every thing has been ordered infinitely for the beſt. And yet, it *ſeems* equally certain, that there muſt have been very noble materials for a *ſecond* part of the *Acts* of the Apoſtles. If, as you obſerve, a book of this ſort had been confined alone to *St. Paul's* hiſtory, it's contents muſt have been very glorious. Among other things, it would have contained his ſecond journey to *Rome,* and the ſeries and reſult of his tranſactions here. Including both his journies, *St. Paul* lived a conſiderable time in this city; teaching *not the chief of the jews only* but *many of the gentiles alſo;* particularly ſeveral *even of Cæſar's houſehold. Here* were his glorious *chains* diſplayed in the preſence of the whole *prætorium:* Hither was he brought, *twice,* before *the face of the lion;* that is, *Nero*:* and after his

long

---

long labours in the miniſtry of the Goſpel, in which I believe he perſevered during thirty years, travelling through many different and remote parts of the *roman* empire, *Here,* at laſt, *he finiſhed his courſe;* and accompliſhed, far more nobly than any of the heathen heroes of this city, his *holy warfare.*

On this account I would humbly ſubmit it to the opinion of proper judges, whether or no thoſe writings of *St. Paul,* which have a relation to this city or country, or at leaſt an extraƐ of the moral parts of them, might not be propoſed to travellers, during their reſidence at *Rome,* as a very uſeful kind of private *ſunday* ſtudies.

All travellers to *Athens,* on viewing the remains of the *Areopagus,* ought certainly to recolleƐt *St. Paul*'s oration there. If we live to make

perhaps alſo, it might be ſaid, on account of that fierce animal's being imagined to be the ſovereign of the beaſts. It is remarkable, that the perſon, who brought to king *Agrippa* the news of *Tiberius's* death, made uſe alſo of the ſame expreſſion: Γλωσσῃ τῃ εβραιων, τεθνηκεν ο λεων, φησιν.

See *Joſephi* Antiq. Jud. lib. 18.

With reſpeƐt to the two trials of *St. Paul,* in the firſt of which he was acquitted by *Nero, Euſebius* makes the following obſervation.

Εικ⊚· γε τοι κατα μεν αρχας ηπιωτερον τε Νερων⊚· διακειμενη, ραν την υπερ δογματ⊚· τε Παυλε δεχεσθαι απολογιαν. Προελθοντ⊚· δε εις αθεμιτες τολμας, μετα των αλλων ᴋ τα κατα των αποϛολων εγχειριϛθηναι.

Hiſt. Eccleſ. lib. ii. Κβ—κε.

the

the tour of *Greece,* and *Afia Minor,* we fhall doubtlefs, at *Athens,* and in many other places, have juft occafion to think on the apoftle's evangelical labours, fufferings, and imprifonments; as well as on the epiftles, which he wrote to or from feveral of the cities in thofe eaftern regions. During our refidence at *Rome,* therefore, why fhould we not, in *like manner,* frequently meditate on thofe particular parts of *St. Paul's* hiftory, which peculiarly relate to this place?

WE have now, for a confiderable fpace of time, been daily ftudying the imperfect characters of the heathen worthies of this city. Yefterday we were bufied in admiring the deaths of *Seneca* and *Thrafeas.* But let us recollect, that the holy apoftle and converter of the heathen world laid down his venerable head on the bloody block, *under the tyranny of the fame Nero,* and *in the fuburbs of this fame city.*

SHALL we be inattentive to *his chains and martyrdom?* Shall we fhut our eyes to *his* inftructions and example? He, in a very high degree, after his Divine Mafter, was a light to lighten even the moft learned part of the gentiles, particularly by his being fo *ready to preach the Gofpel,* not only *at* Athens, *but at* Rome *alfo;* and
likewife

likewife to be the glory of his own people, whether we confider him as an *ifraelite*, or as a *roman* citizen.

From a principle then, both of juftice, and of gratitude, let us endeavour to exprefs, here, fome due refpect to his facred memory. It was for *us*, *gentiles*, that he often bent his knees in prayer; it was for *us*, that he laboured moft inceffantly, and paffed through innumerable perils and pains.

With thefe thoughts I waked, and left my bed by fun-rife, laft *funday* morning. I then immediately withdrew to my clofet: and there, after fome fhort, but I hope not ill addreffed devotion, had the great happinefs to pafs feveral of the calm, ferene, and frefh hours of the day, in reading, *alone, and to my heart*, that divine epiftle, which *St. Paul* wrote from this city to his beloved adopted children at *Philippi*.

While I was reading that epiftle, my mind often returned to you, my dear affociates. Nor can I be forry for that wandering of my thoughts; For I am fure, that *I ought always, upon every remembrance of you, to pray, that your faith and love may abound yet more and more: that ye may be filled with all the fruits of righteoufnefs: that ye may become the children of God. Thus, even thus,*

thus, may the God of peace, that peace which paf-feth all underſtanding, be for ever with you!

O MY valued friends! may that heavenly re-ſignation, which breathes in this apoſtle's writ-ings; may that fervent piety, which was in him, from his youth up, conſtantly accompanied with much learning, and with a conſcience void of of-fence toward God and man; may his great bene-volence to all the nations, through whoſe coun-tries he ever travelled; may his abundant love, even to his enemies, and his unlimited charity to all men, whether *greeks* or *barbarians*, *jews* or *heathens;* although he was perſecuted by them all: may the memory of theſe, his *virtues*, have their due effect; a deep and an indelible impreſſion on your minds!

MAY the influence of his *writings*, and the ex-cellency of his *example*, in all it's fulneſs, deſcend and reſt upon you!

FROM my heart I wiſh you to be happier, than what I dare hope for myſelf: happier, & *in par-vo*, & *in magno;* & *in tempore*, & *in æternitate!*

MAY you be eternally happy; happy, as long as God himſelf will be happy!

May your innocent avocations *here* be, by God's mercy, of such a kind, as to conduct you to that happiness! Many centuries, many thousands of years hence, even from the immense depth of a blessed eternity, may your souls look back with pleasure, to the recollection of your employments at *Rome!* May that retrospect be one part of your felicity, even while your faculties shall be otherwise enraptured with the ecstatic vision of everlasting glory, amidst those *apostles, primitive saints,* and *martyrs,* in some of whose footsteps you are perhaps, *in this place,* now standing!

O my dear friends, you cannot, on this verdant grass-plot, stir one step, where *St. Paul* has not trodden before you. In this place, according to the united testimony, I believe, of all historians, that blessed apostle, saint, and martyr, was called to seal the Gospel with his blood.

Perhaps it was *on this bank,* that *Timotheus* kneeled in prayer, while his master was led up to the block. *There, perhaps, St. Paul* stood, in his last moments; meditating on that heavenly kingdom to which he was then approaching; that third heaven, the glories of which he had already seen.

BUT why, my dear firs, do you look thus earneftly on me? Indeed I am *deeply*, though not *fufficiently*, fenfible, of my infinite unworthinefs *even to pronounce* any of thefe facred names. Every time I make mention of them, my confcience cries out aloud to me, how undeferving I am, even of the ground on which I *ever* tread; or of that air, which *ever* breathes on my face. Yet, let not my utter unfitnefs to preach on thefe or fimilar fubjects abate in the leaft your reverence for them.

*   *   *

IT is perhaps unneceffary, continued *Crito*, after fome paufe, that I fhould thus perfuade you to the ftudy of the works of *St. Paul:* I have great reafon to believe, that the goodnefs of your own hearts hath long ago fuggefted to you, in fome degree, the *propriety* of fuch a ftudy, while at *Rome*.

SOON after our firft arrival here, I remember with great pleafure, that I came by chance into my pupil's apartment one *funday* evening; it was on the 25th of *january*, the converfion of *St. Paul*, when I found him reading the epiftle to *Timotheus*, juft mentioned; that epiftle, in which

the

the heart of a *Paul* pours forth the fulnefs of it's tendernefs, towards this, his darling fon.

My pupil read to me the five or fix concluding verfes of the laft chapter; and upon one of thofe verfes he obferved, that nothing more ftrongly demonftrates the fallacy of the outward appearance of things in this life, than the fact, of fuch a wretch as *Nero*, having fitten in judgment, on fuch a faint as *Paul*. How did they then appear! *St. Paul*, in irons, deferted by his friends*; loaded with contempt and infults by his enemies; *Nero*, feated on the *roman* tribunal, in all the pomp and glitter of imperial fplendour; and furrounded, doubtlefs, with crouds of flattering courtiers.

---

* Εν τη πρωτη μȣ απολογια ȣδεις μοι ζυμπαρεγενετο, αλλα παντες με εγκατελιπον· (μη αυτοις λογισθειη.)

Ο δε Κυρι⊕ μοι παρεςη, κ̃ ενεδυναμωσε με, ινα δι' εμȣ το κηρυγμα πληροφορηθη, κ̃ ακȣση παντα τα εθνη· κ̃ ερρυσθην εκ ςοματ⊕ λεοντ⊕.

Και ρυσεται με ο Κυρι⊕ απο παντ⊕ εργȣ πονηρȣ, κ̃ σωσει εις την βασιλειαν αυτȣ την επȣρανιον. Ω η δοξα εις τȣς αιωνας των αιωνων. Αμην.

Ασπασαι Πρισκαν κ̃ Ακυλαν, κ̃ τον Ονησιφορȣ οικον. Ερας⊕ εμεινεν εν Κορινθω. Τροφιμον δε απελιπον εν Μιλητω ασθενȣντα.

Σπȣδασον προ χειμων⊕ ελθειν. Ασπαζεται σε Ευβȣλ⊕, κ̃ Πȣδης, κ̃ Λιν⊕, κ̃ Κλαυδια, κ̃ οι αδελφοι παντες.

Ο Κυρι⊕ Ιησȣς Χρις⊕ μετα τȣ πνευματ⊕ σȣ. Η χαρις μεθ' υμων. Αμην.

Προς Τιμοθεον δευτερα, της Εφεσιων εκκλησιας πρωτον επισκοπον χειροτονηθεντα, εγραφη απο Ρωμης, οτε εκ δευτερȣ παρεςη Παυλ⊕ τω Καισαρι Νερωνι.

2 Ep. ad Tim. C. iv. 16. &c.

But

BUT *how contrary has been the condition of their
fouls ever fince! How different will be their meeting at the Laft Day!* Let me refer you to what I
find noted on this occafion, in my memorandum
papers: my pupil gave me the hint of it: it confifts of the firft fixteen verfes in the fifth chapter
of the book of *Wifdom* *.

WHILE

---

* **1.** Τοτε ϛησεται εν παρρησια πολλη ο δικαι©·
Κατα προσωπον των θλιψαντων αυτον,
Και των αθετουντων τυς πονυς αυτυ.

2. Ιδοντες, ταραχθησονται φοβω δεινω,
Και εκϛησονται επι τω παραδοξω της σωτηριας.

3. Ερυσιν εαυτοις μετανουντες,
Και δια ϛενοχωριαν πνευματ©· ϛεναζοντες,
Ουτ©· ην ον εσχομεν ποτε, εις γελωτα·
Και εις παραβολην ονειδισμυ.

4. Οι αφρονες τον βιον αυτυ ελογισαμεθα μανιαν,
Και την τελευτην αυτυ ατιμον.

5. Πως κατελογισθη εν υιοις ΘΕΟΥ,
Και εν αγιοις ο κληρ©· αυτυ εϛιν;

6. Αρα επλανθαμεν απο οδυ αληθειας,
Και το της δικαιοσυνης φως υκ ελαμψεν ημιν,
Και ο ηλι©· υκ ανετειλεν ημιν.

7. Ανομιας ενεπλησθημεν τριβοις, κỹ απωλειας,
Και διωδευσαμεν ερημυς αβατυς,
Την δε οδον Κυριυ υκ εγνωμεν.

8. Τι ωφελησεν ημας η υπερηφανια;
Και τι πλυτ©· μετα αλαζονειας Συμβεβληται ημιν;

9. Παρηλθεν εκεινα παντα ως σκια,
Και ως αγγελια παρατρεχυσα·

10. Ως ναυς διερχομενη κυμαινομενον υδωρ,
Ης διαβασης υκ εϛιν ιχν©· ευρειν,
Ουδε ατραπον τροπι©· αυτης εν κυμασιν·

11. Η ως ορνευ διιπταντ©· αερα,
Ουθεν ευρισκεται τεκμηριον πορειας,
Πληγη δε ταρσων μαϛιζομενον πνευμα κυφον
Και σχισομενον βια ροιζυ,

Κινυμενων

WHILE *Crito* was thus fpeaking, his pious pupil held down his blufhing countenance. I am fure, faid he, that both on account of my youth, and of many other more important confiderations, I am really very unworthy of pretending to fpeak on fuch fubjeƈts. Yet, in juftice to my two good young friends here, let me have the pleafure of afluring you, that *their* hearts overflowed with the higheft happinefs this morning, while they were liftening to your inftruƈtions in the bafilica of *St. Paul.* They acknowledged thefe fentiments to me afterwards, though they were filent when on the fpot. Even at prefent *their hearts burn within them.*

LET me add, that a fimilar ardour and pleafure filled their minds, fome few days paft; while

Κινυμενων πτερυγων διωδευθη,
Και μετα τυτο ακ ευρεθη σημειον επιβασεως εν αυτω·
12. Η ως βελυς βληθεντ@ επι σκοπον,
Τμηθεις ο αηρ ευθεως εις εαυτον ανελυθη,
Ως αγνοησαι την διοδον αυτυ.
13. Ουτως κ) ημεις γεννηθεντες εξελιπομεν·
Και αρετης μεν σημειον υδεν εχομεν δειξαι,
Εν δε τη κακια ημων κατεδαπανηθημεν.
14. Οτι ελπις ασεβυς ως φερομεν@ χυς υπο ανεμυ,
Και ως παχνη υπο λαιλαπ@ διωχθεισα λεπτη,
Και ως καπν@ υπο ανεμυ διηχυθη,
Και ως μνεια καταλυτυ μονονμερυ παρωδευσε.
15. Δικαιοι δε εις τον αιωνα ζωσι,
Και εν Κυριω ο μισθ@ αυτων,
Και η φροντις αυτων παρα Υψιςω.
16. Δια τυτο ληψονται το βασιλειον της ευπρεπειας,
Και το διαδημα τυ καλλυς εκ χειρ@ Κυριυ,
Οτι τη δεξια σκεπασει αυτυς,
Και τω βραχιονι υπερασπισει αυτων.

we

we were viewing the beautiful round chapel, built by *Bramante,* on the *Janiculan* hill; on the very fpot where, *it is faid,* St. *Peter* was crucified. But pray, dear fir, what may be your opinion, as to the truth of that hiftory? If we miftake not, it has been controverted.

WE will talk on that fubject, replied *Crito,* if you pleafe, in the afternoon. At prefent let us clofe our morning-ftudies here; for the *maltefe* and *italian* gentlemen, who were with us at St. *Paul's,* are following us hither. Their coach, you fee, has juft ftopped at the gateway leading to thefe chapels. As devotion feems to be the motive of their coming, it will be proper for us to retire.

* * *

THE *englifh* gentlemen now returned to *Rome.* In the way to their lodgings, they vifited the church, and rich chapels, of S. S. *Pudens,* and *Pudentiana.*

THE company dined to-day at the young nobleman's apartments. But they were all remarkably abftemious. After coffee they withdrew, as ufual, to fleep; but not one of them clofed his eyes.

THEY

THEY met again at tea. While they were taking it, the young nobleman defired to look again on the paper, that *Crito* had fhowed them this morning.

WITH deep attention the company reconfidered it's contents, particularly it's conclufion.

AFTER perufing the paper, they walked down, *in filence*, from the *Colle Pinciano*, or *Hortulano**; and, paffing by the church of cardinal *Borromeo*, and the lying-in-hofpital, at the magnificent *Ripetta*, which is on the banks of the *Tiber*, they took boat there, and croffed that narrow, but rapid ftream.

THEY foon landed on the oppofite bank among fome gardens. The whole large fpace indeed, between this part of the *Tiber* and the *Vatican* hill, is at prefent nothing but gardens, fields, and meadows.

IT was then juft that time of the evening, when a rural walk, attended by divine meditations, is moft pleafant.

CRITO, at length, began the converfation; following the train of thought, in which he had

---

* It's modern name is *Monte di Trinità.*

N n 4　　　　　　　　　　been

been engaged at the conclusion of his paper on the subject of *Suffering Virtue.*

THOUGH we are neither able, said he, nor worthy, to meditate on the high and holy subject of our Saviour's passion; yet, let us endeavour to confider and fully contemplate the patience and fortitude of His first followers and disciples: in the fame manner, as, though we cannot fix our eyes on the fun, even while fetting; yet we may view with pleasure the reflection of his light, on the face of the moon, and of *that* evening star.

LET us not imagine, that the deaths of those holy martyrs and faints are less instructive lessons to us, than their lives. By their deaths Providence, as it were, demonstrates to us, that there must be another life. *When we see wicked men prosper, and faints die in dungeons, we are far from doubting of Providence; we are strengthened in the affured belief, that God, who has stamped the marks of infinite wisdom and goodness on all his works, has appointed a just retribution in the world to come. And faith reveals to us, clearly, this important secret. We at present see only one end of the chain, in the conduct of Providence towards men: many links of it are now concealed from our eyes. Let us wait a little, and we shall see, in eternity, God's goodness abundantly justified.*

IN

In the mean time, let us follow the examples of thofe bleffed faints ; their examples of piety to heaven, and charity to man : let us thankfully accept every good gift of Providence; and patiently endure every *feeming* evil, which may be appointed for us, during this fhort and tranfitory ftate.

CRITO now paufing, Permit me, dear fir, faid his pupil, to indulge myfelf in the recolletion of fome happy hours, which I enjoyed about two months ago. Happy I call them, becaufe, during their continuance, my mind was fully engaged in thoughts congenial with yours.

THE day before you began this courfe of *roman* letures, the laft day in *april*, was the feftival of the Afcenfion*. In the afternoon of that day, I attended this our noble young friend, to fee the large piture, which Mr. *Mengs* has defigned and executed, on that glorious fubjet†.

To one reprefentation in that painting, we fhut our eyes. But in relation to the other figures, of the bleffed Virgin, and of the apoftles, who are

* See pages xvi, and xxxiv. of the Introdution to the firft book.

† This piture was at *Rome* in the year 1761 ; but was intended to be removed to *Drefden*, as foon as the war fhould be ended.

there

there defcribed, kneeling and *adoring* our Saviour during his afcent to heaven; on *thefe* our eyes were a long time rivetted.

OUR thoughts entered into the fubject: we dwelt upon it, and were abforpt in it.

AT the inflant of the afcenfion, faid we to each other, how totally muft *thefe* holy perfons have difregarded all the labours, pains, and dangers, with which, during the fhortnefs of human life, innocence and fanctity are fometimes tried! Such alfo were *our* fenfations, while viewing that *picture* only of the Afcenfion.

WE afterwards walked, along this very path, to *St. Peter's.* We found the church full of proceffions, and refounding with facred mufic.

MAY my dear friends in *England,* may my dear friends here pardon me:—I then could not forbear wifhing myfelf in heaven.

SCARCE had *Crito's* pupil uttered thefe laft words, when, recollecting himfelf, and blufhing at the fentiments which fuddenly rifing from the heart, had been unawares expreffed by the lips; he haftened to divert the difcourfe to it's former topic ; the picture of the Afcenfion by Mr. *Mengs.*

CRITO

CRITO joined with him in admiration of moſt parts of that piĉture. He at the ſame time ſpoke, with ſome reſtriĉtion, in favour of church-paintings in general. Provided, ſaid he, thoſe paintings are confined to ſcriptural ſubjeĉts, or to authentic and edifying parts of church hiſtory, I cannot but be of opinion, that they may frequently ſerve to awaken ſome good emotions in the breaſt of the ſpeĉtator.

I HAVE, indeed, of late thought, ſaid the young nobleman, that to conſider thoſe kinds of painting, merely with an *artiſt's* eye, is too cold a method of ſtudying them.

SOME few weeks ago, I took a ſolitary walk to that chapel on *Monte Cælio,* which is enriched with the two famous piĉtures of *Dominichini* and *Guido,* on the ſubjeĉt of *St. Andrew's* martyrdom. I ſat there alone near half an hour; remarking, as well as I was able, the *different* excellencies of each of thoſe maſters. *Dominichini's* piĉture, though not perhaps ſo faultleſs as that of *Guido,* yet has been ſaid, and I think juſtly, to contain equal, if not ſuperiour beauties.

WHILE I was thus amuſing myſelf, an accident happened, which fully inſtruĉted me, that I might
have

have been employing my thoughts there in *a much better* manner.

AN elderly woman, a native of *France*, and of a good family there, entered the chapel. Her drefs was plain, but clean and neat: it feemed to be the proper garb of charity: her looks were remarkably full of benevolence, humility, and devotion. She knelt down immediately before the communion table, and kiffed the pavement. After fome few moments fhe rofe, and walked back to that part of the chapel, where, you know, *Dominichini* has reprefented, on the wall, *St. Andrew,* patiently enduring thofe torments, which ufually preceded crucifixion: *flagellis cæfum.* At the fight fhe burft into tears. Soon, however, recovering herfelf, fhe turned round to the oppofite painting of *Guido.* She fixed her eyes on the apoftle there, joyfully faluting and welcoming his crofs. Her countenance was in that inftant covered with a fmiling calmnefs; and with all the tokens of a meek, refigned, and peaceful mind. She drew a chair, and fat down by *Guido's* picture: She took a book of devotion in her hands, and began to perufe it. I was impertinent enough to look over her fhoulder: it was a tranflation of the treatife *de Imitatione;* and was opened at the 12th chapter of the fecond book.

The

The words, which met my eye, were the following: *Il faut pratiquer la patience, fi vous voulez jouir de la paix du cœur, & meriter une couronne éternelle.*

I REMEMBER that chapter, replied *Crito;* it is a very fine one. I am obliged to you for reminding me of it afrefh. I will read it over again this evening. I have the book in the original; and, indeed, quoted fome lines from it, in the paper which I laid on your table this morning.

IN the mean time, as you have accidentally mentioned the martyrdom of *St. Andrew,* permit me to obferve, that this faint is defcribed in holy writ, as one of the *firft* difciples of the LAMB of GOD.

CRITO now ftopped in his walk, and ftood ftill for fome moments. He took from his pocket the firft volume of the New Teftament; being a fmall edition of the Gofpels and Acts in *greek,* with a *latin* tranflation. He read from it the following lines.

Alterâ die, iterum ftabat Ioannes, & ex difcipulis ejus duo. Et refpiciens Jefum ambulantem, dixit, Ecce AGNUS DEI!

Et

Et audierunt eum duo difcipuli loquentem, &
fecuti funt Jefum—Erat autem Andreas, frater
Simonis Petri, unus ex duobus, qui audierant à
Ioanne, & fecuti fuerant eum. Invenit hic pri-
mum fratrem fuum Simonem, & dixit ei, Inveni-
mus MESSIAM *.

ST. *ANDREW*, my dear friends, at our Saviour's call, *readily* left all things to follow him.
Both in life, and in death, he proved himfelf a
worthy teacher of the doctrine of the Crofs.

THE death of the crofs was appointed for *St.*
Andrew: and, indeed, it is highly fuitable to his
character to think, that he received his crown
with ardent joy.

HE preached the Gofpel in *Greece,* and *there*
laid down his life for it: he confirmed the faith
by his blood fhed on the crofs, at *Patræ,* in
Achaia.

LET us here paufe a little, and reflect on *that*
circumftance.—Is it not probable that *St. Andrew,*
in the hour of his martyrdom, devoutly recollected thofe words, which our Saviour had fpoken to
him, and to *St. Philip,* on a fubject very fimilar?

---

* Evang. *Sti Johannis,* chap. i. v. 35, &c.

It

It was at that *remarkable* time, when some *grecians* expressed their desire of seeing JESUS.

CRITO now turned to the 12th chapter of *St. John;* and desired leave to read the following passage.

Erant autem quidam gentiles (ελληνες), *ex his, qui ascenderant ut adorarent in die festo. Hi ergo accesserunt ad Philippum, qui erat a Bethsaidâ Galilææ, & rogabant eum, dicentes; Domine, volumus* IESUM *videre. Venit Philippus & dicit Andreæ; Andreas, rursum, & Philippus dixerunt Iesu.*

Iesus autem respondit eis, dicens: Venit hora, ut clarificetur Filius Hominis. Amen, amen dico vobis, nisi granum frumenti, cadens in terram, mortuum fuerit, ipsum solum manet: si autem mortuum fuerit, multum fructum affert. Qui amat animam suam, perdet eam; & qui odit animam suam, in hoc mundo, in vitam æternam custodit eam. Si quis mihi ministrat, me sequatur; & ubi sum ego, illic & minister meus erit. Si quis mihi ministraverit, honorificabit eum Pater meus. Nunc anima mea turbata est; & quid dicam? Pater, salvifica me ex hâc horâ? Sed propterea veni in horam hanc. Pater, clarifica nomen tuum.

Venit

Venit ergo vox de cælo: Et clarificavi, & iterum clarificabo. Turba ergo, quæ ſtabat, & audierat, dicebat tonitruum eſſe factum. Alii dicebant, an-gelus ei locutus eſt.

Reſpondit Ieſus, & dixit: Non propter me hæc vox venit, ſed propter vos. Nunc judicium eſt mundi; nunc princeps hujus mundi ejicietur foras. Et ego, ſi exaltatus fuero à terrâ, omnia traham ad me ip-ſum. Hoc autem dicebat, ſignificans quâ morte eſſet moriturus*.

* * *

IT ſeems, continued *Crito,* cloſing the book, to be very obſervable, that as our Saviour him-ſelf, to the utter confuſion of human pride, pa-tiently ſubmitted to the moſt ignominious kind of death; ſo, likewiſe, did all his holy apoſtles.

THE apoſtles and friends of CHRIST were treated, during their lives, as malefactors. They were impriſoned: they were baniſhed: they wan-dered about, being deſtitute; afflicted; torment-ed; hated; deſpiſed: *they,* of whom the world was not worthy. After ſeveral years thus paſſed,

---

* Evang. *Johan.* ch. xii. ver. 20, &c.

they

they, like the prophets and martyrs of the Old Teſtament, were tortured, not accepting deliverance: they were ſlain with the ſword.

OF what then, ought a common chriſtian to complain?

I MADE, yeſterday, ſome extracts from the Imitation, blending them with ſome words of my own; which, if you will give me leave, I will now read to you. They are on this ſlip of paper.

O ingrata anima mea, ceſſa tandem conqueri; conſiderata CHRISTI, *& ſanctorum ejus amicorum, paſſione.*

CHRISTUS *pati voluit, & crucifigi:* chriſtiani autem hodierni, *otium ſibi quærunt, & requiem, & divitias, & longæ vitæ commoda.* Such were not the thoughts of the glorious company of the apoſtles; ſuch were not *their* expectations. *Quid hic circumſpicis, anima, mea? Non eſt* hìc *locus requietionis tuæ. In cæleſtibus debet eſſe tua habitatio in æternùm.*

O Deus meus! verte mihi in amaritudinem omnem conſolationem carnalem, ab æternorum amore me abſtrahentem. Non me decipiat mundus, & brevis gloria ejus: da mihi fortitudinem reſiſtendi,

pati-

*patientiam tolerandi, conſtantiam perſeverandi:
da, pro omnibus mundi conſolationibus, ſuaviſſi-
mam* SPIRITÛS TUI *unctionem.*

MUCH inſtruction might be reaped, from a recollection of a catalogue of the apoſtles, joined
to a ſerious conſideration of what was *their* lot in
this world.

ACCORDING to the accounts, which are moſt
generally received,

1. *St. Peter* was crucified.
2. *St. Andrew* was crucified.
3. *St. Bartholomew* was flayed alive.
4. *St. John* was baniſhed, after having been
   caſt into a cauldron of boiling oil.
5, 6. Two *St. James.* One was beheaded: of
   the other the brains were daſhed out.
7. *St. Philip* was ſtoned.
8. *St. Thomas,* ſtabbed.
9. *St. Matthew,* beheaded.
10. *St. Simon,* crucified.
11. *St. Jude,* ſhot with arrows.
12. *St. Matthias,* ſtabbed.
13. *St. Paul,* beheaded.

Υπαγετε. Ιδυ, ΕΓΩ αποςελλω υμας ως αρνας εν
μεσω λυκων *.

* Sti *Luc.* c. x. 3.

I WISH,

I WISH, said the young nobleman, that you had favoured us with some of these sentiments this morning; while we were admiring the figures of the apostles, painted by the school of *Raphael.* But, I interrupt you.

OF this holy groupe, replied *Crito,* the *first who gained the crown of martyrdom* was St. *James,* the brother of St. *John.* In the beginning of our Saviour's ministry St. *James* had readily left every thing, to obey the divine call. After our Saviour's ascension, he followed his master's path to heaven, doubtless with equal readiness. Enabled, not by the strength of his own resolutions, but by the strength of grace, St. *James* joyfully accepted his Lord's cup of suffering; and was the earliest of all the apostles, who drank of it.

I REMEMBER, said the young nobleman, that in the picture of the ascension, of which your pupil was just now speaking, there was something very peculiarly striking, in the figure and countenance of St. *James.* Pray inform me, where it was that St. *James* suffered, and at what time.

HE suffered at *Jerusalem,* replied *Crito,* a little before *Easter;* in the eleventh or twelfth year after he had attended his Saviour's agony there in the garden of *Gethsemane.*

CLAUDIUS

CLAUDIUS was then emperor of *Rome*, and *Herod Agrippa* was king of *Judæa*. It was that *Herod*, who flew *St. James* with the fword; and, feeing that it pleafed the *jews*, he next proceeded to feize *Peter* alfo; intending, doubtlefs, the fame cruelty to him.

Your mentioning the name of *St. Peter*, reminds me, faid *Crito's* pupil, that, while we were this morning in the valley of *Aquæ Salviæ*, you were afked a queftion relative to *his* hiftory; which you gave us reafon to hope you would confider this afternoon. May I beg of you now, to refolve our doubts on that fubject?

Permit me, faid the eldeft of the young gentlemen, to fecond that motion. We are walking at prefent, in direct and full view of his magnificent bafilica; and, confequently, our thoughts in this converfation very naturally point to him.

With regard to *St. Peter*, replied *Crito*, there are two particular difficulties, which fomewhat difcourage me from attempting to fpeak on the fubject of his life and character.

First, my own great demerits. I am not worthy, indeed, to talk on the virtues of any one of the moft imperfect among good men: much

lefs

lefs fhould I prefume to attempt the defcription of that eminent fanctity, that ftrong faith, that ardent love of God, and zeal for the falvation of human fouls, which infpired the holy perfon, who is always named as *firft*, in the catalogue of the apoftles.

THE other difficulty arifes from this circum-ftance; that *St. Peter's* refidence in this city has been much controverted in modern ages.

I MUST acknowledge, indeed, to my fhame, that I have not yet fufficiently applied myfelf to that important branch of the fcience of divinity, ecclefiaftical hiftory; fo as to be able to give you any full information on this point, and at the fame time to do, what is, perhaps, proper juftice, to the arguments of the writers on both fides of the queftion.

I MIGHT add, that controverfy, however highly ufeful and neceffary upon fome occafions, is, in general, not an agreeable employment. It's dif-cuffions are difficult; and the temper which it fometimes produces, is not that of a chriftian heart. Happy is the ecclefiaftic, who is engaged in the other occupations of a religious life; in the fmoother path of other ftudies; in the ferene feli-cities of devotion; and in the celeftial employ-

ments

ments of that univerfal charity, with which all the true fervants of God are unextinguifhably inflamed: *loving one another, with a pure heart, fervently; and laying afide all malice, and all guile, and hypocrifies, and envies, and all evil fpeakings.*

Yet, on the other hand, furely, the exalted fubjects of this day's converfation ought to impart a generous warmth to our hearts. We ought neither to be afhamed, nor afraid, to confefs our opinion, as to the controverted point in queftion.

Most probably *it is very true*, that *St. Peter* paffed a confiderable part of his life in *Rome:* and, on this account, we ought, during our happy refidence here, frequently to meditate on his virtues, and endeavour to pay due honour and veneration to his bleffed memory.

We juftly reverence *St. Paul*, as the apoftle of the *gentile* world: but let us not forget, that *St. Peter* alfo highly merits the fame title *.

Is it your opinion, faid *Crito's* pupil, that *St. Peter* was really crucified at *Rome?*

---

* See the tenth and eleventh chapters of the *Acts*, and the 7th verfe of the fifteenth chapter.

As

As to the *manner*, replied *Crito*, and the *place* of *St. Peter's* death, my opinion is this:

THAT St. *Peter* was crucified, may be implied from the gofpel of *St. John.* He *glorified God; following* his holy Lord even in *the manner of his death**.

THAT he fuffered *at Rome, all the ancient wri-ters are faid to be unanimous;* and as to the moderns, many learned proteftants agree with the *roman* catholics in this point †.

BOTH thefe points feem indeed *fufficiently clear:* but as to the exact *time* of his fufferings, and the identical fpot in *Rome,* where he breathed out his pious foul, I believe there may be fome real reafon to doubt.

WITH refpect to his interment, it was probably *here,* where his fplendid church now appears. The palaces of the *Cæfars* are in ruins; but the tomb of the *fisherman* is in the higheft glory.

THE tradition, that *St. Peter* was really buried *here,* is greatly corroborated by the teftimony of

---

* See chap. xxi. 15.

† See Dr. *Pearfon's* pofthumous works; Dr. *Cave's* Life of *St. Peter,* and Literary Hiftory, Sæc. Apoft. p. 5 and 7. See alfo *Pool's* Synopfis, on the 18th verfe of the 21ft chapter of *St. John's* Gofpel.

Caius,

Caius, who lived about fifteen hundred and fifty years ago*; and by the indubitable fact, of the emperor *Conſtantine's* having built *here,* in honour of *St. Peter,* a baſilica; which was very ſtately, though I ſuppoſe not comparable to the preſent moſt magnificent ſtructure.

THE baſilica of *St. Peter,* ſaid the young nobleman, which was erected by *Conſtantine,* ſeems, from the plans of it publiſhed by *Bonanni,* to have been very ſimilar to the baſilica of *St. Paul,* which we viſited this morning.

THIS obſervation of the young nobleman recalled ſeveral pious ideas to *Crito's* mind. He recollected ſome of thoſe awful ſentiments, which had filled his heart in the morning, while ſtanding near the ſtairs, that lead down to *St. Paul's* grave.

How ſtriking, ſaid he, is that paſſage in St. *Chryſoſtom's* deſcription of the Laſt Day! Εκειϑεν αρπαγησεται Παυλ☉, εκειϑεν Πετρ☉. Εννοησατε, κ̀ Φριξατε, οιον οψεται Θεαμα Ρωμη τον Παυλον εξαιφνης

---

* Περι των τοπων ενϑα των ειρημειων αποϛολων τα ιερα Cκηνωματα κατατεϑειται, φησιν, Εγω δε τα τροπαια των αποϛολων εχω δειξαι. Εαν γαρ ϑελησης απελϑειν επι τον Cατικανον, η επι την οδον την ωϛιαν ευρησεις τα τροπαια των ταυτην ιδρυσαμενων την εκκλησιαν.

Euſeb. Hiſt. Eccl. β. κε.

See alſo *Euſeb.* lib. ii. c. 25. p. 67. and *Cave's* Appendix to *St. Peter's* Life, p. 47.

αναςαμενον απο της θηκης εκεινης μετα Πετρ8, ἡ αιρομ-
ενον εις την απαντησιν τ8 ΚΥΡΙΟΥ *.

THE idea of the glorious refurrection of *St. Peter,* and of *St. Paul,* feems to have been ftrongly
impreffed on *St. Chryfoftom's* mind. For, in another part of his works†, " What, fays he, was
more glorious, than *Paul?* what more illuftrious
than *Peter?* who travelled over the earth, fowing
every where the feeds of religion?"—But if, in
this world, they were endued with fuch power,
think, what they will be, on that day, when they
fhall have received bodies incorruptible, immortal, and far exceeding all earthly glory; fafhioned
like the glorious body of Chrift, according to the
mighty working, whereby he is able to fubdue all
things to himfelf‡.

*   *   *

You favoured us this morning, faid the eldeft
of the young gentlemen, with a catalogue of the
facred writings, which were compofed by *St.
Paul* while at *Rome.* Give me leave to afk you,
whether *St. Peter* wrote any thing during his refidence here. Did he fow the feeds of religion

---

* See the conclufion of the laft homily on the epiftle to
the *romans.*
† Expofitio in Pfalmum cix.
‡ See *St. Paul's* epiftle to the *philippians,* chap. iii. 21.

here

here with his words and example only; or was his pen alfo employed in thofe glorious labours?

It is faid, replied *Crito*, and I believe truly, that as St. *Paul* affifted *St. Luke* in writing the hiftory of the acts of the apoftles, fo likewife *St. Peter*, while at *Rome*, affifted *St. Mark*, in the compofition and revifal of his Gofpel*. Whence it might be, that fome ancients have attributed that Gofpel to *St. Peter* himfelf. He certainly had a very confiderable fhare in the work. It has been obferved, as an inftance of *St. Peter's* great humility, that in this Gofpel no mention is made of the high commendations, which our Saviour gave to that apoftle, on his confeffing him to be the Son of God: but the hiftory of his fhameful lapfe, and denial of his mafter, is related at full length; with fome particular aggra-

---

* *St. Mark* accompanied *St. Peter* in his apoftolical progrefs, and preached the Gofpel in *Italy* and at *Rome;* where, at the requeft of the chriftians of thofe parts, he compofed his Gofpel.—The converts at *Rome*, not content to have heard *St. Peter* preach, preffed *St. Mark*, his difciple, that he would commit to writing an hiftorical account of what he delivered to them. This he performed, with no lefs faithfulnefs than brevity; all which *St. Peter* perufed, ratified with his authority, and commanded to be publicly read in their religious affemblies.

See Dr. *Cave's* Life of *St. Mark*, folio edition, p. 174, and p. 176, and alfo his Literary Hiftory, v. i. p. 24. *St. Mark* was martyred at *Alexandria*, in the 14th year of *Nero*. But it is related by the *Chronicon Alexandrinum*, as quoted in *Calmet's* dictionary of the Bible, that *St. Mark* was prefent in *Rome*, at the death of *St. Peter* and *St. Paul*.

vations,

vations, of which the other Evangelifts take no notice *.

BUT the only writings, to which *St. Peter's* name is affixed, are his epiftles.

IN relation to the two epiftles of *St. Peter*, I could heartily wifh, that you would allot fome few hours, next faturday or funday, for the diligent perufal of them. The firft of thofe epiftles, you know, is *generally* underftood to have been fent by *St. Peter*, from *this* city †. He is faid to have written the fecond alfo here, while in prifon; *fome little time before the putting off his mortal tabernacle.*

How pleafing will it be to you, in comparing that epiftle with one of St. *Paul's*, to confider both thefe great apoftles as looking forward with

---

* See *Eufeb.* Dem. lib. iii. c. 5. p. 121, 122.

† See *Grotius's* note on the 13th chapter of this epiftle. *De Babylone diffident veteres & novi interpretes. —Veteres Romam interpretantur, ubi Petrum fuiffe, nemo verus chriftianus dubitabit: novi, Babylonem in Chaldæa. Ego veteribus affentior.*

See alfo Dr. *Hammond's* note on the fame paffage, together with his prefaces to both of the epiftles of *St. Peter*.

See alfo *Mill's* Prolegomena to his *Greek* Teftament, p. vii.

See alfo that moft primitive teftimony of *Papias*, ap. *Eufeb.* lib. ii. c. 15. p. 53.

joy to their approaching crowns of everlasting glory *!

I F indeed I might venturously presume to recommend to you any method of preparing your minds for duly meditating on *St. Peter's* martyrdom, it should be this:—

D I L I G E N T L Y study his two epistles; endeavour to enter into their stream of thought, and into the divine spirit itself of the writer.

W H E N you have fully imbibed his sentiments, put your *Greek* Testament into your pocket, and take a walk to this church: let it be about noon, when it is least frequented. Sit down on one of the benches, which stand usually behind *St. Peter's* grave. Meditate then on what you have been reading; re-peruse the most affecting passages; and pray to G O D, of his infinite mercy to inspire into your breasts thoughts and resolutions, worthy of the occasion and place! Pray earnestly: for it will not be a little blessing.

* * *

* The reader is desired to compare part of the second epistle of *St. Peter*, beginning at the 14th verse of the first chapter, with part of *St. Paul's* second epistle to *Timothy*, beginning at verse 6, of chap. iv.

THE

The company were now arrived at the great *Piazza* of the *Vatican:* they advanced towards it's centre; to the bafis of the famous *egyptian* obelifk.

After fome fhort converfation here on other fubjects, *Crito* refumed his former folemn difcourfe.

Within fome few months of the martyrdom of *St. Peter* and *St. Paul*, the *firft general perfecution* broke out. It is one of the honours of the chriftian church, that it's firft perfecutor was a *Nero*.

Great numbers of the friends and difciples of the apoftles were then cruelly tormented, and murdered; as is defcribed in the 15th book of the Annals of *Tacitus*.

Pereuntibus chriftianis, addita ludibria, ut ferarum tergis contecti, laniatu canum interirent, aut crucibus affixi; aut flammandi*; atque ubi defe-

---

* *Stantibus ad palum deftinatis, unco (ne motatione capitis picem ardentem declinarent) gutturi fuffixo, e laminâ ardente pix aut unguen in caput liquefiebat; ita ut rivi pinguedinis humanæ per arenam amphitheatri fulcum facerent. Ad hoc tormentum alludit Juvenalis,* fat. i. ver. 155.

> *Pone Tigellinum, tædâ lucebis in illâ,*
> *Quâ ftantes ardent, qui fixo gutture fumant,*
> *Et latus mediam fulcus diducit arenam.*

Vid. *Hauffii* Annotat. in *Tacitum*.

ciffei

ciffet dies in ufum noĉlurni luminis urerentur.
Cap. 44.

AMONG the fragments of *Seneca,* faid *Crito's*
pupil, there is a paffage, which feems applicable
to the martyrdom of *St. Peter,* and of thefe his
worthy difciples and friends *. It is not in the leaft
improbable, that *Seneca* might be a fpeĉtator of
their fufferings. And from his deep filence in
relation to their doĉtrines, it is very much to be
fufpeĉted, that he was far from condemning them
in his heart; though he was not honeft enough
to declare openly his approbation of them. Pray
excufe the interruption.

YOU are now, my dear friends, refumed *Crito,*
ftanding on the very fpot, where thefe apoftolic
chriftians were martyred. On that point, I believe, all hiftorians and antiquarians agree.

INDEED, the faĉt feems to be paft difpute: for
moft part of the fouthern fide of this great church

* See *Lipfius's* Colleĉtion of thefe fragments, numb. 25.
*Hic eft ille homo honeftus, non apice purpurave, non liĉtorum
infignis minifterio, fed* null are minor (query, if this be not a
falfe reading), *qui cum mortem in vicino videt, non fic pertur-
batur, tanquam rem novam viderit; qui five toto corpore tormenta patienda funt, five flamma ore recipienda eft, five exten-
dendæ per patibulum manus, non quærit quid patiatur, fed
quàm bene.*

ftands

ftands on the ruins of the circus of *Caligula* and *Nero**.

In this part of the *Vatican* valley were the *Domitian* gardens. This obelifk was brought from *Egypt* by *Caligula*, and placed by him, not far diftant from the fpot on which it now ftands, on the *fpina* of his circus. In that circus *Nero*, afterwards, *quæfitiffimis pœnis affecit chriftianos. Hortos enim fuos ei fpectaculo obtulerat, & circenfe ludicrum edebat* †.

It feems fomewhat ftrange, faid the young nobleman, that among all the paintings and fculptures in this moft magnificent church, there are none, which refer to the celebrated and certain martyrdom, of fo many primitive chriftians on this very fpot. What pity is it, that *Raphael* and

---

* See *Bonanni's* defcription of the *Vatican* church, p. 24. and particularly the plan of it, intitled *Tabula* 6 *Ichnographia Bafilicæ antiquæ & novæ, fimul cum Circo Neroniano.*

See alfo abbate *Venuti's Roman* Antiquities, part ii. p. 106.

Fu in quefta valle il Circo di Nerone. Fu quefto fabbricato da Caligola, poi accrefciuto o adornato da Nerone. Nel mezzo vi era l'Obelifco, che ora fi vede nel centro della gran Piazza Vaticana. Crollò a terra ne i tempi barbari, fenza però alcuna lefione del marmo e fino a tempi di Sifto V. giacque proftrato nel fuo antico fito vicino alla Sagreftia della Bafilica Vaticana, fino che nel 1580 *fu transportato nella Piazza.*

See alfo *Severano's* hiftory of the feven churches, p. 92.

I primi martiri Chriftiani furono uccifi in quefto circo, come pare lo accenni Tacito.—The 24th of *June* is the day of their memorial.

† TACIT. *Ann.* l. xv. 44.

Michael

Michael Angelo were not employed here on that fubject!

I heartily wifh they *had* been, replied the eldeft of the young gentlemen. Even our good tutor, I believe, will join in that wifh. Yefter-day, when he was admiring the ftatue of *Seneca*, he expreffed great concern, that *Tacitus* had not preferved the laft difcourfe of that philofopher. If he had, now, before his eyes, fome of the labours of *Michael Angelo's* chiffel, or *Raphael's* pencil, defcriptive of thefe martyrdoms; would he not much more earneftly have contemplated them; and much more ftrongly expreffed his defire, that fome worthy hiftorian had faithfully recorded the dying words of thefe primitive martyrs, and their behaviour in general at their laft hour?

TACITUS, replied *Crito*, prejudiced as he was againft them in general, yet ftrongly afferts their innocence as to the particular crime, for which they moft unjuftly fuffered.

The fpectators alfo of this infernal barbarity, cruel as they were themfelves, and prejudiced in the fame manner; yet, before the horrid long execution was over, felt their hatred to thefe fufferers turned to pity and compaffion.

MISERATIO

MISERATIO oriebatur! fays *Tacitus.* This fofter fentiment feems to have firft flowed from the natural fympathy and irrefiftible meltings of the human heart, on fuch dreadful occafions. But it was certainly much augmented, by the opinion generally entertained of the *innocence* of the fufferers. It was increafed, probably, ftill much more, by the *moving behaviour,* the gentle words, and celeftial afpirations of thefe bleffed primitive faints, and proto-martyrs of *Rome;* who, around this very obelifk, commended their fpirits into the hands of their heavenly Father; in the midft of the heavieft infults, calumnies and tor- ments; full of patience; full of peace; full of the hopes of immortality!

MAY we not, probably, and very juftly apply to them, the defcription of the death of the bleff- ed proto-martyr in *Jerufalem?* And in what bet- ter manner can we conclude this day's meditation, than by recollecting the holy behaviour, both in life and death, of him, who had the honour of being the firft leader of all the noble army of chriftian martyrs? *St. Stephen* abounded with all the primitive virtues: he was remarkable for his faith, for his zeal in the caufe of religion, and for his care of the poor. *St. Stephen,* in his laft hour, being full of the HOLY GHOST, looked up ftedfaftly unto heaven, and faw the heavens opened, and the glory of GOD, and JESUS the Son of Man, ftanding on the right hand of GOD. On *St. Stephen* the people ran with one accord, and caft him out of the city, and flew him, calling upon GOD, and faying, " LORD JESUS! receive my fpirit." And he kneeled down, and cried with a loud voice, " LORD, lay not this fin to their charge." And when he had faid this, he fell afleep!

Αμην, αμην, λεγω υμιν, οτι κλαυσετε κỳ θρηνησετε υμεις, ο δε κοσμος χαρησεται. Υμεις δε λυπηθήσεσθε, αλλ' η λυπη υμων εις χαραν γενησεται*.

Amen! Lord Jefus! *Amen!* So be it! *Fiat mihi, fecundum verbum tuum.*

* Div. JOHAN. cap. xvi. ver. 20.

THE END.

INDEX.

I N D E X.

N. B. The *Churches, Paintings, Statues, Temples, and Villas,* are collected under those respective Heads.

The *Numeral Letters* denote the *Volume,* and the *Figures* the *Page,*

A.

INDEX.

INDEX.

Epicurean

INDEX.

Hormifda,

INDEX.

INDEX.

Robert

INDEX.

INDEX.

Epicurus,

INDEX.

INDEX.

W.

Wales, ravaged by the Romans, ii. 451

Wax-work, by *Caietano Julio,* ii. 148

Westminster abbey, decree of a council held there, i. 351

———— Sepulchres there, ii. 304

———— hall, ii. 79

———— scholars, i. 95

William of Wickham, i. 382

Windsor castle, i. 372

Wolfe, General,---similar to Scipio Africanus, i. 290--- publickly applauded, ii. 396

Wolsey, cardinal, ii. 402

———— his palace at Rome, ii. 403

X.

Xenophon, religious, i. 328--- his writings, 292, 448--- ii. 59

Z.

Zacharias, ii. 18

Zaleucus, i. 5

Zeno, i. 172

Zeuxis, i. 79

Zoroaster, ii. 5

THE END.

A

TRANSLATION

OF THE

QUOTATIONS

IN THE

ROMAN CONVERSATIONS.

VOL. II.

SECOND EDITION.

BOOK III.

CHAP. IV,

Page

2   WE faw, pufh'd backward to his native fource,
    The yellow Tiber roll his rapid courfe,
    With impious ruin threat'ning Vefta's fane,
    And the great monuments of Numa's reign.
                                 Francis.

3 Ye greater guardian Gods of Rome, our prayer,
    And Romulus, and thou, chafte Vefta, hear!
    Ye, who preferve with your propitious powers,
    Etrurian Tiber, and the Roman towers! *Warton.*

4 I had an idea that there were ftatues in Vefta's tem-
    ple, but I was perfectly miftaken: its peculiar dif-

tinction is, the flame which is maintained without intermiffion.

5 He approached the Capitol, with an intention to worfhip the Gods. But when he had entered the temple of Vefta, his whole frame was fuddenly convulfed, either in confequence of fome impulfe from the Deity, or of fome ftings of confcience, from which he was never wholly free.

7 To ferve God in holinefs and righteoufnefs all the days of his life.

8 What fo noble, fo liberal, fo munificent, as to affift the fuppliant, to encourage and protect the perfecuted, and fave them from banifhment.

9 Every man of opulence and diftinction adorned his old age in thus explaining the law. Their houfe was a kind of Oracle for the city, and their doors were crowded by thofe who laboured under embarraffments. Them, as Ennius expreffes himfelf, I exert myfelf to the utmoft to relieve, correcting their mifapprehenfions, and putting them into the true line of proceeding, left they fhould mifcarry through inadvertence.

10 *line* 6. Of all the lawyers the beft pleader, of all the pleaders the beft lawyer.

line 15. I undertake to pronounce Scævola the high prieft, the firft man in the State, both in point of ability and integrity.

13 In Rome itfelf he gained the higheft applaufe for the purity and firmnefs of his provincial adminiftration. The Senate likewife, in a formal decree, made the regulations of Scævola, the fyftem which

fucceeding

fucceeding governors fhould purfue in that province.

15 I think with awe on thy infcrutable proceedings,
who afflictelt the righteous with the wicked, doubtlefs in perfect confiftency with rectitude and juftice.

16 Stretch'd o'er the plain their haplefs friends they found,
Some pale in death, fome gafping on the ground.
With copious flaughter all the fields was dy'd,
And ftreams of gore run thick on ev'ry fide. *Pitt.*

17 In his endeavours to mediate, he was flain.

Now heaps on heaps fall thick on every fide,
And in the cloud of fight, Galefus died :
Good old Galefus! while with earneft care,
He labour'd to prevent the rifing war. *Pitt.*

20 Eight thoufand men had furrendered themfelves to
Sylla. He ordered them to march into the Villa
Publica, as if he was about to incorporate them with
his own foldiers, and at the fame time, ordered the
Senate to affemble in the temple of Bellona. But
death was their inftant doom, and in the horrid maf-
facre fell many who had accidentally come thither
from the country, and even fome of his own party.
Their bodies were thrown into the Tiber. During
the flaughter, Sylla was making a fpeech in the Senate. The Senators hearing the dreadful fhrieks of
fo many thoufands fo bafely put to death, were
thrown into the utmoft alarm; when Sylla, with his
countenance and voice perfectly unruffled, added,
Let us go on with our bufinefs, for only a few fedi-
tious men are fuffering, by my order. Never were
fuch murderous words uttered by man !

Page

21 Miftake not, Romans. Let the conquered be admonifhed not to offend a third time, left a conflagration be the confequence.

22 How irkfome now was his ufurped power!
When the recollection of his enormities harrowed
up his guilty foul, what horrors did he endure, finding by experience for what a prize he had been contending! Before he was in poffeffion of power, he
had to expect folid fatisfaction from it. But on
obtaining the fupreme authority, through the agonies
of his confcience, he loathed and hated what before
the civil wars had fo inflamed his defires. Such
examples fhould be a leffon to mankind, not to rufh
on into dangers from which they cannot retreat ; to
bring their paffions into fubordination ; and to be
ardent only in thofe purfuits, which will not entail
fhame and remorfe.

24 For his country he the more felt, on account of his
mother, by whom in his orphan ftate, he had been
brought up with fuch tendernefs.

26 That firebrand was kindled at Sylla's pile.
Note. Who poffeffed every requifite for the moft
accomplifhed Commander, his mean connexions
excepted.

29 The ordinary concerns of human life, and ftandards
only of common excellence, could not attract his
attention : he was converfant with angels in heaven,
or perfect men on earth.

BOOK

BOOK III.

CHAP. V.

Page

33 This Tribune elect, then very young, was applied to among the laft for his opinion; and with fuch fagacity and energy did he inveigh againft the confpiracy, fo well did he paint the impending dangers of the State, fo happily expatiate on the virtues of the Conful, that the whole Senate concurred in his meafures, and the greater part of his order attended him home.

34 Particularly his orations againft Catiline, at once fo highly finifhed and fo ferviceable to the Commonwealth.

35 Nature defigned him as a model of honour, penetration, temperance, greatnefs of mind, probity, and in fhort, of all the virtues.

36 He did not emulate the effeminate in luxury, the rich in fortune, the factious in fedition. He emulated the wife in the love of wifdom, and particularly moral philofophy; he emulated the brave in valour, the modeft in humility, the abftemious in temperance. Although his conduct was excellent and divine, and his character in the higheft degree refplendent, he enjoyed lefs the reputation, than the reality of virtue: fo that in proportion as he was regardlefs of raifing his name, he became the more celebrated.

37 After Cato had remonftrated with vehemence againft the proceeding as treacherous and difgraceful; Clo-

Page

dius arrogantly and contemptuoufly replied, whatever be the confequence, and how great foever thy
reluctance, thou fhalt fail. And immediately advancing towards to the people, procured a decree
that Cato fhould embark.

42 With ftainlefs luftre virtue fhines,
A bafe repulfe nor knows, nor fears;
Nor claims her honours, nor declines,
As the light air of crowds uncertain veers. *Francis.*

43 Scrutinizing, planning, advifing.

46 *line* 8. So when an aged afh, whofe honours rife
From fome fteep mountain tow'ring to the fkies,
With many an axe by fhouting fwains is ply'd,
Fierce they repeat the ftrokes from ev'ry fide:
The tall tree trembling, as the blows go round,
Bows the high head, and nods to every wound.

Pitt.

line the laft. On one object his mind ever dwelt,
which was reconciliation.

55 Let us no longer ufe the terms, Chance and Fortune: or let us ufe them only, as terms expreffive
of our ignorance. It is God, who prepares effects in
their moft diftant caufes: and who ftrikes thofe
grand blows, the very counter-blow of which extends fo far.

57 Athens! thou deareft city, hail!

59 When contemplating his wifdom and his benevolence, I cannot be filent on fuch a character, nor
can I reftrain my admiration and praife. If any
friend of virtue ever met with a fuperior character
to Socrates, I pronounce him confummately bleffed.

61 That

difperfer

Page

difperfer of forrow and fear. Thou nurfe of devotion. Mayeft thou always prevent us, and render us continually zealous of good works.

———

BOOK III.

CHAP. VI.

73 He was a true Patriot.

74 Radiant in open view, Æneas ftood,
In form and looks, majeftic as a god.   *Pitt.*

78 The boldeft of all innovations, he extinguifhed without confufion or tumult.

79 Hail, Cicero! Thou firft man honoured with this endearing appellation!

81 *Note.* This propofal received the fanction of the Senate.
line 19. He was always watching, and always providing againft every danger : in fhort, he had fully made up his mind, that if in the faithful execution of his office, he fhould lofe his life, he would view it as a noble facrifice.

83 *Note.* On the temples in general, on that of Concord in particular, the vultures fat in crowds. Their appearance was fuited to the occafion, for then thofe maffacres were committed, which filled the whole city with blood.
line the laft. On the very roftra, where he had fo refolutely protected the State, that head was placed,

by

Page

97 He judged that it would ferve the Republic to un-
fold this Philofophy to the Romans ; and that the
honour of the city required fome Latin produ&ions,
on fubje&s fo fublime and interefting.

98 At Rome he devoted himfelf entirely to Philo, feeling an irrefiftible impulfe to the ftudy of Philofophy.
Note. On my arrival at Athens, I fpent fix months
with Antiochus, the moft illuftrious and the beft
informed Philofopher of the old academy: and
under this able inftru&or renewed my application to
Philofophy, to which from my earlieft years I have
been attached, and in which I have been conftantly
labouring to make advances.

99 Here we find a retreat from all anxiety and toil.
Tufculum affords fuch pleafures, that we never fail
to be happy, whenever we repair hither.

101 It is fcarcely to be believed, how much I write, not
only by day, but alfo by night.

102 Which purfued its ftudies in this place.

103 Ye dear, dear ruins! and thou Troy ! declare
If once I trembled or declined the war :
Midft flames and foes a glorious death I fought,
And well deferv'd the death for which I fought.
No hopes of aid in view, and every gate
Poffeft by Greece, at length I yield to fate.
Safe o'er the hill my father I convey,
And bear the venerable load away.   *Pitt.*

104 *line* 10. Corruption.
line 14. The place in which he found medicine for
his foul.
line the laft. The antidote againft gloom and fear.

105 Laurence

Page

105 Laurence Juſtinian, by country a Venetian, in rank a Patrician, in the church of St. George, a Canon. Having been a Regular for thirty years, he was elevated to the epiſcopal chair of Venice, though he had taken ſome pains to be releaſed from the burthen. He was juſtly in high eſteem for his undiſſembled piety towards God, his unbounded charity to the poor, and his ardent zeal ˈfor the ſpread of ⁀ religion.

106 Though they were not the invincible, yet they were powerful auxiliaries of his fortitude and wiſdom.

107 *line* 1. He ſaw the place of that cataſtrophe, according to hiſtory.

line 13. The Eleuſinian myſteries poſſeſſed regenerating virtues.

B O O K   III.

CHAP. VII.

120 *Note*†. He was thruſt into the loweſt dungeon, and killed.

Note ‡. There his life ſtruggled with famine till the ſixth day, and then yielded.

121 *line* 7. Oh my ſon, my friends, who would have imagined, that to theſe abodes of vice and horror we ſhould ever be conſigned! But ah, before us, have theſe galling chains oppreſſed ſuffering virtue!

line 18. Their priſon was more ſacred than any court.

124 The temple of filial piety.

127 Here

Page

127 Here is fcope for your efforts, afpiring young men!
There lies a noble conteft between your parents and
yourfelves; who have received, who have conferred,
the greateft favours. No conteft fo interefting!
Happy the conquerors! Happy even the conquered!
What can be fo fatisfactory to an old man, as to
declare, that he has been exceeded in kind offices by
his fon! What can redound fo much to the honour
of the young man! It is beyond the power of words
to exprefs, or of imagination to conceive, what fu-
perlative, what unfading glory, muft be enfured to
him, who can thus exprefs himfelf: the commands
of my parents I have obeyed; and to their wifhes
have been ever obfequious; but for this I ever muft
contend, that I have not been behind them in the
obfervance of domeftic duties.

128 *line* 12. Nor are there wanting examples to ftimulate
thus to excel.

line 22. In life they did not fo much rejoice, as to be
indebted to their fons for their life.

130 As the fun fhines with peculiar radiance amongft
clouds.

Note. Tanufia concealed her hufband T. Vinius, in a
cheft, and conveyed him to the houfe of their freed-
man Philopæmen, where he was fecreted. Then
fhe revealed the bufinefs to Cæfar, by Octavia,
Cæfar's fifter, by whofe interpofition, many at that
time were faved. He forgave all the parties in this
tranfaction, and moreover raifed Philopæmen to
equeftrian rank.

Lucretius, Ligarius, and Antiftius, were concealed
by their wives. Acilius was redeemed by his wife
from

Page

from the foldiers, having difpofed of all her rich attire for the purpofe. L. Cæfar was faved by his fifter. Servants likewife, fignalized themfelves for their devotion to their mafters; particularly Hirtius and Ventidius. Panopio and Menenius, defired to be fcourged, as fubftitutes for their mafters. Amidft thefe perfecutions, the utmoft affeÉtion was difplayed by the Ligarii, and by other brothers.

---

131 Wives and CHILDREN, and brothers and fervants, anxioufly concerted meafures for their prefervation, and when thefe failed, declined not to DIE WITH THEM.

The Ignatii, father and fon, clafped in each others arms, died by the fame blow : their heads indeed were feparated, but their bodies remained united. Geta, though he had provided himfelf a retreat in a field which he had lately purchafed, left it, in order to perform the funeral rites of his father, who had fallen a viÉtim. Adrian, not profcribed himfelf, hid his profcribed father in a tomb, and watched the opportunity to convey him away in fafety. When Metellus was fitting on the bench with Cæfar, trying the prifoners, it appeared that his own father and fon were in the number. The father was firft brought forward, difhevelled, haggardly, and wretched. Metellus, on recognizing him, leaped from the bench, and embraced him with a groan. O Cæfar, He was thine enemy, but I was thy friend : I beg, that for my fake, my father may be faved ; or if he muft die, that I may be doomed to death with him. Every heart was melted ; Cæfar difcharged

Page

charged the prisoner, though he had been very active against him.

132 From his close covert Nisus rush'd in view,
And sent his voice before him as he flew :
Me, me, to me alone, your rage confine,
Here sheath your javelins, all the guilt was mine.
His only crime, (and oh! can that offend?)
Was too much love to his unhappy friend ! *Pitt.*

———

133 Haste then, my sire, I cry'd, my neck ascend,
With joy beneath your sacred load I bend;
Together will we share, where e'er I go,
One common welfare, or one common woe. *Pitt*

———

134 Charm'd with his virtue, all the Trojan peers,
But more than all, Ascanius melts in tears,
To see the sorrows of a duteous son,
And filial love, a love so like his own. *Pitt.*

135 *Note.* So that he became a rich man.
line 12. Two Sicilian youths, when Ætna, with unusual violence, discharged its torrents upon the fields and cities, and a great part of the island, took their parents on their shoulders : one, the father; the other, the mother. It is related, that the fire made way for them, and that the flame retiring on each side, a passage was left open, through which these most deserving young men made their escape.

136 Now by the goddess led, I bend my way,
Tho' javelins hiss, and flames around me play ;
With sloping fires the flames obliquely fly,
The glancing darts turn innocently by. *Pitt.*

137 You

Page

137 You fee here an old piece of architecture, commonly
called *L'arco di Giano*, with twelve niches in each of
the four fides : this monument, made of uncom-
monly large pieces of Grecian marble joined together, is built in fuch a manner, as is really aftonifhing, each angle is one hundred and two palms, which
makes the whole four hundred and eight.

BOOK III.

CHAP. VIII.

138 *Note**. Temples were built to Janus, with four
fides and four fronts. One ftill remains in the
Forum Boarium.
Note†. Their gilded ftatues are at the forum ; fix
of one fex, and as many of the other.
line the laft. The twelve Gods that protect the city.

139 The twelve Gods who prefide over the fields.

140 *line 5.* Dialogues on hufbandry.
laft lin-s. In a bafon, formed by the retreat of the
mountain, were fituated the country houfe and
gardens of Varro.

141 *line 13.* Varro fixed upon his eftate at Caffino, for
his philofophical retreat. What converfations were
there held ? What ftudies were there purfued ?
What volumes were there compofed ? The laws of
the Romans, the monuments of their anceftors, every
fyftem of wifdom, every fubject in literature.

141 Note.

Page

Page

right. Then befeeching them to confult their own fafety, he retired to fome diftance.

167 Struggling for the liberty of his country, difdaining to think of flight or fhelter, even daring the enemy, prefenting himfelf confpicuoufly to their view, and leading on with ardour the firm and bold——he fell ——exhibiting a prodigy of valour to his foes.

170 Never to defpair of the Commonwealth.

177 What! muft thefe rifing crops barbarians fhare, Thefe well-tilled fields become the fpoils of war? See to what mis'ry difcord drives the fwain! See for what lords we fpread the teeming grain!

Warton.

178 In compliance with your prayers, may Apollo banifh war and famine, and peftilence, from the people and prince, to other countries : to Perfia and Britain.

181 A rich marble fabric.

182 Among thefe worthies thou muft hold the moft confpicuous rank, having been the moft confpicuous for virtue.

187 Difpeopled Egypt fills the wat'ry plain, And the whole Eaftern world o'erfpreads the main.

Pitt.

188 As incenfe, may it afcend before thee, for thy mercies' fake.

BOOK

BOOK IV.

CHAP. I.

Page

193 Who, in cold Hæmus' vales my limbs will lay,
And in the darkeſt thicket hide from day. *Warton.*

194 The mountains riſe, and the plains retire to the
ſtation which thou haſt aſſigned them. O Lord, how
manifold are thy works, in wiſdom haſt thou made
them all.

195 Wherever I caſt my eyes,
I ſee thee Omnipotent God.
I admire thee in thy works,
I ſee thee in myſelf.
The earth, the ſea, the celeſtial ſpheres,
Proclaim thy power.
Thou art every where,
And we all live in thee.

200 *line* 1. Not fair Lariſſa with ſuch tranſport warms,
As pure Albunea's far refounding ſource,
And rapid Anio, headlong in his courſe,
Or Tibur, fenc'd by groves from folar beams,
And fruitful orchards bath'd by ductile ſtreams.

Francis.

line 7. Pan from Arcadia's hills deſcends
To viſit oft my Sabine ſeat,
And here my tender goats defends
From rainy winds, and ſummer's fiery heat.

Francis.

201 On columns, rais'd in modern ſtile,
Why ſhould I plan the lofty pile
To riſe with envied ſtate?

b 2

Why,

Page

　　Why, for a vain, fuperfluous ftore,
　　Which would encumber me the more,
　　Refign my Sabine feat?　　　　　　*Francis.*

206　Sudden, the dire alarm the temple took!
　　The laurels, gates, and lofty mountains fhook.
　　Burft with a dreadful roar, the veils difplay
　　The hallow'd tripods in the face of day.　　*Pitt.*

208　Where Mincio's ftream bedews the verdant fields;
　　And fpreading wide his lingering waters, feeds
　　Around his winding fhores the tender reeds.
　　　　　　　　　　　　　　　　Warton.

　　Note. Two miles from Mantua, is the village
　　Andes, the country of Virgil, now called Pietola.
　　The dukes of Mantoua had there erected, to the
　　memory of Virgil, a moft elegant villa, which was
　　deftroyed in the war of 1701.

209　On the left is given in different pieces, an idea of
　　the moft ancient collections of books. The fixth
　　reprefents Ptolemy Philadelphus, accompanied by
　　Demetrius Phalereus, his librarian, and by Arifteus,
　　who are arranging the famous library of Alexandria.
　　In the feventh, appears Auguftus, walking between
　　Virgil and Horace in the library which he had formed
　　on Mount Palatine, where the ftatue of Varro was
　　placed.

211　Thefe are my views of education. What has gene-
　　rally been obferved of the arts and fciences, is ap-
　　plicable to virtue. To complete moral excellence,
　　three qualities are requifite : inclination, intelligence
　　and habit. By intelligence, I mean, a proper ac-
　　　　　　　　　　　　　　　　quaintance

Page

quaintance with the nature and importance of virtue ; and by habit, the praƈtice of it. The elemen-
tary parts depend upon good inƌruƈtion, its advancement upon care and diligence, and its perfeƈtion on the union of all. In proportion as any
one of thefe is wanting, our virtue will neceffarily
be defeƈtive. The inclination without information
is blind ; and information without the inclination
will be of little avail ; and the attempts to praƈtice
it without both, will be very ineffeƈtual. As in
hufbandry, a good foil is the firƌ objeƈt, and then
a judicious labourer, and laƌtly good feed : fo in
education, the difpofition and genius may be compared to the foil, he that inƌruƈts us to the labourer,
and the principles of wifdom to the feed. (The
fame fimilitude occurs in the gofpel.) Happy and
beloved by the Gods, is that man, who enjoys all
thefe advantages.

221 Virgil with the utmoƌ care and diligence ƌudied
medicine and the mathematics, and in each highly
excelléd, before he came forward to the notice of
the world.

Note, laƌ line. Take me, ye Mufes, your devoted prieƌ,
Whofe charms with holy raptures fire my breaƌ !
Teach me the ways of heav'n, the ƌars to know ;
The radiant fun and moon's eclipfes fhew ;
Whence trembles earth, what force old ocean fwells
To burƌ his bounds, and backward what repels ;
Why wintry funs roll down with rapid flight,
And whence delay retards the lingering night.

Warton.

b 3   222 The

Page

222 The Bucolics were written in honor of Pollio, Varius, Gallus, becaufe in the diftribution of the lands his property was untouched. The Georgics he compofed in honour of Mæcenas. In the Æneid he propofed to celebrate the origin of the Roman ftate and of Auguftus.

223 *line* 17. On the proper improvement of poetry.

line 19. A city is not fecured by gates however numerous and impregnable, if only one be left open for the admiffion of the enemy : nor will temperance in all other inftances avail, if a young man abandon himfelf only to one vice.

224 In regard to the exhibitions of the ftage, the productions of the lyre, and the exercifes of the fchool, he fometimes admits the principles of Pythagoras and Plato. Youth fhould be previoufly and gradually prepared for philofophy, which is the perfeftion of all other accomplifhments : and poetry may ferve as a pleafing introduftion to that ftudy.

225 *line* 1. Strew flowers upon the tomb.

line 16. Behold how tottering nature nods around,
Earth, air, the watry wafte, and heav'n profound !
At once they change——they wear a fmiling face,
And all with joy th' approaching age embrace.

Warton.

BOOK

BOOK IV.

CHAP. II.

Page

227 *Note**. As you advance farther, you enter the beautiful walks of Genfano, which look more like a garden than a public road, on account of the efpaliers of elm trees, which are planted in double rows, with a large fpace between them : there is likewife a beautiful garden belonging to the Capuchin Friars, from which you fee the neighbouring lake of Nemi. That lake, which is four miles in circumference, makes the country fruitful, and extremely pleafant : the walks along its banks are alfo delightful.

Note ‡. His grandfather contented himfelf with bearing the public offices of his borough, and grew old in the quiet enjoyment of a very plentiful eftate.

229 And he became man.

231 To God only and to his angels ought it to be known, and to efcape the obfervation of men.

232 Great multitudes were gathered together to hear, and to be healed by him of their difeafes. But he had retired to the wildernefs to pray.

236 This road and aqueduct were completed by him alone.

237 The prodigies related of Q. Marcius are ftrictly true. Being ordered by the Senate to repair the aqueducts of Appia, Anien, Tepula, he completed

pleted

Page

pleted a new one called by his own name, by means of paffages cut through mountains, in the courfe of his prætorfhip. It was univerfally allowed to be the moft cool and falubrious ftream in the world, and among other prefents to the Gods, was left by Marcius to the city. By a comparifon of all the waters, this fuperiority was afcertained; and as grateful as the aqueduct, called Aqua Virgo was to the touch, was Aqua Martia to the palate and the ftomach. It fupplied the whole city, but was referved entirely for drinking, while the other canals might be ufed for any purpofe. It was in length fixty miles and upwards.

241 Water in fuch abundance is brought by means of thefe aqueducts, that rivers flow through the ftreets and pipes of the city, and almoft every houfe has its fprings and refervoirs. To this bufinefs Marcus Agrippa gave the greateft attention; the city is like-wife indebted to him for many other ornaments.

243 Brafs were the fteps, the beams with brafs were ftrong
The lofty doors, on brazen hinges, rung.   *Pitt.*

---

246 Next with kind gales, the care of every God,
Agrippa leads his fquadron thro' the flood.
A naval crown adorns the warrior's brows,
And fierce he pours amid th' embattled foes. *Pitt.*

---

248 *line* 1. Varius, who foars on Homer's wing,
Agrippa, fhall thy conquefts fing,
Whate'er, infpir'd by his command,
The foldier dared on fea, or land.

But

Page

But we nor tempt with feeble art
Achilles' unrelenting heart,
Nor sage Ulyffes in our lays
Purfues his wanderings thro' the feas.   *Francis.*

248 *line* 18. His courage was moft diftinguifhed : to no
labour or danger by night or by day did he yield.

249 To acts of kindnefs he was ever difpofed. Gentle
and generous to thofe who applied for his favours :
to none auftere and forbidding. On his approach
to Jerufalem, he was met by the people with the
pomp of their moft folemn feftival, and faluted with
cordial acclamations. He facrificed a hecatomb to
Jehovah, and gave entertainment to the people.

255 There is extant an oration of Agrippa on this magnificent defign, fo worthy of the greateft of citizens.

260 That prince was juftly beloved by France and by
his mafter, becaufe he was alike the friend of both.

263 *line* 7. On behalf of ourfelves and the city, we
obey that deftiny which invefts thee with the monarchy : hereby are we much ferved, becaufe we
are not only relieved from civil diffentions, but
likewife fhall enjoy an eftablifhed government.
line the laft. If merit determine, Agrippa moft evidently was the beft of men.

270 Auguftus Cæfar, Emperor, having reduced Egypt
to a Roman province, confecrated this to the fun.

271 *line* 5. Reprefenting Rome as a Goddefs.

line 9. Proud of her fons, fhe lifts her head on high ;
Proud, as the mighty mother of the fky,
When thro' the Phrygian towns, fublime in air,
She rides triumphant in her golden car,

Crown'd

Page

Crown'd with a nodding diadem of tow'rs;
And counts her offspring, the celeſtial pow'rs,
A ſhining train, who fill the bleſt abode.
A hundred ſons, and every ſon a God.   *Pitt.*

271 *laſt line.* I pray thee, wreſt not this child from my arms:
let this child live: how many have I already loſt:
while this ſurvive, I ſhall have ſome ſatisfaction: in
poſſeſſion of this child, I can ſubmit to being be-
reaved of many.

276 Hail, Hail, O Egypt! my tender parent. See the
epitaph of Iſis, in Diodorus Siculus.

278 Nile ſaw the rout: his mantle he unroll'd,
Spread forth his robes, and open'd ev'ry fold,
Expanded wide his arms, with timely care,
And in his kind embrace receiv'd the flying war.
                                                        Pitt.

283 Live, for ever!

288 London very famous for the number of its merchants, and the quantity of its ſtores.

289 Now to a woman chang'd by fate again.   *Pitt.*

BOOK IV.

CHAP. III.

291 Your purchas'd woods, your houſe of ſtate,
Your villa, waſh'd by Tibers wave,
You muſt, my Dellius, yield to fate,
And to your heir theſe high-pil'd treaſures leave.

Whether you boaſt a monarch's birth,
While wealth unbounded round you flows,
Or poor, and ſprung from vulgar earth,
No pity for his victim Pluto knows;   We

Page

  We all muſt tread the paths of fate :
  And ever ſhakes the mortal urn,
  Whoſe lot embarks us, ſoon or late,
  On Charon's boat, ah! never to return.   *Francis.*

292 This juſtly celebrated Mauſoleum, was a tomb by
the river-ſide, on an alabaſter baſe, and to its very
roof cloathed with ever-greens.

294 Then mighty Juno, with a melting eye
Beheld her dreadful anguiſh from the ſky ;
And bade fair Iris, from the ſtarry pole
Fly, and enlarge her agonizing ſoul.
Swift from the glancing ſun the Goddeſs drew
A thouſand mingling colours, as ſhe flew :
Then radiant hover'd o'er the dying fair.
——————The vital ſpirit flies, no more confin'd
Diſſolves in air, and mingles with the wind. *Pitt.*

————

295 *line* 7. ———— The only joy he knows
    ———— The ſolace of his woes.   *Pitt.*

Note. This piece is a moſt chaſte production. The
countenance ſhines with that ſerenity, that ſweet ſatisfaction, which may well be experienced on the
approach to unchanging joy. It is one of Guido's
moſt finiſhed compoſitions : the attitude is very
ſimple, and at the ſame time highly poetical.

298 *line* 3. He was the delight of the Roman people.
    line 21. His mind was active, chearful and vi-
gorous.

299 *line* 1. He was patient of labour : diſinclined to
indulgence : and conſidering his years and temptations, a prodigy of frugality and temperance.

Page

299 *line* 9. He was competent to the ftation, for which he was educating.

line 13. His mother, Octavia, was inconfolable through life. Her mourning weeds fhe never laid afide. Conftantly were her thoughts fixed upon him ; and what fhe was at his funeral, fhe continued to be, all her days.

line 20. Marcellus had already been entrufted by Auguftus with the concerns of government, and had fhared the burden with him ; and was preparing for all the ftrefs which his uncle might choofe to lay upon him, as he well knew that the foundation fhould yield to no load.

300 Bring fragrant flow'rs, the whiteft lilies bring,
With all the purple beauties of the fpring ;
Thefe gifts at leaft, thefe honours I'll beftow
On the dear youth, to pleafe his fhade below. *Pitt.*

301 Not with his ufual promp and flowing eloquence.

302 Who is that young Prince, in whofe countenance majefty and mildnefs are fo happily blended ? With an eye of indifference he looks on the throne. Heav'ns ! What a fudden darknefs fpreads around me ! Death is hovering round him. He is falling at the foot of the throne, which he was about to af-cend. O my fon, thou feeft the pride of the French nation : The Gods will form him of thy royal blood. Ye Gods, do you produce that exquifite flower only to difplay its beauties? Alas, what a virtuous foul would his have proved ! France, under his reign, had been happy. He had promoted peace and plenty. My fon, his days had been numbered by

his

Page

his good actions. He would have loved his people. How will France mourn, when under the fame tomb will be re-united ·the hufband and the wife, the mother and the fon !

304 To the gloomy apartments of Agrippa, was Marcellus configned : Dear in life, united in death. Scarcely was the tomb clofed, when lo! a fifter demands the fame funeral honours! To thefe three fhocks, lo! a fourth fucceeds; and Cæfar's tears now gufh forth for his beloved Drufus. Shut up, ye Fates, this gaping tomb! Shut it up, it yawns infufferably wide.

305 A myrtle of verdure and odour moft exquifite, has fprung on the grave, and raifed its bufhy head, covering the two urns by its branches and its fhade. Every one exclaims, that Ariftonous, in recompence for his virtue, has been changed by the Gods into this beautiful plant. Sophronime undertakes the charge of fprinkling it, and honours it as a Deity. This tree, inftead of growing old, is renovated every ten years : and the Gods by this phænomenon demonftrate, that virtue, which throws fo fweet a perfume on the memory of men, never dies.

306 Who knows, whether it was for his advantage to live longer: or whether his death was not in mercy?

308 For it is neceffary that men be produced, before they can be made happy.
He fhut the temple of Janus four times.

311 *line* 13. To Rome, and to Auguftus Cæfar, the father of his country.

311 *laft*

Page

311 *laſt line.* In the adminiſtration of his government throughout the world.

313 By him they lived, by him they failed, by him enjoyed liberty and proſperity.

317 Never, never, ye holy Gods, may I ſee that day; rather let me be expunged from exiſtence, than that ſuch a blot ſhould attach to my name.

319 Cæſar's houſe eſtabliſh; which ought certainly to be exempt from mortality, and all the ills of life. His ſacred perſon, from the high pinnacle on which he ſtands, is entitled to look down on the world without any apprehenſion.   Death ſhould not preſume to ſeize him, or to enter his abode : nor ſhould a tear ever burſt from his eye.

320 Oh! had I died, when firſt I ſaw the light,
     Or died at leaſt before the nuptial rite.   *Pope.*

322 Druſus was honoured with a cenotaph even on the Rhine.

326 What is the reaſon, Brutus, that, as we are compoſed of body and mind, and the art of healing in regard to the former is ſo much ſtudied, and even aſcribed to an invention of the Gods ; that medicine for the mind ſhould be ſo much neglected ?

328 *line* 3. The brave and good are copies of their kind,
     ——Yet ſage inſtructions, to refine the ſoul,
     And raiſe the genius, wond'rous aid impart,
     Conveying inward as they purely roll,
     Strength to the mind, and vigour to the heart :

     When morals fail, the ſtains of vice diſgrace
     The faireſt honours, and the nobleſt race. *Francis.*

328 *line*

Page

328 *line* 19. Felt how Auguſtus with paternal mind
Fir'd the young Neroes to heroic deeds. *Francis.*

329 No youth, however endowed by nature, and improved by education, ever excelled him. Whether
he ſhone moſt in the arts of war or peace, is dubious:
in the judicious choice of friends, and in his engaging behaviour towards them, he is ſaid to have
been inimitable.

331 While at Rome, Druſus was lamented as a prince of
diſtinguiſhed merit, brave, virtuous, full of goodneſs, and fit to ſucceed Auguſtus: many nations in
Germany rejoiced in his death. He had experienced
on the part of that Prince, (or rather the Roman
army under his command) unparalleled cruelties:
ſo deteſtable was his name among them, that when
they imprecated curſes on an enemy, they wiſhed
that he might fall into the hands of another Druſus.

333 When Auguſtus was informed of what had befallen
Varus, he was very much agitated, both lamenting
the numbers he had loſt, and dreading the fury of
the Germans; who, he expeſted, would pour down
into Italy, and even attack Rome itſelf.

334 Yon chief ſhall vanquiſh all the Grecian pow'rs,
And lay in duſt the proud Corinthian tow'rs.
That chief ſhall ſtretch fair Argos on the plain,
And the proud ſeat of Agamemnon's reign,
O'ercome th' Æacian king, of race divine,
Sprung from the great Achilles' glorious line:
Avenge Minerva's violated fane,
And the great ſpirits of thy fathers ſlain. *Pitt.*

336 He left a noble pattern for young men. Great, in
ſtriking terror into the enemy: great, in proteſting
the rights of the citizen. 339 The

Page

339 The affection of the cities, provinces, and all Italy, for Drufus, was heightened by his death: through whatever town the funeral proceflion paffed, it received all poffible honour, and it entered Rome almoft like a triumph.

340 His body being brought to Rome, was laid in Caius Julius' tomb. (The tomb of Auguftus muft be meant, according to the exprefs words of Dio) His panegyric was pronounced by Auguftus, and every affecting folemnity obferved on the occafion.

345 I now take leave of my work on the tranfactions fubfequent to thofe, which Livy's hiftory comprehends; having my mind abforbed by that nobler and more durable empire, which was founded by Jefus Chrift, and over which he prefides. We are now at the period of his birth, though on the precife day the learned cannot agree: but then the world rather beheld, than acknowledged, its Lord. To his blefling I am entirely indebted, if I have laboured to any purpofe: and I moreover humbly pray, that he would confirm me in this opinion, that all I have written concerning victories, triumphs, and ftates, is deferving of no regard, fhould it have diverted my mind from his holy religion, and made me in any degree inattentive to what it enjoins us to do or to fuffer.

BOOK IV.·

CHAP. IV.

Page

360 *Note.* By his ſtern and proud countenance, his frightful eye-brow, and threatening looks, it is eaſy to know *Caracalla,* repreſented in a buſt of porphyry, with a head of marble.

———

line 11. ——————— Catiline in chains
Roars from the dark abyſs, in endleſs pains:
Sees the grim furies all around him ſpread,
And the black rock ſtill trembling o'er his head,
But in a ſeparate place the juſt remain ;
And aweful Cato rules the godlike train. *Pitt.*

361 The Lord hath led the juſt man by the right way, and hath ſhewn him the kingdom of God. O happy man, whoſe ſoul is in paradiſe, where angels exult, archangels rejoice, and the chorus of ſaints invite to remain with them for ever.

363 By examples of vice and virtue we may improve: warned by the former, we riſe ſuperior to the wicked ! and imitating the latter, may not be inferior to thoſe who are revered and loved.

364 Alas! how did they degenerate.

365 His charaɛter changed with his ſituation. As a private man, he was in reputation, and poſſeſſed the confidence of Auguſtus: he retained the ſemblance of virtue during the life of Germanicus: till the death of his mother, he did not wholly lay aſide his regard to charaɛter, but ſeemed divided between virtue and vice: after that period, he heſitated at nothing, however criminal, however infamous.

366 He had great talents, excelling alike in eloquence and learning. He has left many monuments

of

Page

of his literary improvement. His fortitude and benevolence were confpicuous, and he had an irrefiftible art of conciliating the affeftions of men.

367 *line* 1. Wherever he met with the tombs of great men,
he treated them as though they were altars : he firft
fet about collefting the relicks of the Varian party.

line 14. Trajan raifed an altar to the memory of thofe
who were flain in battles, and there offered annual facrifices.

He reftrained the Legions who were difaf-
fefted to Tiberius, and who would have placed the
government in his hands : difplaying alike his firm
refolution and his filial piety. Thofe legions were
the ftrength of the Empire, and their pleafure was law.
Note. The two bufts of Trajan are of excellent work-
manfhip, and exaftly like the medals : they are both
of white marble, and the firft is all of one piece.

369 *line* 4. When I die, let fire confume the globe.
Note. When Nero repeated this line, he added with em-
phafis, Let the conflagration take place, before I die.
line 8. From fuch a hell, good Lord deliver us.

370 *Note* †. Germanicus defcended from his chariot,
laid afide his triumphal robe, and offered to Jupiter
many white bulls : he afterwards brought to the
temple of Mars the revenger, the ornaments of the
triumph and German fpoils.

Note ‡. At the end of the year an arch was confecrated near the temple of Saturn, on account of the
recovery of the ftandards loft with Varus, under the
command of Germanicus, and with the aufpices of
Tiberius.

Page

371 The ftatues of the rivers were in the proceffion.

372 *Note.* L. Domitius croffed the Elbe with his army, penetrating farther into Germany than any commander before him.

line 22. ' To the empire which extended beyond the ocean, the Rhine was a limit.

374 In the devaftation fpread by fire and fword through a vaft extent of country, mercy was fhewn neither to age nor fex. Slaughter, not captives, was the objeƈt; the defolation, not the fubjeƈtion of the country.

375 A kind of towered crown.

377 The armies of the Germans are not led on as formerly, to irregular attacks, and in detached companies. Their operations now are fyftematic, and in concert. In their long war with us, they have learnt to follow the banner, to march to each others fuccour, and to obey the word of command.

380 Germanicus thought the Mufes more enchanting than Syrens.

381 By all beloved, becaufe a friend to all.

Note. He revived the provinces finking under internal difcord, or the oppreffions of their rulers. He lowered the price of wheat, by opening the public granaries. He went to Alexandria, on account of a fudden and grievous famine.

382 *line* 4. Not being able to endure the fight of his fubjeƈts.

line the laft. Overhearing thofe juft and fevere reflections, with which he was wounded in fecret.

383 *Note.*

Page

383 *Note.* An ifland, with a weftern afpect, command-
ing a full view of the fea, and a moft charming bay :
but the torrents of Mount Vefuvius have defaced
the beauties of the fcene.

384 *line* 3. Vicious indolence, effeminacy, luft, cruelty.
line 9. He found no relief in gay or in folitary
life, but confeffed what torment he endured. A
letter to the Senate he thus begins, " What I fhall
write to you, Confcript Fathers, or how I fhall
write, or in fact what I fhall not write, may the
Gods and Goddeffes inflict more horrible vengeance
than what is already preying upon my vitals, if I
know." Thus his crimes were converted into
pangs : and abundantly true was the argument of
that moft illuftrious fage, Plato, that if the mind of
tyrants could be laid open, wounds and ulcers
would be feen. As the fcourge lacerates the body,
does vice harrow up the mind.

385 Rough Ithaca we fhun, a rocky fhore,
And curfe the land that dire Ulyffes bore. *Pitt.*

386 In Plutarch's book, concerning virtue and vice, a
paffage is applicable to this purpofe : Abroad, pronounced happy : At home, he is in an agony. His
wickednefs having taken poffeffion of his heart,
haunts him night and day, confuming without a
torch, and haftening on premature old age. When
he fleeps, his body may be at reft, but his foul is in
tumult, terror, and diftraction. Where then are
the fweets of vice, if anxiety and horror are thus its
attendants ?

388 The

Page

388 The bones of Agrippina, daughter of Agrippa, grand-daughter of Auguſtus, wife of Germanicus.

391 *Note.* He likewiſe read whole books to the Senate, and made them known to the people, by proclamation; as the orations of Q. Metellus, for the encouragement of matrimony, and Rutilius, about a method of building: to convince them that he was not the firſt, who had attended to theſe ſubjeĉts, but that the ancients too had thought them worthy of their care.

.*line* 13. That they might not think it beneath them to imitate the example of a young man.

393 *Note.* The ancient palace of the old forum.

line 11. With cluſters of virtues was his charaĉter enriched. To his friends moſt dear; dear, however, to all, while he lived, but much more at and after his death.

394 Wherefore reſtrain the tender tear?
Why bluſh to weep for one ſo dear?
Sweet Muſe, of melting voice and lyre,
Do thou the mournful ſong inſpire.

397 I conſider this as the principal deſign of Annals, to record both what has been excellent, and what has been infamous: that virtues may not be loſt in ſilence, and that the dread of the reproach of poſterity, may be a check upon bad words and bad aĉtions.

398 If the immortal Gods had ſuffered him to enjoy the fruit of his viĉtories, no man ever would have returned to his country with greater applauſe.

399 Great Druſus' greater ſon.

Page

400 *line* 6. If they perifh, it is no lofs.

line 14. I have feen the wicked adored on earth: like the cedar, he raifed his audacious front to the fkies. He feemed to have the thunder at his dif- pofal: he trampled under his feet his conquered enemies. I only paffed by —— he was no more. Wretch! God the avenger of innocence, is now weighing thee in the balance, and foon will thy doom be pronounced. Tremble! Thy day is at hand, and thy reign at its clofe. The traitor is dead. He is torn in pieces by an enraged people. What remains of his clotted carcafs, will now be expofed to public view.

402 How deceived was Sejanus in the objeft of his wifhes! While he was afpiring after unbounded honour and wealth, he was erefting a lofty fcaffold for his own punifhment: and the higher it was raifed, the more confpicuous and the more tre- mendous was his fall, when from that eminence he was dafhed to the ground.

403 Through what dangers we arrive to a danger ftill greater! And how long fhall we enjoy the diftinc- tion! To be the friend of God, fhall be my objeft, and that honour I may attain.

405 O for that melody, which enraptured thy breaft! O to approach thine ardours, and to penetrate into thofe myfteries, which ennoble thy verfe! If this be too much for one fo unworthy to expeft, teach me to emulate thee in the fervours of repentance, by which thine awful offence was forgiven. Thus bleffed, I fhall be happier, than if my lyre warbled thine immortal ftrains.

BOOK

BOOK IV.

CHAP. V.

Page

409 Why were not the cataracts of heaven then opened?
Why were not the fountains of the great deep broke
up?

410 *line* 7. They retired to fcenes more tranquil, more fafe,
more ennobling.   There they devoted themfelves to
the ftudy of the fine arts, the cultivation of virtue,
the fubjection of appetite and paffion, the improvement of life and death, and the dignified enjoyment
of the world.

line 21. Numbers fell during the bloody reign of
Caius.

411 *line* 8.   Such was the monfter's delight; on cruelty
alone were his thoughts employed by day and by
night.

line the laft.   That inadvertent expreffion.

413 The origin of the evil.

415 He was lavifh of wealth; and had no hoard but
crimes.

416 *Note* *. With Nero's character we are fhocked; with
Nero's baths we are charmed.

Note †. This building is one of the fineft of ancient
Rome, and is more remarkable than any other, for
its height and fize.   It is built of *travertine* ftones,
joined together without any lime, and fupported by
four large arches, with columns of ruftic work of
the ionic order.   To underftand how magnificent
the

the arches of this monument are, it will be sufficient to know, that the arch which serves as a door, is forty-nine palms long ; and each piece of stone is three palms three inches thick, nine palms five inches, and some two and a half long. The whole of that lofty arch, is only made of twenty-six pieces of stone.

417 Claudius, father of his country, at his own expence, brought to Rome the Claudian stream from the fountains which are called Cæruleus and Curtius, through a course of thirty-five miles ; and the new Anio, through a course of sixty-two miles.

418 His disposition wonderfully varied : sometimes he was cautious and sagacious, sometimes unadvised and rash ; and occasionally frivolous, and like a madman.

420 The savage cruelty of his temper betrayed itself in many things, both great and small. When any were to be put to the torture, he was impatient for the execution, and would have it performed before his eyes. He was much delighted with seeing men engage with wild beasts, and the combatants that perform their parts at noon : so that he would come to the theatre by break of day, and at noon would dismiss the people to dinner, but continue sitting himself. And besides such as were appointed for that bloody work, he would match others with the beasts, or one another, upon slight or sudden occasions, as the carpenters and their assistants, if a machine, or any thing of that nature they had been employed in about the theatre, did not answer the

purpose

Page

purpofe it was defigned for. He likewife obliged one of his nomenclators to that cruel drudgery, and in his toga too. *Clarke.*

421 Once bleft with wealth ———
But now a broken, rough, and dang'rous bay. *Pitt.*

426 He tried every expedient for procuring provifions in the winter feafon.

427 Concerning the title of the work, the learned are not agreed. Beatus Rhenanus, who is faid to have found, and firft to have publifhed it, is fuppofed to have annexed that name to it. And that name Junius, and indeed all retain, treading in the fteps of Dio.

428 He had determined that Gauls, Greeks, Spaniards, Britons, fhould appear in Roman dignity.
Note. Such were the tranfaftions in regard to Britain ; and to induce others to come to terms, it was decreed, that the engagements which Claudius or his officers might conclude, fhould be as valid, as though they were ratified at Rome.

429 To Claudius Cæfar : In commemoration of his exploits in Britain : fubduing its kings without bloodfhed, and compelling them to acknowledge fubjeftion.

430 In Campus Martius he exhibited by imagery the attack and plunder of a town in Britain, with the furrender of its kings : he prefided on the occafion in military pomp.

431 He engaged thirty times with the enemy in Britain.

434 *line* 2. Fighting feparately, all were conquered.
line 5. They fcorned to decline danger.

Page

434 *lin:* 8. Their valour and their liberty funk together.

line 11. Their great exploits by no pen are blazoned.

435 Their minds would have been on fire to fhine in the field, and would have admitted of no reftraints, till they had acquired the glory of their anceftors.

438 Ye happy Bards, whofe rapturous ftrains tranfmit departed heroes to a diftant age, did ye melodioufly chaunt: and there, O Druids, were your favage rites renewed.

440 On the cuftoms of the Germans.

441 Britain was in his time inhabited by an infinite multitude.

442 He was not far behind the moft diftinguifhed of the Romans. Of hereditary fame, or corporeal excellence, he could not boaft : but his dignity was unfullied. Brave and mild, and juft and faithful to friends and foes.

443 Plautius, after his expedition in Britain, which he conducted with great judgement and fuccefs, was applauded by Claudius, and honoured with a triumph. On this occafion, many ftrangers who had been made free of Rome, and Britifh captives, fought in the armour of their refpective countries : and he valued himfelf on the numbers that fell in thefe exhibitions.

445 Caractacus, fleeing hither and thither protefted, that that day, that army would reftore their liberty, or doom them to eternal flavery. He called to their recollection the names of their anceftors who had repelled Cæfar, the dictator ; and affured them, that

by

by fuch valour, they would fave their wives and children, and be free from terrour and tribute.

447 Sweet breeze! The wifh and joy of all, whofe heart not finks in woe! But ah! to me not welcome! Whither wilt thou waft me! Alas! a captive's lot is now my doom!

448 At the Porta Viminalis, behind the other fortifications, are there works thrown up in the form of a Roman camp, accompanied with a fofs and rampire, which are now in a ftate of decay. But that it was a Prætorial camp, Onuphrius and Lipfius fpeaking of the fpot, pronounce; and are herein fupported by antiquaries.   *Donati.*

You fee near *Porta Chiufa* the ruins of a ftately building, which from the outlines, you eafily know to have been the *Caftro Prætorio.* This is alfo indicated by fome pipes which have been found in it, belonging to the aqueduct of *Aqua Martia;* on the infcription of which, mention is made of *Caftro Prætorio. Abate Venuti* adds, *il Signor Piranefi* gives the whole plan of it as it was before it came to ruin, which he fays he took from its remains, and its view in the baffo relievo of the arch of Conftantine, likewife from medals and the defcriptions of ancient writers.   *Efchinardi.*

449 Cæfar, while he difplayed his own glory, conferred honour on his prifoner. For the people were affembled, as to a fplendid entertainment. The Prætorian bands were under arms, in the field before the camp. Then the royal train advancing, the fpoils of war were difplayed : foon appear his brothers,

Page

thers, wife, and daughter, and laſt of all, Caractacus himſelf.

450 Caraɛtacus attempted not to move their pity by
looks, or words, or geſtures : but unembarraſſed
preſented himſelf before the tribunal.

451 By Claudius' permiſſion, he walked through the
city, and obſerving its dimenſions and ſplendour,
exclaimed, Is it poſſible, that with ſuch poſſeſſions
as theſe, you can have any fancy for our poor cottages !

452 If the enemy be rich, they muſt be very covetous;
if poor, very ambitious. The Eaſt and Weſt cannot ſatisfy them. Countries, rich and poor, they
are alike eager to engroſs. They rob, they murder,
they ſeize the government under any pretence ; and
when they have depopulated a country, they call it
peace.

459 He baniſhed the Jews from Rome, that were perpetually making diſturbances, at the inſtigation of
one Chreſtus.

460 The moſt ſlight ſuſpicion, the moſt contemptible
author, could throw him into alarm ; and under the
idea of caution, he proceeded to puniſhment.

464 Under the portico are ſix ſtatues of Sabine women.
The Roman matrons honoured them with ſome religious rites at a feſtival, called Matronalia, on the
firſt of March. Among the different cauſes which
Ovid aſſigns for this feſtival, the firſt is, that the
Sabine women, firſt ſeized and afterwards married
by the Romans, by their tears put a ſtop to a cruel
war,

Page

war, in which were involved their fathers, their brothers, and their hufbands.

465 In the mean time Meffalina, in the gardens of Lucullus, was preparing her fubmiffions, with fome hope that her life might be prolonged : at the fame time, fhe was diftracted with rage, for pride fhe did not abandon to the very laft. Narciffus rufhed from the palace, and orders the centurions to difpatch her : fuch being the emperors pleafure. Evodius was commiffioned for the purpofe. On entering the gardens, he found her ftretched on the ground, attended by her mother, Lepida, whom in her profperity fhe had difregarded, but who felt for her in her extremity. Now was fhe, for the firft time, convinced of her fate, and took the dagger, but trembled fo much, that fhe could not effect the purpofe : fhe was therefore ftabbed by the officer.

469 *line* 14. In early life prudent, early pious, early hufbands, early fathers, early engaged in all the important cares of life.

line 18. The hymenæal hymn is already fet to mufic.

line 20. Thrice happy they, whom love unites
In equal rapture, and fincere delights,
Unbroken by complaints or ftrife,
Even to the lateft hours of life.   *Francis.*

470 Pfalm cxxviii.

478 They grievoufly lamented her, and interred her in great magnificence.

479 Lafcivioufnefs, cruelty, indecency.

480 The

Page

480 The mother and head of all the churches in the city and the world.

481 *Note* The baptiſtery which has the name of Conſtantine, a work of modern times, and made with the ruins of Lateranus's houſe : behind the baptiſtery are ſeen ſome remains of that palace. The columns of porphyry in the baptiſtery, belonged to that palace, as well as thoſe which are in the wall towards the veſtry, and ſupport part of a frieze and old cornice.

line 16. " Thou fool, this night ſhall thy ſoul be required of thee ; then whoſe ſhall thoſe things be, which thou haſt provided."

482 *line* 3. We were witneſſes to the ſudden poverty of many rich men, but it did not occur to us, that we could place no dependance on our own poſſeſſions.

line 9. In thoſe direful times, by Nero's order, a troop ſeized Longinus, and the ſpacious gardens of the opulent Seneca, and inveſted the ſuperb buildings of Lateranus.

line 22. Not revenge, but love for his country, influenced Lateranus in joining the conſpiracy.

483 Nero next ſentenced to death Plautius Lateranus, conſul-elect, and upon ſo ſhort a notice, that he had not an opportunity of taking leave of his children. Dragged to the moſt degrading place of execution, he was killed by Statius, the Tribune.

485 *Note.* Men and women of equeſtrian and ſenatorial dignity, were not now ſeen as at other times, in their diſtinguiſhed ſtation in the theatre, but mingling

with

Page

with the very loweſt claſſes in the ſports which were there exhibited, and contending for the palm in ſuch diverſions. Some engaged voluntarily, ſome reluctantly. Then were ſeen the greateſt families, the Horatii, the Fabii, the Portii, and all the others for whom monuments and temples were raiſed, diſplaying their feats among the common performers. The ſpectators of ſuch degenerated excellence, ſaw with indignation the proceeding, and thus exclaimed to one another: The Macedonians, pointing with their finger, ſaid, This is a deſcendant of Paulus. —— The Greeks, This a deſcendant of Mummius. —— The Sicilians, ſee Claudius. —— Thoſe of Epirus, ſee Appius. —— The Aſiatics, ſee Lucius. —— The Carthaginians, ſee Africanus.

485 *line* 14. Thus was the diſpleaſure of the Gods ſhewn to the Romans.

486 Nor beauteous Helen now, nor Paris blame,
Her guilty charms, or his unhappy flame ;
The Gods, my ſon, th' immortal Gods deſtroy
This glorious empire, and the tow'rs of Troy. *Pitt.*

487 *line* 15. To hear the neighbouring camp reſound with execrations of himſelf, and the applauſes of Galba.

Note. He hurried away in the night to ſome caſtle : on his way, there was ſuch a violent earthquake, that he imagined the earth was opening, and that the ghoſts of thoſe whom he had murdered were gathering round him. He was heard to ſay, wife, mother, father, all demand my death. Having
fiinſhed

Page

finifhed his career of wickednefs, all were fhocked at his enormities.

489 The country about Nomentum is highly fpoken of, particularly an eftate of Seneca, a man of great talents and learning, whofe vineyards have been known to produce, acre by acre, eight pipes of wine.

490 *line 7.* Writers on hufbandry.

line 16. Labour does not agree with our effeminate habits.

Note. The prevailing vices of this city are now regularly tranfmitted from father to fon ; namely, the rage for plays, and the amufements of gladiators and horfemanfhip. How can a mind, occupied in fuch purfuits, attend to the fine arts ?

491 *Note.* He took the utmoft pains to fhine among fidlers, and to be a difgrace to emperors. He was anxious for a crown of olive, or laurel, or parfley, or pine ; but would facrifice the regal diadem.

line 14. And other trifling objects.

line 21. Born for fuch purfuits, I ought to value them : as I have not much time, let it be well employed. What is called old age, is the revolution of a few years. While my frame is vigorous, I fhould apply myfelf diligently to the nobleft concerns. Before old age arrive, may I take care to live well ; and during old age, to die well.

492 On account of the laws of Lycurgus, which were diametrically oppofite to his tafte.

Page

493 They are perpetually in motion, and are grown
restlefs by their changes : their minds are fickened
by their excursion.

497 They had reached the fummit of virtue, and died
merely, on account of their fuperior excellence.

Bareas Soranus was arraigned at the inflance of a
Roman knight, on charges refpecting his pro-con-
fulfhip in Afia, where he had conducted himfelf
with fuch juflice and diligence, as to inflame the an-
tipathy of his prince. The time appointed for his
condemnation was, when Tiridates came to the
city, to be invefted with the jurifdiction of Armenia.

498 His freed-man Phaon, offered him a country-houfe
of his, betwixt the Salarian and Nomentan roads,
about four miles from the town, barefoot as he was,
and in his tunick, only flipping over it an old wea-
ther-beaten cloak, with his head muffled up in it,
and his handkerchief clapped to his face, he
mounted a horfe, with four perfons only to attend
him. When they came to the lane that turned up
to the houfe, they quitted their horfes, and with
much ado he got through fhrubs and bufhes, and a
track through a piece of ground covered with reeds,
to a wall on the back fide of the villa. There
Phaon advifing him to hide himfelf in a fand-pit, he
faid, " he would not go under ground alive :" and
flaying there, till a private paffage into the villa
could be made for him, he took up fome water out
of a ditch, faying, This is Nero's boiling water.

Clarke.

In

Page

In that place of concealment, he fufpected each around him as having a defign upon him, and trembled at every voice, as though it were making enquiries for him. Not a dog could yelp, or a bird twitter, or a leaf move, but he was violently agitated. He was afraid to fpeak to any, left he fhould be overheard by others. Looking round on his few attendants, he called to mind the ftate in which he had been accuftomed to move. So tragic was the prefent fcene, that he need not perfonate murderers and vagabonds as formerly, but only exhibit himfelf. He then affected to relent and retract; but now it was too late.

499 In dying, his eyes darted horror.

501 Nero could not endure the recollection of his crimes, but often confeffed that he was haunted by his mother's figure, and perfecuted by all the furies of hell. And Tiberius is reprefented as the moft miferable of men.

502 A ftatue of Seneca is feen among the wonderful productions of antiquity, in the poffeffion of Cardinalis Borgefii. It is a ftriking refemblance of him expiring in the bath, to his laft breath uttering his golden maxims. It is full of life and fire. The hands and fingers are extended, like a man dictating to writers, precepts of wifdom and fortitude; unreftrained by the pangs of approaching death, happily ftruck off in his countenance by the ingenious artift. His face is not handfome, but bears an African refemblance. The full check, the turgid lip, the diftended noftril, difcover the native of

Corduba,

Page

Corduba, a province of Bætica, contiguous to Africa. But mark his body, worn down by fick-nefs, ftudy, and flender diet; yet inured to regular exercife, and hard labour. Moft happily has the ftatuary united the fkin, emaciated by the fatal draught, and the full veins and mufcles which had been produced by previous exertion.

503 Not without eloquence, even in his laft moments, did he deliver his fentiments to thofe who ftood by him to record them.

507 Its circuit is three miles, or a French league. It is a delicious fpot, in refpeft to plantation, wood, and water: there abound roe-bucks, deer, hares, and pheafants: and every where the ufeful is blended with the agreeable, in perfeft order and elegance.

512 Thrafeas did not recede from what he thought right, though in direft oppofition to the prince.

513 *Note**. Thrafeas did not attend in the council, when not fatisfied with their proceedings.

Note †. Thrafeas always fpoke his mind. Nero might kill him, but could not hurt him. " It is perilous ftriving with princes : their anger is death: Is that all, my Lord, &c."

line 8. After having put to death fo many eminent men, Nero hoped, that by adding Thrafeas to their number, the caufe of virtue would expire.

514 Thrafeas, with a venerable afpeft.

515 *line* 4. Let me think only on hiftorical faßts.

line 12. Without grief and terror.

516 Thrafeas then in the garden, was holding an interview with an illuftrious circle; particularly with

Demetrius,

Page

Demetrius, of whom he was making enquiries concerning the nature of the foul, and the feparation
of foul and body.   When Arulenus, a tribune of
the people, propofed to intercede on his behalf, he
reftrained his zeal, left he fhould expofe himfelf to
danger.   He admonifhed his wife, not to imitate the
example of Arria, and deprive their daughter of her
only refource.   How fuperior is this to Seneca!
The account of his fentence being now brought, he
recommended it to his weeping friends to part, and
not to run any rifque on his account.

516 *Note.* Demetrius, in my opinion, is a great man,
even if he were compared with the greateft.

line 16.   Then advancing towards the portico, he
met the executioners.   He was the more fatisfied,
becaufe he was informed that Helvidius, his fon-in-
law, was only to be confined in Italy.

517 He then took Helvidius and Demetrius into the
chamber, and as the blood gufhed from the veins
of each arm, he fprinkled fome upon the ground,
faying, Let us make a libation to Jove the Deliverer.   He then addreffed himfelf to the officer:
Behold, young man, may the Gods avert the omen,
but thefe are times in which the mind fhould be
fortified with noble examples.   His exit being lingering, he in agony turned to Demetrius.

BOOK IV.

CHAP. VII.

Page

534 Theodofius improved, Honorius completed this temple, confecrated by the remains of Paul, that teacher of mankind.

This church was founded by Conftantine, who built it upon a fpot of ground belonging to Sta. Lucina, a young Roman lady: the burying-ground of the Holy Martyrs was alfo in that place. The Apoftle St. Paul is the firft that was buried in it, by his Difciple Timothy: That burying-ground is under the church, and the fteps leading to it are near the great altar.

535 On the Oftian road, on the left fide of the river, is a fplendid edifice, bearing the infcription of Paul; which a pious Prince dedicated to him at the expence of many talents. The beams are overlaid with gold, fo that the light is reflected, like rays from the fun. The ornamented cieling is fupported by columns of Parian marble, of the fourth order. And there are interfperfed befpangled arches, which have the effect of meadows, in all the gay attire of fpring.

536 I love Rome on this account. Highly is it to be celebrated for its dimenfions, its antiquity, its fplendour, its population, its power, its wealth, and its fucceffes in war: but waving thefe confiderations, I moft revere it as the place, with which Paul correfponded, as the fcene of his labours, and his dying fcene. What charms muft there be in his tomb! O could I now fee his dear remains! the duft of that mouth, by which he fpake before kings and was not afhamed —— the duft of that heart,

Page

heart, which embraced the whole church, and all
nations and people, ardent for the falvation of thofe
about to perifh —— the duft of thofe hands, by
which the epiftles were written —— of thofe feet,
which travelled through the earth, regardlefs of
fatigue, and by which, when fettered, he fhook the
prifon! However, let us not admire him only, but
let us imitate him, that we may be counted worthy
on our departure from this life, to fee him in the
heavens and partake of his glory.

539 He did not write to Timothy, barely to invite him
to come to him, but to renew his exhortations, that
he would difcharge all the duties of a bifhop and a
teacher, with a zeal that might be expected from
one, who was enriched with fo many graces; and
with a noble contempt of all the evils of life : fince
the fpirit of the gofpel is not a fpirit of fear, but of
fortitude and love, and all who will live godly in
Chrift Jefus, muft fuffer perfecution. " Endure
hardnefs as a good foldier of Jefus Chrift."

540 An Arabian hiftorian, relates in his life of Luke,
that he fuffered martyrdom at Rome, foon after
Paul's firft releafe from imprifonment : fuppofing
that if he had lived longer, the hiftory of the Acts
would have been brought down later.

541 He faid in the Hebrew tongue, the lion is dead.
Nero's temper being more mild in the beginning of
his reign, it is probable that he favourably received
Paul's defence; but afterwards, advancing to the
moft audacious impieties, the Apoftles, in common
with many others, fell facrifices to his violence.

544 Happier

Page

Page

By it the antients underftood Rome, where there can be no doubt that Peter lived. The moderns fay, Babylon in Chaldæa. I am of the former opinion.

573 The death of the Chriftians was made a common fport. They were either cloathed with the fkins of wild beafts, and expofed to the fury of the dogs, or fixed to croffes, or confumed by fire. By night they were committed to the flame. Standing at the ftake, they were faftened to it by a hook round the neck. Then burning pitch was poured upon their head, from a red-hot plate : fo that the ftreams of human juices made a furrow in the fand of the Amphitheatre.

574 He is a great man, though not fet off with a crown, with the purple, and the pomp of ftate, who, when he fees his neighbour die, is not alarmed as though the cafe were new : who, whether the body be on the rack, or fire applied to the head, or the hands ftretched on a crofs, does not afk, what pain was endured, but how well it was endured.

575 *Note.* Nero's circus was in the valley, having been firft built by Caligula, and afterwards enlarged and embellifhed by Nero : in the middle of it was that obelifk which is now feen in the centre of the *Vatican place.* It fell to the ground in the dark ages, but without the marble being damaged ; and remained on the fame fpot near the veftry of *Bafilica Vaticana,* till the time of Sixtus the Fifth, when it was brought to the *Vatican place,* in the year 1580.

575 In

Page

575 In that circus, Nero put the Chriftians to the acuteft tortures. He offered his own gardens for the pur-pofe, and prefented fports on the occafion.

577 Pity was kindled.

578 Verily, verily, I fay unto you, that ye fhall weep and lament, but the world fhall rejoice : and ye fhall be forrowful, but your forrow fhall be turned into joy. Amen, be it unto thy fervant according to thy word.

- ## THE END.